Daughters

n Amritsar into an austere and
love with a neighbour, the Pro-
rried. That the Professor even-
er in his home (alongside his
er towards further studies in
her scandalised family. Or even
attle for her own independence
artition and pain around her.

y an Indian writer who prefers
Kapur's sensuous pages re-create
groups sleep in the open air on
in the yard in the dewy cool of
is furtive and urgent because
ag, and women's lives move to a
cooking, washing, weaving and
, chopping and blending . . . This
hagined, aromatic, complex world, a
nday Times

ovingly told. A story of sorrow and
nise. Kapur sets the scene in pre-Parti-

e, and she re-creates that time and the
is a very impressive first novel.' *Literary*

orn in Amritsar. She is a teacher of English
la House College, Delhi University, and has
earching and writing *Difficult Daughters*, her
er five years.

Difficult Daughters

MANJU KAPUR

faber and faber

First published in 1998
by Faber and Faber Limited
3 Queen Square London WC1N 3AU
This paperback edition first published in 1999

Typeset by Faber and Faber Ltd
Printed in England by Mackays of Chatham plc, Chatham, Kent

© Manju Kapur, 1998

Manju Kapur is hereby identified as author of this
work in accordance with Section 77 of the Copyright,
Designs and Patents Act 1988

A CIP record for this book
is available from the British Library

ISBN 0-571-19569-5

2 4 6 8 10 9 7 5 3

for
my mother, her mother
and
my father

I

The one thing I had wanted was not to be like my mother. Now she was gone and I stared at the fire that rose from her shrivelled body, dry-eyed, leaden, half dead myself, while my relatives clustered around the pyre and wept.

When the ashes were cold, my uncle and I went to the ghat to collect them. All around us were tear-stricken people dressed in white, sitting on benches, standing in groups, some with corpses before them, some clustered around bodies burning on daises. The air was smoky, and the breeze blew the stench about. It was not a place to linger in, but I felt unable to move, staring stupidly at the little pile. The inscription on the raised concrete slab announced that a Seth Ram Krishna Dalmia had been burnt there, and his loving widow, brother, and children had labelled this spot in commemoration. On every bench and burning platform, were names and dates, marks of people gone and people left behind. Not a scrap of cement was left unclaimed. I stared again at my mother's ashes and wondered what memorial I could give her. She, who had not wanted to be mourned in any way.

When I die, she said to me, I want my body donated. My eyes, my heart, my kidneys, any organ that can be of use. That way someone will value me after I have gone.

I glared at her, as pain began to gnaw at me.

And, she went on, when I die I want no shor-shaar. I don't want a chauth, I don't want an uthala, I want no one called, no one informed.

Why bother having a funeral at all? I asked. Somebody might actually come.

Why do you deliberately misunderstand me? she countered.

And here, contrary to her wishes, she was being burnt with

1

her organs intact. I walked quickly towards the gate, following my uncle to the car.

'Last Journey', 'Remember God and Death are Beside You Every Moment of Your Life', splashed on the blue exitway under a garish portrait of Shiv, screamed out the impermanence of our lives, while three beggars in saffron robes and matted hair sat on the ground below, tin begging-bowls in front of them.

Going through her papers, I find a bent, scallop-edged photograph, faded brown and sepia. The girl is about fifteen, and stands stiffly before the camera. Her hair straggles untidily, her sari hangs limp and careless on her. I peer at the face and see beauty and a wistful melancholy. Should my memory persist in touching her, the bloom will vanish into the mother I knew, silent, brisk, and bad-tempered.

I stare at this early photograph of an unknown woman and let despair and sorrow run their course. I could not remember a time it had been right between us, and the guilt that her life had kept in check now overwhelmed me.

'You must come and visit us often, Ida, very often,' my relatives said as they left Delhi. 'Now we only are your father and mother.' I decided, yes, I must go to our birthplace, hers and mine, overrun with aunts and uncles still living in the ancestral home.

The train has not yet moved out of the station, but the women squashed next to me in this second-class ladies' compartment are already producing vast quantities of food, puris and parathas wrapped in Britannia-bread waxed paper, aalu ki sabzi in mithai boxes, mango pickle, lemon pickle, little packets of chopped onion and cucumber. Chewing firmly and audibly, they offer me some, but I refuse. They eat and feed their children, pressing another puri, some more vegetables, upon them, followed by water from plastic water-carriers. At stations they shout for tea and cold drinks. From time to time they stare openly at me, middle-aged, alone, and not eating. After the food, their life stories will be spread and consumed, but these are exchanges I am no longer equal to.

I gaze out of the window, and try to whip up some feeling for the landscape. Monotonous fields, buffaloes sitting in muddy ponds edged with slime and lotuses, little brown boys waving at the train as it passes, level-crossings with cars, rickshaws, scooters, buses, and tongas waiting on either side of rickety fences. By and by I am politely asked to get up, so that the berths may be lowered and beddings opened out and spread. By ten o'clock everybody has settled down to sleep. Only the overhead blue night-light remains on.

Once again, I am on my way to the house that, through my childhood, I had slipped into as easily as a second skin. My mother had sent me to Amritsar during all my school holidays, away from my half-siblings, and the proxy warfare conducted on the battlefields of my home.

At six a.m. we reach Amritsar. I gather my things and hasten out to take a rickshaw, avoiding the little family groups, exclaiming, hugging, kissing. No matter how I might rationalize otherwise, I feel my existence as a single woman reverberate desolately on that platform.

The house the cycle rickshaw turns into is an old-fashioned bungalow, with a tall, bushy henna hedge screening a lawn with thick, even grass, ringed with low lemon, papaya and orange trees. The walls protecting the house on the roadside are eight feet high, topped with jagged spikes of coloured glass. The gate is a big, wide, metal sheet, bent and out of shape. To one side is a small doorway for people on foot or cycle.

I step on to the deep, cool, black and white tiled veranda. A couple of old wooden wicker chairs, with their long leg-rests tucked underneath the arms, are lined against the wall. I was born in this house, in one of the small rooms at the back. I sit down on those tiles, and remain there fingering the cracks between them.

I had not told my aunts and uncles I was coming, and, when

3

they see me, I am carried off inside, on a wave of accusations and explanations.

Amritsar was a place I associated with my mother. Without her, I am lost. I look for ways to connect.

I know my relatives feel sorry for me. I am without husband, child or parents. I can see the ancient wheels of my divorce still grinding and clanking in their heads.

He was such a nice man . . .

So educated . . .

But with Virmati for mother, it is not strange that such a thing should happen . . .

Now I show curiosity about them. I wonder how they remember their past. I probe and find that: gold was forty rupees a tola, it cost eight annas to go from Amritsar to Lahore, ten rupees to go from Lahore to Calcutta, six pice to stitch a pyjama, two annas to stitch a shirt, school fees started at four annas a month in the junior classes and ended at one rupee at matric. Ghee was one rupee a seer, milk was four annas a seer, atta was one rupee for twelve seers. The milk had a thick layer of malai, yellow, not white, like nowadays. And when food was cooked, ah, the fragrance of the ghee!

At this point, words fail them.

I had grown up on the mythology of pure ghee, milk, butter, and lassi, and whenever I came to Amritsar, I noticed the fanatical gleam in the eyes of people as they talked of those legendary items. Perhaps, if I could have shared that passion, the barriers of time and space would have melted like pure ghee in the warmth of my palm. But my tastes are different.

I try and ask about my mother, the way she was before I knew her.

There had been eleven of them. The girls: Virmati, Indumati, Gunvati, Hemavati, Vidyavati, and Parvati. The boys: Kailashnath, Gopinath, Krishanath, Prakashnath, and Hiranath.

My relatives are polite, respectful to the dead. I am not satisfied. I dig and dig until they reveal reluctantly.

You know, our mother was always sick, and Virmati, as eldest, had to run the house and look after us.

We depended on her, but she was free with her tongue and her hands. One tight slap she would give for nothing.

She would lash out if we didn't listen. We used to run from her when she came. She was only our sister, but she acted very bossy.

We were scared of her.

She never rested or played with us, she always had some work.

She was so keen to study, *bap re*.

First FA, then BA, then BT on top of that. Even after her marriage, she went for an MA to Government College, Lahore, you know – very good college, not like nowadays. The Oxford of the East they called it.

She studied more than any other girl in this family. Bhai Sahib – your father – was very particular about education.

But why do you want all this? What is past is past. Forget about it. Eat, have another paratha, you are so thin.

My relatives gave me one view of my mother, I wanted another.

II

Ever since Virmati could remember she had been looking after children. It wasn't only baby Parvati to whom she was indispensable, to her younger siblings she was second mother as well. She was impatient and intolerant of fuss. If they didn't eat their meals, on her return home from school she would hunt out the offending brother or sister and shove the cold food down their throats. If they refused to wear the hand-me-down clothes she assigned them, she slapped them briskly. Usually once was enough. Sometimes she tried to be gentle, but it was weary work and she was almost always tired and harassed.

By the time Virmati was ten, she was as attuned to signs of her mother's pregnancies as Kasturi herself. She would redden with shame over her aunt Lajwanti's comments about the litter that was being bred on the other side of the angan wall. She did her best to make sure that none of the smaller children went over to the aunt's side to pee or shit, that they looked neat and tidy when anybody came to visit. This did not improve her temper, or draw her closer to her brothers and sisters, but the children's clean and oiled looks drew admiring comments from those who met them.

At times Virmati yearned for affection, for some sign that she was special. However, when she put her head next to the youngest baby, feeding in the mother's arms, Kasturi would get irritated and push her away. 'Have you seen to their food – milk – clothes – studies?'

Virmati, intent on the baby's little hands and feet, was often not able to hear.

'*Arre,* you think there is all the time in the world for sitting around, doing nothing?'

'I'm just going,' protested Virmati finally. 'Why can't Indumati also take responsibility? Why does it always have to be me?'

'You know they don't listen to her,' snapped Kasturi. 'You are the eldest. If you don't see to things, who will?'

As Virmati got up to go, she realized her silliness. Why did she need to look for gestures when she knew how indispensable she was to her mother and the whole family?

By the time Virmati was sixteen, Kasturi could bear childbirth no more. For the eleventh time it had started, the heaviness in her belly, morning and evening nausea, bile in her throat while eating, hair falling out in clumps, giddiness when she got up suddenly. How trapped could nature make a woman? She turned to God, so bountiful with his gifts, and prayed ferociously for the miracle of a miscarriage. Her sandhya started and ended with this plea, that somehow she should drop the child she was carrying and never conceive again.

Every day, Kasturi entered the dark and slippery bathroom to check whether there was any promising reddish-looking mucus between her thighs. Nothing, always nothing, and tears gathered and flowed in the only privacy she knew. Her life seemed such a burden, her body so difficult to carry. Her sister-in-law's words echoed in her ears, 'Breeding like cats and dogs,' 'Harvest time again.'

Kasturi could not remember a time when she was not tired, when her feet and legs did not ache. Her back curved in towards the base of her spine, and carrying her children was a strain, even when they were very young. Her stomach was soft and spongy, her breasts long and unattractive. Her hair barely snaked down to mid-back, its length and thickness gone with her babies. Her teeth bled when she chewed her morning neem twigs, and she could feel some of them shaking. She had filled the house as her in-laws had wanted, but with another child there would be nothing left of her.

The next day, as she was serving her aunt-in-law her afternoon meal, she groaned a bit and looked faint. The bua looked up sharply.

'One more?' she asked.

Kasturi stared at the floor and blushed.

'*Bap re*. How do you do it?' asked her bua. 'And so sick all the time.'

Kasturi reddened even more at the public betrayals of her flesh.

'I am going to die, Maji, this time. I know it.'

'Don't talk such rubbish, beti,' retorted the older woman sharply. 'God has favoured you.' Kasturi remained silent. From her bones to her mind she felt dull and heavy.

The next morning she called Pinnidatti, her dai.

The dai looked sympathetically at Kasturi's drawn face and shadow-rimmed eyes. 'There is a remedy,' she said at last.

Kasturi looked eager. 'I'll try it.'

'It can be painful.'

'I will die if I have another child,' said Kasturi desperately.

There followed a series of bitter powders and liquids distilled from a dozen different roots and herbs. Kasturi felt sicker than she ever had in her life, she had nausea, cramps, blackouts, and headaches. Soon, soon, she kept repeating to herself as the cramps would come at her morning puja or while she was cooking in the kitchen. These sharp spasms must be the prelude to expulsion, she must be patient. After a month, weary with futile trips to the bathroom, weary of seeing no sign of the blood of delivery on her white, dry, left-hand fingers, she resorted to a twig the dai had given her to insert in her vagina. But still nothing of substance happened.

After the fourth month Kasturi told the dai to let it be. 'God does not wish it. Otherwise why would all this pain not lead to something?'

'The baby is strong,' replied the dai. 'Destined for great things.'

Through her exhaustion, Kasturi wondered at the punishment meted out to her for trying to interfere with the designs of God. She had had strong healthy children, no deaths, no miscarriages; whereas with only two children, her sister-in-law, Lajwanti, had had three spontaneous abortions. Instead of being grateful, she had rebelled, and pain and sickness had been the result.

The excitement she had felt at the birth of her first child

seemed to belong to another life. Everybody then had been considerate of her youth, fears and inexperience. Her mother had been present. Her mother, who had come with all her own food, her dal, rice, flour, ghee, and spices, with her own servant boy to buy fruits and vegetables, to draw her drinking water from the market pump, to help with the household work. Light-as-air she had passed through, with not an anna spent on her, not a grain of wheat or drop of water taken from the house of her son-in-law.

Kasturi's eleventh child was born on a cold December night. A small, puny little girl. The mother looked at the will of God lying next to her, closed her eyes, and let the tiredness of seventeen years of relentless child-bearing wash over her.

Kasturi had no milk. The new-born sucked with all her feeble might on her mother's dry breasts, hanging milkless and flabby against her little chest. Kasturi got a new silver feeding-bottle, with an English nipple, something the other children had not needed. The baby developed a bad case of colic, and Virmati often came home from college to high-pitched, frantic screaming.

When Kasturi was finally allowed out of bed, she was still bleeding heavily. She would have to wash the stains on her bedsheet herself, as the dai had stopped coming. She needed plenty of water, and she worked the pump in the dark and slippery bathroom furiously, shivering in the cold Amritsar December, her frame glistening wetly in the shadows. Though she knew she should hurry out of the bathroom and lie down till the dizziness grew less, rebellion filled her. Why should she look after her body? Hadn't it made her life wretched enough?

The chills and trembling began soon after she reached her bed. Her moaning attracted the attention of the servant who hurriedly asked Chhote Baoji to send for the hakim, Pabiji looked very bad. The hakim declared he could not answer for Kasturi's life if she had any more children. The vaid also said the same thing. A Western-educated allopath declared that repeated births deplete the body, and no medicine could help Kasturi through

9

another pregnancy. She needed to build up her strength, she needed the fresh air of the mountains immediately, as much as she needed to be removed from the crowded and unhealthy bazaar permanently.

It was decided to send Kasturi to Dalhousie. Virmati was seventeen and studying for her FA exams, but since the tail end of her education was in sight, it was felt that missing a little of it to help her mother was quite in order. After all, in a year or so the girl would be married. The family hired a house near the central chowk, and Kasturi shifted with her eldest and youngest daughters to a hill station clean and bracing enough to work wonders with her health.

III

The cottage Suraj Prakash had rented for his wife in the mountains was a pleasant one, with a pointed roof, and a glassed-in front veranda. It was high on the hillside, with a grand view of the valley in front, and washed with cool, bright sun during the day. There were deodar trees, thick and fragrant in the back garden, and blue and pink hydrangea bushes down the path leading to the front door.

Virmati quickly settled into housekeeping for her mother. Compared to her duties at home, her work here with one baby and one mother was comparatively light. She had never had Kasturi so much to herself, and was jealous of each moment with her. The best time was the morning havan. In the clear, chilly greyness of five o'clock, before Paro woke, they sat in front of the tiny prayer fire, their chanting the only noise in the house, the yellow-orange flames the only colour. Unlike Amritsar, there was no reason to be distracted from the peace that both mother and daughter felt as they finished praying and sat watching the small, moving glow of the twigs in the havan kund.

At other times, Virmati's attempts to spin webs of love through her devotion were met by exasperation. Kasturi was not used to so much solicitude.

Towards the evening it often rained. Trapped in the house, Virmati mooned about restlessly, hanging about her mother, playing with the baby, fidgeting with some knitting as she looked out of the window.

'Viru, at least don't ruin whatever knitting I am trying to do,' said Kasturi tartly one evening, 'Why can't you make yourself useful? There is so much sewing to be done for the baby. There are sweaters to be made for the other children. It's a shame that your hands are idle.'

'I'm tired of knitting and sewing,' flared Virmati. 'Besides, I'm here to look after you.'

'I can look after myself.'

'Why did you bring me if you don't need me, Mati?' said Virmati, with a thick lump in her throat.

'What is all this nonsense? In Amritsar you were bad-tempered because you were busy and tired, here you are bad-tempered because you are idle,' retorted Kasturi.

'Maybe I should go back to Amritsar. Pitaji can take me the next time he comes.'

The language of feeling had never flowed between them, and this threat was meant to express all her thwarted yearnings.

'Maybe you should,' said Kasturi crossly. Why was her daughter so restless all the time? In a girl, that spelt disaster.

Virmati left raging. Why was saying anything to her mother so difficult? Maybe it was best to keep silent.

Back in Amritsar, Kasturi's residence in Dalhousie occupied much of Lajwanti's thoughts. She had never seen anybody fussed over as much as that woman. She, too, had been sick after her miscarriages. Had the family offered to send her to the mountains? To her mother's? Anywhere?

'See how they are all running around like mad people between Amritsar and Dalhousie,' she remarked to her husband as he lay on the takht in the angan, having his feet pressed by her.

Chander Prakash twitched his head, but the silence continued.

'How irresponsible to expect to be pampered like this,' persisted Lajwanti. 'Really, some women have no sense. They behave without thinking. I never let my ailments disturb anyone. Only God knew how I suffered.'

Silence. Lajwanti pressed harder to jog her husband's mind a bit. His eyes remained closed.

'Your poor brother,' she proceeded, 'going every month to Dalhousie. In fixing his wife's health he will ruin his own. All the burden of running the shop falls on you while he is away, but you are a saint and will never say anything about your own condition. Where do we, and our two children, stand in front of that woman, and her eleven children?'

Chander Prakash muttered something unintelligible, and Lajwanti brooded over the strain of softness that ran through the men in her in-law's family. Every month her poor brother-in-law made the long trip to Dalhousie. Train to Pathankot, tonga up, money, time and worry, all indulged in so frequently, what good could come of this? As for the children, she was fed up with their wild ways. Last night the cinema chowkidar brought one of the boys home on his shoulders. He had paid an anna to be let in, and had then fallen asleep in the theatre. And where had he found an anna to waste? She resolved to go with Suraj Prakash on his next visit, and let Kasturi know how matters stood. Her policy had always been to be frank and open.

She approached her brother-in-law that evening. 'Praji,' she began as she handed him his glass of milk, 'I worry about Pabiji. That my sister-in-law should do without her family at a time like this! There she is, with just Viru to look after her, *bap re*. We forget that Viru is still a child. But sitting here, what can I do? I feel so helpless, Praji. I must go with you next time in order to relieve her. I know how you worry, merely once a month as you see her. With an elderly woman staying there, you will get peace of mind.'

The cottage Lajwanti saw in Dalhousie increased her concern. She must stay as long as possible, to assist the invalid on her road to recovery. Besides, she herself also needed some rest occasionally.

Suraj Prakash had written to Kasturi about Lajwanti's anxiety about her health, and Kasturi had known that her sister-in-law had come to claim her own share of her lengthy stay at the hill station. She did not mind. Only Virmati objected, with a fierceness that she concealed by a great show of hospitality, and a refusal to let her tai help with Paro in any way.

'Beti, I am here now, you rest,' said Lajwanti frequently to her niece.

'No, no, Taiji. You are here for a holiday,' said Virmati.

'What holiday is it for you, beti, with your mother so sick and needing constant care.'

Virmati was offended by this implication of herself as a pleasure-loving female, and did not reply. If Lajwanti was offended by her niece's rudeness, she hid this fact. She did not want to initiate a longish stay, in a house her brother-in-law was paying for, with a quarrel.

IV

Lajwanti stayed and stayed. She wrote to her daughter in Lahore. She too must come and visit – the climate was so nice, the house big enough, of course your cousin and aunt will be delighted, and you too, my child, need rest, you work so hard.

She then broke the news to Kasturi and Virmati. Kasturi said what was required of her, Shakuntala was family, the house was hers, etc. Virmati asked listlessly, 'How is Shaku Pehnji doing?' And, since she was annoyed with her aunt, added with a touch of viciousness, 'It will be so nice to see her, because when she settles down, we will meet her even less than we do now.'

Normally few dared to mention Shakuntala's unmarried state, each remark was such an insult to the mother.

'How can anyone see her when she has no time? Such a talented teacher, so popular, what an inspiring example she is for the younger ones,' declared Lajwanti, about achievements she herself had never understood or cared for.

'Still, it is the duty of every girl to get married,' remarked Kasturi mildly.

'She lives for others, not herself, but what to do, everybody in our family is like that. And with all this reading-writing, girls are getting married late. It is the will of God,' concluded Lajwanti aggressively.

Shakuntala came, very different from the thin sallow creature she had been in Amritsar.

'I hope I am not disturbing your convalescence, Chachi,' she said teasingly to her aunt.

'Beti,' said Kasturi, in a mock scolding voice, 'how can family disturb? You are getting very modern in your thinking. We hardly get to see you as it is.'

'What to do, Chachi? These colleges really make you work.'

'*Hai re*, beti! What is the need to do a job? A woman's shaan is in her home. Now you have studied and worked enough. Shaadi.' Here Kasturi's eyes glistened with emotion. 'After you get married, Viru can follow.'

At this entry into the hackneyed territory of shaadi, Shakuntala winced.

'Now Chachi,' she said, playfully, 'you know Viru doesn't have to wait for me.'

Kasturi knew of course. There was no question of the line being held up. Six girls to marry was not a joke, and nobody could help those who missed their destiny.

'Another word about shaadi,' continued Shakuntala, 'and I'm going back to Lahore.'

Kasturi laughed indulgently while Lajwanti sniffed disapprovingly in the background. 'When will this girl settle down?' she asked rhetorically. 'All the time in the lab, doing experiments, helping the girls, studying or going to conferences. I tell her she should have been a man.'

Virmati, looking at her glamorous cousin, marvelled at the change Lahore had wrought in her. What did it matter that Shakuntala's features were not good? She looked better than merely pretty. She looked vibrant and intelligent, as though she had a life of her own. Her manner was expansive, she didn't look shyly around for approval when she spoke or acted.

Her dress too had changed from her Amritsar days. When they went visiting she wore her saris in Parsi-style, as Shakuntala called it, with the palla draped over her right shoulder. The saris were of some thin material, foreign, with a woven silk border sewn onto them. The blouses were of the same thin material, with loose sleeves to the elbows. She wore her hair with a side parting, smoothed over her ears into a bun at the back. Her shoes were black, shiny, patent leather with high heels. Her jewellery consisted of a strand of pearls, a single gold bangle on one arm, and a large man's watch on the other.

'She's become a mem,' Kasturi said disapprovingly. 'Study

means developing the mind for the benefit of the family. I studied too, but my mother would have killed me if I had dared even to want to dress in anything other than was bought for me.'

Virmati listened, thrilled to be her mother's confidante, but drawn towards Shakuntala, to one whose responsibilities went beyond a husband and children.

The cousins were taking an evening walk. 'These people don't really understand Viru, how much satisfaction there can be in leading your own life, in being independent. Here we are, fighting for the freedom of the nation, but women are still supposed to marry, and nothing else.'

'But everybody knows how they also go to jail with Gandhiji, don't they, Pehnji?' contradicted Virmati timidly.

'*And* conduct political meetings, demonstrate, join rallies. I wish you could see what all the women are doing in Lahore. But for my mother, marriage is the only choice in life. I so wish I could help her feel better about me.'

The setting sun was colouring the snow on the distant mountains of the Dauladhar range, Paro was looking bright-eyed and kicking her legs in her pram, but for Virmati her cousin's words were the most vivid thing on the horizon.

'My friends are from different backgrounds, and all have families unhappy with their decision not to settle down, as they call it,' continued Shakuntala. 'We travel, entertain ourselves in the evenings, follow each other's work, read papers, attend seminars. One of them is even going abroad for higher studies.'

'I want to be like you, Pehnji,' blurted Virmati. 'If there are two of us, then they will not mind so much.'

'Silly,' said Shakuntala, stopping in the middle of the path. She turned Virmati's face to her, caressed the flushed cheek and tucked the loose strands of hair on either side behind the ears. 'Chachi will say I am a bad influence on you.'

'No, no really,' said Virmati, catching her hand. Maybe here was the clue to her unhappiness. It was useless looking for answers inside the home. One had to look outside. To education, freedom, and the bright lights of Lahore colleges.

Through the ensuing days Virmati followed Shakuntala around. She watched her ride horses, smoke, play cards and badminton, act without her mother's advice, buy anything she wanted without thinking it a waste of money, casually drop in on all the people the family knew. Above all, she never seemed to question or doubt herself in anything.

And suddenly Shakuntala's infrequent visits home changed their complexion. No longer was she the poor, unmarried, elder cousin, who didn't come because she was hiding her face in shame. She didn't come because the glamorous life of metropolitan Lahore was such that she couldn't tear herself away. Besides, it was easier for her in Lahore than in Amritsar, which represented endless prospective bridegrooms, their money and family histories. And more recently represented the lack of bridegrooms, and her mother's conviction of her doom.

When it came time for Shakuntala to leave, Virmati clung to her. 'Maybe I will also one day come to Lahore, Pehnji,' she wept. 'I wish I too could do things. But I am not clever –'

'*Arre*,' exclaimed her cousin patting her on the back, 'times are changing, and women are moving out of the house, so why not you?'

Why not, indeed, thought Virmati, looking at her, almost breathless with admiration and love.

V

Shakuntala's visit planted the seeds of aspiration in Virmati. It was possible to be something other than a wife. Images of Shakuntala Pehnji kept floating through her head, Shakuntala Pehnji who having done her M.Sc. in Chemistry, had gone about tasting the wine of freedom. Wine, whereas all Virmati had ever drunk had been creamy milk in winter, designed to deaden the senses with its richness, and frothy cool lassi with its lacy bubbles in summer. No, she too had to go to Lahore, even if she had to fight her mother who was so sure that her education was practically over.

So far, not much attention had been paid to Virmati's education. As a child she had been sent, a ten-minute walking distance, to the Arya Kanya Mahavidyalaya, situated in a gully so narrow that, with the drains on either side, it took one person, single file. The school was a single set of rooms around a courtyard, with a dark bathroom in a corner. Every morning at nine, the school maidservant collected Virmati from her house, along with others who lived in that area.

The Arya Kanya Mahavidyalaya believed in grinding the essential rituals of life into their pupils' consciousness by daily example. Every morning started with prayer. Virmati loved sitting with her fellow pupils around the fire, chanting the hymns she had grown up hearing her mother say. She loved the sense of harmony she had when they all tossed havan samagri into the fire with the thumb and middle two fingers of their right hand, the feeling of peace that being away from the home and its children brought.

Once she finished Class VIII, Virmati had been sent for higher studies to Stratford College in the Civil Lines, double-storeyed, red-brick, gardened, with gracefully arched corridors.

The first class she had to join was the special class for those girls weak in English. After that, classes IX and X, and then two years to get a Fine Arts degree. And then marriage, said the elders. Thirteen-year-old Virmati listened and felt the thrill of those approaching rites.

But now, sitting in Dalhousie, with only her FA exams to be taken for her education to be over, she began to feel she had not taken the whole process of learning seriously enough. Really, it was the key to – what? She was not sure, but from now on she must work hard, she must practise her English. She could hear her mother telling her not to waste her time, there were more important things to do. Like looking after the children, thought Virmati bitterly, and then, as she thought of Paro's clinging arms around her neck, she began to cry.

Virmati returned to Amritsar with her father. It was obvious that her family didn't wish her to be further educated. Her future lay in her own hands. But eight months in the hills had made a difference, notwithstanding her diligent attempts to study while looking after her mother. Her English had become rusty. When her mother returned from Dalhousie, Paro, now walking and not considered a baby any longer, became more than ever her care. The other children were constantly demanding.

'Viru Pehnji, we need more sugar and flour. You'll have to unlock the storeroom again.'

'Viru Pehnji, must I take this medicine?'

'Pehnji, she hit me, and took my book!'

'It's really mine! Bade Pitaji gave it to me!'

'Viru! Vidya is crying!'

'Pehnji! The uncle in school said to tell you Gopi hasn't done his homework for a month!'

Such statements provided the background chorus of her education, and formed her character even more surely than any book might have done.

Eventually Virmati failed her FA. The struggle to do well in school while doing her duties at home was too much. With tears in her eyes, Virmati stared at the bulletin board. Higher education involved being on one's own. At the Mahavidyalaya, the teacher would pay a visit home if a student was not doing well. There would be hospitality offered, respect shown, slowly the topic would be raised, and dealt with, in the same tactful manner. Here, everything was hard, cold and impersonal.

'Mati,' she said to her mother that evening, 'I've failed.'

'I told you it was too much for you,' said her mother, busy feeding the younger children.

'It's not too much for me,' protested Virmati. 'Not if I have time to study.'

'Ever since we've come back, you have been making difficulties,' said Kasturi crossly. 'You had the kotha storeroom to study in during your exams, and still you fuss. When Shaku used to study there she never complained.'

'Mati, that was long ago. There were hardly any children playing on the roof then. Now the boys fly kites all evening, then they splash water about from the pump, screaming throughout. Even the neighbour's children jump over their wall to our side. Why can't they stay in their own house?'

'Since when have you been so particular about theirs and ours?'

'Yes, but they all dance on my head. Any quarrel and they come to me, any crying or hurt and they come to me. It never ends.'

'Leave your studies if it is going to make you so bad-tempered with your family. You are forgetting what comes first.'

'Is that what I am saying? When Paro comes to the kotha, and wants to join the other children, I leave everything only to make sure she does not fall or hurt herself.'

'Now you are complaining about your sister.'

'I'm not! Please, Mati, remember how hard Shakuntala Pehnji studied. She did so well her teacher in Lahore asked her to stay and teach when she finished her degree. Her mother understood,' said Virmati, not daring to be more direct.

'Now it is you who are eating my head. What good are

21

Shaku's degrees when she is not settled. Will they look after her when she is old?' demanded Kasturi irritably. 'At your age I was already expecting you, not fighting with my mother.'

Kasturi found the fuss Virmati was making about failing unreasonable. It hardly made a difference to the real business of her life, which was getting married and looking after her own home. There was a good Samaji family making enquiries. The boy was a canal engineer and doing well. His aunt lived in Amritsar and she was getting quite persistent. She was sure Virmati's grandfather would approve of the boy's background.

Virmati was over seventeen by this time. She had a long, fine face with large, widely spaced eyes, eyes with a dazed and distant look. Her nose was thin and straight, her colour pale as the inside of a banana stalk. Her lips were full and a natural red, her chin small and rounded. She was short-sighted, and didn't notice when people looked admiringly at her.

VI

Meanwhile Kasturi continued sickly. The temporary respite in her ill health that the hill sojourn had brought about was soon over. Her father-in-law, Lala Diwan Chand, could see that Kasturi had not benefited as much as he had hoped, and that his son was still anxious about his wife.

'We need to think of another solution,' he said on one of his frequent visits to the Amritsar kothi. He had had a busy day. The Jewellers' Association and the Food Grain Merchants' Association had both had meetings. The Swami he had invited to the evening congregation of the Samaj had given an excellent discourse on the Gita, and after that there had been discussion and conversation with friends and associates. Now he was resting with a glass of milk, while his sister was serving him home-made jalebis, fragrant with saffron, crisp, hot, and sweet.

'Maybe she can come and stay with me in the mill house,' he continued, thinking out loud. 'Let her and Viru come.'

'Virmati has already missed too much school,' said the great-aunt, as she sat down to eat what was left. 'And once she finishes, it will be time to get her married. Already people are asking.'

'Don't I know that?' retorted her brother. 'I have been approached, and when the time is right, I will pick a boy from our Samaj, educated and homely. We must be careful, because where the first one leads the others will follow.'

'Marriages are in the hands of God,' sighed his sister, turning her eyes heavenwards.

Lala Diwan Chand gave a small smile. His standing in the community was very high, and he had brought up his family by the same strict principles that had governed a life of austerity and charity. There were no indulgences permitted in his household. No festivals were observed, not even Holi and Diwali. No fancy clothes were ever worn. Their lives were plain, simple and high-minded. Whatever his sister might say, he knew his girls would be prized. Had he allowed himself to consider such things, he would have acknowledged that the faces out of which this simplicity shone were beautiful, and that beauty had its function in attracting the right-minded towards his family. Nobody mentioned anybody's good looks for fear of attracting the evil eye and inflating the child's head, but the good looks were unarguably there.

Here Lala Diwan Chand's thoughts turned to his daughter-in-law. So far, despite the large number of children that Kasturi had produced, and the small number of rooms that his two sons and their families inhabited, there had been no question of moving. But the family vaid had made it clear that Kasturi's listlessness, pallor and lack of appetite would continue unless she was given more fresh air. Uncongested spaces and long walks were what she needed, on a daily basis. The city with its open drains and dampness was an unhealthy place. He himself lived at the mill house in Tarsikka, and he always felt better there. Though his grandchildren and his daughter-in-law often came to visit, it was clearly not enough. He must talk to his sons. Moving such a large household would mean considerable work and expense. Then the thought of leaving the house that the family had lived in for so many years was painful.

Lajwanti had foreseen trouble of this kind years ago, with a heart that became tight and constricted in Kasturi's presence. Ever since her young brother-in-law, Suraj Prakash, had brought his bride home, she had watched how her in-laws danced attendance on her, fussing over her health, duped by that sweet face, when really she was no better than a dog or a cat in season. No better.

Before Kasturi's arrival she had been the only young woman in the house, and everything had been managed peacefully. But within one year of Suraj Prakash's marriage the first child had come, and after that there was no stopping the woman. She remembered, with a bitterness still fresh and sullen, how delighted her father-in-law had been at Kasturi's disgusting breeding. 'Raunaq in the house at last,' he exclaimed, completely ignoring the existence of her two children.

She had tried complaining to him, 'Baoji, the noise. From morning to night I have a headache. Somnath has been forced to go to the storeroom on the kotha to study, and as for Shaku, how is it possible for her to concentrate on her books with all their hoo-hoo, haa-haa, hee-hee?'

'She should play more with her cousins,' commented the grandfather. 'She is too pale.'

'She is very delicate, Baoji, how can she stand it when I can't? Poor Shaku has to walk up and down my back and across my head to relieve the pain,' whispered the girl's mother, pressing her temples.

'I will allow no one to be sick in my house,' replied the father-in-law. 'From tomorrow the tonga will drive both of you every morning to the Company Bagh. One hour of brisk walking in the fresh air will benefit you greatly.'

But how could Lajwanti go? If she were to leave the house every morning, who knew what mischief those children would be up to. They respected nothing, and that woman had no shame. If she wasn't always on the alert they would slip in to pee in her angan, in her rooms, even shit in the gutter outside her kitchen. She had to be there to shout for Kasturi, carefully inspecting while the latter performed an inadequate swabbing job. They even had the nerve to wet her quilt, and though she forced Kasturi to wash the heavy thing there and then, that woman was incapable of cleanliness. She had to be vigilant not only in her own quarters, but upstairs where the latrines were, as well. Her family used to do their morning business before the sweeper came to carry the night soil away. After that, the toilets remained clean for the rest of the day. Now these children would hop across the terrace to her side and mess up the three cubicles, even the cement blocks, so that no one could decently use the place. It was because of their dirt and filth that she had had to demand a separate kitchen from her father-in-law.

At first he hadn't taken her seriously, but when she left the house and refused to return he realized she meant her threats. Gradually she had had to supervise the building of a wall across the angan and then across the common drawing-room in order to protect her space. As for money, that woman was such a blood-sucker, it was but inevitable that her own family would suffer.

Only her husband had begun to see things in their proper per-spective. God had helped her to achieve that.

'I've never seen such a thing,' he would hear when he came home, tired from sitting in the shop all day. 'How hard you have to work! And for whom? Those children! Ha!' A stream of red betel juice would be spat in the gutter.

'Our children, too,' the children's tau initially mumbled. He revelled in their chatter, and frequently kept little surprises for them to discover in his pockets.

'Our children! Now it is all very well, but will they ask after us in our old age!'

'What is to be done? The children are here,' said Chander Prakash.

'*Arre*, what is here is all right, but they go on coming. Every one or two years. It is like a harvest!'

'It is God's will. How is it in our hands?'

'*Bap re*, you are too good-natured. At least we cannot keep watching our money go into their mouths!'

'How can you talk like that? It is common money, after all.'

'And should be divided equally,' said Lajwanti.

'Everyone gets a share,' reasoned her husband.

'And their share is never ending! We are few, our needs are simple. For whom are you working so hard?'

And this conversation with variations to suit the time and place became almost a daily feature in the elder brother's life. What was he to do? His wife was a good woman, she kept his comforts in mind. Eventually he decided to retire. His father was puzzled.

'Not work? What does that mean? We are traders, we are growing.' Chander looked unhappy. 'Are there problems with your brother?' he asked.

'No, no, Baoji.'

'Then?'

'My health,' said Chander.

'Your health?' The father looked amazed. 'What's wrong with your health?'

Chander whimpered something about not wanting to worry his father, which just irritated the old man further.

'Worry, worry! What do you mean? Now my son will decide for me what I should think, is that it?'

'No, Baoji, of course not.'

'I'm still working, looking after the mill in Tarsikka, coming here to the city at least twice a week, and you are talking of sitting back and doing nothing! How will that look in the eyes of the world?' his father said, his temper rising.

'Why should anyone say anything, Baoji? I only said my health was bad. It has been going on for some time now. Maybe a little rest.' By now Chander believed that rest was what he needed, and what he deserved. His responsibilities were not many. He only had one daughter and his son wanted to break away from the Amritsar Lala tradition and enter law or public administration. If his father gave him a monthly pension out of his portion of the family income, he could manage on his own and regain his strength.

Lala Diwan Chand was vehemently opposed to any kind of division in the family. As long as he was alive, everybody would be provided for. But with each new child Kasturi produced, the murmurs of discontent became louder and more persistent.

Finally, worn out by his elder daughter-in-law's increasing quarrelsomeness in the home, and gently supported by his widowed sister, Lala Diwan Chand agreed to pension off his older son with a substantial monthly stipend. His property he refused to divide. He had worked all his life to make it grow, and he was not about to halve and quarter it now. What he thought was a final solution, however, turned out to be the beginning of a long chain of partitions.

The family owned large orchards on the outskirts of Amritsar, on Lepel Griffin Road. It was eventually decided to add to the three rooms already there in order to accommodate the two brothers. Suraj Prakash was pleased at the prospect of shifting. He had been worried about Kasturi, and was relieved to have his father share that concern. Furthermore, his older children were approaching marriageable age, and the openness of the orchard house would make wedding arrangements more convenient. Once the boys married, there would also be ample space to build bedrooms for the new couples.

Lajwanti saw this as a golden opportunity to detach herself, once and for all, from her sister-in-law. Why should the shift to Lepel Griffin Road not be extended to include separate living quarters as well? When Somnath married, there would be plenty of space for him and his wife in a new house, whereas if both the brothers still lived together, there would be no room for anybody. She started to work on her husband.

The next week as Lala Diwan Chand sat with his sons in the small angan of the city house it was obvious that Chander was agitated. Normally quiet and withdrawn, he insisted on speaking before his father had even finished his milk.

'Baoji, the house. We have to think of Shakuntala and Somnath too. Another one should be built side by side. When they get married . . .'

'What is this?' Lala Diwan Chand began to grow angry. 'Let them first get married. Then you will see what I shall do for them. Further separation of the family is impossible! Your brother's children are like your own. One blood flows in them.'

Next weekend, the same agitation, the same hurry to get the words out. 'Baoji, they are eleven, and we are two. How will everything be equal–equal? With two houses . . .' He hesitated and stopped.

'Beta, since when have everybody's needs not been met equally?' demanded his father. 'We do not consider what we can get, but what we need. Have you or your family ever wanted for anything under my roof?' Lala Diwan Chand raised his voice so

28

that the message would reach any ears that were listening.

'But after you, Baoji . . .' persisted Chander Prakash.

Suraj Prakash gasped. His brother was indeed far gone, if he could talk of his father's dying in such an inauspicious manner, and to his face. Lala Diwan Chand's face took on a rigid look as Chander continued, 'It may not be always so. Why create quarrels among our children's children?'

'We are teaching them to do that now,' said Lala Diwan Chand firmly, his eyebrows bristling. 'If *we* cannot live together, how can we expect the younger ones to do so?' Turning to his younger son, he stated, 'I cannot countenance two different units.'

Suraj Prakash looked mute and non-questioning, Lala Diwan Chand looked angry, while Chander Prakash looked stubborn and childish.

Every weekend Lala Diwan Chand was faced by his elder son's persistent harping on this theme. This house thing was beginning to be a nightmare. And yet the pressures to move were great. The needs of his daughter-in-law and his grandchildren demanded it. His fury grew. I have made them, fed them, clothed them, and now they behave like this, he thought. At such a time with the drain on expenses and manpower, to be forced into further construction, further breakup! He was deeply mortified at being manœuvred into this position. He thought of asking his sister to talk to Lajwanti, but dismissed it. Lajwanti was clever, his sister was simple. In the end it would make little difference.

Ultimately he gave in. He could not bear to see Chander work himself into such agonized states. If separation was inevitable, better to do it while he was alive than to have his sons bicker over his property after he was dead. Bitterly he said to his son, 'You realize your house will only be built after the first one has been completed.' And Lajwanti, who had been listening as usual, knew she had won.

The next six months saw construction work being carried out at Lepel Griffin Road. The existing row of three rooms in the orchard had served as a place to eat and have the children nap in when the family had come on day excursions. Now an angan, kitchen, milk-room, dining-room and storerooms were being added behind the main section. The stables, garage and cowshed were connected to the main building by a long, dark passageway. In one corner of the angan, a well was dug with a hand-pump to enclose into a dark and slippery bathing place, lit by a lantern. At a hygienic distance from the house were three sheds with commodes beneath cement platforms.

Every night Suraj Prakash would inform Kasturi about progress on the building. 'The children won't be able to get into mischief there,' she frequently remarked after he finished. Expenditures were always more acceptable if children were involved.

Lajwanti overheard and burned. How like Kasturi to take advantage of her situation even in this. She herself had never used her children as means to any end. But her day would come, and then, after almost twenty years, she would be able to draw her breath in peace.

Knowing that the pattern of their communal life was going to change soon, the three women took care to preserve the norms of peace that had existed in the early days of their joint-family household. The great-aunt was the saddest to leave the old house. She had been living with her brother since he had taken her away from her in-laws' house after she had become a widow at the age of fourteen. He had educated her, entrusted her with his charitable works, and introduced her to the concepts of Dayanand Saraswatiji. One of the rooms in the new house was to be kept exclusively for her. Lala Diwan Chand's only stipulation to his younger son had been that his sister stay with him, where she would receive the dignity and respect that was her due.

Suraj Prakash, Kasturi, their eleven children, and the great-aunt shifted within a year of the doctor's recommendation. Lajwanti refused to go with them. She didn't want to deprive her sister-in-law of any space, she would wait till her own humble dwelling was ready. Of course, she missed her nieces and nephews terribly, but

Fate was always so cruel to her, what could she do? That is why she took the tonga out every evening and went over to visit them in Lepel Griffin Road. Before leaving, she would take a tour of the house going up next door. She questioned the workmen extensively, and complained about everything to Suraj Prakash. It was just to help him, she said. She knew how busy he was, how little time he had, and how unfortunate it was that her own husband's ill health did not allow him to contribute more. Her helpfulness grew so great that Suraj Prakash wrote to Somnath in Lahore to take a more active hand in the building. What with running the business, looking after the construction, and trying to meet Lajwanti's expectations, he began to feel that some of the responsibility should go to the eldest male of the next generation. He was tired and could do no more.

VII

Somnath was used to shuttling between Amritsar and Lahore. He refused to marry until he was established in some profession, though what that profession was going to be, he kept secret. The clearest thing about his future was that he rejected the family jewellery business. His mother often pointed out that it was his duty to see that her old age would not be spent in darkness and loneliness. He at least should settle down. Shakuntala's refusal to marry had caused her enough heartache. Her son owed her grandchildren. At this Somnath would laugh and look hand-some. He wore rings on his fingers, a hint of kaajal in his eyes, perfume made of attar of roses, and silk pyjama-kurtas with Patiala jootis. His mother, looking at him, would regret that so much beauty was being wasted, but despite all the pressure, nothing would induce Somnath to change his mind about mar-riage. Maybe he would go in for the Indian Civil Services. Every-body knew how few Indians were chosen for the ICS and how much concentrated studying the entrance exams required. He could not be disturbed. His mother's sole consolation was that there was an age limit to the ICS.

Somnath agreed at once to Suraj Prakash's request. 'I have been so selfish – relying upon you to look after everybody.'

Suraj Prakash wondered how much debt Somnath had got into in Lahore, that he should acquiesce so easily. Whatever it was, he could only be glad. He had turned fifty and now thought of himself as an old man. His health wasn't good and his growing weight bothered him, though his family were pleased with how healthy he was becoming at last, after a lifetime of leanness.

Somnath, meantime, was looking forward to the change. His mother's lenience meant there had been enough money while he was studying to enable him to frequent clubs, parks, shops, the-atres, and dancing girls and boys. Five years of this kind of life had brought with it a certain kind of boredom, a certain kind of finan-cial obligation towards friends and shopkeepers that he thought would intrude with less troublesome regularity in Amritsar.

Once Somnath shifted to Amritsar, Lajwanti found that his way of building a house was very different from her brother-in-law's. Not only did he refuse to count the number of bricks used every day, and stand in the hot sun while the workers did their work, or go to the gullies of the wholesale markets to get the cheapest materials unless she nagged him a hundred times, but he also had ideas of grandeur of which she did not know what to make. She listened to him indulgently till she saw he intended to put theory into practice, the day he brought home a marble bust of Caesar picked up from an old Italian marble-seller on Mall Road. The fellow was having a sale before leaving Lahore for Italy, he explained to his mother.

'*He* Bhagwan!' exclaimed Lajwanti when she saw two coolies nearly falling under the large, bland shape of Caesar. 'Don't I have enough troubles?'

'The best places in Lahore have them,' said Somnath by way of explanation. 'We will put it in the veranda. Everybody will love it.'

'Those children will break it, and then you will see what good is your love! They cannot leave anything alone.'

And then the fountain arrived, double basins, with a little statue on top. 'Are we building a Taj Mahal?' demanded Lajwanti.

'*Arre*, where is the harm in these decorative things? Just think how it will soothe to look at a fountain splashing in the summer while sitting in the garden,' replied her son.

'But where is the need?' Lajwanti thought her son had gone berserk. How could one spend money on such ostentation? God willing, soon the construction would be over and this madness would stop.

The fountain was followed by a cartload of green tiles with pink embossed roses on them. 'For the kitchen,' elaborated Somnath.

'The kitchen? But who will see the kitchen?' wailed his mother.

'You will,' he said firmly.

He bought green and yellow chandeliers for the two main front rooms, chandeliers with glass roses rising in graceful arcs from the little bowls containing them.

He bought tables of Burma teak and marble, he bought dressing-tables decorated with tiles and mirrors, he bought chairs and cupboards of carved rosewood.

Lajwanti found solace in reflecting that should real trouble come, she could always fall back on her father-in-law. And maybe if her son spent so much time and effort on the house, it meant he would settle down in it, and marry. Give up the nonsense of not doing the jewellery business.

Finally everything was completed and the family finances severely strained. Chander Prakash, Lajwanti and Somnath moved in. A separate room was designated for the use of the absent Shakuntala.

Inside her wonderful house, Lajwanti felt lost. The silence and emptiness seemed eerie. In the comfortable pokyness of the old city home, there was no possibility of feeling alone. The family and servants could always be heard against the sounds of the street coming up through the windows. But here hedge, garden and separate units made her feel abandoned. There were no nephews and nieces to shout at, nobody to scold. Her status had gone.

She started going more often to Kasturi's, but then she couldn't live there. She began to get even more hysterical about her children's not marrying until Somnath in his careless, lordly way invited a tenant without consulting his mother.

'Social service. We don't use all the rooms. And what is the harm in helping others?'

With anybody else, Lajwanti would have lashed out. With her wayward son, she had to be careful.

'How can we hire out part of our home? It is a humiliation.'

34

'Even the best families in Lahore take tenants. From good families. Students.'

'*Bas, bas.* Enough.'

'And this is a professor. They can stay in the three rooms in the back. They can enter from there. You need never see them.'

'*Bap re!* Not see who is living with me! Are you mad?'

'And it will be a little extra income . . .'

'Humph!'

'And you so alone, with only Baoji. It will be some company, some kindness, some money.'

'Who all?' asked Lajwanti tersely.

'Only the mother, father, little baby, sister, grandmother.'

'That's not so few.'

'He's England returned. He has just come to Amritsar from Waltair because his mother wants to stay with him, and the south is too far.'

'That's no reason for them to stay here. Am I running a dharamshala?'

'At least meet them. No harm in that.'

Lajwanti consented by grumbling that from now on she could see she would be nothing in her own house.

They appeared in the afternoon. Lajwanti saw a handsome family, the man tall, wearing a starched dhoti-kurta, his hair brushed back over a wide forehead, tortoiseshell spectacles framing bright, intelligent eyes. Not many touches of the foreign returned about him, she noted with approval. The wife fair, face like the moon, short, round, plump, with her sari covering her head, and falling below the waist.

This Professor – anybody who taught at Arya Sabha College was a professor – had returned from Oxford two years before, and had landed in Amritsar at the request of a friend's father, who was on the board of trustees. The college had long been looking for a good English teacher, for such an important subject they wanted someone with impeccable credentials. They couldn't afford an actual foreigner, nor did it suit their policy to hire one. Theirs was a Hindu college and they intended to keep it that way. An Indian with a British degree was ideal, and Harish Chandra was enticed by a salary of two hundred and thirty rupees; twenty rupees more than he was getting at the college in Waltair. Harish Chandra had a family, and he came to Amritsar without a second thought.

Did Harish Chandra ever think he would fall in love with the Punjab? Had this been predicted, he would have laughed. His heart he had left in England, returning to India reluctantly, and only because of his mother's insistent demands. Harish knew he was his mother's life. An only son, his specialness had tinged the milk he drank and the air he breathed from the moment he had been born. Her death would be on his head if he did not come back. Five years she kept waiting, it's five years since I have seen my son. It had also been five years since he had seen his wife, but his wife had been in no position to enforce her claims. She couldn't write, and besides she hardly knew him.

Harish returned to India, his house, mother and wife, bringing back as much of England as he could. Her art, music and literature followed him in heavy, black, metal sea-chests. First to his home in the United Provinces, and then to Lajwanti's home on Lepel Griffin Road.

VIII

It is December, and time for Virmati's final FA exams. This time
she absolutely must pass. The books spread on a charpai in the
side garden of her family's new house on Lepel Griffin Road
show how conscientiously she has been trying to study. Near
the books is a large kitchen knife. Scattered around are the leafy
tops of carrots, white and red radishes, and a small thali crusted
with lemon juice, salt and chilli powder. Virmati has been raiding
the garden, and her brothers and sisters have been raiding her.
The youngest, Paro, a little under two years old, runs between
Vidyavati, her four-year-old sister, and Virmati, her eighteen-
year-old sister. From time to time they have fought over who has
had the greater share, and Virmati has energetically scolded and
kissed, and sent for more carrots and radishes. It is fun doing all
this, she feels alive. But her books call, and at last she has been
very firm, and told them not to bother her with any more eating.

'I don't want to eat any more gaajjar-mooli, anyway, Pehnji.
Look, I've made all these drawings,' said Vidyavati, pushing
three crumpled sheets at her, which Paro tried to snatch away.

'She'll dirty them!' shouted Vidya, pulling them back. Virmati
quickly put salt and lemon on a radish and gave it to Paro, to distract her, before turning her attention to the artwork clutched
possessively in Vidya's equally grubby hand.

While Virmati tried to do justice to the drawings, she noticed
the woman next door, gesturing and smiling at the two younger
girls. She was carrying a bucket full of washed clothes. It was
Taiji's tenant. 'She's calling you two, Vidu. Go, and take Paro.'

Paro was slowly chewing through her white radish and did
not move.

Virmati became irritated. 'Hurry up now,' she said, roughly
dabbing at Paro's grimy face.

Five minutes later they returned, triumphantly clutching two huge mathris in their hands, carefully balancing dark-green mango-pickle pieces on top of them.

'Pehnji! Look what she gave us! I've never seen such big mathri, have you?'

No, Virmati hadn't. 'Give,' she said.

Vidya gave her a piece of Paro's mathri. 'I told her my sister is studying, and she said people who study need lots of food to nourish the brain.'

Virmati smiled. In that house, at least, study was given full recognition. She took a bite of the crisp, flaky mathri with a small piece of the pickle to complement its bland taste. 'This pickle is really good,' she told her sisters. 'How dry it is! I wonder how they make it with no oil.'

'She said she brought this from her home.'

'We must give her something too. Vidu, pick some carrots and radishes for her. The poor lady probably doesn't get to eat any straight from the garden like we do.'

And so it started with the exchange of food. Neighbourliness demanded this much and these people were so much closer than neighbours, tenants in what was practically their own house. The woman hospitably opened the doors of her kitchen to them. She loved to cook, she loved to see people enjoying the food she made. Bhabhi – sister-in-law – they called her, following her own little daughter's example. But it was Virmati who came most often, followed by Paro, her shadow. The woman noticed how much she liked her husband's music when it was on, and how she would listen, still and lost. Once, when there was nobody in the main room with her husband, she coaxed Virmati in there.

'The oldest girl from next door, and her youngest sister,' she said by way of introduction.

The Professor smiled indulgently at them. 'You like the music?' he inquired, gesturing to the side table, where the gramophone lay with its lid open, its shiny metal arm bobbing up and down over a record. Lots of red, white and blue dust jackets lay on either side.

Virmati nodded. She was too shy to say anything. The Professor put on his sweetest Bach and was rewarded by the look on Virmati's face. This girl has potential, he found himself thinking, while Virmati listened and dreamed more intensely than she ever had of her fiancé, that shadowy figure waiting in the wings to marry her.

'Don't you ever go out?' Virmati asked the woman. They were quite friendly now.

'*Arre*, where to go? He is busy and there is so much to do in the house.'

Virmati nodded. That she could see. There was much the woman was constantly doing, especially in the kitchen.

'What about Darbar Sahib and the Company Bagh? If you live in Amritsar you have to visit these places.'

'When he gets the time . . .'

'I'll take you,' said Virmati impulsively.

The woman smiled politely and said, 'No, no.'

'I will drag you away. You can say I kidnapped you,' laughed Virmati.

They went in Virmati's father's tonga. In the Company Bagh, Virmati mentioned the names of the trees she knew, and she knew practically all of them. They had been part of her nature-study course in school.

'It's good the girls of today know so much,' remarked the woman wistfully. Out of her kitchen, out of her house, the kinds of knowledge she had left her ill-equipped even in a garden.

'My mother, my masi, all studied. It is the rivaz in our family,' said Virmati proudly. 'Even now my father keeps getting my mother books and magazines to read.'

'She is lucky,' sighed the woman. 'For him, too, studies are very important. He even tried to teach me. But I am too old,' she giggled uncertainly.

Virmati thought it very noble of the Professor to try and teach his wife. It showed he really cared for women's education, just like her grandfather.

The woman thought back to the many times her husband had tried to teach her. In the beginning he was patient, it was an impossible situation that his wife should be illiterate. He had decided to start with Hindi; when she had mastered that, she could graduate to English, read the books he liked, become his companion. But the woman found it difficult to learn letters.

'Here,' her husband would say, going over them once, twice. 'Now you read them on your own. Copy them down in this notebook afterwards, that will help you memorize them. We'll do the next lesson tomorrow.'

The woman copied down the letters carefully, but when it came to her husband's daily test, she found she had forgotten which sound went with which letter. Then they would do the whole thing over again, adding a few more letters, because the husband didn't have all the time in the world, and he wanted his wife to become a companion quickly. Meanwhile the life of the house flowed around them. Women were sewing, knitting or preparing food, amidst ripples of talk, while children played in the angan. The younger girls would peep slyly inside the room and titter at seeing her trying to study. She could hear her daughter's baby voice amongst them.

The woman's own mother had never read, nor ever felt the need. She had taught the woman everything she knew. By the time she was ready to leave for her husband's house at the age of twelve, she had mastered the basic items of a pure vegetarian diet. She was quick and inventive with the embroidery and knitting needle, as well as with the sewing-machine. After her marriage, her mother-in-law made sure that she learned the ways of her in-laws' household from the moment of her arrival. All this was part of growing up, she knew, but how was she ever to dream that without the desire to read and write, she was going defenceless into union with a man so unlike the others she knew, who didn't seem to care about her household skills at all? Yet he was impatient and angry when the food was badly cooked, and the house carelessly managed. The woman sighed, and turned her attention back to Virmati still chattering on about trees and their names.

'It's good you know all this,' she repeated. 'My Chhotti, too, will know,' referring to her daughter, about Vidya's age. 'She has already started looking at books. Her father is so keen. She tries to show me.'

Virmati looked startled. That seemed to be against the natural order of things. She couldn't imagine learning anything from any of her sisters. Maybe things were different in the United Provinces where the woman had come from. Hadn't her grandfather always said the women of the Punjab were among the most advanced in the country?

'Chhotti teaches you?' she asked.

'Sometimes. When I have the time. If God wills, I will learn.'

She said nothing about her efforts to meet her husband's standards, her pain when she remained uncomprehending despite his lessons. Her hope now lay in her daughter.

Vaguely Virmati began to feel sorry, she was not sure for whom. It was strange that the Professor's wife couldn't read. She turned the conversation to herself. 'Mati doesn't want me to study further. I have just done my FA exams, you know.'

'And?' inquired the woman.

'Well . . .' blushed Virmati. 'My family found . . .'

'Ah,' said the woman, understanding completely.

'I agreed and in fact I would have been married by now, but then my grandmother, great-aunt really, died. I think she never liked it here after we moved, you know. My grandfather was most upset. Now we have to wait a year and in the meantime I will go on studying. I want to go to Lahore like Shakuntala Pehnji, but I don't know . . .'

'Some things come before studies,' smiled the woman. 'It is the right time.'

'That is what they all say,' grumbled Virmati, for form's sake.

'It is true. You will see later,' said the woman.

This argument was endless, with the lines well laid down for each position. Education versus marriage. They amiably continued along the traditional texts as they finished their tour of the

41

Company Bagh and drove into the older part of Amritsar towards Darbar Sahib.

The woman loved Darbar Sahib. It was so clean and spacious, so gold and white. Despite the people, it was serene, even silent. They did a parikrama around the marble courtyard, and then joined the line that snaked through the temple inside. Clutching the hot halwa parshad and laughing, they felt light and gay.

'Come, let's buy bangles,' suggested Virmati, leading her companion towards the small, dark, paved gully that rose from off one of the corners of the temple.

'No, no, it's getting late. What'll he say?' hesitated the woman, remembering that she ought not to be away from home for so long. Without him.

'What'll he say? Nothing,' challenged Virmati.

'No, no, he'll say nothing,' agreed the woman. 'Like that he is very good, but still . . .' Her voice trailed off. How could she explain all the different qualities of silence that could thicken the air in a house, and that to someone who was not married? It was impossible. She stood distractedly in front of the bangle-seller Virmati led her to.

'How about these?' asked Virmati, pointing to the blue ones, light and dark, rimmed with gold. 'You are so fair, they will suit you.'

'He doesn't like blue,' explained the woman, shaking her head. 'I wear nothing blue.'

Virmati looked at the woman. She and her sisters wore whatever colour they pleased except inauspicious black.

'He must be very particular.'

'He is.'

'Shall we go further up?'

'Oh, no, no. It's getting late,' and the woman turned.

'But you hardly ever come out,' persisted Virmati.

'He worries,' said the woman.

The tonga clattered back. The woman sat silently tense, while Virmati wondered at her state. Reaching the back rented portion of the house, the first thing they saw was the Professor Sahib looking restless. As they came towards him, Virmati exclaimed gaily, 'Here's the treasure you had loaned me. See, I have brought her back safe and sound!'

For a moment he looked startled. Then, his face softened, and the woman scurried off thankfully to the kitchen.

'Perhaps I'll get my tea now,' the Professor said to Virmati.

'The fault is mine,' she replied, elegant still.

'Mine, if you feel blamed.'

Virmati fell silent. She did not know what to say next and turned to go. He called out, 'Stay and have a cup.'

'Oh, no. My milk will be waiting for me at home.'

Her milk. So young, he thought.

'Do please come in,' he repeated courteously, putting polite pressure on her. 'In England they say nothing is so refreshing as a cup of tea. I learnt to like it there.' He was offering a little bit of himself which both flattered and alarmed Virmati.

'I like it already,' she said brightly, as she remained standing safely on the step. 'Indumati makes me tea when I'm not feeling well. With milk and honey, tulsi leaves, black pepper and ginger.'

The Professor winced slightly. 'Ah, I see. The medicinal potion,' he said.

The woman emerged from the kitchen, a silver tray in her hands. On it was a white cup and saucer with small pink roses, and faint green leaves. A fine gold line could be seen around the rim. Matching this was a small jug with bits of steam curling out, and a round sugar bowl with a silver spoon standing straight up in it. On one side bulged the starched teacosy, with white flowers embroidered against a whiter background. Seeing her husband still talking to Virmati, the woman hesitated before him, holding the tray. He gestured inside, and turned again to the guest.

'Are you sure that I have to be so rude as to send you back without anything to eat or drink?'

But the sight of the tea-tray, with its unfamiliar rigmarole, was enough to send Virmati urgently home – really, they are waiting

– to the glass of hot milk that she could sip comfortably and slowly while warming her hands around it. When you talked to him, she thought, the Professor Sahib wasn't formidable. He seemed quite friendly, offering her tea more than once. How was it that the woman was still in awe of him after all those years?

'Pehnji?'

'Yes, Paro?' Virmati was lying on her bed, frowning in concentration before an English book. Her lips were moving, and her finger ran along the lines.

'I got hurt. Look.' And Paro pointed to her knee smudged with dirt and blood. She had been waiting for Virmati to come home from college and see for herself how hurt she was.

'Oh, poor thing,' said Virmati caressing her half-heartedly. Her finger started moving again and Paro pulled at her dupatta.

'Red medicine,' she started wailing. For while the other children had scraped and banged themselves with no after-luxury of medicine, Virmati had always tenderly looked after Paro's hurts, cooking up haldi and ghee to smear on them. Of late she had taken to being more modern and buying red medicine, which was quicker to apply.

'It's not really so bad, Paro. Now don't disturb me, I'm reading. Go and play with Vidya.'

Paro snatched the book from her hands, and threw it on the floor. Virmati leapt off the bed and slapped her.

Paro burst into tears, and fled. She wandered around the house crying, and when her sister still did not come, crept outside her room, and snivelled loudly next to the window. She wouldn't stop until Virmati came and held her as she used to, until she put medicine on her knee as she used to.

Oh God, thought Virmati, what will the Professor Sahib think? I've kept his book for two weeks already, and he was asking me what I thought of it yesterday, and why did I say I've almost finished it, when I'm only beginning. It's impossible to read in this house. She's not even that badly hurt. No one looked at my hurts when I was her age. I've spoilt her. Anger rose inside

44

Virmati, and Paro felt her hands hard and rough, instead of caring and tender, but looking at her sister's face, she was too scared to complain further.

Virmati passed her FA with marks that were respectable enough for a girl, her parents thought. She now wanted to study further. Her parents thought that she had gone far enough. Her fiancé's parents thought she was already well qualified to be the wife of their son, the canal engineer. They didn't want too much education in their daughter-in-law, even though times were changing. Virmati wept and sulked.

'What is the matter with her?' said her mother. 'She was never so keen before.'

'The girl is serious. It is natural,' said her grandfather to her mother.

'For how long can she go on like this? There is Indumati to think of. We can afford to wait for the boys after Indu, but what about her?'

There was no argument against this, but then the canal engineer's father died. There was to be a mourning period, the marriage was again postponed.

Virmati entered AS College, the bastion of male learning. It had four hundred boys to six girls. Virmati was the seventh.

Kasturi spoke to the Professor's wife: 'What are these college-going boys like? Virmati will be among so many of them! So few girls to so many boys! I do not feel easy.'

Kasturi and the woman had become quite friendly, and Kasturi turned to her for advice about her daughter's education.

'Don't worry, Behenji,' said the woman. 'They are all from good families. And they have no time for anything else besides studies. Even learning in the classroom is not enough, they come to him at home. Books, records, pictures, photos, all he shares with them.' Here the woman put her palla across her mouth and uttered a tiny laugh into it. Her husband's popularity was a source of vicarious pleasure for her, but she was modest and did not want Kasturi to think she was boasting about him.

'Well, you know, so if you think it is all right,' hesitated Kasturi.

'Yes, I do,' said the woman. 'Some of them are married, some of them are engaged. They come to him with problems in their personal lives as well.'

'Such as?'

The woman became vague. She wasn't sure, but it had something to do with the books her husband taught, and the way in which he taught them. She herself distrusted books, they had caused her so much misery, but as the Professor's wife she was hardly in a position to say so. It was just that the whole business involved so many other things as well. Students at all hours, students beginning to be dissatisfied with life the way it was, with the brides their parents had chosen. Thank God, Virmati's fiancé was an engineer, an educated, working man. No, no, she assured Kasturi, Virmati's future was safe in AS college.

Virmati always sat in the front row with the four other girls who were in the Professor's class, and that was the only place he saw her in college, flower-like, against a backdrop of male students. The Professor knew the seven girls spent their time between classes in a small room meant for them, next to the principal's office, on the inner side of the courtyard. Through the thin bamboo curtain that covered the door, they could see what was going on in the morning assembly, could see when all the boys had reached their class, and when it was safe to venture forth, heads muffled in dupattas dashing to their reserved seats in the front.

Once, the class had been more than usually full. Virmati, a little late, found no room left in the first row. She hesitated at the door. The Professor, sensing it was she, did not look up as he might ordinarily have done. Ignoring the half-dozen young men who rose to give her their place, Virmati sat on the floor in front of his desk, looking up at him with her large eyes. The Professor drank in the symbolism of her posture greedily. It moved him so deeply that he remembered it in all its detail even when his children had grown up. The murmur and rustle of students with scratching pens, their heads receding in rows, the whirr and click-click of the fans overhead, and the stillness at the heart of it, enclosing him and Virmati, Virmati with her offering eyes in her open face.

Later, when the deed was done, and he was in love with her, insisting on death if she were so cruel as to deny him, he discovered she was myopic. She still stared at him, with that thoughtful, dreamy, not quite seeing gaze. He took her to the eye doctor. Yes, she needed glasses. Not strong ones, just a mild prescription. With them, she looked more studious, less flower-like and appealing. But by then, the Professor's desire to possess had extended to her heart and mind.

IX

'Kailashnath Mama?'

'Yes, Ida?'

'You know the college where my father taught?'

'Who doesn't?'

'I wonder, could you take me there? If it is not too far?'

'Too far? What is too far in Amritsar? This is not a big city like your Delhi. Instead we have a small city, big with bombings and killings. No, I can't take you there. There is a curfew on. Don't you read the papers, or listen to the news?'

I am guilty. I don't. The rawness I feel after my mother's death doesn't allow me to do anything that is not, in some way, connected with her. Ever since coming to Amritsar I have been restlessly pacing the old house. I wish bricks could speak. This must have been where Virmati slept, this must have been where she studied, this must have been the window Paro snivelled at. Those rooms have now been partitioned and divided into sub-units with separate kitchens for each uncle and aunt.

The lichi and the mango orchards are all gone. The Urban Land Ceiling Act has transformed the huge gardens into little suburban plots. The fields where gaajjar-mooli grew have been replaced by ugly concrete houses. They have little gardens and tall hedges to fence out prying eyes. The hand-pump situated at a corner of the old, yellowing house now hangs dry and useless, with rust gathering around the handle. Everything has changed, become smaller and uglier, more developed.

The curfew did partially lift in two days. How terribly Kailash Mama drives, I thought, as we horned and lurched our way through the Amritsar bazaar. The car was an old Morris Minor and the seats had practically worn into the floor over the years.

'They knew how to build cars, the British did. See how solid it still is, not like these shiny tinny Marutis you see everywhere today. Touch them and you have a dent,' shouted Kailash Mama, swerving to avoid a truck that roared past him on the narrow road.

'This is a sturdy car,' I agreed, poking my finger absent-mindedly through a tear in the upholstery.

Mamiji gazed out of the window.

The way to AS College was very crowded, but ultimately not long. In twenty minutes we were there.

'It is certainly centrally located,' I remarked.

'Cycling distance,' said Kailashnath Mama, 'though your mother came in a tonga.'

A high wall surrounds AS College. It has metal spikes at the top, and on top of that, barbed wire.

'Why the barbed wire, Mamaji?'

'One of the students was caught trying to blow up the place. A fanatic. He was planting a bomb in the lab when the lab attendant spotted him. They couldn't dismiss him because of communal tension, so they quickly awarded him his degree, and sent him to his village. He wouldn't settle for anything less than a second class, I believe. Meanwhile the governing body got very frightened about the security of the place, and put barbed wire all over the top. As though the spikes were not enough. Typical of the mindless idiots.'

The three of us are stopped at the spiked, barbed-wire gate and asked our business. To see the college, we said, which made the guard look even more suspicious. But we are well dressed, and used to a certain treatment. Reluctantly, he ushers us into the principal's office.

It is a small room, cramped and poky. The damp, yellowing walls are randomly broken with mementoes of past significance, stern-looking principals, tarnished shields. Shiny brown and beige curtains hang limply over the barred windows. A huge desk takes up half the room, its Sunmica surface glittering with a design of wood whorls and lines. Bright blue rexine chairs surround it, while at the head sits the principal's armchair, heavy, with dirty black cushions.

Kailashnath thought, how different the place was when the Professor Sahib was principal before Independence. Then the office was in the main portion of the college building. After he married Viru, I visited him once or twice in the college, so that Mati would not get to know. His room was a good one, big, windows overlooking the driveway on one side, and courtyard on the other. His desk was of a dark and lustrous wood, and he placed it where he could see his books and whatever else was going on. He took his English classes here, classes that he refused to give up despite his administrative duties, that man was so fond of teaching.

The principal came, murmuring apologies at the zealousness of his guards.

'The times are such,' said Kailashnath.

'Indeed,' agreed the principal.

'So unfortunate,' I added, though no one was listening.

Did we really want to see the college? The principal looked politely disbelieving. Kailashnath enlightened him. I was introduced as the Delhi seeker after local and historical knowledge. The principal sent for the oldest two teachers. He himself had only joined recently, he explained.

We set off, the men striding ahead. Following slowly, at my aunt's pace, I agonized over the valuable information I might be missing.

We walked into the main building. My parents must have walked down these hallways, across these stones, and I felt the past hovering, cliché-like, over that run-down building, beckoning me into its orbit.

The main college buildings were colonial, with classrooms built around a large, brick-paved courtyard, with a raised cement platform at one end.

'This is where we still have assembly,' said the principal.

'How quiet the college is,' I wondered aloud.

'Exams are going on,' explained a teacher to my aunt, courtesy dictating that he ignore the younger woman while addressing the older.

On the way down the corridors, I could see that exams were indeed going on. The desks were arranged in parallel rows, and after years of invigilation in my own college it was not hard to see that many of the students were cheating. Heads furtively bent forwards, backwards, or at acute angles, open exam scripts pushed over the edge of the desk, question papers being dropped on the floor and exchanged. The invigilators were chatting to each other in front of the classroom. In Delhi, students of some men's colleges cheated with open knives on their desks, a threat that the invigilators did not dare confront, but here obviously the rules were better understood by those concerned.

'We have a very high rate of pass,' said the teacher turning to me at last.

I politely commented that that must bring pleasure to them all.

'Yes, ours is considered a good college, though of course it no longer has the reputation it did in your father's time.'

'Oh no. That was the height of the college. Its days of prestige,' said the other teacher.

'I never knew the Professor Sahib,' said the principal. 'But people still tell stories about him.'

We first went to the library. It was housed in a large room running the entire length of the building on the first floor. There were old-fashioned wooden cupboards with glass doors arranged around the walls. In the middle were desks and benches dotted with a few students. The room was cool, even in the middle of summer. The ceilings were high, and the deep, recessed windows covered with wire netting. It looked old and graceful, peaceful and untouched.

'The librarian sits here,' said the principal, going towards a small room at the back. 'Our oldest staff member.'

We approach the librarian. Yes, he remembers the Professor Sahib.

'This library,' he said, gesturing around the big room. 'He made it. He used to buy the books when he was principal.

Whenever he travelled anywhere, he would come back with a suitcase-full for the college. We had the latest and the best.'

The sight of the books drew me, and I wandered over to look at the names on the faded spines in the literature section. A casual glance, and then closer, my gaze held by those muted colours, those old names. From one cupboard to the next I looked. How many of these same titles, the same edition even, had I lived with in my own home? What did he do? Reproduce the home in the college and vice versa?

I took out a familiar-looking volume. Saintsbury on Dryden in the *English Men of Letters* series, published 1915. The date on the library sticker in front was a current one. Did students still read what Saintsbury had to say on Dryden, on his – here I opened the book – on his 'varied cadence and subtly disposed music' and other such fulsome rubbish? Judging from all the underlinings in the book, yes, they did. AS College, the last colonial outpost, where Saintsbury and Gosse were king, where the Beauties of Literature still flourished.

'All his selection,' said the librarian, who had noticed what I was doing.

'Who bought the books after him?' I wanted to know.

The librarian looked apologetic. 'After the Professor Sahib's time we could afford less and less. And now of course, students depend on keys and guides.'

He sounded quite despondent. I told him it was the same in Delhi, but how did that help? Whether there was Saintsbury or Foucault in the library, in the end we teachers were redundant. The vast majority of students were just concerned with their marks, using any means necessary to achieve them, whether knives or cheating, cheap kunjis or mugging up the notes of last year's topper.

Our group of seekers and guides moved on. We stopped at classroom number eight on the ground floor.

'Where he taught.'

It was a large, empty room, resembling a theatre. A few pigeons fluttered around the rafters, the steep rows of benches and desks were of a dark, sombre wood.

'This used to be the most crowded classroom in the entire college.'

'Students used to come from Lahore to hear him.'

'They sat on the window sills.'

'Stood in the corridors, the doorways, trying to hear what he said.'

'But what was so special about what he said?' I was curious. English was English. You could only carry it so far.

'Oh,' said Kailashnath, looking around the classroom where he too had once sat, 'he brought the subject alive. Most of us had never stepped out of Amritsar. The things he talked about, his expression, his way of speaking, we felt we were in another world. Am I right, ji?' he asked turning to the teachers.

They smiled assent.

I walked inside. The ceiling was high, with three faint domes marked into it. Two large windows looked directly upon the green, thick-creepered, college boundary wall. From the inner door and windows one could see the broad veranda, and the courtyard beyond. I climbed the steps and sat on the topmost row, looking down at the stage far beneath me. The coos of pigeons sounded nearer than the conversation of the little group below. They were standing on the podium, around the lectern, where at one time a teacher performed, working his way into the hearts and minds of captive students.

My history had started here, in this classroom. Here it was that my parents must have looked at each other significantly, doomed love in their eyes.

'Imagine my plight,' my father used to say, performer still, first making sure my mother was in earshot. 'Imagine my plight.' And he would roll his eyes, mock alarm and distress crossing his face. 'Your mother engaged to someone else!'

He said nothing about his wife.

Virmati plus fiancé, the Professor plus wife. An invisible quadrangle in a classroom.

X

At what stage did thoughts of the Professor replace the permitted thoughts of her fiancé in Virmati's mind?

That he looked at her, she knew. That he paid attention to her, she was aware. But to think of him was impossible, given the gulf between them, until he bridged it by crying out his need. Eldest and a girl, she was finely tuned to neediness, it called to her blood and bones. He spread his anguish at her feet, and demanded that she do with him as she pleased.

Days passed, and Virmati's confusion grew. She would sometimes wish that . . . but what could she wish? Early marriage, and no education? No Professor, and no love? Her soul revolted and her sufferings increased.

The question of the fiancé loomed large.

'Tell him, tell him.' The Professor became exigent. 'The thought of him in your life is like poison to me.' By now, Virmati had finished her BA and her wedding date was fixed.

'How can I tell him? I hardly meet him. And never alone.'

'Look at me,' urged the Professor, stroking the hair of her bent head. 'It won't matter to him. As you say, he hardly knows you. How can convenience be allowed to come between us? Say you have changed your mind,' he persisted.

Changed her mind? In what world was he living? 'They will think I have gone mad. They have been patient enough with me as it is. And then there is Indu,' she tried to explain.

At this, his face puckered with distress. The grip on her hand tightened, and his fingers, trembling with passion, travelled persuasively up and down her soft arm. Virmati's whole body tightened with tension.

'Don't.'

'Why not?'

'Someone will see. She may come in.'

'No one will see. She's gone out.'

'Still, I don't like it. There are others. They will tell her – them.'

The Professor gently placed his fingers around the thin column of Virmati's neck. 'Don't worry about her,' he pleaded.

'Why not? She is your wife, isn't she?'

The Professor looked crushed and Virmati thought again how it was not his fault, how could he help it if he had been married off at the age of three? Her arms closed around him, and she cushioned his head against her young shoulder.

Later, on her stealthy way home, she felt as usual tainted by her moments with the Professor. The thought of her wedding was always at the back of her mind, splitting her into two socially unacceptable pieces.

As Virmati entered her house, she heard Indumati's voice, 'Pehnji! Here's a letter for you.' The coyness and interest left Virmati no doubt as to whom it was from. Irritated, she grabbed the letter from her sister's hand. She would read it later, after her milk, in the privacy of the second terrace on top of the house.

Respected Virmatiji,

I have been very busy these past two months, so I have not been able to write to you. The bridge project is to be finished soon. Mr White says the work is going very well. He comes once a week to check the position. He spends the night in an ordinary tent and puts up with all the inconveniences. When I apologize, he says that although he holds me responsible for everything that goes on in the project, he will make an exception of the weather and the insects. I smile when he says this. You have to understand the way the British say things.

I will be able to come to Amritsar for a few days on the second of the month in connection with preparations for our marriage. I will call on you and pay my respects to Mataji

and Pitaji, and Bade Baoji. I hope I will be able to meet
Kailashnath also.
　　Respectfully yours,
　　Inderjit

Virmati read this brief letter several times. She searched the
words, but could find no sense that she was important to him, no
impatience to be united with her. But maybe, thought Virmati
indecisively, these things came after marriage?

In her pocket was another letter, part of a correspondence the
Professor had insisted on maintaining, although she hadn't seen
the need.

'But why? You are right here. We see each other almost every
day.'

'Until I am with you every moment of the day I cannot be satisfied. Every thought and feeling I have, I want to share with
you.'

Now, feeling wretched, Virmati unfolded the Professor's latest offering.

Dearest love,
　　How difficult it is to teach while you are sitting before
me! Your face is the fixed point to which my eyes keep
returning. Let the world – the class – notice and remark, I do
not care. You are imprinted on my mind, my heart, my soul
so firmly that until we can be united in a more permanent
way I live in a shadowy insubstantial land.
　　So darling, you can imagine the state I am in these days.
To have your family still labour under the delusion that you
are going to marry some clottish canal engineer agitates me
greatly. Must this situation, so unfair to all, be allowed to
continue? Think how unpleasant it will be for them to hear
of your decision later rather than sooner. Of the canal engineer I say nothing. Anybody who digs in canals all day must
have a soul as dull and uninspiring as the mud he deals in.
What pain will he suffer? He does not even know you, has
never tried to know you. For him, you are a woman that his

family has arranged he should marry. For such men the individual is unimportant. It is the institution they are concerned with. If not you, then someone else.

I am sitting by the window in the sitting-room. I can see great rolls of cumulous clouds pile up in the sky outside. It is going to rain, the whole earth is waiting, joining a waiting lover in his mood. I feel one with it, because no matter what I see or do, there is some connection that can be traced to you. The koel is singing to its mate, a pair of squirrels are running up and down the jamun tree in the corner by the hedge. We too will one day be together. It is the faith I live by.

Till then, I am,
Ever your H.

Virmati put these letters on the parapet and stared at them as they lay indecently side by side; the Professor's crushed from hiding in her pocket, the fiancé's with legitimate public folds. Quickly she tore up the latter and scattered the pieces over the wall. Wasn't her future partner decided by the first touch of a man on her body? Even though in this case it meant humiliating her grandfather, who was publicly associated with female education, betraying her father who had allowed her to study further, and spoiling the marriage chances of her siblings.

Virmati remembered, once upon a time, she had been quite happy to be engaged to someone her elders had chosen. Had she been able to follow the path they had so carefully planned for her, they would have seen to it that the transition into adulthood was as painless as possible. Now all that was over. Oh, why hadn't she married sooner? But deaths in both families had made hers a two-year engagement. In those two years she had fallen against the grain, and whatever might be the consequences, she must continue her course.

'Mati?'
    'Yes?'
    Virmati found it difficult to broach her topic. Instead, she

silently watched her mother work. Kasturi was sitting outside her room, in the veranda that ran along the side of the house. Before her, on the chattai, was a spinning-wheel, on which she was making thread from a pile of cotton. With long, careful movements, her left hand swung back and forth, pulling out the thread from the needle on the spindle. Her right hand slowly turned the wheel. Disturbed by her daughter's unmoving eyes, Kasturi repeated, 'Yes?'

Virmati sat down on the floor and started playing with the cotton. She felt her mother's inaccessibility even more because her hands could not join hers in their work.

'What are you making?' she finally asked.

'I am getting this last khes ready for the beddings you will take with you.'

'I don't think I want so much bedding.'

'It is not your job to decide how much bedding you want and don't want. This is a question of marriage.'

'Maybe we had better wait,' said Virmati desperately, after a pause.

Kasturi's hand faltered in its steady movement, and lumps formed in the thread. Making an irritated tiching sound, she broke it off. 'Are you out of your senses?' she asked harshly. 'Two years is not long enough for you?'

'What is wrong with not wanting to marry?' appealed Virmati, bringing the words out in the open where they wilted in the hostile atmosphere.

Her mother could only stare. Virmati fidgeted, pulled more cotton apart. 'Shakuntala Pehnji never married. Look at her,' she said.

'Shakuntala Pehnji did not have five sisters waiting to get married either. And do you think it makes her mother happy to have her daughter unmarried? She may say what she likes about jobs and modern women, but I know how hard she still tries to find a husband for Shaku, and how bad she feels. You want to do the same to me? To your father and grandfather?'

'No, no,' said Virmati feebly.

'You are the eldest, Viru, your duty is greater. You know how much the younger ones look up to you. Your grandfather and father both have confidence in you, otherwise would they have given you so much freedom? They thought school and college would strengthen you, not change you. Now what will they feel when you want us to break our word and destroy our good name? How will they understand it?'

By now the cotton was almost completely pulled to pieces. Virmati knew being the eldest meant being responsible. It was unfair on the part of her mother to think that, after all those years of looking after them, she could even think of harming her siblings.

'I'm not harming anybody by studying, Mati,' she pleaded.

'You harm by not marrying. What about Indu? How long will she have to wait? What is more, the boy is getting impatient. What about him?'

'Tell him I don't want to marry,' whispered Virmati, hanging her head still lower.

'*Hai re*. After making him wait so long? What were you doing all this time? Sleeping?' Kasturi's voice was rough with exasperation.

'Let Indumati marry. Give her this khes you are making. I don't want any bedding, pots and pans, nothing!' Virmati was growing frantic.

'What nonsense!' exclaimed Kasturi. 'And what about his family? What face are we going to show them? Do you think you find such good boys every day?'

'Mati, please, I want to study . . .' Virmati faltered.

'But you have studied. What else is left?'

'In Lahore . . . I want to go to Lahore . . .'

Kasturi could bear her daughter's foolishness no further. She grabbed her by the hair and banged her head against the wall.

'Maybe this will knock some sense into you!' she cried. 'What crimes did I commit in my last life that I should be cursed with a daughter like you in this one?' She let go of the girl's head, and started to wail, rocking to and fro. The reels of thread spilt from her lap. Virmati moved to pick them up.

Kasturi slapped her hand away. 'Leave them there, you ungrateful girl!' she hissed. 'Otherwise you do just what you want! Why bother with the show of picking up thread! Get away from my sight,' Kasturi's face was purple with fury. As Virmati got up, she said coldly, 'Remember you are going to be married next month, if I have to swallow poison to make you do it!'

Slowly Virmati dragged herself away. As Kasturi watched her daughter's retreating back, the arms swinging uselessly by their sides, the head buried between hunched shoulders, her own despair increased. What had come over the girl? She had always been so good and sensible. How could she not see that her happiness lay in marrying a decent boy, who had waited patiently all these years, to whom the family had given their word? What kind of learning was this, that deprived her of her reason? She too knew the value of education, it had got her her husband, and had filled her hours with the pleasure of reading. In her time, going to school had been a privilege, not to be abused by going against one's parents. How had girls changed so much in just a generation?

XI

Sultanpur, West Punjab, 1904. Kasturi was seven and had been going to the mission school for only a few months when her parents caught her praying to a picture of Christ, something the nice Bengali teacher said she herself did. Her mother had torn the picture, screamed and shouted, and threatened to marry her off, before she brought further disgrace to the family. It was her uncle who intervened.

There was no question of Kasturi becoming a bride, he said. Child marriage is evil. Suppose her husband dies – her life will be over before she knows anything. Their Swami Dayanandji had said that marriage was a union between rational, consenting adults. This was the only way its sanctity could be preserved, and the misery of multiple marriages and child widows avoided. He understood his sister-in-law was upset – praying to a picture of Christ was no small matter, he agreed, it was exactly in this way that the British sought dominion over their minds – but what kind of example would they set the community? All the things the family stood for would be suspect; Dayanandji's convictions must go on living despite the great sage's death twenty-one years ago, otherwise the Arya reform movement would have no life in it.

'That's all very well,' said the irate mother. 'But this witch sitting at home will have nothing better to do than think she is a Christian. Who will marry her then, I would like to know?'

'Sixteen, and the best bridegroom in the Punjab,' said Kasturi's uncle, flapping the advertisements in the *Arya Patrika*, advertisements of educated boys wanting educated girls. 'Till then, she must go to school. I started one for our boys, I will do the same for the girls. Had I done so sooner, there would have been no question of exposing our daughter to Christian schools.'

And he began, transforming the fistfuls of flour housewives donated for the Samaj cause into bricks and letters for his niece, arranging for grants, teachers, students, space, and facilities.

Kasturi never forgot that evening. Over the sound of beds being dragged into the centre of the angan for the night, and the clatter of poles being inserted for mosquito nets, Praji, his eyes on the children's kites that were darkening against the red evening sky, told her that soon she would soar like those very kites. Once she had gained a proper education, she would be on her way to becoming one of the finest flowers of Hindu womanhood.

So the school came about, and Kasturi became the first girl in her family to postpone the arrival of the wedding guests by a tentative assault on learning. Her father, uncle and teacher made sure that this step into modernity was prudent and innocuous. Her head remained modestly bent over her work. No questions, no assertion. She learned reading, writing, balancing household accounts and sewing. Above all, the school ground the rituals of Arya Samaj havan, sandhya and meditation so deeply within her that for the rest of her life she had to start and end the day with them. After five years of this education, it was considered that Kasturi had acquired all that it was ever going to be useful for her to know. She appeared for her first and last outside exam, performed creditably, and graduated at the age of twelve, to stay at home until she married.

During Kasturi's formal schooling it was never forgotten that marriage was her destiny. After she graduated, her education continued in the home. Her mother tried to ensure her future happiness by the impeccable nature of her daughter's qualifications. She was going to please her in-laws.

How?

Let me count the ways.

With all the breads she could make, puris with spicy gram inside, luchis big as plates, kulchas, white and long, tandoori rotis, layers of flaky flour, paranthas, crisp and stuffed. With morrabas, never soggy, and dripping juicy sweet. With seasonal pickles of lemon, mango, carrot, cauliflower, turnip, red chillies, dates, ginger, and raisins. With sherbets of khas, roses, and almonds, with hot and cold spiced milk, with sour black carrot kanji, with lassi, thin, cool and salty, or thick and sweet. With barfis made of nuts and grains soaked overnight, and ground fine between two heavy stones. With sweets made of thickened milk. With papad, the sweet ones made out of ripe mango, the sour ones with raw mango, the ones to be fried with dal and potato. With thread spun, with cloth woven, with durries, small stitched carpets, and phulkaris, with pyjama kurtas, shirts, and salwar kameezes.

With all these accomplishments under her belt, Kasturi spent her free time sewing. If she wasn't doing the family stitching, she was working on the phulkaris for her trousseau. The phulkari stitch was a simple one, it allowed room for her to indulge in hopes (shy), fears (suppressed), speculations (of the unacknowledged), and the bright colours she used, magenta, orange, green, yellow and white, became linked with the desire she secretly felt for her unknown groom.

With her needlework, Kasturi held back worries about the behaviour of an unmarried, educated seventeen-year-old. Her father, in particular, loved watching her. Such gentleness and tranquillity, beauty and modesty were sure to be rewarded by a good husband, he felt, as with her threads and needle Kasturi joined the ranks of women who have stitched hours of waiting into intricate patterns. Her clandestine activity was reading, which she protected from comments about self-absorption by gratifying it at night.

The glimpse that decided the union of Kasturi and Suraj Prakash, the young and enterprising advertiser, came in August, when the weather was hot and humid. His advertisement answered, his background investigated, his presence called for, he arrived at the dry-fruit shop in the forenoon, looking crisp despite the heat, having washed and changed at the station.

Yes, he would do, Kasturi's parents decided late that night.

They had both talked to Suraj Prakash, they had talked to Praji. Should the couple meet? Kasturi's mother was against this. It was highly unlikely that they could have anything to say to each other, and it just created space for whims and fancies to operate.

'Well,' reasoned Lala Jivan Das, 'he has come all the way. He will want to see as well as be seen.'

'See her? He can see her from the window if he is that keen,' said the mother. 'But there is no need for anything else.'

'These are modern times,' Lala Jivan Das tried again. 'Swamiji has said that young people should not get married without knowing each other. The young man has come, and we have been able to judge him for ourselves. Let him also meet Kasturi, it is only natural.'

The mother thought this a strange idea. After all, their girl was not for display.

'No, no,' argued Lala Jivan Das. 'Where is the display in this? Send her in with his glass of milk. She is always doing this for her brothers.'

'Suppose he doesn't like her? Then another will want to see her, and another, and another, and our daughter will get a bad name for nothing.'

Lala Jivan Das looked at his wife in amazement. He supposed it was the tension. 'Not like her? Of course he will like her. What is there to dislike in her? He is an educated man, from a respectable Samaj family, where is the room for liking and disliking? Nonsense!' he exclaimed.

Next morning, Kasturi's mother handed her daughter a glass of milk, with a small plate of barfi, and told her to give it to her brother's friend who had come from Amritsar. Throwing her red dupatta over her head, Kasturi walked towards the baithak, where Suraj Prakash was sitting, waiting, wondering.

There she was, young, thin, her dupatta setting off the colour of her skin. Tendrils of hair framed her face. As she offered him the glass of milk, their eyes met and held for a moment. They looked away, and were consumed by the desire to look again, but how could they? There were so many people around. The blush on their faces became a glow. With this one glance, the final link was forged in the chain of events set in motion years before.

The wedding was fixed for October. On a formal visit to Amritsar, Kasturi's brother came to Suraj Prakash in his shop, with a silver bowl of mishri, a gold guinea and a hundred and one rupees. Suraj Prakash ate the mishri, kept the bowl, sold the guinea, gave the money to his father, and set about making clothes for his wedding.

The preparations in Sultanpur began. There would be fifty to sixty people in the barat to house and feed at regular and steady intervals. Some of the barat intended to stay at least a week because they meant to make a holiday of the whole expedition. Lala Jivan Das pored over the menus, consulting for hours with the halwais. He was a wholesale merchant who dealt in spices such as black pepper, cinnamon, and cumin; sherbets of kewra, rose and khas; dry fruit, especially almonds, pista, cashews, walnuts, raisins, figs, and apricots; pickles, mainly mango and lemon; sweet morabbas in huge jars containing carrots, amla, mangoes, apples, pears and peaches preserved in sticky sugar syrup. His godown was now ransacked for the best it had to offer. There were to be at least four varieties of barfi in different colours – green pista, white almond, brown walnut and pink coconut – for the guests to eat as a side dish with every meal. The freshest spices, rose leaves, and saffron were to flavour the daily glasses of milk they would drink. Special feasting things like dhingri and guchchi to put in the rice and paneer were ordered from the Kashmiri agent in Sultanpur. The expenses were going to be considerable, but Lalaji did not care. How else was he to display his love for Kasturi, his sorrow at her leaving, the worthiness of his son-in-law?

Praji was calm. He had done his duty, kept his word. He was aware that the cause for which he had done so much, education in Sultanpur, was talked over in many homes after Suraj Prakash had made his visit and won his bride. It was rumoured that he

65

had a wonderful jewellery business in Amritsar, that he was a sanatak, having graduated from a gurukul in Kangri, that he had no mother, only an old widowed aunt, and of course everyone was aware of how he had come to Sultanpur himself, with no running-after by the girl's side. If education had started the whole process, there was a lot to be said for it. Already Praji had more people showing an interest in the girl's school, and more willing promises of donations than ever before.

Kasturi and her mother spent hours alternately crying and preparing the trousseau. Most of it was taken (along with the big metal trunks) from the trousseaus of Kasturi's two elder brothers' wives. Nobody thought of asking them whether they minded or not, such territorial attachments were frowned upon as being contrary to family spirit. Looking at the two sets of bed frames with delicately painted legs, Kasturi felt the twinge of dread in her grow stronger. The initiation into womanhood, intimacy, procreation, all this was going to be hers at last, on home-made sheets of fine Manchester cotton, embroidered pillowcases, brightly woven kheses that her mother had spun in red, yellow, brown and black. The base of the bedding was a strong thick durrie, especially made to order from the Jammu jail. For warmth in the winter months she had six mattresses, stuffed with cotton from her family's fields. In another trunk, padded with old cloth, were a hundred and one vessels and utensils. There were small, delicately moulded tashtris for snacks; kansa thalis and katoris gleaming their mock silver shine; brass, cone-shaped glasses; huge karhais and patilas to cook in. A small suitcase contained her clothes – six sets of salwar kameezes. A wife was not for show, after all.

XII

Virmati and the Professor, in a room in a friend's house, a meeting that has been arranged with some difficulty.

Virmati to the Professor, 'I can't do it, I simply can't. We will have to forget about the whole thing. At home they will not listen to any more arguments.'

The Professor turned Virmati towards himself, and cupped her face in his hands. He took off her glasses, then stroked her face, with small, caressing gestures. He kissed her eyes, her nose, her soft, full mouth. All Virmati's feelings were focused on his touch. As he smoothed the hair back from her forehead, and tucked the untidy strands behind her ears, she sank towards him.

'Darling Vir,' said the Professor, leading her to the white-sheeted takht that was against the wall of the room. 'You must be firm. I know how difficult it is for you, but you must be firm.'

'I can go on being firm, but the doli will be at the door, and I will leave my house in it,' said Virmati, choking and hiccuping in a burst of sobs. She threw her dupatta over her head, and rocked back and forth, her arms tight around herself.

The Professor tried to turn her rigid face towards him. Not succeeding, he took her hand and spreading her fingers, pressed his lips to the white spot where they joined. Virmati tried to snatch her hand back, but the Professor laced her fingers with his own so tightly she could feel the blood going from them. Once more she struggled against his grip.

'Soon things will be all right. Then you will see. We will one day be together,' said the Professor, holding onto the kissed hand with conviction.

Virmati could not imagine how things were going to become all right, and she noticed that the Professor made no suggestions either.

'It will never be,' she muttered desolately to herself. Her situation was hopeless. Even crying was no good. She pulled away her hand and this time he let go, laying it gently in her lap.

'Good girl,' said the Professor, as her sobs decreased, and she grew less rigid. He transferred his kisses to her eyes.

'Smile at me,' he begged.

With great effort, Virmati twisted the corners of her mouth.

Cycling home, it was clear to her that she could not depend upon the Professor to sort out any domestic situation. It was up to her. At home, everybody assumed that her listlessness had to do with bridal nerves, and treated her with a tact rare in her family. Even Paro and Vidya, wild with excitement, were subdued before their sister's absent-mindedness.

The morning after meeting the Professor, Virmati woke to find the verandas washed with blowing winds of rain. The grounds around the house were swirling with muddy brown waters, little waves lurching against the veranda steps. Inside Virmati kept bumping into one or the other of her brothers and sisters. They were all housebound, no school, no college, no work for any of them today. All of them had something to say to her, all of them wanted her to join in the excitement of the more-than-usual rain. Some of them were dancing about on the veranda, making dashes into the pool below, some of them were darting up and down from the roof. All were wet. Paro came running up to her.

'Pehnji, come. Mati's making pakoras in the kitchen!'

It was ideal weather for pakoras, there could be no two opinions about that, thought Virmati sadly. She was sure that the woman would be also frying them for her husband, daughter, mother and sister-in-law.

'What kind is she making?' she asked Paro, dully.

'Oh, the usual. Onion, potato, green chilli, spinach, brinjal and pumpkin.'

Ah, pumpkin, potato, onion, and green chilli pakoras! Sweet, salty and sharp, with the sourness of chutney slathered on their golden crisp shells. But now what was the use of anything?

'Indu Pehnji and Vidya are in the kitchen, helping Mati. Gopi Praji is there too, trying to finish the pakoras by himself. Come, Pehnji, before they are all gone! I was waiting for you before I ate any!' Paro tried to make her lagging sister walk faster by pulling her dupatta.

'I am coming, Paru,' said Virmati. And she did hurry a little, despite her heaviness of heart.

In the kitchen all was noise and hot frying smells. Big pieces of wood were sticking out of the fire that was crackling under a large heavy kaddhai, half full of foaming oil. Indumati and a dripping Hemavati were cutting vegetables, sitting on wooden pattris on the floor. Gunvati was concentrating on cutting pumpkin pieces to the required thinness, and Vidya, young and inexperienced in the art of fine slicing, was vigorously grating a long, green lauki. Her body swayed back and forth over the grater. Kasturi was standing over the kaddhai, at one end of the kitchen, wielding a long, black-handled ladle. Some children were on the floor, on their pattris, with small tables in front of them, eating, swallowing, gulping, fighting pakoras. Paro quickly took her place, Virmati joined Indu in the cutting.

'You eat now, Indu,' she said. 'You must have cut long enough.'

'No, no, Pehnji. After all, you are here for only a few days now.'

'Yes, yes, Pehnji,' giggled Hema. 'Let us do some seva for you, for a change.'

Virmati silently sat next to Paro, taking the little girl in her lap. She hugged her tightly, putting her cheek next to her damp hair. Paro, in response, stuck a pakora into her sister's mouth, carefully smearing it with green tomato chutney first.

'Nice, no?' she asked.

'Yes, darling,' said Virmati, eating with small, careful chews, for she had no appetite.

'It will be an auspicious omen if it rains on your wedding, Pehnji,' said Hemavati.

It seemed to Virmati that her family could talk of nothing else but her wedding. Every word they said had so little relation to her inner life that she felt fraudulent even listening to them, passively, immorally silent. If they knew what she was really like, would they tolerate her? Look upon her lovingly, do seva for her, think of her comfort – even Paro, would she push a pakora into her mouth? Would anyone let her?

XIII

In 1849 the British formally annexed Punjab, completing a process that had begun with the death of Maharaja Ranjit Singh ten years earlier. They set about establishing their control in a manner that would persuade the Punjabis that, of all possible political options, British rule was best. From the 1880s they started building canals, twisting the five rivers into courses that would change the demography of the area as well as the dry colour of the earth. Acres and acres of arable land were created in order to provide: gifts in return for the horses and soldiers that the military needed; the revenues that the administration needed; and the picture of a contented peasantry that the Raj morally needed.

The Upper Bari Doab Canal was among the first to be built, harnessing the Ravi at Madhopur Head. Broad, muddy and silent, the river flowed in its straight canal lines to Tibri, where it branched off into three equally straight subdivisions. The Kasoor Branch flowed past the village of Tarsikka where there was a small oil mill which Lala Diwan Chand bought in 1910.

Lala Diwan Chand loved Tarsikka, and he grew ambitious for the place. To the existing mill, which was for extracting mustard and rape-seed oil, he added a gin and a flour unit. And as his grandchildren grew, he kept adding to the place. They needed fresh fruit and vegetables which his six-acre garden would provide. He planted trees of mango, mausambi, cheekoo, jamun, pear, pomegranate, lemon, papaya, malta, loquat, lichi, and mulberry. In winter there were rows of seasonal vegetables. To house his frequently visiting grandchildren, he built a block of four large rooms bordered by a wide veranda in the middle of the garden. The kitchen was on one side with the hand-pump near the entrance. The outhouses were in the back, far from the house, kitchen, vegetables, fruit trees, and everything else. A

71

great boundary wall, with huge, iron-studded gates in the front surrounded the whole property.

Four shops, of cloth, vegetables, dry goods, and freshly made sweets and savouries just inside the mill entrance served basic needs. The shops, the stables for the tongas, the garages for a car and twenty-seater bus, together with Lala Diwan Chand's small office, formed a square in front. To get to the house, one had to cross a little bridge which spanned the narrow canal inlet that flowed from the main branch into the mill.

This canal stream, deep though narrow, ran through one end of the garden, and was a great attraction for Lala Diwan Chand's grandchildren. They spent every minute they could in or around it, swimming and eating. The boys would raid the garden for litchis, loquat and mangoes, which they sank in the water in buckets to cool. After everybody had had their fill of fruit, the boys would go to the halwai for pakoras. With spots of grease spreading on the wrapping paper, they would run back, the hot pakoras in their hands, to be pounced upon by the rest and sent back for more.

At one end of the garden, next to the bridge, Lala Diwan Chand had built an enclosure so that the daughters of the house could swim in privacy, sheltered from any eye that might glance upon their fair bodies in wet and revealing clothes. Their sense of modesty prevented them from following their brothers, who sometimes preferred to go to the big canal outside, where lay vaster, grander spaces of muddy water.

The day after the floods and pakoras, Virmati could be seen trying to leave her house in the late afternoon. Just as she thought she had reached the gate unseen, Paro pounced on her.

'Pehnji! I'm also coming!'

Virmati looked at her grubby sister. Paro had smudges of dirt all over, and her hair was loosened untidily from her plait. Wordlessly she bent down to put her face next to hers for a moment, tightly holding the thin child body, with its small round stomach.

'Pehnji?' said Paro, a little surprised.

Virmati's chest heaved. Paro couldn't believe that her strong sister might be crying. The very unusualness of it was enough to start her lips quivering.

'Pehnji?' she sniffed, wriggling around, trying to catch a glimpse of Virmati's face. 'Pehnji, don't cry. What's happened?' and her own tears began to fall.

Virmati set her down by the side of the gate.

'I'm not feeling well,' she explained, as she dried Paro's smooth round cheeks with the end of her dupatta.

'Oh. I thought because you are getting married, but then it is only afterwards you cry, no?'

Virmati's mouth twisted a little. 'Yes, darling. Only afterwards.'

'Where are you going? I'm also coming!'

'Not now, darling,' said Virmati, looking at this youngest of her sisters, almost a daughter, trying to memorize every line of her little face. As Paro started to protest, she added quickly, 'I'll bring you a notebook and coloured pencils. All right?'

'All right,' said Paro, distracted but doubtful. She was suspicious of such largesse. 'But tell me, where are you going, and why can't I . . .'

Before she could say anything more, Virmati had slipped out of the gate and left. She walked swiftly down Lepel Griffin Road, her head bent, her feet intent on avoiding the big, squishy mud puddles that laced the pathway. The watery overflow of the previous day had left rubbish residues on the road, and it was beginning to stink in the sun. What must it be like in the city, thought Virmati, where even on ordinary days the drains were always clogged and full. Her mind wandered to the thousands of mosquitoes that hovered around the drains and all the fruit and halwai stalls in the market. Then to her father's shop, the old house, her old school, her new house, her new college, incoherent pictures jumbling about in her unhappy mind.

At the nearest crossing from Lepel Griffin Road, Virmati hailed a tonga. She was afraid she was going to be late for the bus, but she was looking for signs from God and refused to urge the tonga-wallah to go any faster. If the bus was there at Hall Gate it meant that even God had declared that she was getting too burdensome for her family. Ah, there it was. Dear grand-father, your kindness to your fellows in providing them with this shuttle service between Amritsar and Tarsikka, for a four-anna one-way fare will also take me to my death. And seeing her fate resound prophetically in every step she took, Virmati climbed slowly and heavily into the twenty-seater bus. An old villager sitting next to a vacant seat got up because Virmati's status entitled her to sit either with her own kind, or alone. As he shuffled to the front and squatted next to the driver's seat, Virmati gratefully took his place, glad to be out of sight of the other passengers.

'Bibiji,' asked the driver who had recognized her, 'is anyone else coming?'

'No, no,' said Virmati, confused, 'no one is coming.'

The bus started, and Virmati fixed her gaze on the moving world beyond the window. The ride was smooth. Lala Diwan Chand believed in keeping his vehicles well. Virmati's inert body rocked to and fro as she stared at Paro's face, planted on the scenery outside. She could see the details of the tear marks she had tried to wipe away, see the big eyes fixed on hers as she promised coloured pencils, a notebook. How would Paro get these things? She would think her sister had forgotten. The scenery blurred as Virmati's eyes grew hot and began to prickle. She hoped Paro would not think badly of her when she grew up.

Soon Kailashnath would finish his game of capturing rival kites on the roof, and give her letter to the Professor. She had composed it with unusual care, trying to make sure there were no grammatical or spelling mistakes in it. She knew those annoyed him.

'I want you to be perfect,' the Professor had told her. And she had blushed with pleasure. Nobody else had ever seen her as someone who could be perfect.

Of course, he would grieve at her going, she knew that. But then, there was always his wife for him to turn to. Strange to think they had been friends once.

It was growing dark as the bus turned off from the main road into the dirt path that bordered the side of the Kasoor Branch Lower Canal. The sun was setting, and the sky was a splendid series of serried colours, gold, pink, orange, red, purple, merging one into the other, a perfect monsoon sunset. The trees along the canal stood out, their leaves looking subdued and shadowy against the brilliance of the sky. If Virmati could, she would live with Bade Baoji in Tarsikka, and never go to Amritsar. But the luxury of living how and where one wanted was only for the old. When the responsibilities of life were over and the right to choice earned.

From the bus windows, Virmati could see that the canal was full after the previous day's rain. In the slanting evening light the swift, muddy waters were faintly tinged with pink. Little frothy waves slapped against the walls. Virmati had times out of number cooled herself in this canal, sat on its banks to eat pakoras, to bite into hot, roasted corn smeared with lemon and spicy masala, to munch peanuts and see the shells swirling about in the water, to suck mangoes and watch the seeds and skins sink. Now its separate life struck her, the waters going strangely and mysteriously on, having a being in which her own would soon be inextricably mingled.

The bus, which had been stopping at intervals to let villagers off, finally crossed one of the bridges that spanned the canal leading towards her grandfather's mill. A few furlongs down, it stopped before the gates, its horn blaring shrilly before the massive shut doors. As Virmati got off, the conductor shouted to the chowki-dar, 'Tell Bade Baoji that Chhoti Bibiji has come.'

'I'll tell him myself, Sukhdev,' said Virmati.

She bought some pencils and a long notebook bound in red cloth. From the munshi sitting in the small front office, she borrowed a scratchy nib pen, and dipped it in the small glass ink-well on his desk. The ink was the pale kind made from a tablet dissolved in water, and she had to go over her letters several times. 'Parvati' she wrote on the copy, though it was difficult, the nib kept sputtering and dividing down the middle. The whole compound had seen her by now, but she supposed that was inevitable.

'Send these things to the kothi,' she told the chowkidar as she stepped through the small inner door set in the gates.

Briskly she walked up to the canal path, her dupatta fluttering in the pleasant dusk breeze. She turned left at the bridge, away from the direction from which the bus had come. It was more isolated here, and there were fewer chances of anybody seeing her. Now that she was actually going to merge her body with the canal she felt her confusion clearing. Her briskness increased as the chowkidar stepped out from behind the gate to stare thoughtfully at her disappearing figure.

The place where the canal branches off is secluded and shady. The water pours into a small artificial waterfall, down under the pathway which rises a little to become a bridge. If you lean over it on the big canal side, you can see the gates that, lifting and falling, regulate the size of the stream that enters the mill. On the other side you can see the water emerging, whirling around in foaming eddies before straightening out for its onward course. As children, Virmati and her sisters loved to first throw things down one side of the bridge and then rush over to the other to see them emerge.

Virmati walked a little beyond this point. She took off her chappals and folded her dupatta on top of them. She stared into the water. She knew that the spot where she was standing was where the water began to feel the strong pull of the small canal. Though a good swimmer, she did not expect to be able to resist the current. She hoped Paro would get the little presents, she hoped the Professor would forget her, she hoped her family would forgive her. With these thoughts she held her nose and jumped.

The Professor was on his last cup of tea that evening. He was sitting in the angan looking at the sky. His wife, watching him from the kitchen, could tell from his face how absorbed he was in the beauty of the sunset. His glasses, raised upwards, reflected the brilliant colours he was contemplating. In all her life she had never known anybody as crazy about beauty as her husband. He could talk about it at great length and in such detail that listeners would go away feeling that till the Professor had spoken, they had never really seen anything. She had heard him enough times to be able to predict the feelings of all involved. When the woman saw Kailashnath come to see the Professor, she thought, 'Now they will discuss the sunset, and then he will tell him about colours, paintings, and whatnot.'

She was about to turn her attention back to the cooking when she saw Kailashnath hand the Professor something. Her lips tightened, and the movement of her hands grew mechanical and listless in the dough she was kneading in the thali between her feet. She was suspicious, but what could she do with her suspicions? Even such a trivial thing as Virmati's brother handing something to her husband was enough to unsettle her for the evening. She made up her mind to visit Kasturi the next day and make inquiries about Virmati's wedding, and could she do anything to help?

The Professor was by now getting up and making for his room. The woman finished kneading the dough, and got up to take his tea tray inside. All the breakable china on it she would wash and dry herself. Wash, so that the servant boy wouldn't get a chance to crack or chip anything; dry, so that there wouldn't be the water stains he hated on the crockery. Sometimes she would pass her fingers gently over the rim of the cup, thinking that his lips had rested there. She did this now. Suddenly she heard his tread, hasty, rapid coming towards the kitchen. She blushed and quickly put the cup down. The Professor lurched in and the woman stammered, 'What . . . what's the matter? Are you all right?'

'Vir – Virmati,' the Professor trembled over the name.

The woman moved the tea things about on the tray.

'Vir –' he tried again.

She put the tray down with a bang.

77

'Tell them . . . Hurry, go tell her mother . . .' Here the Professor choked, and looked terrible in his wife's eyes.

'What is she telling you that her mother doesn't already know?' asked the woman as snappishly as she dared. 'You lie down. I will make you some desi tea.'

She started to peel the potatoes. She would do the tea things later. Dinner had to be served, her family had to be fed, no matter what Virmati had done.

The sight of her peeling shook the Professor into articulation. 'I'm telling you to go, and you sit here cooking!' he cried.

'To say what?' she asked, still not looking at him.

'Tell them she's gone to Tarsikka – perhaps to drown herself in the canal. They must move fast to save her!' The Professor's voice broke and wordlessly he pushed his wife out towards the other house.

He watched her out of sight, then shut the door of his room and let his head fall heavily against its smooth wooden surface. His foremost feeling was impotence. He had only a cycle. Why had she gone so far? Tarsikka was sixteen miles away. He had to rely on them – what else could he do? He was . . . he was nothing now . . . not a rescuer, not a lover, nothing in this matter of life and death. Why had she decided on this awful step? Didn't she trust him? Didn't she know how much she meant to him? He had told her of his love a thousand times. Now it could no longer be a secret, he had to tell his wife so she could tell that family. Well, let everybody know. With Viru not there, nothing mattered. With no strength to remain standing, he gradually slipped onto the floor, where he remained a long time, his head cradled on his arms.

The first thing that flashed into the woman's head was 'Good.' And then, 'But she'll make sure we are never free of her.' She had made certain of this with her letter, clinging to her husband even in death, making them all suffer.

And then fear took over. Here she was wishing evil of others. Surely this would rebound on her, just as Kekayi's evil wishes had in the end destroyed her in the Ramayan. A person's life or death was in God's hands, and in an effort to collect herself and avoid her thoughts she hurried to Kasturi's house. The woman knew she would find Kasturi with her older daughters in the kitchen across the courtyard, preparing the evening meal. She walked towards the back entrance, dread mixed with righteous triumph at this opportunity, wondering what phrases to use. Hadn't her husband himself sent her? If there was any irregularity here, it was not her fault.

In the kitchen, Paro was bothering her mother. 'When is Pehnji coming, Mati, when? She promised to bring me something.'

'How do I know where your sister has gone and died?' asked Kasturi irritably, wiping the smoke tears from her eyes.

'Tell me, *na*,' said Paro insistently, dragging her mother's palla off her.

Kasturi turned to take a tired, half-hearted swipe at her youngest daughter. 'Didn't you hear? Just wait till she does come. She should be here at this time instead of out of the house. She is old enough to know better. Really, I give my daughters too much freedom. And this is the result!'

'Come here, Paro,' said Indu, as Paro prepared to sulk. 'Here, help me knead this dough.' She tore off a piece and gave it to her.

Paro sat down, and absently started to pinch and pull the damp dough between her fingers. 'Oh, there's that Pabi from the other house,' she remarked, half to herself, half to the others.

As the woman came in, Indu nudged Paro to give her a wooden patla. Kasturi felt a little surprised. This was not the time for neighbourly visits.

The woman meantime was wondering how she was going to break her news, among the sisters and everybody? The bearer of messages from her husband about their daughter? It wasn't fair she should be put in a situation like this, she should also be at home cooking. That was her right, to be able to cook for her family, to be left in peace to fuss over their eating habits, to cater to their likes and dislikes, to do just what Kasturi was doing with her daughters. As a preliminary she let tears gather in her eyes.

'*Arre, arre,*' exclaimed Kasturi, putting down her ladle, and cleaning her hands by flicking some water on them from the glass next to the dough. The sisters stared at her.

The woman threw her palla over her face and rocked back and forth, moaning.

'*Bas, bas,*' said Kasturi, rubbing her on the back.

'Oh Bhenji! It is my unlucky kismet that has brought me here. Everybody's curses will be upon my head!'

'No, no,' said Kasturi soothingly, one eye on the cooking vegetables.

'Bhenji, I am so ashamed. I am so unlucky! What will you think?'

'I think? Why? Indu, just stir the sabzi, and add a little water,' said Kasturi.

'He told me . . . told me . . .' The woman stumbled over the words amid sobs.

'Yes? He told you what?' asked Kasturi in the same even tone.

The woman's purpose was to convey news. Her words came rushing out. 'He told me to tell you that maybe Virmati has gone to Tarsikka . . . That maybe she has done something to herself. Oh, Bhenji, please forgive me!' As she gave her news, her sobs subsided. She no longer had the greater right to cry.

Kasturi's hand slipped from the woman's shoulder. She turned to stare at the fire under the cooking. In the silence, Paro could be heard shouting, 'It's not true. She was going to bring me something from the city! Mati, it's not true! Indu Pehnji, it's not true!'

'Ssh, Paro,' Indu tried to keep her quiet. 'You can't talk like that to Pabiji!'

'But she's saying things about Pehnji,' whispered Paro hoarsely. 'I saw her in the evening before she went and she *promised* me –'

'All right, all right. Now shush,' whispered Indu back.

Kasturi got up heavily. She did not want to expose her daughters to more. It was bad enough, this information coming from outside the home. 'We must go and see her father,' she said, her voice lacking all expression. 'Please come.' And with none of her usual politeness she left the woman to follow her out of the kitchen. At the doorway she turned back once to say, 'Indu, just see the sabzi doesn't burn, put the dal on afterwards. Start making the rotis. Use the fresh butter in the doli, the old one is for ghee.'

'*Han*,' said Indu, stopping Paro from following her mother.

The bus driver and the conductor of Lala Diwan Chand's twenty-seater both belonged to the same village. By the time they had locked the bus and deposited the keys at the big house, the bright colours of the sky had faded to dull purple and grey and the trees had begun to absorb the darkness of the night. They had to hurry if they were to get home while there was still light to see. As they stepped through the small door of the big gate, the chowkidar exclaimed, 'Pyare Lal and Mahan Singh! Chhoti Pibiji came alone in the bus, and has gone up to the canal by herself. On your way home, just make sure –'

There was no need to say more. The men started quickly up the high embankment that bordered the big canal.

Virmati's chappals were still warm when they reached the small bridge that spanned the branch stream.

Kasturi was sitting tensely in the veranda. Her daughters were silently waiting with her. Suraj Prakash and Kailashnath had left for Tarsikka in Lala Diwan Chand's car, the car he kept to be used for special occasions.

Soon Lajwanti came to join them.

'Any news yet?' she asked, as the daughters made way for her. The girls shook their heads. Kasturi's tears began to fall.

'No, no,' consoled Lajwanti, throwing her heavy arm around Kasturi's shoulders. 'God will send her back to us. Everything is in his hands. You must not cry. It is a bad omen.'

'How could she do this? What will happen to us all? To these girls? Where did we go wrong?'

Kasturi cried on, saying all the things she knew Lajwanti

would be thinking, saying them with a heart full of grief and angry shame that she had to be talking like this about her own daughter, and the eldest in the family too. And Bade Baoji, who had championed her cause, what would he think? As for herself, she could never wipe out the stigma of having a child thoughtless enough to contemplate ending her life without consideration for what her family would suffer. Then there was the Professor, how did he know before her own family? She trembled at what she might find out.

Lala Diwan Chand was surprised when, on coming home from work that day, he was handed a notebook and pencils with 'Parvati' scrawled on the package.

'Who brought this?' he asked.

'The munshi,' said Ram Lal, the servant, old, faithful and slightly stupid.

'Yes, but why?' asked Lala Diwan Chand patiently. 'Didn't he say anything?'

'No.'

'Call the munshi,' said Lala Diwan Chand, 'and quickly. From his quarters. Faster!' he shouted uncharacteristically, at Ram Lal's slow-moving back.

The munshi's arrival a few minutes later produced an explanation that left Lala Diwan Chand seething with exasperation. His eldest granddaughter was here and he hadn't even known. The munshi's 'We thought you knew, Baoji, or would I not be the first to tell you, Baoji?' left him struggling to control his temper. Where was she? This was no time to be away from home. If some trouble had caused her to come to him at Tarsikka, why didn't she follow her impulse to its logical conclusion? He got up and hastened towards the gate.

Virmati was meanwhile walking down the canal bank. Through her burning sense of shame she saw her back as it presented itself to those two men, the hollow in the curve of her spine, the rounded buttocks stretching the wet fabric, the long, swelling thighs, with the material gathered between the legs.

Hadn't she seen her sisters' wet backs times out of number when they had been swimming in their salwar kameezes? She tried to wrap her dry dupatta around her, but the thin material soon got soaked. Her path was dotted with drops that were quickly absorbed into the soil. Her saviours followed at a respectful distance, also dotting the soil with water that dripped from their clothes. They ignored Virmati's low, repeated requests to be left alone. She was thankful for their help, she said, she had slipped and was all right now. No, no, they said, what would Baoji say? Virmati had no answer to that, only further blankness at the thought of her grandfather.

By now the car containing Kailashnath and Suraj Prakash had turned into the mud path bordering the canal. The increased bumping of the car meant an increase in Suraj Prakash's nausea, a nausea that had risen within him since their departure from Amritsar almost forty-five minutes earlier.

'We are almost there,' Kailashnath tried to be consoling.

Suraj Prakash said nothing, only hunched up tighter in his seat.

'Have faith, Pitaji. Everything is in God's hands.' Kailashnath was worried by his father's silence. Suraj Prakash was looking ashen and the son thought suddenly, my father is an old man, and may Virmati be cursed for what she has done today. His hands whitened over the steering wheel, and he pressed the accelerator, making the car bump even more and his father turn even paler. By this time it was almost dark, and they had come within sight of the bridge they would have to cross to reach the mill.

The Professor's wife was banging on his door.

'Open, open,' he could hear her shouting. Her voice seemed to come from far away, too faint and tiny for him to pay any attention.

And then, 'Your food is ready. It's getting cold.'

The woman is mad with her obsession about food, thought the Professor wearily.

Shrilly, it came. 'Something has happened.' Shrieks and shouts.

'He's gone and done something inside! He is ill, he is sick, he has fainted. *Hai re, hai re!*'

Footsteps receded at a run and immediately came back compounded. This time multiple bangs on the door, and a crescendo of wailing.

Finally the Professor surfaced. His eyes were dazed and red, his usually carefully done hair wild and dishevelled. 'What is it?' he demanded cantankerously. 'I was sleeping.'

His authority in the house meant that nobody openly questioned this statement.

Virmati was not the first to see her grandfather almost running towards her. Her head was too bent. Instead, 'Baoji!' exclaimed Pyare Lal.

'Baoji!' echoed Mahan Singh.

No sooner did he reach them than they overwhelmed him with their choric accounts. Sukhdev had said, they had hurried, they had seen, they had jumped and they had, by the grace of God, been able to rescue, a little later and . . . Here they broke off to invoke the name of God again.

Lala Diwan Chand praised them. Their presence of mind had averted an untimely accident. The canals were not safe in the monsoon, and they themselves must be careful when walking along them. People could slip. The men agreed. And now they should go home, went on Lala Diwan Chand, it was late enough.

As he talked, his hands were unwrapping the chaddor from around himself and transferring it to Virmati's shoulders. He did this without giving her more than a cursory glance. His gaze was fixed on the men, as theirs was on him. Since Lala Diwan Chand's arrival, Virmati had become invisible, and, burning from gazes, imagined or real, she was grateful.

They walked back in the dark, together. Lala Diwan Chand could feel the girl's agitation, and in their solitude he felt no need to press her for any explanation. That could come later. It was probably pre-marriage nerves that accounted for her strange behaviour. He hoped her parents were treating her with gentleness and understanding. Maybe he should have visited Amritsar more often, she might have opened her heart to him.

Tears gathered in Virmati's eyes as she felt her grandfather's love float around her. And then fear. What would he feel when he really knew. Meanwhile as Lala Diwan Chand put his arm around her, he could sense that she was crying, and he caressed her damp head. This affectionate gesture was more than Virmati could bear. 'Baoji . . . forgive me,' broke from her, but then at the sight of Sukhdev, up near the bridge with a lantern, she fell silent.

'Go, beti, go inside,' said Lala Diwan Chand gently, nudging his granddaughter away. 'I'll just have a word with him.'

Head bent and covered, Virmati scurried down the rise into the small door of the gate. Once inside the house, she snatched a lantern and searched the dressing-table drawer for her mother's cupboard keys. She needed to change, she could not face the world wet a second longer.

Inside the cupboard were a few simple sets of salwar kameezes. Virmati had just put one on and hung her own clothes to dry on the line in the veranda, when she heard the sound of a car entering the outer compound. Her hands shook. That was for her, she knew, but she hadn't thought they would come so soon.

Darkness fell over the house on Lepel Griffin Road. Virmati's family was still on the veranda, waiting for the car to come back. Till then, no one could bear the thought of doing anything. Lajwanti had her arm around her sister-in-law, the girls were clustered around the two older women. Kasturi's eyes were closed. Her fingers were moving along her rosary and nobody wanted to disturb her by saying anything.

Virmati was in the back seat of the car, watching the heads of her father and brother in front. She longed to say she was sorry, to have her father make some gesture towards her as her grandfather had done, but through the long ride back their backs were a stiff wall to her, cold and unrelenting. To block them out, she stared at the scenery, and dug up the image of the Professor.

Only a few hours ago she had left with such brave thoughts of renunciation. Now she was being brought back with her selfless impulses counting for nothing. How had they found out so quickly? Maybe Kailash had opened the letter meant for the Professor, and that was why they were so silent. They knew.

The car turned and lit up the shut gates of the house. As Kailashnath jumped out, Gopinath dragged them open from inside, his round face blinking in the glare. Running to the side of the car, he peered in, and 'She's back, she's back!' he shouted, rushing to the veranda. 'Sssh,' they cautioned. Did he want to publish their shame to the whole world?

The family was together again. There was no need for any more silence. Words broke forth in great torrents as the sequence of events was pieced together. United, the family talked. United, they raged and grieved, united they questioned.

Why? Why had she done this thing? Why run away? And worst of all, why tell a total stranger of her intention, and leave them to find out from an outsider what she was doing? And what about her relatives that-were-going-to-be? Didn't she owe them a moment's worth of consideration? Was this all her education had taught her? To put herself before others, and damn the rest? How would Bade Baoji bear it? How could anyone in their right senses bear the humiliation?

Kasturi said she would be grateful if her daughter could enlighten her as to the cause of all this tamasha, or were strangers going to perform that kind office once more?

'I want to study.' How weak and fragile that statement sounded, even to Virmati, as it left her hesitant lips, and fell on the sceptical ears of the family.

Kasturi hit her. Across her face, from cheek to cheek. 'For this, I let you go to college. So that you are ruined permanently? Are you mad?'

Lajwanti interrupted, her own daughter in mind. 'Pabiji, there is something else going on. Who has been influencing her? She has been taught by somebody – that much is clear. Otherwise Viru is hardly the academic type.'

'She's very good at learning other things, I can see,' Kasturi shouted, implicitly accepting Lajwanti's evaluation. 'Or how would she learn to run away, as though there were something wrong with her home and with us, to throw herself in a canal to be pulled out by servants?'

'*Achcha, achcha*,' Suraj Prakash made neutral noises. 'Maybe she was in great difficulty, but she should have come to us, that was her mistake. Why did you do this? Tell us, beti, whatever is in your heart?'

'Study,' mumbled Virmati like a mantra. She swallowed. 'Study . . .'

'For such a little thing?' said her father. 'You did this for such a little thing?'

'And not marry.' Virmati's face twisted. 'I don't want to marry.'

'But why? You know every girl has to go to her own home. This is your right, and our duty. As it is, we have taken our time, not wishing to hurry you. We have let you study, as much as any girl has studied in Amritsar.'

'I know, Pitaji.' Oh, why was he so good to her? Why did he speak so gently? She preferred the way the others spoke.

'Then, what is it? The boy, too, is good.'

She had to say something. 'The boy,' she said. 'I do not like the boy.'

Kasturi sprang forward to hit her again. Lajwanti held her back. 'Were you dreaming till now?' screamed the angry mother. 'The barat is coming, and she says she doesn't like the boy!'

'She is hiding something,' repeated Lajwanti.

'This girl will throw mud on our whole family, make us fall so low we will have no name left,' moaned Kasturi.

Virmati hung her head. Her silence though was not one of acquiescence, but refusal. She would not marry.

Finally they locked Virmati in the godown and arranged for Indu to marry Inderjit.

XIV

I can write to you because Paro got me paper, pen and ink tablet. I asked her for my study books and something to practise writing with. Please, otherwise I would go mad, alone in this place. I think Paro still has some feeling for me because she agreed. Maybe one day I will be able to show you what I have written, though my scribbles are so silly it doesn't matter if they are read or not.

The first time Paro crept up to my window, she asked me why I was locked up, what had I done that was so bad? What could I say? I could only cry, which made her cry too. Now she doesn't ask.

Time stands still in this large, dark room where they have put me. When it rains, I sit next to the small window, usually on a bin of rice. Sometimes the breeze blows a few welcome drops on my face. Long ago I used to dance and run in the rain when nobody was looking. Now I pine for drops.

They say men are not to be trusted. That I am giving up my life for nothing. That because I am stupid and foolish, they have to lock me up to save me from myself and you.

Indu is going to marry Inderjit. You must have heard that already. She will be happy, I know. Inderjit is a good boy, his family is good. Do you remember how jealous you used to be of him? See, it has all come to nothing.

I don't think they will let me attend the wedding, nor do I want to. What face will I show all those people who were almost my own? I feel safer here.

The evening is coming. The light in the angan grows dimmer and more mellow. You have taught me to notice such things. Before, I saw without any eyes. With my food will come a lantern, and then shadows will cover the walls. I go to sleep early, and get up with the sun. The first thing I do is my sandhya, slowly, and with great concentration.

It is the next day. Alone, my thoughts flow vacantly about in my head. This godown reminds me of my grandfather's in Sultanpur. It was always dim and mysterious, the only source of light was criss-crossed with bars, from the opening in the angan floor upstairs. I thought it the biggest, most wonderful room in the whole world, unlike this one, a place of imprisonment, with nothing but potatoes, onions, dal, rice, wheat, and winter quilts.

That one was full of – oh, all kinds of things. My grand-father dealt in spices, dry fruit, pickles, and morabbas, all of which we weren't supposed to touch. That's what he said, but sitting in his little office that opened on to one side of the godown, do you think my grandfather didn't know we were helping ourselves from the sacks and jars, and running into the outer courtyard to eat what we had stolen?

What has happened to that girl? Her family used to love her, how has she lost it all?

V.

Tuesday, 5 September, 1939

Precious love,

That little girl is the one I love, running wild and free through her grandfather's godown, and straight into my heart, where I hope to keep her forever!

Dearest, how could you? What I went through! Next time you contemplate such a thing, take me with you because it is now abundantly clear that I cannot, cannot live without you. Not in this world, or in the next.

I don't care how melodramatic that sounds. The threat of losing you makes all priorities clear. God, what hell have I been through. To be forced to put on a mask and pretend normalcy, when my deepest instincts were to scream and dash my head against the wall.

My darling, I feel I am responsible for driving you to this desperate measure. You must have felt so alone in those last few hours, a tragic irony when you are what I hold most dear on earth, when your face is the constant shadow in my mind. Those few, dreadful hours when I thought I had lost you are moments I wouldn't wish on my worst enemy.

First the fears, then the assurance that you were all right, then the fears again as to what was happening to you, and now this certainty, that you, my brave one, are locked in the godown while I roam at leisure – a free man ostensibly, but actually with every fibre of my being, next to you, by your side.

Oh, I knew what was happening to you. I have a wife who is a very good neighbour in times of trouble, and who doesn't hesitate to share the news she has been able to gather. Yes, I have a wife, very generous with her information, and therefore I knew you were locked up, that you refused to marry Inderjit, that Indu is going to preserve the family integrity. Bit by bit these nuggets fall, while she is feeding me, for we hardly meet otherwise. Bit by bit, while she looks closely at my face, where not a muscle twitches. Everybody is very upset, and your grandfather avoids coming to Amritsar, he is so ashamed. You have disgraced the family. Your sisters' chances of marriage are ruined. Indu is getting married, true, she says (though I don't say a word – she provides her own arguments), but that was settled before, and what about all the others? She doesn't dare say too much, but she doesn't leave the topic alone either.

I thank God there is some way of communicating with you. Your angel of a sister came. 'Pehnji has sent some work for you to correct,' she said, chewing her plait and standing on one leg. Then she added, 'You can send it back corrected, if you have the time.' I think God at least looks after lovers, no matter how the world treats them.

Enough, I can hear them coming back from a film, *Tulsidas*. One rupee was well spent to get the house to myself, to pour out my heart to you undisturbed, to let you know that I am ever, ever yours.

Later. The house is quiet. They have discussed the film non-stop, mainly gossip about Leela Chitnis. The war that Britain declared the day before yesterday on Germany after the attack on Poland leaves them unmoved, though every radio shop in Amritsar is thronged with people waiting for the latest news. London is being evacuated, the Army and the Navy are being mobilized. Churchill talks about defending everything sacred to man, freedom and democracy, all the ideals that are blatantly disregarded here every day. Ha! The left hand refuses to know what the right is doing.

Oh! I forgot to mention that soon we have to move. Our gracious landlady, your aunt, said her son is so worried about her health, she needs peace and quiet, and of course a most troublesome tenant out!

I have to live on Lepel Griffin Road or nowhere. Wild horses cannot drag me far from you. I need a little time, I said. That is all right, she said, and my wife hovered in the background and tried to keep the smile off her face.

Sweetheart,

Your H.

A morning, and the rains have stopped.

Paro got your letter, saying briefly, 'He has corrected your work.' I took it, and continued in a calm voice to talk to her. This enforced stillness increases my self-control.

At first I was afraid of involving Paro. She is so young, not yet five. I told her that she must not talk about me to anybody because they are angry with me, and everything I do earns their disapproval. Fortunately, she believed me, as why should she not? She can see for herself how it is.

Indu has married and gone away. Because of the family shame it was a small, brief affair. I was allowed to help dress her, and during the time of the vida, they let me say goodbye. Indu feels strongly that she should not be getting married before me. But the wrong I have done seems irreparable. Either our commitment is dishonoured, or the second daughter gets married first.

To be with my sisters again, and that too on such an important occasion, was almost as it used to be. However, nothing can take you back in time, and I noticed, though I didn't want to, how well they managed without me, how strained their conversation was in my presence.

As far as Inderjit is concerned, I don't feel I have done him any wrong. He has got Indu, who will make him an infinitely better wife. As for me, I know I have failed in my duty and I will be punished one day. Nobody can escape their karma. Maybe what is happening to me now is part of it, and there is no use protesting.

My fate is cast, and I am free now. I feel far more peaceful in the godown than I did in the days before I went to the river. Then, the confusion in my mind was terrible. I couldn't think, and all I heard around me was talk of my marriage. If I was to be a rubber doll for others to move as they willed, then I didn't want to live. I thought of what you taught us about Sydney Carton, and how noble and fine he seemed at the moment of his death. His last words echoed in my ears all that day. So you of all people should understand my actions!

I will wait a while before I give this to Paro. I dread her getting into trouble. People will say I am not satisfied with my own corruption, but I must start on my innocent sister too.

Many days later. Each day I say to myself. Not today. Wait one more day. You can wait one more day. But now I think it's all right, Paro can take it.

On Mahatmaji's birthday, they allowed me to join them in

spinning. We spun the whole morning. It was nice to be able to do this again. I asked Pitaji if I could do this inside, and as he agreed he looked so sad.

Mati and Pitaji want me to promise I will have nothing more to do with you, then they will let me out. Soon you are going away, they say, and then you will forget me. A man who is already married and a traitor to his wife can never give happiness to any woman. He is a worldly person caught in his own desires. Nothing solid.

The nights are beginning to get cold, and I now sleep with them. In the day they still lock me in the godown. Each time I hear the doors shut, I burn with anger and humiliation. What have I done? I am just like the sacks of wheat and dal here, without my own life. Mati blames it all on college. She should have married after Inter, she keeps saying. See what this reading has done to her. She feels she knows more than her own father and mother. It seems I have given a setback to the Arya Samaj effort to educate girls.

Moti Cottage
Lepel Griffin Road
Wednesday, 25 October

Vir, love,

Paro came with the letter safe and sound. I kissed it over and over, imagining it was your hand under my lips, and not the cold paper.

We are *both* buffeted by the winds of opposition, my darling. Friends tell me in indirect ways to give you up. After the passionate ardour of romance dies down, wives are all the same. How does it matter who is managing the house and looking after the children. Keep her as a friend, they counsel in their infinite wisdom, but why do you want to *marry* her?

What can I say? I feel sorry for them, because they do not know what it is to feel united with what one holds dearest on this earth, they cannot be elevated above the *practical* and the *convenient*. Before such worldly-wise souls, I do not reason. I only tell them I am committed, and I change the subject.

You see from the address that we have shifted. Though I derived some meagre comfort from being physically near you, I could no longer stay in that house. The situation was getting impossible. At least now there won't be those toings and froings between my wife and your mother – what a deadly combination. I was always apprehensive that you would be treated harshly as a result of what my wife said and yet I was powerless to stop these neighbourly visits. My mother too gave me no peace. She feels it deeply that her eldest son, the pride of her heart, should consider a second marriage. She has brought Ganga up, whereas you would be a stranger to her and the family ways. They do not recognize that I need the companionship of an educated, thinking woman nor that I feel lonely and desolate among all these people who care for me.

We spent our first Dussehra here. We did a small puja at noon. That evening we went to see Ravana, Meghnath and Kumbhkarna being burnt. In Ferozepur an effigy of Hitler was also included amongst the demon trio, but Amritsar is obviously more traditional. The aviation grounds were crowded, but we managed to push ourselves to a good viewing place.

Here, in Moti Cottage, my heart stretches far in your direction to pull you towards me to this place you haven't seen. I will describe it, and then, when you imagine me in it, imagine amid the noise and hubbub of a large household, a solitary, isolated man, yearning for you, always, always. At times I think I cannot bear it, and then the thought of what you are going through for the sake of our love makes me feel ashamed of my impatience.

The garden is small, but it has space enough for four fruit trees, malta, mango, mulberry, and mithha. (I wonder if the owner has an attachment to fruits beginning with 'm'!) In the middle of the garden is a small brick platform, cemented over so we can avoid sitting on wet grass if we want to. The two large rooms in front are a drawing-room and a bedroom with an attached dressing-room. At the back stretches the kitchen, storerooms, bathing-rooms, cowshed, all in a row. And in the middle of the angan is this most wonderful tank! A tube-well fills it and in the summer it promises delightful relief from the heat.

Night falls, and my hand aches. Today I have corrected over fifty essays – in an effort to clear the backlog of work that had piled up during these past few weeks. If you knew how difficult it has been for me to function even minimally! Teaching has been a colossal strain, correction impossible. Only now, with your letters which I read and reread constantly, do I feel a whole man again.

H.

Next day but one.

Yesterday was busy with the College Students' Association elections. I wonder, darling, whether any of your brothers unbent enough to tell you what happened in college ten days ago. Democracy in its most 'popular' form! A quarrel erupted between the two rival factions, which turned into fisticuffs before any of the staff could be informed. Very soon the whole central courtyard resembled the Kurukshetra battlefield. MM rushed to intervene and found himself in the pathway of a flying missile. Obviously throwing things at a principal will not do, even for the rowdiest boy, and this incident served to sober them up.

Next day, at assembly, MM gave the most spirited lecture I have ever heard him make. Talked about the microcosm mirroring the macrocosm, and if this was the Indian conception of elections, perhaps the British were right in declaring us too immature for independence.

The boys apologized profusely, and the elections were

scheduled for yesterday, with all the staff on duty to ensure no mishap.

How are you, my dearest? I long for our separation to be over, to see you, touch you again. Till then, I lead a restless life. Family, teaching, friends, reading, nothing absorbs me for long. I write on, wanting, needing to share everything with you, despite the fact that there is no messenger, praying that some way will be found.

Wednesday, 15 November, 1939

D.!

There is a god who looks after lovers, there is! Kanhiya Lal came over to pay his respects. Normally I encourage my students to visit, but I was too depressed to talk much to him. As he was leaving, he asked me discreetly whether there was anything he could do for me. I hesitated, then took the plunge. I said I needed a letter delivered.

'What am I there for?' he demanded, clicking his tongue.

'It is a complicated matter . . .' I know he is friendly with your brothers, and wondered whether it was fair to put him in the position of go-between.

'Any little difficulty, any problem, and I will consider it my privilege, my pleeyure . . .' (I have not been able to make him say 'pleasure'.) 'I will come this evening,' he ended impetuously and left without giving me a chance to say anything. He has a delicate perception that pleases me.

How was your Diwali, sweetheart? We saw the Golden Temple, wondrous with lights, its aquatic reflection adding to its ethereal beauty. It was so romantic, I missed you more than I can say, and the pain made me surly and bad-tempered with the others.

This Diwali was the most expensive I have ever known, though I didn't like to stint on sweets or oil lamps, especially as I had called the usual number of people. If this continues we shall all be forced to tighten our belts. Ever since the war started, prices have risen at an alarming rate. The quality of goods has gone down, and fines have not helped the increasing adulteration.

Our old life recedes further and further away. Attempts are being made in Europe by the smaller countries, mostly Belgium and Holland, to bring about peace. After ten weeks of war, Britain remains strong, at least according to Churchill, and they might be successful in convincing Germany about a cease-fire. I hope this time peace will emerge as a result of these efforts. So far it has been a term bandied about by both sides, with how much sincerity the results show.

Ever your H.

Moti Cottage
Saturday, 25 November, 1939

Love,

A feeling of depression pervades me. Money problems increase day by day. The war is said to be costing Britain six million pounds daily. The price of gold has gone up dramatically, and it is all the more imperative that I redeem my mother's jewellery as quickly as possible. Some of it I have already done, she mortgaged it in stages you know, to finance my upkeep in England. It is only when I have fulfilled my responsibilities that I can consider myself a free man.

Kanhiya Lal came today. He said he had not known how hostile the opposition to our relationship was. (All this in a roundabout way. I think he is afraid of wounding my feelings!) He approached Kailashnath, who kept saying your parents and grandfather were grievously hurt, and in society one couldn't go on thinking of oneself alone. The same thinking that perpetrates the most ghastly personal tragedies. What is society made up of, but individuals?

Finally, Kanhiya managed to persuade Kailash to let him

97

see you – to make you see reason, he said. He reports you as silent, very silent, darling. He met you in the drawing-room, along with one of your younger brothers, your eyes followed the letter he managed to hide under the cover of the takht.

Kanhiya feels thrown into the role of both Machiavelli and Cupid. As I imagined, he is uneasy about having to deceive his friend. On the other hand he wants to serve the teacher at whose feet he has sat. (This is the way he puts it.) He cannot be accused of personal motivation, so that eases his conscience somewhat. Poor fellow! That my difficulties should involve my students! But it can't be helped. My loneliness is so great, my desire for you so acute that these niceties get brushed aside.

Soon it will be my birthday. My thirtieth. At Moti Cottage, we will do a puja, and feed thirty brahmins. Any other form of celebration would seem callous disregard of the lives being lost. Not a day passes without some news of ships sunk, and aircraft shot down.

When I look back, I feel I have achieved so little of what I wanted! My debts are unredeemed, and my family's ineptitude in matters of learning and self-improvement is as glaring as ever. When I see how eagerly my students learn, how they hang upon my every word, sadness comes upon me. Those who are my nearest ones are those whom I can help the least. *She* was the first with whom I tried, and the first with whom I failed.

The war drags on. Moral polarities become more evident to all, from Gandhi to Malik. How can the British claim to be sincere about defending democracy when they refuse to give up their control over India. Some in the staff-room feel that Britain is as much an imperial, expansionist power as Germany. Others feel there is a qualitative difference, and that notwithstanding our political disagreements, we should support Britain. Enriched or impoverished, we have been so interlinked these past two hundred years that the symbiosis goes beyond a simple definition of right and wrong. How can we turn our backs, and say the war is your business, not ours?

Malik, our economist, remarked yesterday that whether we turned our backs on Britain or not, we were going to end up financing this war, in one way or another. No country could afford to go on fighting on the scale Britain was. Sooner or later she would have to draw on her resources, and that was her Empire. Either through taxes (but Malik didn't think the taxes would go very far, that would make her too unpopular) or through other means, we would be vitally affected. We could flatter ourselves with the illusion that we had a choice about support. The truth of the matter was that we had been involved since the moment war was declared.

We thought of the unprecedented rise in prices, and voiced no dissent.

It seems aeons since I heard from you, darling. Shifting from your aunt's house has lengthened the distance between us, and made my heart more anxious.

H.

Morning.

I was so surprised when Kailash brought Kanhiya Lal here to see me two weeks ago! I didn't say much to him. We sat in the baithak, and I managed to take the letter he hid without anyone noticing. I fed upon it eagerly. Nobody here cares to discuss anything seriously with me.

They have moved me to the terrace. The godown was getting very cold. Before they sent me up, they asked me again if I would marry. I should be grateful, they said, for a decent man with a sound family background. Someone as fallen as I would not find it easy to get a home. My mother keeps saying that all my education has achieved is the destruction of my family. How I am supposed to respond, I don't know.

After the godown, this is like a new life for me. I can breathe and think more clearly with the great sky above me.

The sun feels soft and warm. At one end of the terrace is a neem tree, where I can sit when it gets too hot in the afternoons, almost in its branches. There is a little store in the corner that is used for keeping the charpais, bedding, mosquito nets and poles, and this serves me when I need a room.

This long period is the first time in my life I have been left completely to myself. Away from my brothers and sisters, away from household activity, I feel strange, one pea alone in a whole long pod, no use to anybody. I have to get used to it, for this is my fate.

All I have is your letters. They are the only sign anybody cares for me. My family tells me they are doing this for my good. I feel, since I have caused them so much grief, why don't they just let me go away and never see me again. God will provide – there are things I can do. When I suggested this, they got very angry. They want nothing from me but an agreement to marry.

V.

Moti Cottage
Tuesday, 12 December, 1939

Viru sweetheart,

You must write more. The frequency of communication is so limited that the volume of our correspondence has to compensate. And then darling, what is this curious habit of not addressing me?

Forgive this cavilling. I am disturbed and not hearing from you makes it worse. My family is putting pressure on me to leave Amritsar. They say even if I cannot find a job for three hundred rupees a month in Kanpur, the living expenses will be cheaper in the family home. My brother's children also need me, there is no one who can guide them like I can, my mother will feel more settled, it will be easier to arrange my sister's marriage, etc., etc.

Yesterday a huge demonstration was held at Jallianwala

Bagh criticizing the Punjab Government for not controlling prices and checking profiteering. With so much agitation there is bound to be some positive outcome. Then they will have less reason to pressurize me to move.

My bua has arrived from Kanpur. Apparently my mother had asked her to get my horoscope read by a more learned astrologer than our pujari. Although I do not believe in all this nonsense, my horoscope has turned out to be an unexpected ally in our union! This my sister Guddiya told me, as she was giving me breakfast. Normally she just leaves the tray in the room and goes, but today she hovered around.

'Guddiya?' I said. 'Is something the matter?' I thought she might be having a problem with the last book I gave her to read.

She smiled. 'Bhaiyaji, they were discussing your horoscope.'

'And?' I pricked up my ears.

'The Moon and Venus are together in the seventh house –'

'What does that mean?'

'You don't know, Bhaiyaji?' she exclaimed. 'Why, the seventh house is the house of marriage – among many other things!'

Even this ten-year-old girl knows such a thing. How we fill our children's heads with rubbish!

'So?'

'So, in your case, they are inspected by the tenth aspect of Saturn, therefore two marriages!' And she ran off giggling and looking very naughty.

Next day, next instalment.

'Bhaiyaji,' she said.

'Guddo,' I said, catching her by the arm, and holding her chin with my hand. 'Let me see if you know how to give news. Imagine you are writing a composition.'

'Who will read it? It is not like "My Favourite Book" or "My Holiday", is it?'

'Never mind,' I said. 'Compositions are supposed to teach

you how to tell things clearly.'

She told me that she had heard (or made it her business to hear) Buaji tell Ammaji that even if she tried she could not stop my second marriage. Fate worked in strange ways, and she should accept whatever happened with good grace. Amma kept crying throughout but Buaji said that you were from a good family, how much worse would it have been if I had come home with an English mem? And she said I was doing my duty by the family, and trying to pay back my debts as fast as possible, even though no one had ever asked me for the money. If they tried to restrict me too much, they might end up losing me altogether.

I could not have put my case half so well! I told Guddiya that I was very satisfied with her powers of expression. She looked pleased and ran away.

Friday, 15 December, 1939

K.L. is coming tomorrow. I do not know how many more times he will be allowed to see you. Even this much has been an unexpected piece of good fortune.

Darling, you say your family is questioning your years of studying. One of the benefits of education is that it teaches us to think for ourselves. Even if we arrive at the same conclusions that have been presented to us, our faith in those beliefs are stronger for having been personally thought out. If, as sometimes happens, our education leads us to question some of the value systems by which we live, that is not to say that we are destroying tradition. The tradition that refuses to entertain doubt, or remains impervious to new thoughts and ideas, becomes a prison rather than a sustaining life force. Even the smallest one of us has a social function, but that function is not to follow blindly beliefs that may not be valid.

Do you know how an earthworm lives? It inhabits an extremely limited space, its whole life is spent within the darkness of the soil. It can neither feel nor see. Uneducated people are like that. We are being murderers towards ourselves if we do not develop our intellect. Any part of us that is not used will atrophy and die – the same is true of our minds. Remember, it was through your desire to learn that we were first drawn to each other.

Then Vir, consider, what is it that takes me away from the woman I live with? Apart from the planets in the house of marriage, of course! She is a good woman, runs the house to perfection, looks after my family as though they were her own. Despite all this, I am lonely, lonely, lonely. We have nothing in common. I once wanted to share my interests with my wife, felt her pain at my estrangement from her. But she will not change. Will not – cannot – I do not know.

Who is responsible for this state of affairs? Society, which deems that their sons should be educated, but not their daughters. Society that decides that children – babies really – should be married at the ages of two and three as we were. As a result, both of us needlessly suffer for no fault of ours. I cannot be an adherent to stultifying tradition after this, but Viru, you must make up your own mind about these matters. You are intelligent and capable.

This has been a very long letter – to make up for your very short one! Do not disappoint me again, in this respect, darling.

All my love,
H.

Thursday, 4 January, 1940

Vir, darling,

So long, and no word from you! It is with an uneasy heart that I contemplate this silence. Kanhiya said you had no letter for him. He said nothing else, and I did not like to probe further.

Today is the last day of the Scout Mela. It has been almost a

two-week affair, with seven thousand scouts and guides con-
gregating from all over India. I would have thought a more
natural venue would have been Lahore, but I suppose the
powers that be thought that Amritsar should get its fair share
of (what?) attention, I suppose. One can hardly call it culture.

Thanks to the Scout Mela, Amritsar was graced with the
presence of Jawaharlal. We Indians have an innate need to
worship, I think. The day he came, the market shut. At
Malviya Nagar, where he was to give his address, two lakh
people congregated. Two lakh! Imagine! By the time J.L.
came, they were so excited they broke the cordon and
swarmed all around him. Such was the press and swell of the
crowd that he even fell off his horse. His pleas for order, as
well as repeated injunctions over the loudspeakers, had no
effect. In the end he left in disgust. The crowd disbanded and
collected at Jallianwala Bagh where rumour had it he would
appear. At five, J.L. finally came back and gave his speech!

I give you these snippets of news, but my heart is not in it.
Please Viru, write to me. That I should have to plead with
you! I will send K.L. again to your house, and again and
again, until I hear from you. This misgiving that I feel within
me is hard to bear.

H.

Can it really be a mystery to you why I have not written?

They have told me that your wife is pregnant. Apparently Ganga had come to announce the happy news. At
first I did not believe it. How could it be true?

They have let me out of the little room on the terrace. I cried
when I left. That was my house of dreams, when I still believed
in you. Thank God their problems are over, Mati said, and my
daughter is safe. Now she has to come to her senses

On her next visit she asked to see me. They forced me to go.

When I saw her I could see that it was true. Mati told her it
will be a boy, and this is what every man wants, even if he is

educated. She blushed, and smiled, and I knew that the place next to you was rightfully hers.

Tell K. there is no need for him to visit.

I understand. She is your wife after all.

Goodbye, goodbye forever,

V.

No, Viru no. Will you brusquely cut me off, will you really condemn me without a word from my side? Day and night I move with your invisible presence next to me, my love for you quickening my heartbeat with life and vitality. What you imagine happened seems so insignificant, hardly worth talking about in comparison to what I feel.

I find it hard to unravel the tissue of domestic strife and obligations that I find I am the centre of, but I must try.

You will say, why did I not walk away, why did I succumb? You think I am no longer faithful – that I am incapable of it – that I want a son, and believe the things the whole world tells you to believe.

It was not for a son that this happened. It was not because I wished to reaffirm the physical bond between my wife and me.

My love, what can you understand of these things? You who are so innocent and inexperienced.

Picture to yourself a man so in love, he cannot call his soul his own. Out of consideration to his family, he tries to hide his deep involvement with the girl. They are used to his preoccupied demeanour, no one is close enough to know the state of his emotions.

Then one day the girl tries to commit suicide. The man breaks down completely, the inmates of his house become privy to his secret. His wife cries, threatens, demands reassurance. She does all this softly, bit by bit, with half-sentences, and tear-filled eyes. She burns the food. His mother takes her part.

The man needs to be left in peace. What has happened to

his loved one has so shattered him he finds it difficult to think coherently, finds it difficult to resist the relentless appeal to what was made out to be his moral responsibilities.

He does what he can to bring back domestic harmony. He feels guilty about ignoring the suffering of one who is also in a way blameless. An act is performed mechanically, with what result you have already seen.

Sweetest, it does no one any credit, the story that I have had to reveal to you. Yet I was vulnerable, and in this moment of weakness it seemed I could not in all conscience ignore the claims of those around me.

Vir, revile me as you wish, curse me, berate me. Only do not punish me so harshly as to deny me yourself. If I have sinned against you, it has never been in spirit, my darling, never that. My love and devotion has remained ever yours, it is that which gives my life its meaning.

This time I have called Kanhiya Lal, and begged him to take this letter to you, as soon as was feasible. I had to tell him that there was a misunderstanding between us, and he must insist you read it. I know your feeling for me will not allow you to refuse this plea.

I enclose a small poem. Not as part of my letter, but rather as a supplement to it. You are too perceptive a reader not to sense its application to my poor situation.

I live only when I hear from you again.

Still, and forever, your

H.

LOVE'S UNITY

How can I tell thee when I love thee best?
In rapture or repose? How shall I say?
I only know I love thee every way,
Plumed for love's flight, or folded in love's nest.
See, what is day but night bedewed with rest?
And what the night except the tired-out day?

And 'tis love's difference, not love's decay,
If now I dawn, now fade, upon thy breast.
Self-torturing sweet! Is't not the self-same sun
Wanes in the west that flameth in the east,
His fervour nowise altered nor decreased?
So rounds my love, returning where begun,
And still beginning, never most nor least,
But fixedly various, all love's parts in one.

Thursday, 1 February, 1940

Please do not go on sending K.L. with demands for a reply.
It is kind of you to show such interest in me, and to try and
educate me by sending me poems, but I am still not advanced
enough to understand them. It seems to me the poem is saying that you can do what you like so long as you go on saying you love. I know this cannot be true. In my family
marriages are not made like this.

Now I know there is still some life in your feelings for
your wife – as it is proper there should be – it would be very
wrong of me to come between you, especially when there is
going to be another baby. But for the pregnancy, I would
never have known.

What has happened has happened for the good. In which
world was I living, to be so caught up in the illusion of your
love? Just as you must do your duty to your family, and
your wife, so too I must do my duty to mine. My people
have always been straightforward people, Pitaji and Bade
Baoji have always been known for their honesty and high
standards. People blindly trust my father in business, our
community respects us. I am proud that I belong to such a
family, and I must keep up its traditions.

I am going to Lahore to do my BT. I want to be a teacher
like you and Shakuntala Pehnji. Perhaps my family will also
benefit by what I do, as yours has done. As for me, I never

stopped learning from you, whether it was in the classroom or outside.

Mati says at least I wouldn't be at home to remind her of the eternal disgrace I am to everybody. I, too, want a fresh start. It will be a great relief for me to leave this house. Maybe Bade Baoji will consent to come here after I have gone.

I hear them say to each other, 'Poor thing, it is not her fault she has been taken in. She is so simple. Once she is out of here, the situation will improve.' They haven't talked so nicely about me in a long time.

I have learnt from my experience, but this much I also know. You did not mean to deceive me. What has happened is God's will. I was unreasonable ever to mind.

I thought you would appreciate the fact that I was not going to stop my studies – you were always so pleased when I learned anything.

V.

Wednesday, 7 February, 1940

Sweetheart,

For that you will always be, no matter what you say – how can I stop writing to you? How cease begging, pleading, imploring you to have a little mercy upon me? You are the air I breathe – you may as well ask me to avoid eating or reading.

And the tone of your last letter, how cold, how indifferent, how determined. You thank me for my interest in you. Good God! Can I be merely interested in someone whom I have banded round my heart with hoops of steel! That is doing me a gross injustice, darling! I had rather you abused, damned, anything but this deadly polite tone.

At another time I would have rejoiced that you are going to Lahore. I have a friend there – you remember I used to talk about him sometimes – the one who teaches in Government

College, we were at Oxford together. He was responsible for bringing me to Amritsar. His father was asked by someone on the AS College board to recommend an English teacher.

Can this be of interest to you now, when your calmness strikes terror in my heart, when it seems immaterial to you whether we meet or don't? I, who love you so truly and so ardently have become an enemy in your eyes. I cannot bear this. I realize I am repeating myself, but the pain I feel is not subject to variety.

Sweetheart, I do not send K.L. with the intention of extracting a reply. I am too miserable, too deeply troubled. Any distance from you, not physical distance, for that we have experienced and survived, but any alienation of the spirit, leaves me but half a man.

I must hear from you soon, I must. Every minute of the day will be passed in waiting.

Yours, ever and always,
H.

27 February, 1940

Dear Sir,

It is not as though I do not value your friendship. Nor do I purposely sound cold and cruel, as you put it. I just described what seemed obvious.

When I first heard, how I suffered, how I cried. I thought, this is the real punishment for what I have done. I had to be strong to bear the pain, silently, without anyone knowing. I did not want them to believe I was so stupid that no matter what you did, I would go on fighting with them over you. I had already caused enough grief by trying to be different from what was expected of me. No, it is better to do as they tell you. It is safer. Then the family protects you if things go wrong. At least I would not be as lonely as now.

So it hurts when you talk of my not caring for your misery.

Do you really think I could so quickly forget all you were to me? It's only that you were not mine to care for.

Shakuntala Pehnji has suggested Rai Bahadur Sohan Lal Training College for Women. It is small, attached to a school in the same compound, and away from the fashionable part of the city. They have approved the place. All I want is a change from my old life and the chance to do something useful. I do not mean ever to marry.

I have heard that a hostel has opened for girls in the medical college. There *are* families who want a career for their daughters. Nobody wanted anything for me except a husband.

How is your wife? She looks very nice these days. The way she walks, I too think you will have a son. I see her talking to Mati sometimes, but thankfully she has not sent for me again.

I do not think we need to write to each other after this.

V.

XV

Who would go with Virmati to Lahore? Kasturi rejected all the possibilities that offered themselves to her. Suraj Prakash could not leave the shop, Kailashnath was too young, Somnath too irresponsible. Shakuntala Pehnji had offered, but how could Kasturi expect a young, unmarried niece, already corrupted by Lahore, to recognize any lurking invitation to sin?

No, Kasturi had to go herself. If fate saw fit to rub chillies in her wound, she must resign herself to that. She made one last attempt to make her daughter see reason before they departed.

'If you cannot consider your duty to us, at least consider yourself. There is a time in the cycle of life for everything. If you wilfully ignore it like this, what will happen to you? A woman without her own home and family is a woman without moorings.'

Virmati had nothing to say. That tone, those reproaches had but to start for her to go deaf.

'When I was your age,' continued Kasturi, 'girls only left their house when they married. And beyond a certain age . . .' Her voice quavered and she stopped, looking at her daughter helplessly.

Virmati noticed the tears in her mother's voice, but she kept her head turned away. She had made a decision, and there were certain things she would not see.

'God has put you on earth to punish me,' concluded Kasturi harshly, disappointment pinching lines around her tense mouth.

The train ride was a silent one. The Inter class in which they sat was almost empty. No strangers' voices dropped into their midst, no questions were asked as to where they were going and why. From time to time Virmati glanced furtively at her mother, and the wall she encountered forbade her from making the attentive gestures that might have made the journey bearable for both.

An hour later, Lahore.

Kasturi leaned out of the window, anxiously scanning the platform for Shakuntala. Virmati hugged the bag in her lap and thought, I've come, I'm going to be on my own, this is a new beginning. She was filled with a lightness that made her useless in collecting the luggage, irritating her mother further.

By now, Shakuntala Pehnji had spotted them. Embraces, exclamations followed, with the usual remarks of how thin the younger one was looking, tossed from Kasturi to Shakuntala to Virmati. A coolie piled their luggage on his head, and the trio made their way to a precious tonga waiting.

'Why precious, Pehnji?' enquired Virmati.

The luggage was stored under the wooden bench, and the women squeezed onto the back seat, as Shakuntala gave details of the tonga strike, the insistence of the authorities on three passengers instead of four, the new demand that all tonga-wallahs be licensed, the indignation of the tonga-wallahs – were the horses of more importance than the men driving them? – the subsequent agitation, and the difficulty of finding transport. This explanation over, Shakuntala started commenting on the places they passed. From time to time, Kasturi grunted to show that she was listening.

At the sight of the passing scenery, the weight of her mother's displeasure lifted a little from Virmati. She was seeing the fabled city at last. They passed the Mall, Chief's College, Nedou's Hotel, the Botanical Gardens, Lawrence Gardens, the Gymkhana Club, Queen Victoria's massive statue with its delicate canopy of carved marble, the Assembly, the GPO, the majestic-looking courts which looked like palaces, while Shakuntala murmured and pointed to all of the above.

From time to time Shakuntala looked Virmati over. She thought the girl looked older, the shy, open look she had seen in Dalhousie was gone. She was glad that her family was at last waking up to the fact that women had to take their place in the world, but must it always be when marriage hadn't worked out? Work was not second best, though she didn't expect anybody from Amritsar to understand that.

'Chachi,' she said, turning towards her aunt. 'You will not regret sending Viru to Lahore.'

'Beti,' said Kasturi, 'what is there to hide from you? What else is left this wretched girl but study?'

Shakuntala smiled bitterly to herself. 'She will become a teacher and help others. Chachi, you know how important education is to Bade Baoji. In time, maybe he will even be pleased with her.' Virmati devoured this sympathetic crumb, and yearned for more.

Kasturi said tartly that where Virmati was concerned no course of action was right, the girl was so stubborn and independent, no matter what they did for her, she wasn't grateful. When she had been young, eighth-class pass had satisfied her, but her daughter thought she was too special to follow family ways.

Virmati stared fixedly at King Edward Medical College coming up, with a statue, she presumed, of the king in front. Her eyes were hot and burning. She was trying to live within a moral code, but her mother would never understand that. Scenes from last evening stabbed her mind. She had carried all the letters the Professor had ever sent her to the kotha. At the furthest point where the topmost branches of the neem tree could touch her face, she watched them burn undisturbed. When the fire had finished its job, she collected the ashes and flung them towards her aunt's house, where he had once lived, watching the tiny black specks of her lost love float about. She would leave him to his pregnant wife and get on with the rest of her life. Nevertheless, despite her resolution and her pain, she was still considered the black sheep of the family.

Past Government College, past DAV College, on and on the tonga went. The grand buildings receded, and to Virmati's dismay they entered a more congested part. Finally they reached a high brick wall, with a small, painted sign proclaiming that these were the premises of the RBSL School and College. To one side was a black gate, with the usual pedestrian opening let into it. The tonga-wallah stopped just inside, and demanded one rupee as fare. Infuriated, Kasturi paid the unreasonable sum to avoid the greater humiliation of her niece paying first.

Mother and daughter looked around speculatively. Kasturi was relieved. A plain no-nonsense place. None of those poems in stone and brick they had been passing. A good Arya Samaj institution.

Virmati thought she should have known that the poems in stone and brick would not be for her. Still, any place was welcome, any place that promised to bring sense and purpose to her life.

The compound housed several buildings. A brick-paved walk led to the administrative unit, low, white, and wide-verandaed. On the right was a dusty playing field, with two basketball nets hanging desultorily on either side. Beyond that was a large, double-storeyed, red-brick school. Far to the left was the smaller teacher-training college, and behind both of these was the teachers' hostel.

They met the principal in white khadi with a greying bun. She spun her charkha daily, was a staunch supporter of the struggle for swarajya, Gandhi, female education, and everything being bettered. She assured Kasturi that all the girls staying there were like her daughters, and consequently she had her eye firmly fixed on each one. This was a respectable institution, with a reputation to maintain.

Kasturi allowed herself to relax. Perhaps her worries had been unfounded. Her daughter would be all right here.

The formalities over, the group walked through the narrow entranceway of the teachers' hostel. A door was unlocked to a small room containing two string beds, a cupboard, two desks, two chairs, and a small window from where one could see the mud of the playing field. Though the room was dark and gloomy, it was bordered by a pleasant corridor-veranda towards the inside. The angan beyond was spacious, with a badminton court painted on its grey, cemented surface. In a corner was a large mulberry tree.

'These used to be single rooms, but now the new girls have to share. Your room-mate will come tomorrow.'

Virmati looked around and saw autonomy and freedom. The ache in her heart lessened a bit.

Kasturi looked around, a tightness in her throat. My poor girl, for this she wouldn't marry. For living in a solitary, poky little room in a strange city, for eating hostel food, for the loneliness of single life.

Shakuntala looked around with satisfaction. The room was dismal, and she knew enough of her family to be sure it met her aunt's requirements.

Just to be sure her daughter would be able to pursue her studies undisturbed, Kasturi departed to have a small private talk with the principal. Virmati knew what her mother was going to say, and she was angry. She was to be supervised like a jailbird on parole. Marriage was acceptable to her family, but not independence.

There was silence in the room. Virmati started fiddling with her things, while her cousin looked at her thoughtfully before putting her arms around her. Virmati was startled. Shakuntala had never been demonstrative.

'I didn't want to say anything in front of Chachi, but I know that whatever happened could not have been your fault. You are not the kind of girl to give up an engagement casually,' said Shakuntala lightly.

Virmati did not know what to say. That part of her life was closed. Discussing it might bring back the pain.

'You will find, Viru, that in Lahore people are not so narrow-minded. It is a pity the man was married, but you have done the right thing. Together we will face the family. After all, I have experience in resisting pressures. Don't worry, I am on your side.' Shakuntala squeezed Virmati closer and added, 'Now tell me all about it. What actually happened?'

Virmati squirmed.

'Nothing happened,' she mumbled.

Shakuntala looked incredulous. Virmati felt hunted.

Shakuntala had been a source of inspiration, she wanted to be like her. Now she noticed the hunger in her eyes, the avidness on her face. She waited uncomfortably for her mother to come, and as a way of putting Shakuntala off, cried instead. It wasn't difficult once she started.

When the goodbyes took place, Kasturi, moved by the tears in her daughter's eyes, unbent enough to give her an affectionate farewell.

XVI

The next day Swarna Lata, the room-mate, came. Her name meant golden creeper, and she crept around Virmati without tightening her grip and shone on her as long as they were together, because she was generous and had plenty to give from a life that was full.

'Do you have anything to eat?' she now asked as she started unpacking.

'Why yes,' said Virmati, eager and wanting to make friends. 'Mathri, pickle, mango and lemon, namak-para.'

Later, as they ate the fresh, flaky mathri and lemon pickle made from garden lemons, covered in large red chilli flakes, Virmati asked delicately, 'Your mother? Didn't she send anything with you?'

Swarna sighed.' She's annoyed with me.'

Virmati pricked up her ears.

'You look too nice for anybody to be cross with,' she probed.

'I wish my mother thought so.' Swarna licked her fingers. 'It's only because of my father that I am here. My mother wanted me to marry. She said I had done my BA and that was enough. Where was all this study going to end?'

Virmati positively glowed. 'And then?' she asked, hands suspended in mid-air, a drop of oil dangling from the dull-gold lemon piece.

'Then what? I love Lahore. All my friends are here, all my activities. I had to stay here, and so I decided to do an MA. I wrote and told my parents. There was not a moment to lose. They'd already begun to send me photographs of prospective husbands! Each looking uglier than the last.'

'Didn't they try and stop you?' asked Virmati wistfully.

'They had no choice.' Swarna arched her brows, totally in control of her life. 'I was very clear that I wanted to do something besides getting married. I told my parents that if they would support me for two more years I would be grateful. Otherwise I would be forced to offer satyagraha along with other Congress workers against the British. And go on offering it until taken to prison. Free food and lodging at the hands of the imperialists.'

Virmati stared at her in amazement. 'They weren't *very* angry?'

'They probably were. I don't know. But they agreed because they knew I meant what I said. Which was just as well, because I am too insignificant for our rulers to arrest. They would have let me off with a fine at the most, and money I didn't have.'

Swarna Lata got up from Virmati's bed, where they had been eating, and brushed the crumbs from her khadi kurta.

'Thank God all that is over,' said Swarna Lata. 'It was quite unpleasant while it lasted. I prefer not to quarrel with my parents, but sometimes there is no alternative.'

'Yes,' agreed Virmati dejectedly, 'sometimes there isn't.'

A few days later, Shakuntala cycled down to the RBSL College during visiting hours, to check on her cousin.

Virmati greeted her cautiously.

'Settled in nicely?' enquired Shakuntala solicitously.

'Everything is very homely,' stated Virmati firmly. 'And the food is really not bad.'

Shakuntala at once looked interested. 'What do they give you?' she demanded.

'Mornings, toast and milk. Lunch, dal, rice, chappatti, vegetable, dahi, sometimes a sweet dish, for tea, pakora or mathri, for dinner, dal, sabzi, sometimes with paneer, rice, chappatti.'

'Sounds good. Chachi will be pleased. And your room-mate? What is she like?'

At this Virmati gushed, 'Oh Pehnji, she is very nice. I am so lucky she is staying in this hostel, even though she doesn't study here. Her parents also wanted her to get married, but she is doing an MA because she wants to do something with her life first.'

'*Hoon*,' grunted Shakuntala.

'Come and meet her,' said Virmati, grabbing her cousin by the arm and pulling her towards the hostel. 'Luckily she is in.'

But the meeting was not a success. 'I must say she is rather plain,' remarked Shakuntala as they left the room.

Virmati looked at her a little coldly. Fancy Pehnji going so much by looks. Anybody would be impressed by Swarna's eyes behind her glasses, eyes that refused to smile just because they were looked at. And what about the intelligence in her round face, and the friendliness that was frank and open?

'But Swarna is not who I want to talk about,' went on Shakuntala. 'What about *him*? Has he tried to get in touch with you yet?'

'Of course not, Pehnji,' said Virmati resentfully. 'Besides how would he when . . .' She stopped.

'Doesn't he know you are here?'

Virmati wished her cousin would talk of something else. 'I'm so lucky to be here,' she said quickly. 'Thank you, Pehnji, for helping me.'

'*Arre,* where is the need for thanks in the family?' responded Shakuntala, flicking Virmati's cheek with her finger. 'And thank God there is no quota system in SL. In Government colleges, the quota is so high that good Hindu students have to wait until the Muslim quota is full, though of course their quota is hardly ever filled because those people don't like to study . . .'

'How do you know, Pehnji?' Virmati enquired timidly. 'Maybe they have other difficulties?'

Shakuntala looked surprised. 'Everybody knows that,' she said firmly.

I wonder if Swarna does, thought Virmati as Shakuntala swept on. 'And only then are the Hindu girls, really good students some of them, allowed seats. Miss Dutta – we eat with her – says the quota system is part of politics, and we mustn't get upset about something we can do nothing about.'

The girls parted at the gates, Virmati wondering a little sadly whether she would ever feel the way she used to about Shakuntala Pehnji.

*

In Amritsar, the Professor's thoughts kept circling around Virmati. Had she forgotten him? It was obvious she was trying to. Away from him, away from all associations of their relationship, who knew how quickly the unthinkable might be accomplished?

An open invitation from his friend, Syed Husain, to use his house as his own, went a long way in helping the Professor achieve his objective. Syed Husain was married, had regrets, and was involved with a specific alternative. A situation enough like the Professor's own to make each one eager to help the other.

'Stay here and meet her,' said Syed Husain, the friend. The Professor was sitting in his drawing-room, in his house on the campus of Government College.

'It is so difficult,' said the Professor gloomily. 'I write to her but she doesn't reply.'

'Oh?' Syed looked surprised. 'Don't they open letters?'

'I was lucky. The BT girls have their letters opened only on random occasions. Even though I had taken the precaution of signing myself as a female, she was extremely annoyed. She wrote back only once and asked me – me, imagine! – if I was trying to get her expelled before she had even started her course of study.'

There was a brief silence as the bearer came in with the tea service. The Professor looked at the tray and bearer appreciatively. Both were completely uniformed – down to the white gloves on the hands of the man, the small, gleaming slop bowl, and lace-embroidered milk-jug holder on the tea tray. Syed knew how to live well, thought the Professor wistfully. The set must have cost at least a hundred rupees.

'Lay siege to her,' declared Syed as he poured the tea.

'How?' asked Harish. 'I'll never be allowed in there. Her mother couldn't have rushed to put me on the list of acceptable male visitors,' he added drily.

'Faint heart never won fair lady,' laughed Syed. 'Remember the women we went out with in Oxford? You had no problem with them!'

'Virmati is different,' complained the Professor. 'She is so serious. Just because I'm still living with my wife, she chooses to doubt me. And then, she's staying in a fortress, so that it is impossible to meet her and explain things.'

'These women don't understand our predicament,' said Syed understandingly.

'I could convince her, I'm sure of that,' said Harish. 'It's her family that has poisoned her. And then the difficulty of managing contact with her is proving insuperable. It is certainly not easier here than it was in Amritsar.'

'Persistence is all you need, Harish. She'll come around eventually. Wait and see for a few weeks.'

It took slightly longer than that. The Professor wrote and wrote. He pretended he was a girl in all his letters. He used different names, different references that he was sure she would understand. He said he would risk everything to come and see her: 'My parents are unwilling to send me to Lahore to study further, but when a girl has been educated so far, it is foolish to not pursue the subject, and I am so far determined that nothing should stop me. What do you think, Virmati?' was how he put it.

Virmati understood the meaning of the letters and grew fearful of discovery. The Professor was very exigent. The first time he called, he posed as one of her brothers. Virmati, guessing who it was, said she was unwell and couldn't come out. The second time he asked Syed's lady-friend to call her out of the hostel. Virmati, embarrassed by a strange woman's appeals, came, but she only spoke a few words, cold, confused and tentative. She refused to go out with them, but the reproachful glances out of her large eyes left the Professor full of hope and joy.

'She's coming around, Syed, she's coming around,' he announced to his friend, who was naturally very interested in the outcome of the whole thing.

'What did I tell you, Harish?' said Syed, triumph in his manner. 'It was just a matter of time.'

The Professor's third visit to the college passed without his managing to meet Virmati. For just before his entrance to the compound gate he saw Kasturi being escorted outside by her.

He could see the mother look angry and turn Virmati back to the hostel, talking all the while. He could see Virmati vehemently shake her head. It was obviously impossible to see her now, so he hailed a tonga and left.

The fourth visit was successful.

The first thing they discussed was the Professor's baby. A boy, a few months old. She had heard about the birth in detail from Kasturi, what a difficult time the woman had had of it, but how it was all worthwhile, God be praised, a son had come into that family, and every well-wisher must rejoice.

'I am happy for you,' said Virmati twisting her dupatta round and round in her fingers, till the cotton looked as though it had never been ironed.

'It is my mother who is really happy,' said the Professor quickly. 'She keeps saying how grateful she is to God for allowing her to see her grandson before she dies.'

The boy in the eating place they were sitting in brought them hot kachoris with green mint and coriander chutney. Virmati looked at them miserably, crisp, flaky, brown kachoris for which she had no appetite.

'Please don't take out your anger on that innocent baby,' said the Professor in a low voice. 'You are everything to me. All the sons and daughters in the world are nothing next to you.'

Virmati was sure she should not believe him. Even allowing for the fact that he might be telling the truth, was it desirable for a man to abandon his children for the love of a woman? And what about her? The daughter had been bad enough. Now she would be ruining one more child's life. How could she do it?

'Please, Hari,' and her voice trembled with the weight of months of unshed tears.

'Darling,' The Professor showed his desperation. 'Co-wives are part of our social traditions. If you refuse me, you will be changing nothing. I don't live with her in any meaningful way.'

Virmati gazed at him.

'No, I don't,' repeated the Professor. 'That night was the only night. And I told you how it happened.'

Virmati looked away. Were they really arguing about a single night?

'And I never will,' he continued. 'There is a void in my heart and in my home that you alone can fill.'

By now Virmati's kachoris were a mass of crumbs, and her fingers shone with ghee as she continued to desiccate them.

'In time you will forget,' she said, but even to herself she sounded trite. She wished she had greater power over words. Forgetting or remembering was not the issue, but she didn't know how else to express herself.

'Never,' said the Professor, leaning forward. 'Never.'

When the Professor first took Virmati to the guest room in Syed Husain's house, it was after hours of haggling.

'Why do you want to be alone with me?' she asked suspiciously.

'Darling, it is not so unusual for lovers to want to be alone,' Harish explained. 'We were a few times in Amritsar, remember.'

'Yes, but that was before –'

'For heaven's sakes, Viru, will you never stop bringing up the past? Why do you always want to torture me?'

Virmati looked mulish.

'Besides, there is no other place to meet. We can't spend all our time in public places.'

Virmati had no answer to that. They were walking down Anarkalli. The area was crowded. They would have something to eat, and then they would go in separate tongas to their respective destinations. It was unsatisfactory. The Lawrence Gardens would have been nicer, but they were considerably farther away. Reluctantly she agreed to go to his friend Syed Husain's place. It was a red-brick house, with a small angan at the back and a garden in front. The high, green, mehndi hedge all around made it look reassuringly private to Virmati's apprehensive eyes.

*

And now they were in the guest room.

'What if someone sees?' Virmati asked, trying for more sophistication in her nervous tone.

'Here, nobody cares who comes and goes,' replied the Professor soothingly.

'But suppose someone does?'

The Professor pointed to the curtains. 'We are safe from prying eyes, my love,' he said. 'Take off your shoes. They must be hurting you. I know you hate shoes.'

'I bought these at a sale for three rupees, fifteen annas,' said Virmati in explanation. 'One rupee less.'

The Professor did not reply. Instead he bent to slide off her sturdy black shoes. Hastily, not wanting his hands on her feet, Virmati bobbed down to take them off herself. 'It's all right,' she mumbled.

'Would you like something to eat or drink? The bearer here is very nice.'

More people to see. 'No, no,' stammered Virmati, 'it's all right.'

Harish sat next to her and held her hands. 'Why are you so nervous, darling?' he asked. 'Do you feel you should not be with me?'

Virmati remained silent.

'Though that's a question I dare not ask,' the Professor continued, playing with a little ring she was wearing on her finger, twisting it, pulling it on and off. 'You have been too cruel to me once already. Once? Why, more than once.' He laughed, and carried her hand to his mouth.

'If you don't like the way I think, then go away,' said Virmati pettishly, putting her arms firmly down by her sides.

The Professor slid down so he could look into her eyes, her head was so bent. 'It's not in my power to like or dislike, Viru. Whatever you do, I must accept. But for God's sake do not put me through that misery again!' His voice had become husky with pleading, so low she had to strain to hear him. He lay down his head in her lap, his arms around her waist.

Virmati sat the way she was. The Professor lowered his hands, and began to caress the round caps of her knees. Feeling the weight of the Professor's head, and the proximity of his moving hands, the muscles in Virmati's legs grew tense and she shifted uneasily.

The Professor tightened his grip. His hands inched higher.

'Don't,' she whispered. 'Please.'

'Why? Aren't you mine? And I yours? Body and soul, heart and mind? I worship you, Viru, I want to express it, that's all.' The Professor got up and pressed his lips to her throat, her ears, her chin, her lips, murmuring endearments while his breath came faster. He seemed to be in a trance. Dazed, Virmati didn't think it would be fair to bring up the fact of his existing wife and children. But this wasn't right either.

'Then marry me,' she said, trying to push him away. 'Marry me and make it clear to everybody.'

'I will, I will, darling, I will. Just give me time.'

His hands held her face, stroked her hair, pushed her against the pillows, wandered lightly over her body, still so tight and miserable. They drew light circles on her skin, loosened the drawstring of her salwar, opened the hooks of her kameez.

She cried afterwards, but not much. He dried those tears while she thought, he was right, she was meant to be his, what was the point in foolishly denying it on the basis of an outmoded morality? The words recalled Swarna Lata, and she smiled.

The Professor looked at her lovingly. 'Good girl,' he said as he traced the tears from her cheek with his thumb and forefinger.

Their meetings continued along these general lines, though not as much time was spent on the preliminaries.

The eve of Diwali. The Professor was in Lahore for two days, an exercise which had caused much grief in his own home, for of course they saw through the flimsy excuses he made. The girl had bewitched him, his madness was not yet over, rather it seemed to be increasing every day.

The day before, he had spent hours in Anarkalli, going to all the sari shops, choosing the best possible sari that his fifty-rupee budget would allow. An exquisite sari draped around an exquisite body like his Virmati's would be a mighty reflector of his taste. Finally he chose a heavy south Indian silk, with the traditional small orange, black and red checks, and a border of black and gold. It would set off her fairness to perfection, he thought. He could hardly wait to see her in it.

In the parcel he made, he enclosed a small red lipstick. Coty's. He liked a little make-up on women. Virmati always wore kaajal, emphasizing her eyes, but an added touch of lipstick would supplement the original high colour of her lips.

On Diwali evening, the 31st of October that year, the couple found themselves strolling in Anarkalli, like so many others. Everything around them was vibrating with life and glitter, the men and women in new silk, the shops in lights. Virmati was wearing the sari with small checks, the palla draped modestly around the back of her head and her shoulders. Her face glowed. This was the first Diwali they had spent together, and she saw it as a step towards public statement, matrimony and the fruition of love. The Professor looked upon her with the eyes of a Pygmalion. My Galatea, he thought, and in a burst of desire snaked a hand under her light shawl, around her smooth elbow, pressing her breast at the same time.

'Aren't the lights wonderful, darling?' he asked.

'Yes,' she said breathlessly.

The Professor gently increased the pressure of his hand. Virmati's step faltered. 'Are you all right, darling?' he asked. Her momentary loss of balance allowed his thumb to rub across her nipple. He could feel how erect it was beneath the soft material of her blouse.

By now they were passing a shoe shop. 'Bhalla Shoe Company' it said, in bright lights on the front, which was lit with thousands of electric bulbs and had life-sized portraits of two ladies perched on a map of India. They represented unity between the Hindus and the Muslims, and had the motto 'Unity, Industry and Freedom' written under them.

'Oh, look,' said Virmati, edging closer to have a better look, and incidentally disentangling herself from the Professor. 'What good thoughts these people have. And such a noble message on Diwali. If everybody thought like this, there would be unity in our country today.' Tears came to her eyes at the thought, and she looked so appealing that the Professor felt that the whole crowd would soon be looking at Virmati rather than at the display.

'Come this way, Viru,' he said. 'This vulgar and meaningless display of unity is too much to stomach.'

Virmati felt a coldness come over her. 'How do you know it is meaningless?' she asked, half objecting, half pleading.

'These are banias. Do you think with all their taboos there is any scope for unity? They write this in the window, but I'm sure if you ask Messrs Bhalla if they would partake of a meal at the house of their Muslim neighbour they would be horrified.'

'But surely you don't have to eat in another person's house to be friendly with them?' cried Virmati.

The Professor looked at Virmati a little impatiently. 'Can't you see, it's not only a question of eating. It's a question of trust. Take Syed. He knows I am a vegetarian and when I come to visit him, he especially prepares food for me with his own hands. It's a labour of love. Were I to reject it, I would be saying that no matter what you do for me, there are certain things I cannot accept because of who you are. Now is that right, my love?'

Virmati was getting confused. She tried to remember what she had been saying, and persisted with her argument. 'But what has that got to do with the message in the shoe shop. Even if we don't eat in each other's houses, tolerance is still possible.'

The Professor laughed elegantly and indulgently at Viru's arguments. 'I see Lahore has made you an idealist,' he said.

Virmati was silent. Were her thoughts idealistic, and not worth taking seriously?

By this time they had reached Bhojwani's, the biggest and oldest bookshop in Lahore. It was famous throughout the Punjab for its up-to-date arrivals in the arts and the sciences. Librarians patronized it, and as both owner and son were graduates of English Literature from Government College, those sections

were particularly fine. On entering, the Professor's face lit up
and he withdrew his hand from Virmati's elbow.

Looking around, Virmati could see why. Bookshelves lined
the high-ceilinged room from top to bottom. In the middle was a
large rectangular pillar, also lined with books. Two ladders
leaned against the walls, and in the corner was a staircase going
up to the second-hand section.

The Professor dived into this paradise with an 'I'll just look
around, darling', emerging fifteen minutes later to ask the attendant if the owner was around.

'One moment, sir.'

The owner appeared, a Sindhi gentleman. Tall, fair, middle-
aged, round glasses, with an I-love-books air.

'I have a small budget from my college,' murmured the Professor to Mr Bhojwani senior.

'Ah, sir, which college?' asked the man. He recognized most
of the institutional book-buyers who came to his shop, but the
Professor was new to him.

'AS College, Amritsar,' said the Professor, with a slight hint
of defensiveness.

Virmati, standing behind him, recognized that tone. Throw in
a further note of apology, and it became the tone he used when
they discussed marriage. He's like that about other things also,
she noted, dispassionately.

'Ah, good place,' responded Mr Bhojwani, professionally.

As they bought and sold, discussed prices, lists and future
transactions, Virmati wandered to the doorway of the shop.
Though it was crowded outside, there were not many people in
the bookshop. Few, it seemed, associated Diwali with the buying
of books, even though it was the day of Saraswati as well as Lak-
shmi. She turned her head and saw the Professor's distinguished-
looking head, hair brushed back from high forehead, suit
immaculate and English, glasses earnest and gleaming, and felt
enclosed in a cocoon of exclusivity. Feeling her glance upon him,
the Professor looked up at her and smiled. She smiled back,
brushing away that feeling of irritation over the Hindu and Mus-

lim question, blanking out her observation at his apologetic tone about his college.

December, 1940. Congress leaders in the satyagraha movement are arrested on a daily basis. Their names appear in the papers, and if their prison centres are changed their names appear again. Various Muslims, Hindus, and Sikhs continue to declare the Partition scheme fantastic and un-Nationalistic, while the Muslim League presses on with its demands. Food adulteration in Lahore persists without check, think the bitter inhabitants, while the city is declared to be the most expensive in the whole of Punjab. German efforts to bury London under mountains of rubble continue, and money, goods, arms, men flow out of India to support the war.

That year, the Roerich exhibition was one of the major culture events of the season. Its inauguration by Sir Douglas Young, Chief Justice of Punjab, specially attended by the Punjab premier, Sir Sikander Hyatt Khan, provided a mingling ground for Indian and British celebrities. The exhibition, in a wing of the Lahore Museum, was a father–son affair, with both Professor Roerich and his son Svetoslav displaying paintings on opposite walls. Comparisons, contrasts, and an occasion for a wealth of commentary by art lovers. Of course the Professor made it a point to come to Lahore while it was on, and of course he took Virmati to see it with him. Excitement filled Virmati at the idea. What would she wear?

'Your Diwali sari,' said Harish.

She would also wear red on her lips, from the lipstick she had squashed while trying to wrench the cover off. She would drape the sari over her head, because he said it framed her face like a Madonna's. He would look at her with that look in his eyes. She blushed now, thinking of it, and then she blushed at her thoughts.

At the museum the paintings were mostly mountains and portraits. People were walking about, talking softly, staring at the paintings, standing back, going forwards, even writing little notes about them. The Professor, on entering the gallery, assumed the same intent look he wore on entering bookshops. He made towards the table which had the brochures. Left to herself, Virmati gave a quick glance around. Vivid, majestic, bright, I do like them, she thought. Imagine painting so many scenes of our mountains, and him a Russian. Maybe they reminded him of home.

Slowly, they started circulating. Alternating his gaze between brochure and painting, the Professor pinned Virmati to him with his low voice, telling her just what to look for, what to admire, what to criticize. Virmati listened, looked, wondered. Of course, all that the Professor was saying must be true, he was older and so much more refined and civilized. He knew.

'Notice,' he was saying, 'notice that in almost every picture there are unobtrusive symbols that represent love, peace, or a sense of humanity. See, there is Lord Buddha, there is Christ, there is a Cross hidden in the peaks of that mountain. Now what do you think that means?'

Virmati tried hard to think what it might mean. Her mind registered nothing but blankness. Why would the painter want to put a Cross on a mountain? She could not conceive.

'Perhaps he is trying to imply that we should live peacefully on earth?' the Professor suggested, with a glance at Virmati.

'Oh, how clever!' exclaimed Virmati. Her own imagination was a literal one.

'But a little obvious, I think,' went on the Professor. 'The function of the artist is different from that of the propagandist. Here he is being prescriptive.'

Virmati wondered why the Professor, of all people, should disapprove of that, then suppressed the thought. 'But perhaps with a war on, he might think it important to say this?' she ventured timidly.

The Professor looked pleased. 'A very timely reflection,' he said.

'And it says here,' said Virmati, encouraged, seizing the brochure from the Professor's hand, 'that Set – Shet – how do you say it?'

'Sv, it's Svet-o-slav.'

'Yes. Here it says he is exhibiting at –' Virmati skipped Milwaukee and said, 'America also.'

'True.'

'There also people must be liking the message. So many people dying, it is frightening. And it has been going on for so long!'

'Darling, you are so sweet,' caressed the Professor, putting his arm around her for a moment. 'But the true test of great art is its ability to express the inner realities of life, those realities that don't change according to time and place, that have a universal application.'

'Ah,' said Virmati.

By now they had been at the exhibition for almost forty minutes. The Professor glanced at the gold watch on his wrist. There was not much time left. He guided Virmati out of the hall, and hailed a tonga.

The evening raced to its expected climax in Syed Husain's guest room. There was some pressure for hurry, as Virmati had to be back by eight. Her sense of guilt, her fear of her family, her terror of being exposed, prevented her from ever taking the risk of squeezing through the bars of the hostel gate as Swarna did, though the Professor did urge it a few times.

XVII

Virmati loved doing her BT. It took up her day from nine to three – theory classes in the morning, practical teaching in the attached SL girls' school in the afternoon. She even thrived on the hostel mess, despite her mother's predictions that, deprived of home cooking, she would grow thin and sick. When Swarna commented on how well she was looking, Virmati replied, 'Maybe they really are using pure ghee as they say. Otherwise, how could I gain weight?'

'Rubbish,' said Swarna Lata. 'You can't get pure ghee in Lahore any more. It's all mixed with vegetable oils.'

'Then vegetable oils must be good for the health,' said Virmati complacently, refusing to get agitated even about pure ghee.

'When there are more outlets for food at controlled prices, then at least one won't be paying such high sums for adulterated stuff,' said Swarna.

There was a pause. Virmati felt uncomfortable as she always did when Swarna started talking about the many things she was involved in. Finally she asked, 'Wasn't your Diwali demonstration in Krishna Nagar a success?'

'Oh,' said Swarna, 'it was a success all right. That is, a lot of people participated. We drafted a petition, but government rationing and fair-price shops still show no signs of materializing. I wish you had joined us.'

'I can't be like you, knowing what to say. I do not know how to convince people. I'm not clever.'

'You don't have to be clever to fight,' snorted Swarna. 'Besides, I think you are intelligent.'

Virmati didn't believe her. 'We are just *seedhe-saadhe* people,' she said righteously.

'For heaven's sake, what does that have to do with it?'

Virmati thought that the trouble with leaving home was that one had to explain perfectly obvious things. In her family the banner of simplicity, once unfurled, functioned as a deterrent to argument rather than a stimulant.

Swarna Lata scowled at her. 'It is people like you who create trouble by letting others do your thinking.'

Virmati looked bewildered at this hostility. Swarna Lata sighed. 'Sorry. I'm in a foul mood and I'm taking it out on you. It's just that today I met, or rather didn't meet, but saw, a friend who was once extremely dear to me. She cut me dead. I'm not surprised, but it hurts, hurts almost as much as it did a year ago. My friends would say I am still too bourgeois.'

'How dare anybody cut you dead?' cried Virmati, ignorant of bourgeois traits.

Despite her tension, Swarna Lata smiled to herself. It was true, Virmati was simple. She made no demands beyond the ones of basic amicability.

'I'll tell you. Come, let's go for a walk.' They moved outside into the moist and cool November night. From the angan they could see the brilliant stars in the piece of sky framed by the hostel buildings.

'Ashrafi and I were like that,' Swarna continued, lifting twisted fingers in front of Viru's face. 'We were doing English Honours together at Lahore College for Women. It was around April last year at the time of the student elections. My friends persuaded me to stand for senior studentship. It was the first time that a nationalist like me was nominated. The English principal, Miss Dean, usually saw to it that the elected leader was somebody who went along with their line of thinking, but it was done behind the scenes to give the whole process a façade of democracy.'

'But you are hardly pro-British,' laughed Viru, who was well acquainted with her friend's politics.

'Exactly. They didn't want me. Too much khadi-wearing, too many speeches about our cause in the debating society. And our cause included the Muslims. Time and again I said that the

Muslim League and the Congress should come together, that we were one, that it was the British we should fight, and not each other. I was not alone. Plenty in the college thought like I did.'

Virmati thought, this is what is going on around me. This is the life I should be involved in. Not useless love and a doubtful marriage. 'What happened then?' she asked in a subdued tone.

'Shortly after I was nominated, I found that Ashrafi was standing against me! The principal had persuaded her – how, I never found out. Why she never told me, I never found that out either. And we used to share everything.'

Virmati understood betrayal. 'She couldn't have been much of a friend,' she remarked vehemently.

'No, she was, she really was. But obviously there was something deeper than friendship at work here.'

'What? What could be deeper than friendship?'

'What a baby you are, Viru! So many things are deeper than friendship. In this case it must have been religious identity, maybe Muslim fear and insecurity. They must have told her she would be disloyal to the Muslim cause. I didn't want to stand against Ashrafi, but my group said we had to win this election if it was the last thing we did. So you see, ultimately I too put something before friendship.'

'It's not the same thing,' muttered Virmati.

'Maybe Ashrafi thought it was. Anyway, for the first time our college was divided along communal lines. For the first time.'

'Did you win?'

'I did. There were more Hindus, Sikhs, Christians in the College than Muslims and most of them voted for me. Much good that victory did me. The whole year it was like dust and ashes in my mouth. Ashrafi stopped talking to me. Initially I tried to discuss it with her, surely our feelings for each other were strong enough to survive an election! What rubbish I was talking. We were pawns to forces beyond us. I did learn a valuable lesson, though. I now know better than to presume on the permanence of any relationship.'

Virmati felt tears come to her eyes as she heard this. Despite all their differences, they shared common experiences.

'Obviously she still hasn't forgiven me. I hear she's joined the youth wing of the Muslim League. Ashrafi! The most apolitical person that was! How does one stop thinking of someone one used to love, Viru? How does one stop remembering?' Swarna shook herself, adding, 'It's something I have to get used to, I suppose. It happens all the time.'

Virmati stared at Swarna. What a girl! Her opinions seemed to come from inside herself, her thoughts, ideas and feelings blended without any horrible sense of dislocation. She was committed, articulate. Would the Professor want her to be like Swarna? She didn't want to do anything that would alter the Professor's undying love for her. Maybe she could be like Swarna from the inside, secretly.

Gopinath Mama helps me unearth a little old lady who used to know my mother while she was studying in Lahore.

Swarna Lata Sondhi lived in a small set of rooms on the second floor of an old house near Eden Gate. She was shrivelled with age, her eyes red-rimmed and watery. She walked with a stick, and was delighted to see me.

'Yes, I remember your mother, though we didn't keep up after she finished her BT and left Lahore. Maybe, I think, yes she did come back for an MA, but I'm not sure. There was so much happening at the time . . .'

'But you also left Lahore, didn't you, auntie?'

Her voice fluttered and trembled over the division that had ploughed furrows of blood through her generation.

'We had to . . . had to . . . though we hadn't believed – never believed – things would come to such a pass. Lahore was our city – our home. Whether it went to India or Pakistan was irrelevant, we didn't care. Nothing was going to make us forsake it. Leaders of both sides claimed – again and again – minorities would be safe. They said to quit would feed communalism. We assumed that ourselves. We had always co-existed. Why not now?'

'And . . .?'

When they received the worried, secret warning from a Muslim friend they too hastily departed. They had seen too much arson, looting, and people drunk with the lust of killing to feel exceptions. As it was, they were hanging on by a long emotional thread that needed but one direct threat to snap.

So she and her husband fled, planning their return once the absurd trouble was over. Like thousands of others, abandoning their land, houses, furniture, carpets, linen, dishes, jewellery, pets, cars, books, gardens. Those things were never forgotten and around them crystallized an aura that borrowed its lustre from tears that were too inadequate to shed. Too much had been lost, too many people had died.

Swarna Lata Sondhi stoops towards me. 'If I only knew', she said, 'how little Ashrafi's loss would mean to me later, when it was drowned in the sea of all those other losses, I never would have wasted so much time crying over her. As 1947 drew near, friends like her went – increasingly, as the divisions of Hindus and Muslims were exploited by both the Congress and the Muslim League. I threw myself into my work. Yes, and I also got to thinking that agonizing over personal sentiments was a time-consuming bourgeois luxury. There is a lot to be said for that attitude, dear.'

'I am sure there is,' I reply. 'But what exactly did you do, auntie?'

'After Rameshwari Nehru was arrested in 1942, she handed over charge to Perrin Barucha – shall I spell that out for you, dear?' And the old eyes peer uncertainly over spectacles at my illegible handwriting.

'No, that's all right. I think I've got it.'

'Perrin Barucha and her girls. I was one of them.'

'You must have been pioneers.' I am full of admiration for this frail, incredible female.

'Oh, not really,' she said modestly. 'That was the time when people were very aware of what was happening around them. I got involved with IPTA, we agitated against rising prices, we organized singing squads with songs based on folk songs to arouse awareness, we wanted rationing centres opened, we wanted profiteers punished, we wanted more equality between men and women, and we were against, *totally* against, segregation on religious lines.'

Swarna Lata's nostalgia is so strong that I feel it too. We live in the long shadow of those times, I thought as I sit before her, my pen my votive offering to her age and history. Her death will further dwindle those who can still remember an undivided India. I lean towards her soft, quavering memories and the difference between her and my mother becomes increasingly marked. 'No use thinking about the past,' had been my mother's axiom, blanketing everything in oblivion. So far as Lahore was concerned, the subject of other people's eloquence, there was nothing but a void, though it had been a place she had studied much in.

I want to go to Lahore, I want to see the place where my mother was educated after so much trouble. I want to see the place that had been the Mecca for all Punjabis. Lahore, where students gathered on the river, around the mausoleums, through the mall, in the gardens, the shopping areas, the eating places, the theatres. Where anybody with brains in their head went to study. To learn, to meet people, hear leaders, be in contact with social, political, fashionable trends. The centre of Punjab, its heart and soul, and how much else besides.

Going to Lahore is not easy. It takes me two months. The queues in the visa section are long, the atmosphere between the two countries as usual hostile. When I finally arrive, I understand the look in people's eyes whenever there is talk of the fabled city.

It is clean, leafy, cool and beautiful. The institutions I visit are massive, ornate, touched by Gothic, and I am in love with everything between the sky and the grass from my very first hour there. As for the people, I had never seen so many good-looking ones together. I look at them possessively, a Punjabi Hindu hunger in my eyes – a hunger about a region I'd hardly thought about – until I thumbed through the pages of people's memories, and saw my questions as a bookmark in their leaves.

And the Oxford of the East. I saw Government College Lahore, first from the road. I walk up an incline towards it and look at the Gothic spire narrowing into the sky, a superb statement of its colonial heritage. This place must have been something in its heyday. Students dressed in maroon blazers and grey pants pass me as I wander around full of lust and longing, my eyes glassy with desire for the best shot to imprint on my film, certain I would fail to capture the ultimate vision.

I walk reverently through a narrow, arched corridor, leading into the inner courtyard, not quite a courtyard, because one side is bordered by a path, with wide, serried, stone steps sloping down to an open-air theatre. Beyond and below I can see the boys' hostel, a double-storeyed red-brick building. Yellow leaves fall on the students who are pacing up and down the path in front, open books held before them. I climb the stairs flanking the library, into a gallery with classrooms on either side, enter one, slide into an aisled bench and put my arms on the wooden table in front. This is where my mother sat and waited out the periods of time that fate had employed to divide her from her married life.

Here she faced the black-robed Professor and tried to concentrate on what he was saying. Here her eyes fastened on the two fans whirring on their long poles suspended from the rafters. Here she gazed at the peaked ventilators, and the tops of the green trees beyond the veranda. I drink in all these details; I take photographs of every turn in the staircase, the corridors, the classrooms, outer and inner aspects, knowing I may never be able to come again.

XVIII

Winter in Lahore, and conferences take place fast and furious in the city. Important people arrive, inaugurate them, make speeches, have their photographs printed in the newspapers, along with an account of what they said, and then move on. In one month alone there is the Anti-Pakistan Conference, the Arya Bhasha Sammelan Conference, the Urdu Conference, the India History Conference, the Punjab Azad Christian Conference, the All India Sikh League. The atmosphere is charged, and voices reverberate with self-awareness.

On a very cold Saturday in January, 1941, the weatherman forecast rain and fog during the day, accompanied by strong surface winds. By afternoon, the girls in RBSL College Hostel were able to admire the accuracy of his predictions.

'It's raining, Swarna,' stated Virmati tentatively.

'I know,' replied Swarna noncommittally.

Virmati wriggled further into her quilt till it was over her shoulders. Her shawl was wrapped around her head. Her fingers and toes were freezing, and her nose was running. It was just her luck, she thought, that the Punjab Women's Student Conference was being held on the coldest day of the year, and that she was committed to going. She had been excited about it, but on days like this she preferred to stay in bed. Of course Swarna wouldn't object if she didn't come, but what would she think? She looked at her a little apprehensively now, as if her thoughts were transparent.

'Don't come if you don't want to,' said Swarna, at precisely that moment.

Virmati jumped slightly. 'No, no,' she said.

'It is a terrible day,' went on Swarna. 'There are sure to be others – not coming because of the rain.'

'Perhaps, then . . . um . . . you?' Virmati suggested tentatively.

'I? Good heavens, no. I don't let the weather decide for me.'

'Will your Mohini Datta be there?'

'Of course. Auntie is speaking, and I too am making a little speech.'

Virmati was torn between hurt and admiration. Swarna Lata was going to make a speech, and hadn't even mentioned it to her. She was used to Harish's attitude to speechmaking – preparation, rehearsal, studied approach, subsequent assessment – and she considered public appearances a specialized activity, to be preceded by a lot of fanfare.

'Aren't you nervous?' she asked.

Swarna Lata smiled. 'I am – a little,' she admitted. 'But I consider the message more important than the person, you know. I'll repeat it for you back here, if you like.'

'What's a little rain?' declared Virmati.

'Well, hurry then. Tongas will be difficult in this weather.'

Clenching her teeth, Virmati bravely left the warmth of her bed. She pulled on her morning socks, still a little damp, groped for her shoes under the bed, dragged on the thick sweater Indu had knitted for her, and struggled into the tight sleeves of her coat.

'Better take your umbrella also,' said Swarna Lata, gesturing outside.

The girls hurried across the SL quadrangle, holding their coats, clutching umbrellas, the wind driving the rain sideways onto them.

'There are some girls from my class singing for this function,' volunteered Virmati, her breath emerging whitely in the air as she spoke.

'I hope the rain won't stop them,' smiled Swarna Lata.

Not everybody is like you, Swarna, thought Virmati. I'm not, though I wish I were. But when Harish is here, I stop thinking of other things. And when he is not here, all I do is wait for him to come. How long do we have to be secret man and wife, hidden from the eyes of the world. I hate it, but what can I do?

Virmati wished she could discuss all this with Swarna, but she felt too shy. It was not as though Swarna was unaware of her relationship with Harish, but she was too afraid of Swarna's contempt to go into the myriad instances of where she felt she had been weak or wronged. In a dim, obscure way, Virmati longed for that open-hearted conversation between friends that relieved the mind, and strengthened faith in oneself, but she had always found it difficult to articulate her feelings.

By this time a miserable-looking tonga had appeared, with its miserable, shivering horse. The driver agreed to take them at three times the usual price.

'Beggars can't be choosers,' said Swarna as they jumped onto the back seat.

How true, thought Virmati.

The tonga slowly creaked from side to side, with spurts of speed as the driver thrust his hand between the horse's hind legs and twisted its genitals. Although the rain had stopped, the sky was heavily clouded, and it was dark for three-thirty in the afternoon. In the slushy, muddy portico of Lajpat Rai Hall, Virmati started to sneeze, her feet damp in spite of socks and closed shoes. Swarna looked at her speculatively but was soon swept inside by eager cries, and 'Why are you late? She's already here.'

Virmati made her own way more slowly. Despite the cold and rain, the hall was packed with girls seated on the floor almost up to the stage. More were standing against the walls. She edged her way towards a space at the back, hoping she would be able to hear Swarna from where she was.

The girls around her seemed to know what was going on. 'Look, there's Leela Mehta. She's sick and still she's come. That's why she's got that heavy scarf around her neck.'

'Naturally. She's the guiding spirit of the women's conference. Half of the girls have come to hear her.'

'Despite the weather.'

'All the rain in the world could not have kept me away today. See.' The girl held up her foot with the wet, muddy paoncha of her salwar showing.

'What's so special about muddy salwars that you should show

me yours?' said the first girl, pushing her friend's foot down. 'Almost everybody is damp and dirty. I must say we are a committed lot.' And the first girl gazed around the hall with some satisfaction.

'That we are. My poor parents rue the day they sent me to Lahore to study,' said the second girl, laughing.

'Look, there's Sita Rallia, and there's Noor Ahmed, and there's Mary Singh, and there's Mohini Datta, sitting right next to Swarna Lata Anand, and you can only think of your Mrs Mehta. And there's Pheroz Shroff.'

At Mohini Datta's name, Virmati peered at the women sitting on the stage. The woman beside Swarna was short and bulky with a dark, heavy-set face. Even silent, she gave out strength and confidence, an older more definite version of all the things that coalesced in Swarna. What was she? A nationalist, leftist, or Communist? She had forgotten, though Swarna had enthused about Mohini Datta more than once. Virmati sighed. They all seemed so remote from her.

The Inquilab Zindabad was sung, and Virmati looked up, tears in her eyes. The song was so moving. The students' flag, representing freedom, peace and progress, was unfurled. There was a hush in the hall and it was clear most of the girls identified with it. Now Mohini Datta was explaining the meaning of the flag, how freedom was necessary for the development of the human spirit, how war especially affected women, how progress was their object so that freedom could be enjoyed by all classes of people, even the lowest of the low.

Am I free, thought Virmati. I came here to be free, but I am not like these women. They are using their minds, organizing, participating in conferences, politically active, while my time is spent being in love. Wasting it. Well, not wasting time, no, of course not, but then how come I never have a moment for anything else? Swarna does. And she even has a 'friend', who lives in the city. Thank God Hari lives in Amritsar. Otherwise I would be completely engulfed. But isn't that what I want? What'll happen when we marry?

Now there was Mrs Leela Mehta speaking, the woman her neighbour had come to hear – and according to her, half the girls in the hall. She got up, a commanding presence, looking taller for the scarf wrapped around her head, her voice husky and carrying. She was to inaugurate the conference.

'I am a student like you, engaged in studying the book of life in the university of the world,' she started. Loud cheers, as Virmati's eyes glazed over in thinking of her own lessons in the university of the world. She saw instead of the crowded hall, images of herself and the Professor embracing, kissing, his tongue pushing its way into her mouth in a way she had initially found very strange, and then liked, enough even to reciprocate. He always started this way, before undoing her kameez, or sliding his hands against her breasts. Making her so dizzy with kissing, she could no longer think.

Leela Mehta's short speech was concluding. Virmati tried to concentrate. 'And lastly,' she thundered, 'we want not only degrees but constructive work. We demand the right, the privilege of doing something for our country. Friends, comrades . . .' and here her voice dropped dramatically. 'That is the real Inquilab. Not slogan shouting. Not posturing, and empty speechmaking. If you, the hope of the future generation, can achieve some difference in the lives of your fellow men, then indeed you are the true wealth of your nation.' The hall broke out into thunderous applause as she sat down.

Virmati's hands clapped too, as loud and as long as the others. Then Miss Saubhagya Sehgal, chairman of the reception committee, gave the welcome address. I didn't know we were still at the welcome stage, thought Virmati. Miss Sehgal regretted that the leaders of India were keeping back progressive forces and doing their utmost, though in vain, to come to a compromise with British imperialism. She praised the students' involvement in the satyagraha movement, as a result of which 360 students in Bengal were already in jail.

Begum Saba Malik, in the presidential chair, felt that the traditional view of women was changing as girls continued the freedom struggle. But, she went on to say, communalism had unfortunately been strengthened by the Congress accepting ministries and creating jealousies in people like Mr Jinnah and Mr Savarkar. Miss Noor Ahmed said the masses ought to be organized on the basis of their economic position, rather than on religious grounds.

One after another, voices spoke into the microphone, voices from Foreman Christian College, Kinnaird College, Lahore College for Women, Rawalpindi College, Fateh Chand College for Women. All the women had such strong opinions. Virmati was amazed at how large an area of life these women wanted to appropriate for themselves. Strikes, academic freedom, the war, peace, rural upliftment, mass consciousness, high prices due to the war, the medium of instruction, the Congress Committee, the Muslim League, anti-imperialism, Independence Day movement, rally, speeches. Virmati's head was swimming. They were talking a language she had yet to learn. She began to feel stifled. Her legs had gone to sleep. She shifted uncomfortably on her haunches, the cold from her feet seeping into her despite the heat of the bodies around her. She felt out of place, an outcaste amongst all these women. She thought of Harish who loved her. She must be satisfied with that.

These larger spaces were not for her. She felt an impostor sitting in the hall. Again, scenes from her private life came unbidden before her eyes. She could feel the pressure of the Professor's thighs against her own. At such moments the meaning of her life seemed perfectly plain. She just had to follow that memory upwards, to feel him thrusting inside her, strong and large, as she moaned and arched with pleasure.

Oh, there was Swarna getting up. She was walking to the lectern, damp and bedraggled, looking directly at the girls.

'We are at the moment engaged in an effort that is purely symbolic,' she said. 'The leaders of the Congress Party are daily being tried under the Defence of India Act, an act that forces one to realize the very divergent interpretations attached to the word "country". The outcome predetermined, they are forced into the confines of narrow prison cells. Hundreds of students share their fate, hundreds more will no doubt join them before their time is over.

'And yet, friends, how representative is this movement? Where are the masses that should be part of it? The cruel divisions that arise from economic differences make their effect felt in this arena as well.

'As women, it is our duty, no, not duty, that word has unpleasant connotations. It is our privilege to be able to give ourselves to the unity of our country. Not only to the unity between rich and poor, but between Muslim and Hindu, between Sikh and Christian. Artificial barriers have been created amongst us to gain power over insecure and fearful minds. Let the politics of religion not blind us to this fact.

'We know what it is like to have our freedom threatened. The ban on strikes, particularly in Kinnaird and Khalsa Colleges is an attempt to muzzle the student movement, to stifle our voices. We know their efforts will be in vain. Our united front will prove that. But we must not falter, or be cowed down.'

Heavy applause broke out as Swarna finished speaking. As the final resolutions were being formulated, Virmati wondered about her friend. She had known she was well known, but had not realized the extent of her reputation. Her heart felt dull and heavy within her. The whole afternoon had been interminable. She wondered whether she would ever get out, ever see the sky again.

At last the final resolution was moved, seconded, and adopted. The crowd around her began to heave and rise. Some of the girls left, but many moved towards the stage. They haven't had enough, thought Virmati resentfully. She could see a group of people clustered around Swarna, could then see Swarna and her cluster join the bigger one around Leela Mehta and Mohini Datta. Should she wait or go? She hung about irresolutely for a few minutes and then made her way slowly out of the hall. Once outside, she gulped in the cold, fresh, rain dampness, her lungs getting rid of the moistness produced by the myriad breathers inside. She carefully made her way down the slippery steps, and decided to walk to the hostel.

On her arrival back at her room Virmati immediately dived for her bed, the rumpled quilt waiting as she had left it, the sheets now clammy. She lay there, her limbs too heavy for movement, drifting uneasily in and out of a dazed sleep, when at nine the door swung open with a bang, and Swarna came in, humming, with all the brightness of a woman who has come from a fruitful engagement with the world.

'Oh, Viru! Why didn't you wait for me?' she exclaimed. 'I thought we were coming back together. You could have met auntie also,' she went on, taking off her shoes, and flinging herself next to Virmati to tuck her icy-cold feet under her quilt. 'She invited us all for tea, and Mary and Sarla made pakoras. We also had an impromptu meeting, that's why it took so long.'

Virmati shifted her feet away from Swarna's. She was feeling too ill to respond.

'I almost got into trouble with the warden, you know,' continued Swarna chattily. 'Coming late, and all. Fortunately the weather was enough excuse. And she knew about the Women's Conference meeting. The press was there too. Did you notice?'

'No.'

'It'll be out in the papers tomorrow. I'll read them in college, next to the fire. I love doing that.' Swarna laughed happily. 'There is bound to be a picture of auntie. Shall I get you one on my way home?'

This roused Virmati somewhat. 'If I start spending one anna on the newspaper, my mother will kill me.'

'I'll buy it for you.' Swarna leaned over and rumpled her hair, looking at her affectionately. 'Don't look so upset. Now go to sleep. For the first time today my feet are warm!' With this she slid off the bed to her corner of the room, putting off the main light and switching on her small table lamp.

Virmati tried to sleep but couldn't. She lay still, she tossed and turned. Cold and shivering, her thoughts slipped out of their normal grooves and wandered disjointedly. The faint light coming in from the veranda burned her eyes. Swarna was speaking. Mohini Datta was standing next to her. There were songs, gestures. That song sounded like the Internationale. She should have learned at least one of the three versions. Then she too would be part – part of what Swarna was. Other friends crowding around her . . . crowding her out. Their gaze washed around her, through her. Swarna, Swarna Lata, look at me. Ah! she won't look. Why should she? In her heart she despises me, but we're living together, she has to pretend.

He's there, knocking. Writing, let me in, let me in. Answer. Answer. Now I'll have to write. Write, write. Quotations of love, faith, duty, devotion. I must reread his letters more often . . . more often. There's so much to learn . . . so much to learn. But we are one. One. One. Our one body. Twisting in the curtained gloom of Syed Husain's house. Where I'm not cold but warm.

Virmati's fever increased. She wanted water, but could not speak. Her lips felt swollen, her throat parched. Tears of illness and self-pity gathered under her shut lids and oozed over her cheeks. Beneath the quilt and all her sweaters her limbs felt heavy and damp. She groaned and wondered that Swarna did not wake. But Swarna was tired and slept like a stone.

Virmati was sick for days. Swarna cared for her when she could, and the neighbouring girls looked in. The warden kept a check, the principal expressed her concern, the doctor was called. He said her blood was drying up, her liver was weak. He prescribed medicine, tonic, compounds. Virmati just had one request to make of the RBSL authorities. She begged them not to disturb her parents, she was sure she would get well soon. Privately she hid the medicine, she didn't want any drugs suppressing her symptoms. Let it all come out. Nature cure was what her family believed in, and she had never in her life taken anything remotely resembling a pill. She drank lots of water to wash away the fever. Sometimes she asked for tea.

The Professor was upset and irritated. Why was Virmati so

147

careless of her health? And what was she doing going to women's meetings anyway? She was in Lahore to study, not fritter away her energies. Though it was important that Virmati be exposed to the latest in political and social trends, she must not overdo it. He scolded her lovingly in letters. Virmati responded in wobbly, apologetic paragraphs. Harish would have more time to spend with his family. What nonsense, replied Harish. All he wanted in the world was to be with her, and this time in Lahore was such a wonderful opportunity. She was depriving him, she was depriving herself. He hoped he could say without vanity that she was depriving herself.

They met after two months. Virmati had grown very thin. Nature cure, though healthy, takes its toll from the flesh. The Professor looked at her. He could not speak. He had thought of Virmati's fair skin so often, its rosy overtones, with faint yellow-ivory undertints. Now it was more yellow than rose, and he could feel the outline of her ribs. Tenderly he gathered her to him, and whispered into her hair, 'Darling, it's been hell for both of us, your being so ill.'

'I couldn't help it,' Virmati whispered back, rubbing her hand across his throat, liking the feel of his voice beneath her fingers.

'You're too delicate to go out much in the cold, sweetheart. You must be careful for my sake.'

'It's the first time this has happened.'

'Still.'

Virmati pulled the Professor closer to her, and tugged at his hair. 'I was dying for love of you,' she teased. Loving him, and hoping to distract him at the same time.

The Professor smiled delightedly, looking like a boy in his pleasure. He continued to caress her, feeling her like a precious thing, arousing her, drawing a shawl closer around her. They lay silently together, while the late afternoon sun shone green and pale through the bushes outside Syed Husain's guest room.

'Soon your course will be finishing here, my love.' The Professor's words dropped with an unpleasant sound into Virmati's deep contentment. She didn't know why, unless the very slight uncertainity in his voice was the cause.

Her stillness became stiller. 'And what are your plans for me?' she inquired carefully.

His hands went on in their steady, stroking movements. 'It would be a shame to waste your degree.'

Virmati drew away from him and sat up. 'I'm cold,' she announced, and moved towards her clothes.

'Viru!' exclaimed the Professor.

'I have to go.'

'What's wrong? All of a sudden . . . you jump up and behave as though I have committed a crime.'

'There is more than one way to commit a crime.'

'What have I done?'

'Can't you see?' asked Virmati, fumbling with her clothes.

'No, I can't. Tell me.'

'Hari –' Virmati spat out the name. 'How long is it you say you've been in love with me?'

'Three years.'

'I break my engagement because of you, blacken my family's name, am locked up inside my house, get sent to Lahore because no one knows what to do with me. Here I am in the position of being your secret wife, full of shame, wondering what people will say if they find out, not being able to live in peace, study in peace . . . and why? Because I am an idiot.'

'No, no, Viru –'

'Now you want to prolong the situation. Why don't we get married? You say your family makes no difference. But still you want to continue in this way. Be honest with me. I can bear anything but this continuous irresolution. Swarna is right. Men do take advantage of women!'

Virmati had only to mention Swarna Lata for the Professor to explode, and he shouted, shaking with anger, 'What does this Swarna Lata know of my situation, pray? How does she know of the difficulties I face at home? How do *you* know of them, Viru? I come to you as a haven. Except for this, my life is hell! Hell!

Tantrums, sulks, sly accusations. My mother, sister, daughter, all she has turned against me. And now you are doing the same thing.' He turned away and dropped his head in his hands.

Virmati felt trapped. What had she been saying, was it so unreasonable? Why was he looking so sad? How could she leave him like this? Slowly she moved towards Harish, and slowly she took him in her arms.

Going back to the hostel in a tonga, Virmati bit her lip to prevent her tears from falling. What was the matter with her? It was not her way to burst forth in anger or in crying. She supposed it was the weakness after her illness. It had been ecstatic in the beginning. And then he had said 'What are you going to do after your degree?' She felt again the cold, despairing recognition that her future plans must not include marriage. Only this series of furtive meetings in borrowed places. Did he think that would satisfy her for ever? Far better to be like Swarna, involved in other people, and waiting for no man.

'What's the matter, Viru?' Swarna could see that she was agitated. Normally the occasions when Swarna did eat in the mess were precious to Virmati, but today she remained withdrawn through most of the meal.

'Nothing,' said Virmati.

Swarna asked no more questions, but after dinner she asked Virmati to come with her for a walk before they settled down for the night. The weather was mild enough now to stay outside for a while. As they were walking, she reached for Virmati's hand. 'What is it, Viru?' she asked gently. 'You are obviously miserable. I usually don't have time for us to spend together, but I care about what is happening to you. Now tell me. Otherwise I shall feel terribly guilty.'

'It's him,' said Virmati reluctantly. She thought to discuss him an act of treachery, but the heavy burden on her heart was weighing her down.

'He came today?'

'Yes.'

'Then?'

'Well,' stumbled Virmati. 'First when he came . . . in the beginning it was all right. But I have to think about the future, even if he doesn't. If we don't get married, it cannot go on. I have to consider. My family has been so patient.'

'Viru, you have chosen him with your eyes open. I am sure he will eventually justify your faith in him,' said Swarna after a little pause.

Virmati briefly wondered how much actual choosing had gone into her relationship with the Professor. Swarna exercised such options in everything. Choosing a 'friend' who understood her need to be independent, choosing her political leanings, choosing to stand for senior studentship despite the unpleasantness about Ashrafi, choosing to stay in Lahore though her parents wanted her to come home and get married. How could she explain her own actions?

Swarna said thoughtfully, 'His wife must be presenting a real problem, Viru. What does he say?'

'That's it. He doesn't say anything, only looks hurt when I bring up the topic. As though I don't trust him.'

'Give him credit for not abandoning his wife. In my work I hear so many stories of men taking two or more wives, and the women left helpless, often with small children.'

'But I can't go on waiting. And I can't – don't want to – marry anybody else.'

'Marriage is not the only thing in life, Viru. The war – the satyagraha movement – because of these things, women are coming out of their homes. Taking jobs, fighting, going to jail. Wake up from your stale dream.'

'I wish people in Amritsar talked to me like this,' said Virmati.

'I wish people in Delhi would talk to *me* like this,' laughed Swarna. 'But they don't. So here we are. Responsible for our own futures.'

'You think he will never marry me?'

'I don't know, but why sit around waiting?'

'In my family there is only marriage for girls.'

'Most families look upon the marriage of a daughter as a sacred duty – or sacred burden. We are lucky we're living in times when women can do something else. Even in Europe women gain more respect during wartime. And here we have that war, and our satyagraha as well.'

'Perhaps I should go to prison, and help the freedom movement.'

'It might make him think a little. But students are not yet supposed to offer satyagraha. Maybe a little fine?'

'How do I do that?'

'Offer provocation, but not too much. There are ways. Besides, you're not a prominent figure, and they will not want you to take up valuable jail space. One look at your lovely eyes and they'll do nothing more than fine you. They need the money, and what better way to collect it? They have already got over two lakhs this way.'

'My family – ?'

'If it keeps you out of the Professor's way, I am convinced they'll offer thanks to Gandhiji.'

They went on walking, up down, up down, around the trees of the playing field. Their feet sent up faint clouds of dust, the dew still hadn't fallen enough to dampen the ground thoroughly. The moon was a clear, thin curve in the sky. It was so peaceful. Why can't I be content with what I have? thought Virmati. Swarna's words gave her some comfort. But that meant thinking of a life for herself without marriage, which was strange and not quite right. It meant she would be alone, and she wasn't sure she was capable of it.

Next morning saw a slight postponement in Virmati's plan to get fined or arrested. Her studies were her passport to independence, not just her passport to sleeping with the Professor. They were worthy of more respect. She would wait till her exams were over.

XIX

Virmati did not do well in her exams. She had memorized the theory, history, psychology, and modern practice of education till she could churn them out in her sleep, but that preciously guarded horde of information vanished from her mind the day she discovered that the egg in her uterus had mated with a sperm and was swelling with popping cells, in an insistent, anti-intellectual life of its own.

'Oh God,' she moaned, as she stared at the brown, viscous mass in the cracked white china toilet. She reached up to pull the chain dangling overhead, but another wave of nausea passed over her, and she leaned forwards to heave and retch again. This time there was no discharge except a thin trickle of foul, yellowish bile.

Quickly she calculated dates. When was the last time she had surreptitiously rinsed out the old cloths that were recycled to soak up the blood? The water from the tap had been cold then, it was that far back. She was certain she was pregnant. With this certainty, the nausea came again, ripping through her throat, salivating her tongue. She thought of all the hours she had spent over her practical files, her teaching charts, making sure that they were complete and decorative. What would happen to her BT now? What would they say at home if they found out? She shuddered as, supporting herself with one hand against the wall, she staggered slowly out of the bathroom. Thankfully Swarna had left the room. She sank onto her bed and started to cry, with sobs that racked her body as much as her vomiting had done, except that they lasted much longer.

When she stopped, she remained on the bed in a trance. How had this come about? Harish had assured her that it would not happen. She had raised the topic once, carefully, in a playful, casual manner. 'Maybe a child of ours will decide the marriage date.'

He had looked at her and frowned. 'No, Viru, we cannot allow ourselves to be pawns in the skeins of fate.' He laced her fingers within his own, 'She clings hard, but soon they will see it is all futile.'

Virmati gripped the arm that was around her. 'Suppose it happens to me, like those women you hear about, who die trying to get rid of it. There was a woman we had, a widow from Tarsikka. She got pregnant from the cook, though he said she was lying, and Mati was going to dismiss them both, but before she could, the woman died in horrible agony.'

'What talk is this? Are we poor, uneducated, unenlightened clods, to leave such things to chance? Don't you trust me?'

He drew her onto his lap, and in an effort to increase her trust, gently and delicately fondled her, while taking off her clothes. When he talked and looked like that, she could not argue further. She had to prove she trusted him. Fulfilment lay in their union.

Now, each of Harish's words echoed in her mind with an irony he had taught her to recognize in Shakespeare's texts. Tragic irony, comic irony, how he had loved to expand on them. Which species was this? It lacked the epic proportions of tragedy, and the love–courtship–marriage theme of comedy. In either case, she was the Fool, that much at least was certain.

Virmati shook herself. She must see him. But how? His last visit had been about ten days ago, and she had told him not to come till her exams were over. She had to do well, and he distracted her. She must go to Amritsar instead. Slowly she got up and started a letter to her mother.

Within a week an answer arrived. The envelope that Virmati eagerly grabbed from the V-shaped slot in the cubby holes outside the dining-room was a thick one. As she tore it open, out slid two folded pieces of paper covered with her mother's large round hand. One was a short note to herself – so at last you have remembered you have a home – and the other a formal note to the warden requesting permission for her daughter to leave the hostel for the prep leave.

That evening saw the warden scrutinizing the letter carefully, turning it over, reading through it again. Then she examined Virmati.

'Are you all right?' she asked severely. 'Your parents will not like it if you fall ill.'

'Madam, it is the studies. I will be better at home.'

The warden frowned. If Virmati was going to be ill again, she would be better off at home. As the BT course was over, permission was given, and Virmati left.

'Goodbye, Swarna,' she said, the tears which were always at the base of her throat creeping into her eyes.

Swarna looked at her strangely. Did she have an inkling, did she suspect? She who worked with women in the Lakkar Hatti, she who could detect early signs of pregnancy as well as anyone.

'Yes, she was pregnant,' said my old lady slowly, carefully. 'Though she only told me when she had to.'

'How was that? You were good friends, weren't you?' I asked naïvely to encourage the flow of words.

'Good friends?' she asked, the mockery in her tone shaming me in my artless pose. 'Yes, we were good friends. But Viru knew, yes, she knew that what she had done would be seen by me as a social setback for women. Good God! This was the very thing the men were afraid of, even the mothers. Education led to independence and loose conduct. Things were better than they used to be, but these fears took a long time to remove. You should have seen some of the buildings that passed for girls' schools. Dark one or two-room holes, no ventilation, no playground, all in the name of keeping them safe.'

Poor Virmati, I thought, how she must have suffered. Whatever did they do in those days when these accidents occurred? How was it kept a secret, when women could smell a pregnancy a mile off, just as Virmati smelt Ganga's, or Lajwanti smelt Kasturi's.

'Tell me, whatever did she do?' I said leaning closer to Swarna Lata's white-framed face. 'I don't think she married . . .? Or at least not right then.'

Swarna Lata snorted. 'Oh no, she didn't marry till he was good and ready, and that wasn't then.'

'Did her family find out?'

'I don't think so, because she came back, which they would not have allowed her to do had they known. In the end I helped her, it came to that . . . poor thing. Her pride prevented her from asking me first. Though if she had stopped to reflect, it would have been obvious that Lahore was a better place than Amritsar for these things, and I a better . . .' Swarna Lata broke off, and didn't continue. I remained silent. The shroud of secrecy my mother carried all her life now protected her in death, as I drew back from violating her with my knowledge.

I knew, Mother, what it was like to have an abortion. Prabhakar had insisted I have one. In denying that incipient little thing in my belly, he sowed the seeds of our breakup – as perhaps he meant to do. Yes, I knew what it was like. I had lain awake nights wondering why he wanted me to have an abortion, worrying whether he was having an affair, feeling unloved, because he didn't want a baby from me.

'Show it to her,' he had told the doctor. 'She thinks she is killing something.'

They thrust a stainless-steel bowl under my nose. It was full of floating blood and plasma. 'That is all it is, you silly girl.' I threw up in the red plastic basin kept under the bed.

It was never the same afterwards. That death haunted me for years, but Prabhakar was very careful, and I never conceived again. Now I have nothing. Mother, I never told you this, because you thought Prabhakar was so wonderful, and I was glad that in the choice of my husband I had pleased you. Why should I burden you with my heartaches when you had enough of your own? You believed too strongly in the convention that a mother has no place in a daughter's home to stay with me, so you never really got to see the dynamics of our relationship close at hand. That was some consolation to me, though it meant that you were the more upset when the marriage terminated. He was what you respected, a successful academic, a writer of books, a connoisseur of culture, a disseminator of knowledge. Like my father.

How many times had you declared that I would be lucky if I found a husband like my father? I had agreed with you. My father was on a pedestal so high that to breathe that rarefied atmosphere was an honour.

For Virmati, the drive to the railway station was torture. The driver of the tonga, a young man, was reeking of coconut oil and a heavy, rose perfume. Feeling queasy, Virmati pulled her dupatta around her nose, and put a pinch of churran in her mouth from the bottle she kept in her handbag. The sour, salty taste helped, but by the time she reached the station her tongue was blistered with the amount she had eaten.

The hour's journey between Lahore and Amritsar passed quickly. As Virmati gazed at the familiar fields of the Punjab countryside, crossed by the horizontal bars of the train window, it seemed to her that her miseries had just started. What was the crisis that had impelled her towards the river compared to this? Now that way out was not possible. Once tried, it had lost its power as a solution.

Amritsar Station, and Virmati lingered in the compartment, forlorn, as she watched other platform reunions. Quickly she decided her condition was making her maudlin, and with clenched jaw, she swung down her leather attaché case from the overhead rack and marched up the stairs, across the overhead platform, down another staircase, and outside into the mêlée of tonga-drivers clamouring for customers. She chose one, fixed the fare to Lepel Griffin Road, and throughout the ride stared unseeingly at the trees lining Grosvenor Road and the grassy stretches of the Company Gardens. Whatever happened, she could not allow any further stigma to taint the family name.

The tonga pulled up in front of the heavy metal gates of the house with its side door slightly ajar. Virmati stared blankly at it. It had been several months since she had visited home. The atmosphere wasn't so conducive . . . she had to study hard . . . she couldn't be distracted . . . those secret visits of Harish . . . those precious moments snatched in Syed Husain's guest room.

'Bibiji, you said this was the address.' The tonga-driver sounded impatient.

Wordlessly, Virmati paid the man his four annas, and got down. As the driver manoeuvred his horse around, he saw her still standing before the gates, holding her attaché case. She looked so lost, he regretted the missed opportunity of asking for an anna more than the agreed fare.

Evening time. Many of the family were sitting out in the angan, on the string beds pulled from the eating room where they were kept stacked. Virmati was with them, but she wished she could be by herself in front of the house, watching the evening pigeons, flapping wings imperceptible, circling in great, low, black wheels against the purple sky. She had missed this evening sight in Lahore, no orchards near SL College to attract such large numbers. But her absence would have been minded. Already, first day at home and she is wandering off by herself, independent as usual. Virmati could even hear the tone of voice in which this would be said. So she sat with them and peeled potatoes for dinner.

Thud, thud, thud, the potatoes dropped one by one into the brass patila between the two beds. The pile of potato peel on the brick floor grew slowly, to be gathered and fed to the cows later. Paro was sitting as close to Virmati as she could, her small, crossed legs pressed against Virmati's knee, absent-mindedly separating some coriander leaves from their stalks. Virmati was enjoying the smell of the torn leaves, and she forgot to admonish Paro for doing her work so badly. Paro, meanwhile, thinking that her sister had become very nice after her stay in Lahore, broke through the low buzz of the women, asking in her high, clear voice, 'Pehnji, why do you have to go away so soon? This time I'm also coming.'

'*Arre wah!*' exclaimed Lajwanti, clearing her throat and expertly spitting into the narrow gutter running around the angan. 'Your sister is too busy to bother with the likes of her family. Even when she became an aunt she didn't come. Shaku said she tried to bring her along when she came, but it was no use.'

Virmati glanced guiltily at her sister. Indu was nursing her baby on the next bed, the little head bobbing up and down under her sari palla. Her face had become rounder, and she shone like the full moon, happy, tranquil and undisturbed.

The family said nothing, and Virmati sensed they were waiting for her reply.

'How can I compare with Shakuntala Pehnji?' temporized Virmati after a silence. 'She has brains. It is stupid people like me who have to study all the time, though it means my family think I neglect them. But that is not true! They are always in my heart.'

'No child of mine is fortunate enough to be compared with Shakuntala,' murmured Kasturi deprecatingly. Lajwanti's face darkened. References to Shakuntala's unmarried state lurked beneath seemingly innocent statements and she was ever watchful.

'After the exams, Pehnji'll be back with us,' said Gunvati, smiling placidly at Virmati, and shaking her head ever so slightly to remind Virmati that she must not mind what her aunt said, it was just her way. Having an unmarried daughter nearing thirty was a fate so devastating that it must excuse any loss of temper.

Lajwanti looked at the sky and flung a long, perfectly curled potato peel casually to the ground.

'*Arre,*' she remarked to her sister-in-law, 'whatever happened to that woman? Has there been any news from her?'

'Which woman?' asked Kasturi, sifting through the dal, checking for dirt and small stones.

'Oh, that one. You know. The one who had the baby boy recently.' Lajwanti clicked her tongue in exasperation. 'Oof, what is the name? Why, every day she used to come!'

'Oh yes,' said Kasturi, reluctantly. 'That one.'

'She came to meet us one, two weeks back,' broke in Gunvati. 'Came to take her leave, I think.'

'Oh?' said Lajwanti. 'At last she has managed to make him see sense?'

Virmati froze. They were lying. He would have told her.

'She explained that his classes were over,' said Kasturi, carefully tossing the dal in the air, and shaking the thali. 'They could now go home for the little baby's mundan. Everybody was dying to see.'

'Who wouldn't want to see that little chand ka tukra? Such fairness I've hardly seen before. How happy his father must be with his little prince!' enthused Lajwanti.

After a pause Kasturi added, 'Everybody has gone. The whole house is shut up.'

'If she has any sense, it will be permanent,' said Lajwanti, hawking and spitting again.

'It is not up to her, Taiji,' said Gunvati.

'That girl was too simple. She didn't even know how to keep a husband,' snorted Lajwanti disapprovingly. By now she had peeled and cut her last potato. She got up to leave and the strings of the bed moaned as they suddenly went limp without her weight.

After dinner, Virmati did not linger in the angan where everybody was gathered. Instead, quickly changing into her night clothes and pulling Paro behind her, she climbed the narrow staircase with its steep uncomfortable brick steps to the kotha. At the doorway, she stopped, while Paro wriggled past her, and ran to switch on the light of the storeroom. At the sight of the familiar place, Virmati felt a longing for the relative simplicity of being locked up. That punishment should have been saved for now, she thought. It would have been far more appropriate.

'Pehnji!' called Paro. 'These charpais are too heavy for me.'

'Then why are you doing it all alone?' scolded Virmati. 'Can't you wait for me?'

'But you are not coming, you're just standing there,' pointed out Paro.

Virmati joined her in the storeroom, and together they dragged the six charpais out, flung rolls of mattresses, pillows and sheets onto them, spread them, and then started to wedge poles for the mosquito nets crosswise between the legs of each bed.

'Do you have to do this in Lahore, Pehnji?' asked Paro.

'No, we sleep inside.'

'Inside? All the time! Chee! Do you like Lahore, Pehnji?'

'Yes.'

'Are you glad you went there?'

'Yes.'

'Everybody says you are studying more than anybody in the family, Pehnji.'

'Really? Then what do they think Shakuntala Pehnji has been doing? Killing flies? And that too when she is First Class M.Sc.'

'But they talk more about you.'

'Oh?'

'About your getting married. Why, why not, when, who, where! Oof! All the time! Then Pitaji says the nation needs teachers. Imagine!'

Virmati was concentrating on looping the ends of the mosquito nets around the poles. Paro continued chattering. 'Won't they be surprised to find the beds all done, Pehnji? Usually, Kailash and Gunvati do them.'

'When I am here, I do them. Have you forgotten so fast, Paro?'

'No, Pehnji. But for so long you are not here . . .'

'Well, now I am.'

Virmati motioned Paro into one of the beds and slipped in next to her, carefully tucking the mosquito net beneath the mattress so that no treacherous gap would allow the insects in.

'Now go to sleep, Paro,' she said firmly, for Paro was all ready to go on with her stream of talk. 'My journey has made me very tired.'

For a long time Virmati lay on the damp coolness of the thick khadi sheets, surrounded by the white net cocoon that once used to make her feel so safe. The moon was bright and made her ache with sadness for herself, for that thing inside her that she couldn't name for fear of making it more real. Tears started sliding down her cheeks, and she cried, letting her breath out in small gasps in order not to wake Paro. From the gardens below she could hear crickets chirping in their thousands. The scent of the raat-ki-rani, so strong on moonlit nights, came floating up to her. The beauty added to her pain. She wished it were hot and uncomfortable and ugly.

Eventually her tears stopped, and she lay drained and corpse-like. The other sleepers had long since come and settled down. She was the only one awake. Like Lady Macbeth, she had murdered sleep. How Harish's face had glowed as he murmured, tasted almost, 'the multitudinous seas incarnadine / Making the green one red', so that the stretched-out vowel sounds seemed to contain the mysteries of life. Given all that, she might as well wander around like Lady Macbeth. Quietly she got up, rearranged the thick sheet around Paro, and made her way down the ladder connecting the two terraces. On the lower terrace she was by herself, and could appear as distraught as she liked. Restless, she paced round and round.

Everything she could see from the roof was a reminder of some stage or another in her past. There at the water pump they had played as children in the summer, building miniature canals and dams, there were the fruit trees they had climbed, hiding from the mali, there her tai's house, where the Professor had been a tenant, where she and her brother used to go for help with their English lessons, there the gate through which she had walked that fateful day, two years ago, to throw herself into the canal at Tarsikka. And right above, in the store-cum-bedroom, she had been kept locked by her mother because she had been so bad.

In Lahore she had thought that, once home, things would become clear, she would be able to meet Harish, think and plan. She had not considered what she would do beyond seeing him, and it turned out he wasn't even there. What was she to do now? Even if she could get word to him, would he rush back and marry her? In time for there to be no disgrace? When he hadn't married her for so long? What world was she living in?

Rapidly Virmati walked up and down the terrace, the firmness and lightness of her tread ensuring that she made no noise. Gradually her mind grew empty. She began to be more wholly alive to the brilliance of the moonlight, to the faint moist touch of the night air, to the fragrance of the raat-ki-rani, and the soft, quick flap-flap of her slippers. Whatever it was, she thought, she would be able to tackle her problems on her own. She had lived away from home for almost a year, she had seen women growing in power and strength, claiming responsibility for their lives, declaring that society would be better off if its females were effective and capable. Why had she been so upset to learn of Harish's absence? She would solve her problems on her own. She was worthy of independence.

In this calmer state, she became aware of the fatigue of her body. She looked around her and smiled. How long it seemed since that morning! She had travelled so far. It was time to sleep.

Next morning, Virmati vomited quietly in the outhouse and hoped that nobody would notice. As she emerged, lota in hand, she felt exhausted. The mood of the night before vanished in lethargy. Her body felt stale, the burden of its separate life loathsome and repulsive.

If only she could get rid of it, just go back in time, to that fateful moment – how long ago was it? Two months, six weeks? She had always been irregular and, preoccupied with other things, she had not bothered to keep track of her dates. She had depended on Harish to protect her. Wasn't it his duty, having drawn her into this situation?

'Pehnji!' Paro's young, untroubled voice could be heard.

'Coming, bebu.' Virmati mentally prepared herself for another day of appearing normal as she walked quickly towards the house, listlessly swinging her brass toilet lota.

Eating breakfast was agony. Paro sat beside her on her small, flat, wooden patra, and lovingly insisted on doling out spoonfuls of fresh white butter and watching them melt into clear pools on the hot parantha. 'Everybody says how thin you have become, Pehnji,' she said. With the help of almost as much mango pickle as butter, Virmati managed to eat one parantha, chewing slowly, concentrating on getting each mouthful successfully down. Her lassi she made very watery, with two green chillies sliced into it.

'Green chillies?' exclaimed Paro. 'In lassi?'

Virmati was aware of Kasturi's eyes turned momentarily towards her, in an appraising glance.

'I learnt this in the hostel,' explained Virmati. 'A Madrassi girl there showed us how to drink it with green chillies, ginger, and fried mustard seeds. Very tasty. I'll make it for everybody, sometime.'

Paro smiled, and Kasturi turned back to her paranthas. Virmati decided she could not stay long. She could not endure more attention, more meals, more hiding.

It was evening, and Virmati was wandering confusedly outside in the garden. Desperately, she thought of how she felt last night. But that upsurge of confidence only tantalized her with its memory. In its place was a hollow helplessness she tried to fight. She needed help quickly. What about the dai who used to come for her mother? An old Muslim woman, she used to come every day after the children were born, to wash her mother's clothes, massage her abdomen with ghee, and bind it tightly with cloth. Her hands were gentle, practised hands. But how could she get in touch with her? It had always been her great-aunt who had managed that side of things.

Indu had had her baby girl in a hospital. The father had not wanted any dai, or home birth. She would go where Indu went, but silently, secretly, with her face veiled, her thighs open, for that little growing thing to be wrenched out of her.

But why was she thinking like this? Virmati gave herself a small shake. Maybe she could send word to Harish, get his address from Kanhiya. Harish would want to be involved. It wasn't only her. After all, it wasn't only her . . .

The next morning, Virmati set out quietly on a bicycle to meet Kanhiya. She had never been to Kanhiya's house, and knew that her unaccompanied appearance there would seem odd to his family. As she had expected, she was looked at strangely. The mother's 'Beti, we have heard so much about you, I feel like you are the daughter of this house,' came with an edge to its tone. Then, 'Kanhiya? Oh no, he is not here. Studies all day long now, poor boy, now that the exams are near, sometimes in one friend's house, sometimes in another's. But who would know the ways of these boys better than you . . . with so many brothers. I will tell him.'

Later, to her husband, she commented, 'Those people don't know how to keep their daughters in order. Just think! Virmati came here to meet Kanhiya! Alone! No brother, uncle, cousin, nobody. So shameless! The poor boy must be protected from her. Are you listening?'

The husband grunted. His wife was from a village, and tended to take these things too seriously. After all, women were going alone to jails without their men folk. They could surely visit a family friend, and that too in his own house, in front of his mother. Still, he was not one to interfere.

Virmati waited anxiously for Kanhiya to return her call. Nothing happened. When she asked her brother about him in a circumspect way, Kailashnath said tersely that he had no time for idle students. Virmati was nonplussed. Next day she visited the house again, but with similar results.

That night, Virmati lingered in the angan next to her father after the children had eaten and dispersed. Her father's charpai was already spread, the movement of the white mosquito net testifying to the small breezes blowing.

'Pitaji,' said Virmati.

Suraj Prakash glanced at her. Virmati noticed how dark the shadows under his eyes had grown, how puffy his face looked. Her heart contracted. In all her troubles, he had never raised his voice to her, had never directly communicated any of the humiliation her mother kept assuring her he was feeling.

'*Han*, beti?'

'Pitaji, in Lahore all the girls wear at least two – two bangles. I also want a pair.' Virmati said, pouting slightly, and holding out bare wrists for him to see.

'It was you who insisted on leaving behind your jewellery when you left, beti.'

'I know, Pitaji. But now that I am almost a teacher, it doesn't look nice, such bare arms.'

'Bare arms never did, but were you one to listen?'

Her father's gentle way of speaking deprived this statement of any sting. 'So you want one pair or two?' he continued.

'Just one, Pitaji.'

Virmati's Amritsar visit was soon over. She had to go back to Lahore, take her exams, do well. Indu embraced her again and again with tears in her eyes. Kasturi said, 'I hope you do well and justify all the fuss that has been made over your studies.' Kailash hugged her awkwardly. The younger ones waited impatiently for her to go, so they could run off and play. Paro insisted on coming to the station.

Back to college, the books in her attaché case unread, the problem in her belly unsolved. That night, with legs trembling, mouth dry, praying fervently for no contempt, she told Swarna.

'I've missed two months, Swarna,' she said, desperately plunging her information into a slight lull in the conversation, her face burning, her eyes focused on her twitching hands.

Swarna said nothing, merely looked, careful in that moment of non-surprise, to betray no shock, only the routine 'Are you sure?'

Virmati nodded miserably. She braced herself for the questions Swarna was bound to ask, questions about the father, and where was he, and why was he not . . . perfectly legitimate questions, questions she herself would have shot off like bullets to one in a similar situation.

'And he . . .?' Delicately put, but Virmati was not in a state where delicacy could spare her feelings. She turned even redder, but forced herself to look at Swarna.

'He . . . he doesn't know,' she stammered. 'Otherwise . . .'

Virmati's voice fell, as she hoped Swarna would understand how it might be if only he had been there.

'And now?' asked Swarna, looking at the shame on the face of the woman before her, whose family was to be feared, whose lover was invisible in her time of need, and who in the end had to turn to her, a room-mate of eight months.

Virmati mutely gestured towards her belly and shook her head.

The next day Swarna came back to the hostel, bursting with news.

'Auntie says it is illegal. No doctor in Mayo Hospital will touch you.'

'But I don't have to go to such a big hospital,' said Virmati diffidently. 'Just a small place.'

'The trouble is, these hospitals and clinics are the safest places. Everything is done properly, but it is also public and recorded. If something happens to you, there could be trouble.'

'What can happen to me?'

'Something did happen just recently in Mayo. The doctor pulled out the woman's intestines along with the foetus.'

'*Bap re*. How did he do that? Are you sure?'

'God knows. Anyway, that's what Auntie told me. Thank goodness both were English, she said, otherwise Indian doctors would have got a bad name.'

'Anyway,' said Virmati quickly, 'I don't wish Auntie or you to bother in any way, especially as it seems to be so difficult. I'll manage myself.'

'How will you do that?' asked Swarna tartly.

'I'll go to a dai.'

'Dais are very dangerous,' said Swarna firmly. 'Auntie says it is the after-care that is neglected. The method itself may be effective, but the things they use are not clean. Their hands . . .' Here Swarna shuddered.

Virmati smiled grimly.

'What choice do I have, Swarna?' she asked, getting up and starting to gather her books. 'Now I have to study. The exams are about to start, and God alone knows how I will manage. If I don't pass, I cannot hold my head up in Amritsar, let alone other things . . .'

Virmati approached her exams in a haze of sickness and worry. She had heard stories of women sometimes bleeding to death after these home-done abortions. She was frightened, but as soon as her exams were over she would go in search of a dai. For now, she had to finish what she had come to Lahore to do. Let the corpse on the funeral pyre be a qualified BT at least.

And then, 'Viru! Viru!' Triumph glowed in Swarna's face.

'What?' asked Virmati, raising her head from her book with an effort.

'Guess!'

Virmati turned away irritated. 'I have to study,' she said in a strained voice. 'Where is the time for guessing?'

Though Swarna looked surprised, Virmati added no palliative.

'Oh, ho! You're so touchy!' she exclaimed. 'And here I've got good news for you. Auntie has arranged it all! Now, what do you say?'

The news penetrated Virmati's bent head. Arranged it all. She had hardly hoped to be let off so easily. She remained still, unable to say anything.

Swarna shook her, 'Have you gone dumb? Aren't you happy. It was not easy to get Auntie to do it, but neither does she want you exposed, or in danger, which she felt certain you would be. I had to tell her about it, Viru! She wouldn't have done it otherwise. There will be two meetings with the doctor, both in her house. It seems that's the best way to do it, the most private. In the hospital it would have cost at least a hundred, but because of Auntie, here it will only be fifty.'

'When?' Virmati forced herself to ask.

'When? Oh, soon. Soon. Better to get it over, no? But the first meeting, to make sure you are . . . you know . . . though I said you are . . . but still the doctor needs to see. The meeting is fixed for day after.'

Day after, the two girls cycled to Miss Datta's house. There they had tea with a gentleman. A man, thought Virmati dismayed, the doctor is a man. She hadn't actually considered this aspect, but now the thought of exposing herself clinically to a male made her grow hot with shame. What must his opinion of her be? She felt apprehension knot her stomach.

'Shall we go to the guest room?' said Miss Datta when the tea had finished. 'We can be absolutely private there.'

The trio made their way out of the house and into the guest room with its separate entrance. It was sparsely furnished, with a bed, a cupboard, and a desk placed against each wall.

'She should take her salwar off and lie down so I can examine her,' said the doctor delicately to the older woman.

Virmati did as she heard with stiff hands, fumbling under her kameez with the tapes of her salwar, not daring to use the bathroom since it was not offered.

'Relax, relax,' said the doctor briskly, throwing a sheet over her, wriggling his hand into a rubber glove, smearing cream on, and parting her knees with Auntie looking on. 'Now,' he said, as the internal examination began, 'Breathe deeply.'

'I'm trying,' gasped Virmati.

The doctor pushed his hand in deeper. Pain shot through Virmati's abdomen, and she involuntarily clenched her thighs together.

'Relax,' insisted the doctor. 'Otherwise it will hurt. Now, breathe deeply.'

Virmati shut her eyes and breathed deeply, and thought, Mati was right, I cannot escape punishment for what I have done.

The doctor put his hand on Virmati's abdomen and pressed. As Virmati stiffened, he pressed harder, moving his hand in a circular motion.

'Yes, yes,' she heard through the tension of her rigid muscles, 'growing nicely. About ten weeks, I'd say. You can get up now.'

Virmati hastily tied her salwar, and they moved back to the drawing-room. Swarna smiled at her warmly. Virmati sat next to her, and started fidgeting with the lace doily that covered the sofa arm.

The doctor asked her a few routine questions, date of last period, any complications in her gynaecological history, number of pregnancies, which Virmati answered with averted eyes.

'When will it be possible, doctor?' asked Miss Datta after he had finished. 'There is some urgency about the matter.'

'The sooner the better,' said the doctor jovially, addressing himself entirely to Miss Datta. 'The girl is healthy, the foetus is healthy, there will be no problem anywhere.'

'Day after, then?' said Miss Datta, looking at Swarna for a moment with her eyebrows raised.

'I think so, Auntie,' said Swarna quickly.

'Very good. The girl should be here at eight in the morning, with a completely empty stomach. Not even water after midnight.' The doctor rose to go. 'She is lucky to have someone like you to look after her. Otherwise I have seen so many of these cases . . .' he shuddered. 'They go to these quack dais, and then come to us bleeding and lacerated. Sometimes there is very little we can do.'

'He is a good man,' said Miss Datta with a sigh as the doctor went. 'At one time our brothers studied together, right here in Mayo College. He is very fond of me.'

Virmati knew she was not expected to make any kind of response. All that was required was gratitude, which she most abjectly felt. Her mind saw each hour sluggishly dragging along till the day after, when deliverance from this unwanted burden would come. That a child of their union, the result of all those speeches on freedom and the right to individuality, the sanctity of human love and the tyranny of social and religious restraints, should meet its end like this! Glancing at her, Swarna saw tears in her eyes.

'I think Viru is tired, Auntie. We'll go now.'

Riding home, Virmati wished the road could swallow her up. Her nothingness was total. She felt severed from the body that was causing her friend's friends so much trouble. They were kind, they didn't say anything outright, but she knew herself to be a crawling worm dependent on other people's good wishes for survival.

The next day was an exam. Mechanically Virmati answered the questions. The fans suspended on their long poles whirred overhead, but she was sweating despite that. Her mouth was dry, and the cautious sips of water she took from the glass in front of her did nothing to relieve her thirst.

The invigilator brushed past Virmati's table, and stood behind her, looking at what she had written. Virmati tried to make the pen in her hand move faster, some of the knowledge she had gained during the year was bound to be relevant, and in a daze she wrote whatever she remembered. The main thing was to finish, somehow get this torture over, so that there would be no distractions from the more major, body-wrenching torture of tomorrow.

That night Virmati could not sleep. She was in misery, and longed for Harish's presence. At least she could talk to him, or more realistically listen to his beautiful words. He would have found something to say, something that would have made her feel better.

What she was doing – killing their child – was it right? If she could have presented Harish with a pregnancy she was sure that all his doubts and vacillations about marrying would be resolved. But she scorned such tactics, and even if she didn't, it was too late to avoid the shame that an early baby would bring.

As she tossed and turned, one thought kept recurring. By

this time tomorrow it will all be over, over.

But suppose it was over in a very final sense? Suppose she died? She got up from her bed, and looked around. There was a dim light coming in from the weak bulb in the corridor. Her glance fell on a fruit knife lying on the table along with some apples. Absent-mindedly she picked it up and walked outside. She sat down on the parapet and looked at the empty courtyard. Everybody was sleeping peacefully, everybody except for her. She picked up the knife and slowly slashed at the soft skin on her calf. If she could brand her name there, that would mean she could survive the pain of tomorrow. But by the time she had carved out 'V' there was too much blood for her to finish.

Next morning the girls took a tonga at seven in the morning.

'I think we had better,' Virmati had said to Swarna the night before, 'I may not be able to cycle back.'

Swarna looked concerned, and on the way to Miss Datta's held Virmati's sweaty hand in her own warm, dry one. The clip-clop of the horse's hooves was the only sound between them. With an effort, Virmati pushed her thoughts to beyond the event.

'I have these bangles to sell,' she said, showing Swarna her wrist.

'Is that why you came back with them!' exclaimed Swarna.

Virmati nodded.

'But won't they mind?'

'I have no other money. I have to.'

'What will you tell them?'

'War effort. Something like that.' As an afterthought Virmati added, 'Even Shaku Pehnji gave a bangle when they came collecting in her college.'

'Hers is a government college. Nobody will come collecting from the RBSL institution.'

'Still.'

Both girls looked at the narrow gold bangles glinting on Virmati's arms. The evening before she left, her father had got her this new pair from the shop, the latest design, he said as he gave them to her, not the old heavy stuff he supposed she was getting too modern for. They were flattish and had small flowers carved onto them, interspersed with green and red enamel leaves. Slowly Virmati took them off and pressed them into Swarna's lap.

'Keep them,' she said. 'In case –' Swarna tried to resist, but Virmati grabbed her wrist and slipped them on.

They reached the house before either girl could think of anything more to say.

Virmati lay on the bed of Miss Datta's guest room, salwar off, legs spread, sheet swathed, in a repeat of the earlier scenario. Miss Datta was standing behind her, Swarna was in the outer room, the doctor was saying reassuring nothings. His tone told her that much, she was too terrified to follow his actual words. Something about planning to teach after her BT? She gulped and made a noise which passed for an answer. By now a needle was approaching her, a hand was laid on her wrist. It is all my karma, hovered around in her mind as her tense lids closed on her weary eyes.

An hour later, Virmati drifted back. Still on the same bed, legs down, alone in the room. There was tape on her wrist, some raw wetness between her legs, and relief! She was alive! The condition of her body was now commensurate with her social position.

Virmati had not reckoned on the discomfort she would feel. The dull ache in her abdomen, the increased soreness when she tried to go anywhere on her bicycle, and of course all that wretched blood meant that she could not ignore her body, even now when everything was over.

That was all she wanted to do. Forget. Forget, forget, forget. She felt a deep emptiness inside her, which she construed as yearning for the Professor. Oh, how she longed to meet him, to throw herself on his chest, babble out her story, feel his love and sympathy, his regret that he wasn't there pouring over her in a great tidal wave that would cleanse her of all guilt and sorrow!

With these feelings, she did her practicals. They were conducted during the regular class hours of the SL school. The examiner who sat in the back row of the class, could he tell that she had just had an abortion?

Only with Swarna could she be comfortable. Swarna who knew what she was, and didn't condemn.

'What will he say?' Swarna once asked curiously.

'He? Oh, he'll be very sorry.'

'I hope they won't mind about the bangles.'

Virmati's face clouded for a moment. She regretted the bangles. She had known that her father had given her those exquisitely crafted pieces with care and love.

'I'll have to say that when everybody was giving, I also had to. Our brave British soldiers need support from the Nazi menace.'

Swarna snorted. 'It's an imperialist war,' she said.

'I do not think that will be their response,' said Virmati.

It wasn't. 'Next you will rob your father's entire shop for the war. How is it any concern of yours? Have you seen?' Shrill, angry tones echoed across the angan. The father disturbed and withdrawn. 'Tell her, ji. She thinks she can dispose of what is given to her, when and where she likes. One can't trust her with anything.'

Virmati was stung. Silently she swore she would never take another gold article from her family as long as she lived. When Indu was married, she had been covered with jewellery. But as for her, they grudged her everything. Nothing was hers, not her body, her future, not even a pair of paltry, insignificant gold bangles.

She turned towards her father. He sat there slumped in his chair in the angan, looking tired as usual. Normally her mother, so concerned about his health, tried to keep domestic worries from him, but the loss of something gold could not be regarded as a mere household matter. This was business. The children were quiet, stilled by the shouting and the anger.

So Virmati's year at Lahore ended much as it had begun, with the displeasure of her elders gathered thick about her head. This time, though, she found it harder to accept their disapproval without question.

'She's become so independent,' she heard her mother complain to her aunt when they were sitting together preparing for the evening meal.

Virmati refused to acknowledge this. She went on picking the little nuggets of dirt from the rice, tossing it into the air without looking at the older women. Yes, she was independent. Her body had gone through knives and abortion, what could happen to her now that she could not bear?

XX

'Why didn't you at least inform me?'

Virmati was not in Harish's arms. She was instead standing stiffly by her cycle near the bushes on the road parallel to his house. Harish was standing near her, twisting her handlebars in agitation and whispering, though it was evening and a casual passer-by would have had to strain even to make out who they were.

'How could I?' said Virmati as normally as she could. 'Where were you for me to tell?'

'Oh, if only I had known! If only I had dreamt!'

'But you were away so long. And didn't even leave me your address.'

'But you said you didn't want to be disturbed during your exams. And that meant a whole month. I was determined that your wishes should be honoured.'

'And you honoured them well,' said Virmati with uncharacteristic irony. 'Without even telling me!'

'I did write to you, Viru!'

'By then it was too late.'

'Darling, what could I do? My mother insisted the baby's mundan be done in the village, nobody there has seen him, you know, and I thought it was a good opportunity to go, since you had decided I should leave you alone. Now you are being unfair!'

'Then to be away so long!'

'It was only a month . . . how can you blame me for that? And then you know that I try and please them in little things, since in the large . . .'

'Meantime I go through this! You once promised this would never happen!'

'I can't help it if something happened. I was always so careful.'

Obviously not enough, rose to Virmati's lips, but she swallowed the words. What good would blaming do? Would it change anything? Bring back the baby? Undo that act on the charpai in the spare room of Miss Datta's house?

A great depression settled over her. She felt more alone than ever.

'I must go, or they will miss me,' she said.

The Professor pressed a letter into her hand as she left. She could feel him watching her as she slowly started to ride home. She tucked those pages of love inside the front of her kameez, and thought that now he hardly needed letters to attach her to him. She was his for life, whether he ever married her or not. Her body was marked by him, she could never look elsewhere, never entertain another choice.

XXI

In the hill state of Sirmaur lived a forward-looking queen, Pratibha. She was educated, and her mind itched for matter to engage
itself on. She heard Gandhiji's call, and cast spinning-wheels
amongst the people. She laid her ear to the ground, and heard the
rumble of change vibrating through the earth. Her people too
must march with the times, and for girls who might find it difficult to march, a school must be provided. It was started in the
palace precincts. Teachers were found among the educated
locals, women who were widowed or childless; their salary, ten
rupees a month. The queen's patronage – the stick of her displeasure, the carrot of her pleasure – was often the only inducement
for families to send their daughters away for such wasteful, time-
consuming activities.

Five years after its inception the school had expanded enough
to move outside the palace walls. A double-storeyed clinic
nearby was vacated. The large lower room became the school
hall, the smaller rooms on top were converted into classrooms.
There was a yard in front, a spreading banyan tree in one corner,
with a brick platform around it, and steep businesslike steps
leading down from the path above. A heavy gate was added and a
board put up, proclaiming this to be the Pratibha Kanya
Vidyalaya.

Further up on the hill a cottage was built for the principal. It
had two rooms with a small garden overlooking the valley
below. It was sufficiently off the winding path to be totally private, and to guarantee complete solitude in the contemplation of
the beauties of nature.

Getting somebody suitably qualified to fill the post of principal proved more complicated.

The Maharani was particular. 'Find a woman with teacher's

training, and some experience,' she demanded. Her prime minister, whose profession included the task of being perpetually obliging, thought of all the people he knew. Among them was a fellow Samajist, Lala Diwan Chand in Amritsar. His granddaughter had gone in for teacher training. As far as he knew, the girl was not married. Some scandal about it – hence her unusual circumstances. If nothing materialized for Pratibha's school by his next visit to Amritsar, he would make discreet enquiries.

The prime minister of Sirmaur State sat in the drawing-room of Lala Diwan Chand's home, exchanging courtesies with the family as he slowly sipped his sherbet.

How does one persuade people to do things they have never done? From the inception of the school he had been doing just that, with families of students, families of teachers, and now with Virmati's family. He looked around him. The large, long, high-ceilinged drawing-room of the bungalow at Lepel Griffin Road was not the kind of room that invited departure. Nor were the vast stretches of orchard that he could catch a glimpse of through the windows. He started.

'It is unusual to have a daughter so highly qualified,' he complimented carefully. 'BA, with a BT from Lahore. Very few of our girls are allowed to go in for higher studies. You should see the poor teachers of our school. Some fifth pass, some eighth, at the most matric pass. What can we do? You are an example for others to follow.'

'Bhai Sahib, you know how times are changing. With the boys becoming educated, and often opting for professional careers, there is the need for girls to keep up with them. Otherwise, where is the compatibility?' said Suraj Prakash.

Kasturi thought how disastrously educating Virmati had misfired, and said nothing.

'Exactly. I knew Lala Diwan Chand's family would be able to understand this,' said their visitor. 'So when the Rani Sahiba asked me to recommend someone for principal, I naturally thought of your eldest daughter. Ours is a small state and we need the help of people like you to aid us on the path to progress.'

'Bhai Sahib! We did not educate her to send her away to work. She is still so simple and inexperienced.'

'Bhaiji,' said the Diwan, 'today the young must also take part in leadership. These are difficult times. What with the war and our struggle, can we afford not to use every capable hand we have. Virmati is qualified and from an impeccable background! Can I think of anybody better? You tell me.'

'Lahore was near, but now, so far away from home – who knows what might happen?'

'She will be like my own daughter, and Nahan like her own home,' said the Diwan Sahib. 'The Maharani is interested in fostering education for girls, and the principal of her school will have a lot of status. People will treat her like Sita.'

The Diwan Sahib repeated all the arguments he had used to persuade, in variation, to make the idea familiar and palatable. Then with murmurs about the pleasure the Maharani and he would have at meeting them in Nahan, he left.

Later. Kasturi and Suraj Prakash between themselves.

'How can we let her go?' demanded Kasturi, frightened at this further, unlooked-for development in her daughter's educational career.

'What is the harm? You heard Bhai Sahib,' replied Suraj Prakash placatingly, trusting in the word of a Samaj member.

'She is so young.' Kasturi had no doubt as to what her daughter should be doing. She should stay at home until she had sense enough to get married.

'If she is not going to get married, she might as well do something.'

That was true enough. Ever since Virmati had come home from Lahore, looking wan and pale, there had been this problem. All that studying was not good for her health, but the girl was past listening to anyone. What to do with her? The topic of marriage had come up again, only to be met with violent hysteria on

Virmati's part. After the Tarsikka episode, the family were too wary to force anything against her will.

'What kind of *kismet* is ours that our eldest daughter remain unmarried like this? After Indu, it is now Gunvati's turn, but still that girl sits there, stubborn as a rock, never mind the disgrace or what the whole world is thinking, or what her future will be,' said Kasturi miserably.

'Let her go,' said Suraj Prakash cleverly. 'Here she is still too near him. We can never be sure. Such an influence he had, and may still have –'

Kasturi retorted sharply. 'He cast an evil eye on her. With simple people such as us, he could do anything! Even with a baby son he is not settled. Such a depraved being I would not wish on my worst enemy!'

'All the more reason to send her away, then.'

Kasturi grunted. 'We always end up discussing that man whenever we talk about Viru. My ears have grown thick and hard hearing his name.'

The Diwan Sahib wanted an answer before he left Amritsar, and the question of Virmati's future had to be discussed with all the elders of the family. Much time was spent in talking, and finally even Virmati's opinion was sought.

She considered the matter dispassionately. Leaving her home meant leaving reproaches and her mother's silent disapproval. Leaving discussions of Gunvati's marriage, discussions tinged with sadness, and she the reprobate.

As for the Professor, it was difficult to meet. On the road, hurried words, the fear that someone might see, the shadow of what had happened hanging heavy and gloomy between them.

Her BT had left her restless and dissatisfied, hungry to work, and anxious to broaden her horizons. She had had a taste of freedom in Lahore, it was hard to come back to the old life when she was not the old person any more.

She told her family she would be very glad to serve the cause of the nation's literacy.

This resolved, Suraj Prakash returned the Diwan Sahib's visit. It was decided that Virmati would return to Nahan with him. Kailash would also go along, look things over, settle her in.

And that is how Virmati found herself in the train leaving Amritsar, her feet on her bedroll, her metal box pushed behind it, its lock faintly clinking with the motion of the train.

Nahan, clean and prosperous, was ruled by an enlightened royal couple. Their foundry was the biggest in Northern India, and provided plenty of jobs. It was a place where the pathways were cobbled, the drains all covered, where a mashal followed the sweeper twice a day with a water bag to wash the dirt off the streets. Where leaves were not allowed to drift.

I am firm on the tracks of my mother, and I am talking to a lawyer who assures me he knows all there is to know, because he and his have lived in Nahan since time immemorial. At the leaves I raise my eyebrows slightly.

'Not even a leaf?'

'Not even a leaf,' came the categorical reply. Never mind that now the streets are filthy and grimy balloons of yellow, blue and grey plastic bags swirl around piles of garbage at every bend and turn of the city.

'Spitting was a crime.'

'Really?'

'Really.' The eyes misted over, and the voice became soft, laden with memories of a mythic time when public cleanliness existed.

'It was never too hot. In summer, as soon as the temperature rose above thirty-two degrees, it rained; in winter the forest cover kept us warm. The water we had was real mineral water, piped straight from the springs, none of these suspect underground sources for us. You can see for yourself what a miracle our plumbing was when you consider that the water supply laid for 6,000 people is serving 35,000 people today!'

I nod vigorously and take notes of everything he says. Even

now, it is clear that underneath the dirt and congestion Nahan was indeed picturesque.

The principal's house, which I got the school chowkidar to open for me, was an abandoned little two-room cottage, the doors rotten white with damp and falling off their hinges. There is a strong, mouldy smell inside, and bat and lizard droppings dot the dirt-crusted floor. The view was of gentle, rolling hills covered in haze. 'But from October on, when the air is clear, you can see the snow-covered peaks,' explained the wizened old chowkidar to me.

'Why doesn't anybody use this?' I ask.

'It is too small to house a family. Long ago someone lived here alone, but all sorts of people used to visit her at all hours. They never hired a single woman after that.'

Into this model of civic amenities and progressive rule came Virmati, excited about independence, still not knowing that for her love and autonomy could never co-exist.

Virmati was charmed by Nahan. She heard the sounds of the foundry floating up at all hours, and felt herself at one with the working people of the world. She stood in her tiny garden and looked across the valley, turned her head and looked towards the school of which she was headmistress, and sensed her singleness and her power. She was twenty-three and the youngest amongst her staff. Her qualifications, BA and BT from Lahore, were so impressive that the Maharani had dispensed with the usual interview prior to the appointment.

Later on, when she did see her, she felt she had made a mistake. The girl was too pretty. Aloud she complained about Virmati's youth and single status to her prime minister.

'I know the family,' he replied. 'The girl is good.'

'I do not wish for trouble, Mantri Sahib. It will be very bad for the school. We will take months trying to salvage what has been built so carefully.'

'I am responsible for that,' replied the prime minister. 'Meanwhile if the Rani Sahiba does not approve, we can look for someone else,' he added carefully, to protect himself.

'No, let it be,' said the Maharani after some thought. 'We will try her and see. But the first hint of anything, she goes.'

'Of course,' said the Mantri.

There were about two hundred and fifty girls in the Pratibha Kanya Vidyalaya. They came from the homes of traders, shopkeepers, bankers, teachers, and the state employees of Sirmaur. Virmati found the school surprisingly easy to administer. After all, she had grown up shouldering responsibility and she discovered that those talents did equally well for larger things. She supervised the accounts, gave appointments to parents, held weekly meetings with the teachers, monthly meetings with the prime minister, and very occasional meetings with the Maharani Pratibha. In the evenings, when she was briskly walking around the hillside, she would think of what she had done in the day and feel the satisfaction of achievement.

Virmati's other major duty in the school was teaching. She taught English Literature and Household to classes IX and X. Household was hygiene, nutrition, domestic management, health care, and enough applied maths to balance a budget. The prime minister, keen to implement the maharanee's ideas, publicized the soundness of female education through Household, a traditional subject taught in a scientific way by the principal herself.

So Virmati ran her school, ran her home, and passed the days busy and happy. From time to time she felt a sharp pang of longing for the Professor. But she had lived with this for so long she would have felt uncomfortable without it. His letters were particularly ardent. Her description of the place had fired his imagination more than hers, and he talked much of romance and beauty. He came to be the spectre that lay between her and her life as principal, so that she too began to look upon her stay there as a period of waiting rather than the beginning of a career.

He wrote every day. The very sight of her name in his distinctive hand, centred so neatly on the pale blue envelopes, was enough to set her face on fire, which she did her best to downplay by briskly ordering the peon about.

Of course, the lover cannot be content with words alone. He must come, he must see, he must feel.

'I'm coming,' he wrote.

'No,' she wrote back.

'I must. You have no idea how drab and monotonous my days and nights are. Nothing can relieve them – nothing except the hope of meeting you.'

'What about your family?' she replied.

'I live and die for you,' he said, evading the issue as usual.

He came travelling up to Ambala by train, and caught the Nahan bus from there. At the Jamuna the waters were too high for the vehicle to cross. All the passengers descended and waded through, the river swirling around their legs. Behind them came two coolies, who moved back and forth with the heavy luggage till it was all transported. Waiting beyond was the bus that had unloaded in a similar fashion some hours ago. This they boarded while those passengers took theirs. Leaving British India for the Punjab Hill States, on to bad roads, with potholes abounding like scars in a pock-marked face, the Professor thought how much Viru was worth this journey, and how she would look when she saw him.

From the station the Professor found out that it was just a fifteen-minute walk to the school. Fifteen minutes to savour the anticipation of their meeting.

There she was, solitary at evening time in the cottage, sitting on the grassy patch in front, the tea he had taught her to drink in a cup beside her. The low iron gate creaked as he opened it, but she was lost in her thoughts and didn't look up. He crept forward, and softly laid a hand on her neck, just under her roll of hair. She turned with a start.

They said nothing then, just looked, drinking the other up with long, deep glances, dead in that moment to everything else.

Arjun, what did you see when you hit the eye of the bird with the arrow, the eye that all your brothers missed?

Guruji, I saw nothing, just the black dot in the centre.

So Harish saw nothing but Virmati.

A flying arrow aimed at a still bird.

Slowly they moved inside the cottage to finish the embrace their eyes had started.

Later, 'This is such a beautiful place,' said the Professor. 'Complete and self-contained. If I had known, I would have come earlier.'

'No,' Virmati replied hastily.

'Why, darling, what do you mean?'

'You can't stay here.'

'Why not? If *I* can't, then who? And here you are so independent.'

'Not so that I can ignore what everybody thinks.'

'No one will know. I'll be very quiet.'

'There is an eye in every leaf. And why is it that suddenly you do not care what everybody thinks?'

The answer burned within her, because I am the only one who will be affected. It remained unspoken because she didn't want a quarrel in which she inevitably ended up conciliating. Instead she grew cross and irritable, while he started to sulk.

'Very well, then. I know where I am not wanted,' said the Professor. 'I am a stranger here, and quite at your mercy.'

Virmati's face grew taut at the unfairness of this remark, but suppressing still more unprofitable words, she picked up his small attaché case and strode outside. It was getting late, and respectability required that she make arrangements for her guest before night suggestively presented itself.

The purple light was shading into blackness as Virmati and the Professor walked silently down the hill towards the vicinity of the palace where the prime minister stayed. Virmati had made up her mind to request him to host Harish. In fact, throughout the passion of their reunion this question had been nagging her. Where was he going to stay?

As they waited in the angan outside the main living quarters of the prime minister's house, Virmati stared moodily at the tulsi growing prominently in an urn in the middle. The prime minister was a conservative man, he was not going to like this.

He came and listened to Virmati's stammered explanations with courtesy. 'Unexpected visit? I see.'

'He was passing through,' Virmati elaborated. The Professor looked as stupid as it was possible for a man with a noble forehead and elegantly brushed hair to look.

'He must stay here of course, beti,' said the Diwan Sahib.

'Thank you, ji,' said Virmati.

'I am grateful for your hospitality,' said the Professor stiffly.

The Professor stayed one more day and then left. He felt the Diwan Sahib's eye on him and he didn't like it. Besides, Virmati was not behaving properly. Let her get more securely established, he thought, and then he would come.

The rest of the year passed. Virmati cultivated friendships with some of the teachers, visited them in their homes in the winding gullies. All of them wanted to know why she wasn't married. Young and pretty, and coming from a good family – what could be the problem? It bothered them. They wished her well. Virmati grew glib talking about her career, and the need for dedication when one was teaching.

'That's all very well, but you can do the same when you are married,' said one of the teachers she was closest to.

'Everything is in the hands of God,' said Virmati.

Meanwhile Swarna's letters were full of Mrs Asaf Ali, Congress leaders in jail, the Left now in the hands of the Socialists, disturbances everywhere, trains being stopped, hartals paralysing the nation, we are united, they can't stop us now. She had also got a job as a teacher in her old college.

When Virmati read these letters, she wondered why Swarna even bothered with the likes of her. She had so little to offer in exchange. 'I am fine. Everything is the same here. How are you?'

And then came Swarna's note saying she was married. He had accepted all her conditions. She was going to be allowed to continue her other activities, remain treasurer of the Women's Conference, go on working for the Party. Everything to do with the house they would share as much as possible. She owed it to her parents to marry. They had let her have her way in everything else.

Miss Datta liked the boy. He would do, she said.

Virmati grew restless. In class she looked at her students, and looked at the poem in her hand. Why was she teaching them 'The Daffodils'? She who had never seen a daffodil? This was Harish's cup of tea, not hers. Swarna asked what it was like in Nahan. Like nothing. Like being suspended in time, in anticipation for her life to start, with the noise of the foundry as background music.

She wrote to the Professor that she was sick and tired of waiting for him. If he couldn't make up his mind to marry her, then she might as well devote herself seriously to her career. Nahan was not the place to do it. Either in Lahore or, if her family didn't agree, Jullunder.

The Professor came as soon as he was able. This time he arrived at the cottage after dark. He had come prepared with a torch.

'Viru,' he called sweetly, knocking at the window-panes.

Alone inside, Virmati started. 'Who is it?' she called, nervously.

'It is me,' cooed the Professor. 'Open the door and let me in.'

Virmati shivered. The voice was his. But without notice, and so late. Was this the commitment she was looking for? She opened the door a crack, and showed the Professor her white face and falling plait in the dark space between door and frame.

The Professor snaked his hand and foot in between the space and pushed. The door gave way a little. Virmati found herself resisting.

'Why have you come?' she asked. 'First tell me. Why have

you come? Is it going to be the same story all over again?'

'Whatever do you mean, darling? Let me in, will you?' He pushed harder. Now more of his leg was inside.

'No, I won't. Not until you answer me,' cried Virmati, her voice low and passionate. 'All this time you have never been straight with me.'

'First let me come in. How can we talk like this?'

Virmati's hold slackened, and the Professor stepped inside and shut the door behind him.

'Come here, darling,' he caressed. 'Be reasonable.' Inside, a hurricane light was burning. The room was full of dark shadows. The electricity had gone.

'I want to know where I stand before anything else,' she insisted, backing into the room behind. In her hurry she didn't lift the curtain high enough, and it got caught in the door, preventing it from closing. In a flash the Professor was through. He pinned her between his arms, against the wall. She tried to push him away. 'This is not an answer,' she said angrily.

'Viru, I love you more than you love me, that much is obvious,' panted the Professor. 'It's been almost six months – I can think of nothing else and here you torture me with your questions and answers!'

'It is you who are torturing me!' she cried almost in a fit. Against her will, the tears started to come. And against her will, he forced her legs apart with his own, pushing his knee upwards between her soft thighs. With one hand he cupped her face, trying to prise her lips open with his tongue, while the other hand fumbled underneath her kameez for the drawstring that tied her salwar.

'No,' protested Virmati, as strongly as she was able.

The salwar was undone, and his hand was making stroking movements on her belly, before embarking on its more probing journey downwards.

'Viru, Viru, Viru, I love you my sweetest darling,' the Professor murmured, saying her name over and over again.

'Then prove it,' said Virmati hoarsely, growing feebler by the minute.

'That is just what I am doing.'

This was the first time they had spent the whole night together. No fear of curfew, or of home, no fear of anybody hearing anything. For a brief moment Virmati lived that night as though there was no tomorrow. In bed, they had looked at one another and smiled, the love flowing thick and strong between them. He kissed the strands of wet hair on her face, he gently dried the sweat away with the palm of his hand. While she slept within the circle of his arms, he caressed and stroked her. Intermittently waking, she felt her year at Nahan melt away into nothingness.

Towards the east side of Nahan was a long walk, which left the town at the temple tank to reappear after a round of the hill. Early next morning the couple were walking briskly down this scenic route, while tension began to gnaw at Virmati. Suppose there was some trouble? But what else could she have done? I don't care, she thought defiantly.

By now they had reached the middle of their walk. The Professor's attention was caught by two stone canopies over what looked like raised graves. Raised high, almost at eye level, they were in a grassy clearing a little below the road, with steps cut into the side of the hill.

'What is that?' asked the Professor, stopping to look.

'Graves,' said Virmati.

'Oh, how charming,' exclaimed the Professor, as he led the way down the shallow stone steps, overgrown with grass.

Virmati followed. Was it charming? She supposed it was. He usually had an eye for the charming, beautiful, lovely, quaint, picturesque. She tried to see through his eyes when he pointed things out to her. After all these years she was getting quite good at the exercise.

The Professor opened the tiny entrance gate and made for the first grave. It was covered by a thick slab of good-quality Italian

marble. Fine dark lines were visible under the smooth softly
shinning stone. The letters were neatly carved and filled with
black. Slowly he read out:

Sacred
†
To the Memory of
Edwin Pearsall
Medical Officer
to
H.H. of Sirmoor
For 11 Years
Died 19th Nov. 1883
Aged 50
Trusting in the Lord

'What a lovely place to be finally laid to rest!'

'*Hoon*,' said Virmati absently, who saw nothing so remark-
able about the gravestones.

'Such peace and stillness. Look darling, they are right on the
edge of this little promontory. As though poised between this
world and the next.'

'I wonder whose is the other one?' asked Virmati, going to look.

'Viru, Viru! Been here this long, and never thought of explor-
ing!' remonstrated the Professor affectionately.

'I was waiting for you,' said Virmati coldly at being dragged
from lover to pupil.

'It must be his wife's. Whose else could it be? So close and so
similar as they are to one another.'

Indeed it was. On an identical slab, carved in the same way,
were the words:

Louisa Pearsall
Relict of
Dr Edwin Pearsall
Resident of Nahan

191

For 38 Years
After the Death of
Her Husband In Order at Last
To Rest Beside Him
Died 19th October 1921
Aged 87 Years

—

And with the Morn
Those Angel Faces Smile
Which I have Loved Long Since
And Lost Awhile

'What does that mean?' asked Virmati.

'What?'

'The poem at the end. What does she mean by losing angel faces? How can they smile at her in the morning if she has lost them?'

'Darling, you won't be able to understand if you think literally.'

'Oh, I wish these authors would say what they mean!' cried Virmati pettishly.

'But then all the beauty would go. The depth! The resonance!'

'They should still say what they mean,' repeated Virmati stubbornly.

'Look,' explained the Professor. 'By "Morn" the poet means the death of the body, and the ascendance of the soul to heaven. And the loss of angel faces refers to this life on earth, which separates us from the life of the spirits that we know before we are born. It reminds one of Wordsworth's "And not in utter nakedness / But trailing clouds of glory do we come / From God who is our home". A common theme of religious poetry, and since all religions share a spiritual component, this is a theme we can recognize, and empathize with.' The Professor was in his element and unaware that Virmati was irritated.

'Silly woman!' she blurted. 'Staying for thirty-eight years. Just because her husband had died here.'

'Viru!' exclaimed the Professor. 'That is love. So often love is manifested in waiting. Remember Anne's beautiful lines in *Persuasion*? "All the privileges I claim for my sex . . . is that of loving longest, when existence or when hope has gone!"'

How fondly he says those words, thought Virmati resentfully. He must have read them a thousand times. 'No,' she continued out loud, firmly avoiding English Literature, 'you are right. She was not silly. She was clever. She must have been quite comfortably off. That is why she didn't go. Old and ugly, as the English become, red and wrinkled by the time they reach forty. Here the Maharaja would have looked after her. And paid for this expensive gravestone. Could a doctor's widow get this gravestone and this view anywhere else, despite all the angels she has lost and found?'

'This is very cynical of you, Virmati,' commented the Professor gravely.

'Perhaps my life has made me cynical,' replied Virmati equally gravely.

'I will not pretend to not understand you, sweetheart,' said the Professor earnestly. 'Indeed I do, too well. I know the trials you have gone through for me. I appreciate them, more than you think, as a lifetime of loving will prove!'

'If it ever begins, that is.'

Virmati could not understand what was happening to her. Last night had been so wonderful, she wanted that bliss to continue. While he was with her, it seemed her life as a teacher was insubstantial, but she wanted more material to their togetherness. She didn't want there to be any constraints in their intimacy, but now, letting him know how she felt, instead of calming her, only served to increase the number of devils raging inside. She started again.

'You think it's so easy for me!' She turned on him. 'It isn't! People wondering all the time. Why I'm not married. What should I say? That my lover is a coward? That he is waiting for permission from his family to bring home a second wife?'

Virmati had never dared to say so much. She stopped. She

hadn't realized how angry and humiliated she was, and her eyes filled with tears.

The Professor flushed. How dare she insult him like this? He knew men whose second marriages had been condemned socially, resulting in nothing but humiliation and misery to everybody. And she was blaming him for being careful! All he had taught her had led to this! Such insensitivity. And after last night too, when he thought she had felt as much as he did. He started to walk away.

Virmati watched him go. She turned slowly and looked across the valley. Harish was right. It *was* beautiful. A peaceful resting place. It was a great pity she couldn't die straight away and rest there too. She fell down on the grass and closed her eyes, crying noiselessly for a long time, her face pressed against the earth. Her body felt too heavy for her to lift and take home. It would have to remain there, where it had dropped.

Virmati realized – and thought how stupid she was not to have realized earlier – that to have a man stay with you is to invite certain consequences, though poetic justice might demand that the distress caused by that visit should allow those consequences to dissolve. But they didn't. They assumed very tangible voices. These swirled around her figure, and very soon, without her knowing, became loud and threatening.

The prime minister called her about a month after the Professor's visit. As Virmati walked to his residence butterflies danced in her stomach, and the sunshine on her seemed less pleasant than usual. She had a nasty presentiment about this meeting. She had seen the prime minister only recently, and normally he didn't see her so soon.

She rounded the corner of the hill, and there it was, the prime minister's house. Broad stone steps led up to it, flanked by curved stone balustrades. At the top were small, seated lions, and big iron gates between. Through them she could see the marble entrance-way, with grass and flowers growing on either side, and further steps leading up into the house. As she approached, her gait grew slow and irresolute, so that by the time she reached the side entrance, the one she usually used, she was dawdling.

Slowly she entered and slowly she followed the servant, who left her in the selfsame angan where she had waited with Harish more than a year ago. There was the tulsi, looking even more bedraggled despite its decorative pot. Oh, why couldn't Harish have stayed there again? But then she dismissed these thoughts. Her life was so tangled, it was impossible to focus on any one particular that should have been different.

The servant reappeared. She was to follow him to the Diwan Sahib's living quarters instead of the little office in which they usually met. They went through a narrow corridor on to the kitchen angan, skirted the zennana angan, passed the massive formal drawing-room, to an adjacent drawing-room, smaller but also richly furnished. Apprehensive, Virmati took in the crimson carpet, hunting pictures, swords, crystal chandeliers, and heavy rosewood furniture with brocade coverings. She had had no idea the diwan sahib lived so well. She went up to one of the pictures. It was in black and white, in a carved wooden frame, with a gold edge, crowded with English men, women, horses and dogs on leashes. In faint, double black letters underneath was inscribed *The Hunt*.

The Diwan Sahib came and found her staring short-sightedly at it.

'Like it?' he asked pleasantly.

'Oh yes,' she replied. 'The horses and the dogs – so lifelike.' Then she paused, confused. Saying something was lifelike was not supposed to be an aesthetic yardstick, that much she now knew. But what else to say. She looked again at the picture.

'The British love dogs and horses, don't they?' she hazarded tentatively.

The Diwan Sahib smiled. 'Sit down,' he said.

Virmati sat on the edge of one of the brocaded rosewood chairs. She looked down nervously.

'Beti,' he started, 'you know I am like a father to you. Your parents sent you here on my recommendation. I am responsible for you to the Maharani as well as to them.'

He has found out about Harish staying the night, thought Virmati gloomily.

'If there is anything bothering you, or any difficulty, you must tell me,' continued the Diwan Sahib, looking at the principal's head bent intently on the carpet.

'No, no, there is nothing,' mumbled Virmati.

'This is a small place. People are traditional, and when anything out of the ordinary happens, they talk.'

Virmati cleared her throat. 'Talk?' she repeated. 'Yes, I suppose they would.' She wished he would say what he meant and get it over with. She was not accustomed to tact. Her family usually hit her with a sledge-hammer, and when not satisfied with the results, hit her again.

'So when a man stays with you, and that too overnight, there is gossip. And you know how bad any hint of scandal can be for a school. It is important to set a good example, particularly because there is so much readiness to suppose that education encourages girls to be independent and wayward.' He hesitated and added, 'You know our people are simple. When they see something like this, they jump to obvious conclusions. They do not know what else to believe. And a bad example is set.'

'I see,' said Virmati tonelessly.

The Diwan Sahib waited a moment before reiterating patiently, 'The situation then becomes very delicate.'

Virmati could see she was expected to say something. The truth was out of the question, so she tried a lie. 'He is a friend of the family's. He came late, and then we couldn't think of disturbing you.'

The Diwan Sahib frowned. 'Don't you have some further studying to do?' he asked after a little reflection. 'Maybe after this term is over, you can do it.'

Virmati stood up. 'Of course I have to study more,' she said wildly. 'In Shantineketan.' That was the furthest spot she could think of on the spur of the moment.

'Excellent, excellent.' The Diwan Sahib could not have looked more pleased. 'I'll inform the Maharani of your plans. She will be sorry to lose you, but we cannot keep young people here against their will.'

Virmati hardly heard him. She started walking quickly out. She hated him, hated herself. Why couldn't he come out and say she was dismissed, instead of trapping her like that? She would be glad to leave this stifling place. She would go to Shantineketan, if that was the last thing she did. She would never go back to Amritsar. What face did she have left to show there?

Two months were left before the end of term. Virmati worked steadily and avoided the small set of friends she had built up during the year and a half she had spent there. The Professor continued to write to her.

She wrote back as normally as she could. She didn't want to risk the Professor's visiting Nahan again. When she left it would be with her head held high.

When Virmati paid the prime minister her final visit he was as cordial as he had always been. He told her there was no need for her to take leave of the Maharani, she was much preoccupied with her husband's affairs. The teaching staff of the school gave her a small farewell party, where her plans for future study were politely discussed. None of them asked her about marriage the way they used to.

On the morning of 30 April, Virmati was packed and ready. She had come with a suitcase and a bedroll, and at the end of two years the only addition to her luggage was the packet of Harish's letters. She latched the front door behind her and stood in the dewy grass of her small garden. She looked over the low mountains and gentle valley for the last time, and involuntary tears rolled down her cheeks. Then, looking straight ahead, she walked out of the gate, and down the hill, towards the bus stop, followed by the coolie, hurrying to keep pace with her quick step.

The bus to Ambala, the train to Calcutta. How many new beginnings had her relationship with the Professor led her to? That sense of hope was beginning to feel stale. Still, with every mile she travelled she felt stronger. There was a life of dedication and service ahead of her, and in that she would forge her identity.

The women in her compartment were all older. She could feel their curious looks without even turning around from the window. The smell of their food and the clattering of lids from tiffin carriers made her mouth water. She knew if she became the least bit friendly, they would hospitably offer all they had to eat, but in return feel entitled to ask her a thousand probing questions. So she remained where she was, drool wetting the corners of her mouth, but with a will stronger than her appetite.

At Delhi, Virmati had to wait seventeen hours before the connecting train to Calcutta. She knew Harish's poet friend lived in the Civil Lines, and she decided to look him up. His family was old and established, she was confident that she would find the house.

The poet was nonplussed. He had not heard, he hinted delicately, when she had washed, and been served some sherbet.

Nobody had, retorted Virmati.

'But why? Has something happened?'

'The same thing that has been happening for so many years,' she replied. 'You know your friend. What can I tell you? I ask one thing only. How long can I go on waiting? People talk. They are bound to. I know his position is difficult. But so is mine.'

'You mean you are not going to marry him?'

'I mean I cannot wait for ever.'

'This cannot be allowed to happen. Aren't you going to see him again?' he pleaded.

'No.'

He remained silent.

'No. How can I? It is over – absolutely over,' she repeated, staring uncompromisingly at the milky white sherbet in her glass.

'Bhabhi,' the word broke from the poet. At this moment Virmati was less than ever his Bhabhi, but the poet was too wrapped up in his role as saviour of romance to notice the expressionless look on her face. 'Bhabhi,' he repeated, 'let me write to him. I cannot bear to see my friend ruin his life. Bhabhi, I appeal to you, delay your departure for three or four days. After that I will not stop you. My mother will be so happy. She has often talked of inviting him here.'

Virmati hesitated. Shantineketan was calling, but –

The poet pressed home his point. 'After so long, a few more days will be of no consequence. How can you rush into something that will affect your whole life?'

'Rush!' exclaimed Virmati, hurt and astonished. 'Is that what you think?'

The poet made calming gestures with his hands, soothing noises with his mouth, but Virmati continued sharply, 'Do you think I would rush into something like this?' She bit her lip and turned away her head. How could she really talk of all that had happened between them, how many times he had promised her solutions, and how many times she had believed him. Nevertheless her training, her sense of obligation, made it difficult for her to ignore her host's request.

Virmati was a silent guest at the house of the poet. She was acutely aware of her lack of standing. She didn't think the Professor would come. After all, he had had more than five years to make up his mind. Still, she didn't want to appear petulant and unreasonable, so she waited for five days to pass and helped the poet's mother every evening in the kitchen.

Meanwhile the Professor had received his friend's urgent telegram. 'Come. Virmati here. On her way to Shantineketan. Urgent. Come at once.' He felt uneasy. Why was Virmati on her way to Shantineketan? He had been expecting her back in Amritsar for the holidays.

During dinner his wife noticed how preoccupied he looked. Hardly any words passed between them, and she was in a state of perpetual hunger to know what he was thinking. Today she associated his distracted air with the telegram. It must be something to do with that witch, what else. The familiar knot inside her tightened, and she prayed to God, like she did every day, morning and night, to keep her home safe from outsiders, safe till her children grew up and married. Then God could do what he liked with her. She would accept.

The next day the Professor informed Ganga that he was leaving by the night train, and she should pack two sets of clothes for him, one pant-shirt-tie-socks-shoes, one dhoti-kurta-jooti.

'Where are you going?' she asked fearfully.

'I have work somewhere. Have you ever shown any interest in it that I should tell you now?' he snapped at her, as he disappeared into the drawing-room to collect some papers.

Subdued and miserable, she started packing his suitcase. Her son jumped on the bed and insisted on helping. He was by now three years old, fair and handsome, with a straight nose, rosy mouth, gleaming little white teeth, and his father's large eyes. His hair tended to curl, and she kept it slightly long so that it framed his face. Such a picture he was; could anyone, let alone a father, resist him? As the mother gazed at him, the burning love she had for the boy helped to relieve some of the anguish in her heart.

'Munna!' she scolded, pretending to slap his hand, as he started to play with the things in the suitcase, 'Oho, what a nuisance this child is!' she exclaimed. But she didn't take him off the bed, and he didn't stop throwing his father's clothes about.

When the Professor returned, the wife turned brightly to him and said, pointing to the mess, 'Look, even he doesn't want you to go.'

Harish smiled, and said, 'You attend to him. I'll do it myself.'

'No, no, I'll do it.'

'No, he's quite right. You should be looking after him, not me. Wisdom from the mouths – in this case, gestures – of babes, you see.' The Professor started picking his things off the floor, dusting them, packing quickly.

The woman did not have the courage to say anything more. She returned to the kitchen, so preoccupied that Giri had to fuss a lot to get her attention.

*

It was the last day of Virmati's stay in Delhi. 'Bhai,' she told the poet, 'I have booked myself on the noon train tomorrow. I thank you for your hospitality and concern.'

'But he is coming. I know it. I have sent him a telegram.'

Virmati remained quiet. When Harish came, she greeted him formally, and then withdrew into the kitchen. There the tears sprang to her eyes, and stayed, causing her to cut her hands with the knife she was using to chop the spinach. Luckily the leaves were green, and the blood went unnoticed in the dark colour of the cooking water.

Harish and the poet were arguing.

'You must marry her now, or she will be lost to you forever.'

'What can I do? I am hemmed in and tortured on all sides. I know I have been unfair to her – I know. And yet what can I do?' Harish turned an agitated face to the poet. 'Everybody will condemn me, her. My children will never accept it, nor my mother. You know the constraints. Surely I need not explain myself to *you*!'

'No, no,' reassured the poet quickly. 'I am not asking for explanations. It is difficult, I know. But my friend, there is a time for action, and in your case that time is undeniably before you. Or,' he paused, 'be prepared to let her go.'

Harish looked distraught. 'What can I do?' he asked helplessly. 'My wife, my son . . .'

The poet tich-tiched in exasperation. 'Bhai, what can they do? Now you get married. Nothing is simpler. A pundit will be arranged – that's all you really need. You can take the pheras here – right here where you are sitting, in this angan. If you can't bring yourself to do this, you will never see her again.'

Harish's face lengthened. 'Imagine going to Shantineketan! What will she learn there compared to what *I* can teach her?'

'Then teach her and be done with it! Now it's settled.' The poet slapped Harish on the back a couple of times as he got up. 'Enough discussion. Expect to be married tomorrow.'

Harish remained sunk in his chair.

The next morning a pundit was arranged, and the puja samagri bought. The groom, throwing himself into the spirit of the thing, decided that his bride had to be dressed in something suited to the occasion. Accordingly he took her out and chose a deep red and gold tissue sari with tiny woven silver flowers in the traditional Banarsi style. He draped it around her head in the shop, and his heart took a turn at how beautiful she looked. The bride, for her part, managed to smile at him. The only thing she said she wanted were the red ivory bangles that the women of her family wore when they married.

In the evening the wedding ceremony proceeded smoothly. The poet's parents did the kanya-daan, the seven pheras were taken, the couple pronounced man and wife. As Virmati rubbed her eyes, watering from the smoke, she knew, rather than felt, that the burden of the past five years had lifted.

XXII

Brides in trains travelling to homes they have never seen, fear in their hearts. Years ago, Kasturi had done it.

Two days after her wedding, Kasturi was escorted to the station, amid crying relatives and sober-faced baratis. She was frightened by this journey from which no return was possible. Her mother has assured her that Suraj Prakash will be kind, that she will be happy in her *own* home. Kasturi trusts her mother, but the pain of leaving all that she has ever known is more than the seventeen-year-old can bear. At the same time she accepts her grief stoically, for she knows she has been but a guest in her parents' house; this separation is ordained from birth.

Ultimately Kasturi had to be half-carried into the train, she was crying so hard. The train starts, but Kasturi was a bride, she could not lean out of the window and wave a last goodbye to her father and brothers. Her husband is in another compartment with the men, strange women surround her. She now belongs to them, and they systematically chuck her under the chin, saying, 'Don't cry, soon you will forget, wait and see, I was like this too, poor thing.' She is part of the tradition of weeping brides, and her sorrow is not taken seriously.

The landscape passed, but Kasturi's head was sunk beneath a heavy, gold-embroidered dupatta and all she could see were the bangles on her arms, gold interspersed with wedding ivory, painted with red and black circles. Long, elaborate kalira hung from them, tinkling whenever her hands moved. Her motion-lessness cramped her; unused to sitting with her legs dangling, her feet hurt. At a station some jalebis were pressed into her hands, lay there soggily and were finally taken away.

At Amritsar Station, Kasturi didn't dare look around her. Down the long staircase she walked with bent head and tiny, faltering steps, supported by women on either side, into a tonga, with soft, cloth-covered seats and painted sides. Squeezed between the wives of two of the groom's second cousins with fretful children on their laps, Kasturi felt sick with tension and dread. What was it going to be like, so far from home, with no one she knew?

The streets became narrower as they approached the inner-city area. The bazaar was congested. There were tonga-wallahs shouting to be let through, coolies with baskets and bundles on their heads, and open carts piled with merchandise in any available space. The narrow drains were exposed, there were children squatting over them, fruit peels and flies were all over. The buildings rising above the shops looked solid and substantial, with delicate wrought-iron balconies overlooking the street.

'Here, the Muslim side of the street,' murmured one of her companions, trying to keep her daughter's hands away from the tonga wheel. Kasturi was surprised at how big and fine the houses were. In Sultanpur the Muslims were mostly poor, and the only one she had known well had been her mother's dai.

'Yours is the first house on the Hindu side,' chorused the women. 'Your father-in-law built a well behind his house for the whole street to use. You are lucky to get such a family.'

The tonga passed by an imposing gateway of red stone. The pointing out continued:

'Your father-in-law built that gate. It leads to the Samaj head-quarters. He has also established a school which runs there during the day.'

Kasturi thought of her uncle. It was reassuring to know that the family she was going to was somewhat similar to her own. The women went on:

'Education is very important for him.'

'Only an educated bride would do for his son.'

'Someone who would carry on Arya Samaj traditions.'

'Who understood her duties to the community. Fees, books, food, jobs, midday meals for who-all, who-all. His daughter-in-law will have to see to that.'

'It's lucky the family is so small. At least the kitchen work will be easy for her.'

Kasturi was indignant. Did they think any kitchen work was beyond her? She came from a good family where girls were taught housekeeping from the time they could walk. All of a sudden Kasturi felt grateful to her mother for those long hours she had spent in the kitchen, cutting, peeling, chopping, slicing, pounding, wrapping, mixing, kneading, baking, roasting, stirring and frying (deep plus shallow). It paid to know these things.

'Here, here, this way,' commanded one of the women, 'now stop, stop,' and the tonga clattered to a halt. While they haggled with the tonga-wallah, Kasturi peeped through the veil the women pulled lower over her face. She saw a narrow gully lined with gold and silversmiths working in tiny cubicles on either side. At the far end were sheds with some cows and a horse and buggy. Mosquitoes buzzed around her, and she could smell urine. This was to be her new home. There were flowers hung across a dark entranceway and a crowd of people swept her inside the narrow spiral staircase that led to the living quarters above. Round and round they climbed the high steps that Kasturi could hardly see. At the top was a narrow landing that ran the length of the rooms. Kasturi was jostled along this into a small angan and the two rooms beyond that she was told were hers. Eased onto a bed, her chin is held up, her veil thrown back for a better look.

'She *is* old. Must be sixteen at least.'

'Seventeen. And he chose her himself. Through an advertisement!'

'Nowadays they all want to decide who they will marry!'

'Look at her colour! So fair. Like a mem's.'

'Isn't she rather thin?'

'Her hair is straggly.'

'When a young boy sees, what does he know?' they laugh.

Her hands are seized, turned around and examined. Her bangles counted.

'Such few gold bangles! Look at the crude designs!' Kasturi shrinks a little more into her clothes.

'How can Sultanpur compare with Amritsar, after all!'

In the midst of all this someone sat down heavily and pulled her face violently onto her shoulder. 'She's just come, poor little thing! *Arre*, such looks, such colour has to have some fault or the evil eye will fall on my pretty one! As for bangles, what need does she have of fine bangles in a jeweller's family? She is a jewel, that is enough!'

'Your aunt-in-law is too good!' the women tell Kasturi. 'Look at her,' and the bride's chin is forced up a little more.

The chatter flows on. Food was brought and Kasturi fed by hands eager, impatient, loving, critical. Women and children are presented to her, their relationships spelt out. Her jewellery is carefully examined before being sent down to the shop to be sold. Her boxes are arranged around the room, in the next few days it will be decided what is to be used, what stored, and what given away.

Night falls, and Kasturi's husband is ushered in to her, thus beginning her long years of childbearing.

Now Kasturi's daughter was undertaking a journey to a similar destination in a train that chugged over the flat North Indian plain towards Amritsar. The landscape was silvered over by a shiny moon. Coyotes could be heard along with the hiss of the engine and the clank of the wheels. In their Inter-class compartment the bride and groom lay silently on their berths and tried to sleep.

Harish was uncomfortable. He dreaded facing his family, but then, he thought mutinously, hadn't he done his duty by all of them? Though he had married Virmati, no one could accuse him of precipitate action. Above him her hand dangled, moving gently with the rocking of the train. He could make out the ivory wedding bangles slipping over her narrow wrist in the dim light. It was a delicate hand with long thin fingers, and he stared at it like a talisman and felt himself soothed with the achievement of his desires. There was no need to touch, it was enough to see, and know that it was his.

Virmati was sure that neither parents nor grandfather would ever forgive her. The process of rejection that had started with Tarsikka would be completed. Let them damn her as they might, at least she had this new life. The thought of her husband, asleep in the berth below, made her eyes go soft with tenderness. She promised herself a blissful marriage; after all, they had gone through so much to be together. Her husband would be everything to her. This was the way it should be, and she was pleased to finally detect a recognizable pattern in her life.

She did not as yet think about the home she was going to. That, which she had fought and yearned for, was hers. Virmati was not overly given to speculation, despite an intensive education, and at that moment she believed herself happy.

It was early morning when the train steamed into the station. It felt strange to Virmati to follow the Professor into a tonga, and listen to him give directions for Moti Cottage. They rattled over the familiar roads, past the Company Bagh and towards the crossing. Here, instead of the customary left on Lepel Griffin Road, they turned right. Finally Virmati broke the silence.

'Do they know?' she asked.

'What?'

'That we are married, of course. What else?' Nervousness made her sound harsh.

'How can they know? I did not know myself.'

It had been a long time since Virmati had actually seen any of the Professor's family, a long time since they had been anything but abstract figures in their conversation. Now this seemed a lacuna in her imagination, these were people she would have to eat with, live with, be with, perhaps for the rest of her life. At the thought that, within a few minutes, she was going to their house, to be presented as his second wife, panic set in and her palms began to sweat.

The tonga drew up outside Moti Cottage, and the Professor paid the agreed price leisurely. Then he jumped down and held out a hand. Virmati took it reluctantly, her eyes on a little boy who was making mud houses on the raised platform in the garden. He saw his father and got up, shouting 'Pitu!' and then, seeing a strange lady with him, ran inside. Virmati could see the dark stain of mud and water on his flapping white kurta as he ran.

The Professor now waited to be discovered. He moved at a snail's pace towards the front door. By the time he reached the veranda, his wife had appeared, with her son, Giridhar, three, her daughter, Chhotti, ten, and her sister-in-law, Guddiya, thirteen, ranged solemnly behind her. Kishori Devi came last, with slow deliberate steps. Virmati could feel herself being taken in, the sindhur in the parting of her hair that the Professor had himself put, her tikka, the sari palla over her head, the red ivory bangles from her wedding ceremony. The wife's eyes wrinkled with tears, her mouth worked, and she turned, clutching at her mother-in-law for a moment, before stumbling inside. His mother looked at him accusingly. Harish responded by pushing Virmati forwards.

'Here, Amma,' he said, 'your new bahu.'

Kishori Devi's eyes blurred. She could make out the terrified look on the face beside her son's, but she had no sympathy for her. All this was her fault. If she had not gone after him, he would not have strayed, the family would not be torn apart now.

Kishori Devi turned away her head from the silent, stricken pair before her. She knew she could only bow before the inevitable. In her heart she could hear the wife's sobs, see her crumpled face, innocent and still young. Her life was over, she would be lamenting bitterly in some hidden corner of the house. She felt Ganga's claims deep within her, closely identified with her own. How could she possibly console her? Her grandson pulled at her sari. She picked him up, and Virmati could hear him whispering 'Who is this *gandi* lady? Send her away.' The grandmother, afraid that her son would hear, smacked the little boy's back lightly.

'Munna, come, come here,' said the Professor to his son.

Kishori Devi pushed Giridhar towards his father. The son resisted. Harish bent forwards and pulled him towards himself.

'Here,' he said. 'Your new mother.' He turned the boy's face to Virmati.

Virmati held out a shaking apologetic hand to caress him. Giridhar shrank into his father's shoulder.

'Come in,' said Kishori Devi finally, breaking into this exchange. She opened the door of the formal seating area, used for all the Professor's guests.

Virmati sat nervously on the edge of an armchair. Her sari palla slipped off her head, and revealed the thick glossy knot of hair at the nape of her neck. Her red marriage bangles clinked with tentative sounds. The Professor smiled at her reassuringly, before following his mother into the next room where most of them slept.

'Beta,' began Kishori Devi, 'at least you could have told me you were going for this reason. So suddenly to bring a new wife home! Is it fair to that one, or even this one?'

'What to do, Amma? It was unexpected,' said the Professor helplessly.

'This is marriage, not a game. You must have thought *something*.'

'Amma, you know how many years I have been involved. It is five years now. How long could she wait?' he said plaintively.

'Oh! So it is *she*! We don't matter any more!'

'There is no need to talk like that,' he replied, stung.

'What about your wife, your children?' demanded Kishori Devi. 'How could you do this to them?'

Harish got angry. 'I do what I can for everybody. But, to satisfy all of you, I am supposed to live my life tied to a woman with whom I have nothing in common. Who cannot even read. Who keeps a ghunghat in front of my friends.'

'She is a wife, not a showpiece,' retorted his mother sharply.

The son maintained a sulky silence, while Kishori Devi thought wearily that there was no use saying anything. What was done was done, and hadn't it been predicted in his horoscope, and hadn't she seen it coming these five years?

'We can move to a separate house, if it is going to be such a problem here,' said Harish abruptly.

Kishori Devi knew that he could not afford to keep two separate households. He had just finished paying back the debts she had incurred in sending him to Oxford, he was supporting his sister, and she herself had been living with him ever since he had come to Amritsar. She looked at his downcast, harassed face, and her expression softened. He was a good son. How was it his fault if he was caught in the trap of some shameless young Punjabi? Her daughter-in-law was exemplary, thrifty, efficient, industrious and respectful, but if this was to be her fate, what could anyone do? She would have to accept it.

Kishori Devi got up heavily and sighed. 'Go, go to your new bride,' she said with slightly less hostility than before. 'I have to manage this household, to which you have given such little preparation.' She moved towards the back of the house, while Harish thankfully escaped through the curtains of the bedroom to the front.

Ganga was hunched over her knees, with some vegetables before her, pretending, with slow distracted movements, to work. She was too experienced to cut her fingers like Virmati had the day before, but she certainly wanted to. Not only cut her fingers, but slash her throat. May the new bride slip in the blood, and break her head in the kitchen from where she had served him so long.

'Beti,' said Kishori Devi.

'Ji,' responded Ganga automatically.

Kishori Devi settled herself on a patla next to her daughter-in-law with many groans. '*He* Bhagwan, we are all in your hands,' she started, her eyes towards the ceiling. 'Who can predict anything, or decide anything on their own? Whatever happens is for some ultimate good, even if we do not understand it at the moment.'

A suppressed sob broke out from Ganga. Kishori Devi went on, 'In this life we can do nothing but our duty. Serve our elders, look after our children, walk along the path that has been marked for us, and not pine and yearn for those things we cannot have. Since our destiny is predetermined, that is the only way we can know any peace. Duty is our guide, and our strength. How can we control the things outside us? We can only control ourselves. Ganga, beti,' and here she turned tenderly towards her, 'you have been a good girl –'

The tears Ganga was determined not to show anybody, started pouring down her face. She buried her face between her raised knees, and wept as though her heart would break.

'What have I done,' she wailed, 'that God should punish me like this?'

'Beti,' pleaded her mother-in-law, stroking her trembling back gently, 'calm yourself.'

'You tell me, Amma,' demanded Ganga hoarsely, lifting her miserable, streaming eyes and runny nose to the older woman. 'Tell me, what did I do wrong?'

'Who can tell why this has happened? Something in his past life, or yours, or hers, or mine. We do not know, we cannot.'

Ganga continued to abandon herself to her crying, wiping her face with her sari end from time to time. Kishori Devi sat next to her patiently, waiting for her to stop. She had her arm around her, and pressed the younger woman close. Finally she felt Ganga quieten down.

'We have to accept – this is our lot in life,' repeated Kishori Devi sympathetically but firmly. There was a silence while her mind moved to the practical aspects of the problem.

The house had just one bedroom and it was shared by the Professor (on one bed) and Ganga, Chhotti and Giri (on the other). Kishori Devi and her daughter, Guddiya, used the veranda that bordered it. It was very inconvenient to give the Professor and Virmati this big room – it was right in the centre, and besides there wasn't enough space for everybody in the rest of the house. No, the only thing to do, would be to move Harish and his bride to the dressing-room, off the bedroom. It was small, but it did have a largish window, and presumably they wouldn't object. Then everybody else could share the big bedroom to keep Ganga company.

On summer nights all of them usually slept on the roof. Now two charpais would have to be brought down so Harish could sleep separately in the garden with his new wife.

'We have to decide about things,' she said, getting up. She knew her daughter-in-law would understand.

Meanwhile, 'Come and see your new surroundings,' proposed Harish pulling Virmati up by one arm and into the front garden, where he showed her the mausambi, mango, mitha and mulberry trees. Virmati was tired and depressed. Now that she was actually in Harish's house for the first time, she could see it was going to be difficult to live separately from everybody else. Where would she sleep, how would they manage? *Gandi*, wicked, go away, that is what the little boy had said. She looked at Harish, her brow wrinkled with unhappiness.

'I should never have married you,' she said slowly, 'and it's too late now. I've never seen it so clearly. It's not fair.' She faltered and stopped. How many times in their past relationship had she said those very same words. I should not, cannot, will not marry you. It will not be fair. And now she had married him, but the old words were still springing to her lips, so many futile noises in the air.

'It will take time to adjust, dearest. Naturally you feel strange. Come, let us go for a walk.'

She turned her aching feet obediently towards the gate. They went out and walked silently down the tree-lined road, towards nothing, away from a situation neither could escape. At the end of that road lay Virmati's old house. How far she was from it! Though married, she was dispossessed. Well so be it. She would walk tight-lipped, mute, on the path her destiny had carved out for her.

Thus ended the first day of her married life.

XXIII

That night, the newly wed couple made love quietly and furtively in the dressing-room before moving to their charpais outside. At each sound Virmati made, the Professor grew tense and whispered 'ssh' in her ear.

'Why do you keep saying "ssh"?' she asked angrily after a while. Even in Lahore he hadn't been so paranoid.

'They'll hear,' he whispered again and gestured to the doors, two feet away from their bed.

'Let them. After all, we are married.' His hand was over her mouth and she could hardly get the words out.

She felt his weight grow limp and heavy on her.

'What's the matter?' she asked, speaking as softly as she could to please him. She tried to turn his face towards her so she could see him.

'We can't rub their noses in the fact. It's difficult enough as it is,' he said in a low, troubled voice, all his attention focused on the other side of the door.

Next morning at five, as it was beginning to get light, the couple rose, and slipped out of their mosquito nets. The earth was still cool, the grass dewy, the birds were twittering and cooing. Virmati sleepily made her way to the toilet, the last room at the back of the angan. Coming out, she could see Ganga squatting next to the pump. She hesitated next to her bent back, but Ganga looked fixedly in the other direction, viciously spitting out bits of the neem twig she was using to clean her teeth. Quietly, on feet of lead, Virmati moved towards her husband in the garden.

Tea was brought on a tray by the mother and deposited silently on a little table next to them. Virmati felt uneasy, she was not used to being served by older women. Then, looking at the tray, she felt even more distressed. There was only tea there, no milk, which she was used to having in the mornings. How could her system be properly evacuated with this unhealthy stuff? She looked anxiously at the Professor.

'What is it, darling?' he asked affectionately.

'You know I drink milk in the mornings,' she said, pouting a little.

'And you know I drink tea. I thought you liked to drink tea with me.'

'Yes, once in a while, I do. But in the mornings I *always* drink milk. Otherwise I can't – you know – I can't –'

'Oh, I'm sure you can, if you try,' he replied.

'How would you like it if I asked you to change your habits?' asked Virmati, looking upset. She was twenty-five. How could her body relearn something as basic as this?

'I would do anything for you,' said the Professor, holding her hand.

'Except this.'

The Professor said nothing, but continued holding Virmati's hand with an abstracted air.

'So, I'm not to get milk,' she persisted.

'Let the dust settle down, sweetheart. If I start saying you want this and you want that, it will only make the whole thing worse.'

'And what am I supposed to do all day?' Virmati asked as she watched Harish get ready for college in the little dressing-room.

The Professor looked at her. 'You can read, you can visit your friends, or your family, if you like.'

'Family? I have no family left. After what I have done to them.'

'You have done nothing.'

Did he really think so, she wondered.

'I'll be back soon,' he continued. 'By lunch. And in the evening we'll go out.'

'Should I help Ammaji in the kitchen?' she asked doubtfully as she walked with him to the gate.

'Why bother yourself with these things?' replied Harish impatiently. 'You are a thinking girl. Let those others handle the housework.'

He smiled at her lovingly and left, leaving her to pass a day alone in a place where her pariah status was announced with every averted look.

Virmati thought she would feel better after she had had a bath, and got ready. She gathered her own dirty clothes and looked around for Harish's. They were not there. Last night, she had flung hers along with his, on the old wooden clothes-horse in the corner of the room, but now his seemed to have vanished. She searched under the bed, in his suitcase, and then made her way to the bathing room.

The small bathroom was swabbed dry, with two brass *taslas*, a brass bucket, and the big round wooden rod used for beating clothes clean stacked neatly in a corner. An alcove within the wall contained some reetha for washing the hair, and a thick, yellow cake of Sunlight. There was nothing else there. She must have done them, thought Virmati grimly, as she pounded her own lonely, single set at the pump. Later, as she was hanging them out to dry, she noticed his, right there in the middle of the line, between some small and some large female ones.

Virmati spent the morning in the little dressing-room, reading. By lunch-time the Professor had come home, and the mother served them lunch on the bed. Whatever little appetite Virmati had was taken away by the humiliation of being served before everybody else like a guest, and that too by her husband's mother, whom, in the proper course of events, she should be serving.

In the evening, Virmati went to the angan to bring the clothes in. The line was bare except for her own, hanging forlornly at the end. She took them down, and clenched her lip. She wondered drearily whether this isolation would continue till the end of her life.

'Harish, who washes your clothes?' she asked later.

'I don't really know. Amma, perhaps. Or she. Probably she. Why? How is it important?'

'She's still doing it.'

'Let her, if she wants to.'

'She picks them up, folds them, I imagine, gets them ironed too?'

'She's a housewife, you know. Somebody has to do these things.' Harish was getting irritated.

'What else does she do?'

'Oh, nothing much.' Harish gestured vaguely round the room. 'Just little small things here and there.'

Virmati was soon able to form a more accurate picture for herself. From washing his clothes to polishing his shoes, to tidying his desk, dusting his precious books, filling his fountain pens with ink, putting his records back in their jackets, mending his clothes, stitching his shirts and kurtas, hemming his dhotis, seeing that they were properly starched – Ganga did it all. His sleek and well-kept air was due to her. When his friends came, he sent orders to the kitchen that their favourite samosas – kachoris – pakoras – mathris should be made. Along with the khas, almond or rosewater sherbet of the season. All the effort of pounding, grinding, mixing, chopping, cutting, shaping, frying was hers. Was this Harish's idea of nothing much? And what about her? What kind of wife was she going to be if everything was done by Ganga?

The next day she tried to get up early, before the sun was up. She was going to wash Harish's clothes, come what may.

'Where are you going?' murmured Harish sleepily, as he heard the rustle of her getting out of bed.

'To have a bath. To get ready,' she replied.

Harish sat up in astonishment. 'Now?' he asked. 'But it's still dark. Why don't you wait till I've gone?'

'I'm used to early habits,' said Virmati primly.

'Of course, darling,' said Harish. 'But you get up early and be with me. After all, that is why we married. To be together.'

'Maybe so. But people have to bathe. Or is there some reason why you don't want me to have a bath?'

The Professor hesitated. 'Let them all finish,' he said. 'My mother bathes at five. Right after her toilet.'

'So, she'll be finished by now.'

'And then the children. Their school, you know.'

'I'll be before them.'

'And then her,' he said reluctantly. 'She has to bathe before she enters the kitchen.'

'So I have to be last,' said Virmati, sounding mean and petulant even to herself.

'But I also stay out of the way, sweetheart. Why do you want to make life difficult? Do you doubt that I love you with my whole being?' He tried to draw her next to him. She resisted.

Finally she said in a whisper, 'She continues to wash your clothes.'

'And?' asked Harish in surprise.

'And? And – what? As your wife, am I to do nothing for you? Just be in your bed?'

Harish looked upset. 'You are my other self. Let her wash my clothes, if she feels like it. It has nothing to do with me. I don't want a washerwoman. I want a companion.'

He took her hand, and they tip-toed inside to their dressing-room. Harish locked the door and, drawing her on to his lap, began to kiss her solicitously. 'I love you, Viru, I love you,' he breathed into her ear, 'and I always will.'

Later, there was a gentle thup-thup on the door, accompanied by the sound of a tray being put down. Virmati flushed with embarrassment. Their room locked, so early, everybody would know what they were doing.

'The tea has come. Why don't you bring it in?' said Harish, stretching and yawning on the bed.

Virmati got up and unlocked the door as noiselessly as she could. Even in her own room she felt raw and exposed. She put her nose a fraction of an inch outside.

There lay the tea-tray on a small table, covered with a spotless white napkin with white embroidery. Underneath was the delicate bone china with the faint green leaves and small pink roses. Virmati picked it up. This tray was really Ganga's. To think there had been a time when she had associated it with Harish, and only with Harish!

After tea, Harish wanted to go for a walk. That was his daily routine. 'I'll wait for you outside,' he said as he wrapped his cotton chaddor around himself.

'All right.'

'And do your hair,' he added.

Virmati edged past the bed, to pull her comb out of her suitcase. Her hair scattered easily, she knew, and now it was almost all out of her plait. Harish would not want her to appear untidy. There were so many eyes watching her.

The day passed, empty like the day before. Virmati had a bath, washed her own clothes – his, of course, were already done – read, and waited. The room she was in was so small, she had to force herself to concentrate on the print of her book in order not to feel stifled. Once or twice she went out. Giridhar, sitting on the bed with his grandmother, fell silent when he saw her, and looked at her with his big, round eyes. Kishori Devi, her face blank, muttered under her breath, as though each word was an effort, 'What do you want?'

She tried to be friends with Guddiya. After all, Guddiya was her sister-in-law. She was not affected, like the others, by her marriage.

'Guddiya.'

'*Hoon*, didi.'

'Let's talk.'

'I have to do my homework.'

'Shall I help you with your lessons? I used to teach girls just like you, you know.'

'Why aren't you teaching them now?'

'Right now, I am here. I want to teach you. Shall I?'

'I have to help Bhabhi in the kitchen.'

Guddiya always had something to do with either her mother, her bhabhi, or her bosom buddy, her niece, and soon Virmati had to give up with her. Though not overtly hostile, in the warring factions that existed in the house, she belonged to the opposite side.

She tried with Giridhar. He was young enough to be won over, she thought.

'Come here, beta,' she said, one day when no one was looking. The door of the dressing-room was open and he peeped in, his bright eyes curious.

Giridhar didn't move, just stared and sucked his thumb.

'Bad habit,' said Virmati instinctively. 'Take it out. Here, look.' She quickly drew some figures on a piece of paper.

The boy inched forward and stopped.

'Come,' said Virmati, 'here's paper, I'll show you how to draw.' If only she could teach Giridhar to come to her! She would have someone in the house.

'Giri . . . Giri . . .' Virmati could hear Ganga's voice calling sharply.

And then a pair of hands snatched the little boy up, scolding violently. 'What are you doing here? Who asked you to give trouble where you are not wanted?' A slap followed, loud wails, Kishori Devi's voice remonstrating, Ganga screaming, 'You want her to take him away too. One is not enough for that . . . that . . .'

Through Virmati's heart hammered, that is how they talk of me, think of me.

It was only when Harish came home that Virmati felt free to move about in the house in the areas that were considered his. The big front room, where he sat, read, listened to music and entertained guests, the front garden, and the little dressing-room where they slept. When Ganga saw her, she would turn her face away, or what was worse, would stare intensely at her, her eyes moist, her lip trembling, her big red bindi flashing accusingly. Occasionally, at night, she could hear both the women arguing, and sounds of Ganga crying.

Virmati paid a single visit home. One morning, when she felt she could bear the dressing-room no longer, she started off, her heart in her mouth. What would they say? On her arrival in Amritsar, she had written and told them she was married, but nobody had come to see her, not one brother or sister, not any of the young ones to whom she had practically been a mother. They were justifiably angry with her, but she realized she had transgressed, she was willing to make amends. Full of a desperate hope, Virmati shuffled down Lepel Griffin Road.

When she reached the house she walked around the back, where the cows were kept. Her thoughts were confused. At this point, she felt far closer to her family than she had before her marriage. Groping irresolutely around the compound, it did not seem possible that the link was severed. Those bricks and leaves were mingled in the blood and breath of her body.

Virmati entered the angan from the narrow entranceway between the cowshed and the house. She stood there silently, while the weak tears she despised gathered in her eyes. Only her mother would be at home this time, her mother who might be hating her.

'Get out of here! Why bother to come now?' Kasturi's harsh words hit Virmati, and she bent her head, hoping this was just the initial reaction, her mother was understandably hurt.

'Didn't you hear me?'

Virmati remained standing. Kasturi came closer.

'It would have been better if you had drowned in the canal than live to disgrace us like this!'

'Mati – Mati –' choked Virmati. 'I shouldn't have –'

'Why are you telling *me* you shouldn't have? What had I been telling you for five years? But no! You were too conceited to listen to anybody – why should you? – you are so *educated*, aren't you?'

Virmati looked at her mother's face. The eyes were cold and narrowed, the brows contorted with rage. There was implacable hostility there. She thought she should die with the pain she felt.

'I shouldn't have come,' she managed bitterly. 'I should have known what to expect.'

Kasturi grew red with rage. 'Yes, you should have, you shameless –' she shouted.

She took off her chappal, and raised it. Involuntarily Virmati ducked, and took the blows on her back.

'You've destroyed our family, you *badmash*, you *randi*! You've blackened our face everywhere! For this I gave you birth? Because of you there is shame on our family, shame on me, shame on Bade Pitaji! But what do you care, brazen that you are!'

Virmati was backing out of the corridor, trying to free herself from the brutal grip her mother had on her arm.

'Pehnji!' It was Paro's cry. Virmati turned around. There was Parvati pulling at her mother's sari. 'Mati, leave her – leave her, Mati, leave her.'

Kasturi turned on her furiously. 'Protecting your sister, are you? You think she cares for you? For anyone besides herself?'

Parvati's pale face became paler. 'Let her go, Mati,' she wept.

Kasturi pushed Virmati so hard that she fell. 'Who is keeping her? Let her go to her cheap, dishonoured home! Could we ever stop her? Go! What are you waiting for?'

Virmati got up and faced Kasturi. 'I'm going.' Her heart was breaking but her voice was determined, 'You will never see me again.'

With a last look at Paro, whose face was twisted with grief, she turned and left.

That afternoon, after lunch, the Professor turned to Virmati and asked, 'And what did you do in the morning?'

'Nothing,' she replied drearily. 'I did nothing.'

'You should go out more,' he said, looking suspiciously at her red eyes. 'See, you are losing your appetite with being so inactive.'

'It sometimes happens,' she replied.

'Well, see that it doesn't. I don't like to see my wife looking so listless. What will people think?'

Ever since the visit home, Virmati had felt blank and dazed. She didn't know how to tell the Professor what had happened, she could barely understand it herself. Were all ties between herself and her family broken? After all those years of care, concern, sacrifice, and responsibility? They had flung her away, what could he do about that? She looked at her husband, her lids heavy and swollen. 'I'll soon be all right,' she said.

'Good girl.' In his experience these troubles that women had with each other generally sorted themselves out. He patted Virmati lightly on the head as he got up to wash his hands and rinse his mouth.

In the big house on Lepel Griffin Road, Kasturi spent the rest of the morning brooding in the kitchen. Paro sat miserably on her patla next to her.

'Where has she gone, Mati?' she asked once.

'How should I know where that good-for-nothing has gone and died?' snapped Kasturi.

'But she was here,' ventured Paro timidly.

'She's chosen to leave us. How should we now know where she is?'

Parvati tried to digest this information. Didn't her sister care for her family any more? Why did people always say these things about Viru Pehnji?

'She's married – now are you satisfied? Betrayed us. Made sure we are all ruined. Understand?' continued Kasturi in a frenzy of bad temper.

'I understand,' said Paro appeasingly. She wished Pehnji had not gone like that. Weddings, she knew, were different. She remembered Indumati's marriage. It had been arranged quickly, but still there had been the excitement of dressing up, new clothes for everybody, all the more wonderful because of its novelty. There had been mehendi, lots of food, and guests, and staying up late, and with Virmati not there, hardly any supervision.

Gunvati's marriage last year had followed the same pattern, but on a larger scale. All the relatives had come. Her two mamas, mamis, cousins from Sultanpur, her masi and cousins from Pherozabad, her father's family, and all the important aunts and uncles from the Samaj, without whom no major function was complete.

And now Virmati was married away from home, beaten by her mother, and declared dead. What had happened?

'Was it really so bad, Masi?' I am trying to get my youngest aunt to remember the time when my mother married. It is an uphill task. My aunt has had arthritis for so long that most of her memories are those of physical suffering. The hands that lie folded in her lap are twisted, with the bones sticking out in peaks. Her face is dark and bloated with the cortisone she has had over the years, her hair is cut short, because she cannot lift her arms high enough to do it any more. Most of it has fallen out anyway, what is left barely covers the shiny, brown patches of her scalp.

Parvati looks irritated. 'She is gone, and you are asking about her marriage? Why didn't you wake up earlier, when she was here and could tell you herself?'

'She never talked much about herself, Masi.' I feel obliged to defend myself. 'When I asked her anything, she would say she remembered nothing. No matter how hard I pressed it was always the same answer.'

'She had such a sharp mind when she was young,' says Parvati Masi accusingly.

'My father used to say she had read a lot . . .' I offer this observation doubtfully, uncertain of its relevance.

'She was the only one in the whole family to get an MA, and that too from Government College, Lahore. But your father complained that she didn't remember anything – such a pity he said, that she didn't study systematically, when she has read such a lot. As though that was all to life . . .' Parvati Masi snorts.

'And?' I am curious to know what she thinks.

'Nothing. He was a learned man, a cultured man. He had a great deal of influence over everybody he knew.'

I drink all this in.

'But –'

'Yes?' I say encouragingly. Why has Parvati Masi fallen silent?

'Why are you asking me these things?' She turns abruptly towards me. 'Both dead and gone. I have nothing to say, nothing.'

I notice she has tears in her eyes. Now I am going to cry myself. Why is it so hard to get information about my mother, something about her life.

'What is there to say?' says Parvati less aggressively. 'He came to Amritsar like a person from another world. He dazzled his students. Small-town people. And then his glance fell on your mother. What chance did she have after that? She was a simple girl at heart.'

I hate the word 'simple'. Nobody has any business to live in the world and know nothing about its ways.

'A simple girl,' repeated my aunt, the harsh lines on her face softening.

One evening as Paro was playing at the back of the house, beyond the cowsheds, she thought she heard someone call her name, 'Paro, Paro!' twice in a voice very like her sister's. She looked around but could see no one. Panic-stricken, she ran inside. Had Pehnji killed herself because of what had happened, and come to haunt them as a ghost? Her mother had said Pehnji had been born to create trouble. Maybe one lifetime was not enough for all of it, and she was working out the remainder.

Next day, on her way home from school in the tonga, she saw Virmati standing at the crossroads where Lawrence Road meets Lepel Griffin Road. She looks very real, thought Paro with relief, maybe she isn't dead. The tonga entered the side gates of the house, and Parvati quickly jumped off. Then she ventured cautiously on the main road, and walked towards the crossing.

There stood Virmati, half-hidden by the trunk of a big neem tree. She looked sad and despondent, much like the woman who had come to the house a few days ago, and not like the loving sister who had cared for her ever since she could remember.

'Pehnji!' she cried, running towards her.

'Paru!' cried Virmati, 'Paru!' She held her arms open. Paro jumped into them and buried her face into the thin young shoulder.

'Pehnji – you are not dead, are you?' asked Paro.

'You also think I should be, darling?' asked Virmati hiding her face in Paro's neck. Just to hold her sister in her arms was balm to her tormented mind.

'No Pehnji – but they are talking like that. And last night I heard a voice that I thought was like yours, but there was nobody there, and I thought . . .' Parvati's voice trailed off.

'Oh, sweetheart, that was me. I was calling you. But you didn't hear.'

'I was so frightened.'

Just then, a tonga cloppered around the turning, and Virmati instinctively withdrew behind the tree again. It was adding to her humiliation to be seen talking to her sister on the road.

'Sweetheart, can you come to my house, just for a little while. Then we can walk back.'

'Your house?' asked Parvati.

'My house. It is down the road here.'

'How come?'

'My husband lives there,' said Virmati, holding Parvati's hand and walking down the road with her. 'Come, I will show you.'

'Why didn't you get married from home, Pehnji?'

Virmati didn't say anything. Paro looked at her face, and then said to cheer her up, 'Kailash is getting married soon, Pehnji. Then you will come?'

Virmati stopped walking. That was how far she had come from her family, how much they hated her. She was not to be invited for her own brother's wedding, when the furthest, most removed relative would be pressed to come. She started to cry.

'It's not nice, Pehnji, being married?' asked Paro after a while.

'It's very nice, darling,' said Virmati bravely.

'Then why do you keep crying? And Mati too, whenever she talks of you.'

'I miss you all. Very much. I think of you all the time. That is why I'm crying, although I am so happy.' Saying this, Virmati dabbed her eyes and blew her nose with the end of her dupatta.

Paro thought she had better not ask any more questions. People were always talking of the time when she would get married, but if her beloved Pehnji were anything to go by, all it produced was storms and tears.

By June it was very hot. The Professor's college duties were over, he had corrected his share of the exam papers as quickly as possible, so as to be with Virmati. For him, it was a joy to have her waiting when he came home, to have her eat with him, sleep with him, move with him in his rhythms through the day. He reflected how wisely he had acted. There was no more tension, no more indecision. Even the social opprobrium was not expressed openly. He glanced fondly at his wife as she lay with her eyes closed, next to him on the bed. Every part of her was desirable, even the perspiration that beaded her forehead and upper lip. He quietly got up to lock the door.

Virmati was not sleeping. Her lids were shut, and her thoughts were wandering. How much cooler it would be in the kothi now, how inviting in summer were the large gardens and sprawling orchards. And then the mangoes, lichis and loquats, the juicy mornings and evenings when they glutted themselves on fruit fresh from their own trees, and on the melons and watermelons brought home by their father every day. She could almost feel the taste in her mouth, almost hear the laughing and quarrelling of her brothers and sisters that accompanied these marathon eating sessions. Unconsciously her mouth half opened when Harish put his tongue in it and clamped it shut again.

Afterwards they lay together, hotter than ever.

'I've been thinking, Viru,' said Harish. 'Why not invite the poet here?'

'Here?' asked Virmati. Moti Cottage did not strike her as a

particularly inviting place. 'Where's the room for another person?' she asked tartly.

'That's not like you, Viru. You are usually so accommodating.'

'The place has to be mine to accommodate, no?'

'Yes, yes, but he is a very understanding fellow. Besides the last visit to him was so rushed.'

The Professor did not elaborate on the role the poet had played in his marriage. But he felt a debt to him and he wanted to show his appreciation by showering him with hospitality. His home was the poet's home, wherever he may be, and in whatever circumstances. He owed all his present happiness to him.

'However understanding, he needs a place to sleep in, and he needs the bathroom *sometimes*,' remarked Virmati in the middle of the Professor's thoughts.

'Viru, what's wrong with you? Why, we had the poet stay with us for two months when we were staying in your aunt's house, and there was even less space there. Don't you remember?'

'No.'

'Well, he did. Really, I'm surprised that you are talking like this.'

So was Virmati. When had actual accommodation ever been a reason for not having a guest over, or making him feel welcome? In the short time since her marriage she had learned to look at space in a new way; to define it and mark it, to think of what was hers and what wasn't in ways that would have been unthinkable in the fluid areas of her maternal home. She felt contrite.

'Call him,' she said. Another stranger in the house might even be a relief.

Harish kissed her lovingly. 'He will be delighted with you,' he said. 'Now I have a partner I can be proud of.'

'A woman's happiness lies in giving her husband happiness,' remarked Virmati, in a language she had learned long ago.

The languid summer drew on. With an acknowledged guest in the house, Virmati found it easier to bear her status as the unacknowledged one. She talked and laughed with the poet, and imagined her voice floating to those ears inside. She ate all those crisp, hot, spicy delicacies that Ganga so excelled in, she drank the thandai and sherbets, khus, rose, almond and kewra, that her hands had prepared. When the poet smacked his lips, she looked complacent along with her husband. Yes, their house was well known for its hospitality and generous feeding of guests. Other friends of Harish's would drop by in the evening. They would discuss the war, the prices, the fate of Hitler, the Allied invasions, the turning of the economy into war-based efforts for the British. Then they would drift to topics nearer home, the fines the hoarders and adulterers were having to pay in the marketplace, the shortages of paper they were all facing, the hilarious advice by the Government that they should use pencils instead of ink and spend endless amounts of time rubbing out what they had written so they could use the paper again. And they would discuss poetry. The poet would say a couplet in Hindi, and in a moment or two, Harish would toss it back to him in English. Then Harish would compose doggerel verse in English, and the poet would translate it into Hindi, and they would try and see whose invention would fail first.

Virmati was the only woman in these gatherings. It felt strange to be so isolated from women, but then, she told herself, she was taking her place beside her husband in the true sense of the word.

The tank at Moti Cottage was built along one end of the angan, a raised concrete triangle with a depth of about five feet. Four narrow, high steps led up to it. The broad tube-well pipe from which water gushed forth was balanced on the boundary wall.

This tank was the centre of the Professor's summer entertainments. He would fill it as often as possible, and spend the two days it took to fill inviting all his friends to bathe. Mangoes were bought and left to cool overnight. Later his guests would suck them while they swam. For Ganga, all this usually meant additional cooking, but it also resulted in having the Professor much nearer than usual – the tank was within earshot of the kitchen.

Virmati was the only adult female of the Professor's family to enter the water, fully dressed in salwar kameez, of course. Any hesitation she might have had about other men seeing her wet was ridiculed by the Professor, who was never tired of pointing out that he expected his wife to be a companion to him. Also, she thought, what else was there for her to do?

The beginning of July and the coming of the monsoon drove the poet back to Lucknow. It was no longer possible to sit pleasantly together in the garden, it was no longer possible to swim in the tank – and he wanted to be in time for the last of the Lucknow Dussehris. The ones in Amritsar were not as good.

As Virmati waved goodbye to the poet, she thought how much she was going to miss the distraction he provided. Every day her outsider position was trumpeted in thousands of ways that Harish could not even begin to notice. She was trying to become thick-skinned but she found it difficult.

That night there was a little too much salt in Virmati's lassi. She took hers thick, while the Professor took his thin and watery, several glasses to her one. As she drank, she made a face, and poured half a glass of water in it.

'What is it?' asked the Professor.

'Oh, nothing,' she said.

The next night, again too much salt. This time, she made a face, and left it.

'What is it?' repeated the Professor.

'Too much salt,' said Virmati.

'Are you sure?' In all his experience of Ganga's cooking, the Professor could not recall such an oversight.

'Taste it.' Virmati held out her glass to her husband. He took a cautious sip.

'It's not that much,' he said. 'Some people like a little more salt.'

'But I don't, and it used to be all right,' she said doubtfully.

She tried drinking it sweet, but there was a little too much sugar. Fool I was, to expect anything else, she thought.

She complained to her husband, who finally complained to his mother, who said, 'Ganga's work has increased of late, she is doing her best. If people could be understanding it would be easier on her.'

In the end Virmati gave up drinking lassi, or eating anything that her husband didn't eat, because hers was always too sweet, too salty, too fried, too soggy, too stale and, if possible, too dirty.

'Why can't I make my own meals?' she occasionally, hopelessly asked. She had once tried going into the kitchen, but there had been such weeping and wailing that day, such ritual rinsing of every pot and pan to wash away her polluted touch, that she felt intimidated. It was clear that not an inch of that territory was going to be yielded. If Virmati had the bed, Ganga was going to have the house. Even Harish said, 'Poor thing, you have me, let her have the kitchen.' Virmati looked at the domain of her kingdom and was forced to be content.

'So much is happening these days,' he said. 'Why don't you work as a volunteer at one of those agencies? Making socks and packing supplies for our wounded boys?'

'Anything to get me out of the house.'

'No. Anything to make you happy.'

Virmati did get a job, but not as a volunteer. Opposite AS College was a primary school, housed on the ground floor of an old building. As before, Virmati's qualifications made her an excellent choice for principal, while marriage added acceptability. Nobody thought much about her youth or beauty now.

At home, things continued the same. If it rained, her things were never brought in. If the dhobi came while she was in school, her clothes were never given, if she was late coming home, there was never any food kept for her. Whenever she tried to play with any of the children, it was 'Giridhar, come here. Don't disturb your new mother.' Or to Giridhar, when she was with the Professor, 'Go quietly to your Pitaji. See that you don't make your new mother angry. She is the one you have to love now.'

Virmati was reluctant to bring these instances to Harish's

attention, because somehow that never seemed to improve matters, only made them worse. And then some were so minor that talking about them exaggerated everything except the hurt.

Chhotti particularly carried on the battle. Quick and intelligent, she perceived things in a way that Giridhar never could. She was fiercely protective of her mother.

'Bhabhi, what's the matter,' she would say when Virmati was in earshot. 'Are you feeling sad? I'll look after you.' And she would sit in her mother's lap, and pull her sari palla over her eyes.

Once she said, 'See, I'm making you a bride. Then he will marry you.' That was when Ganga slapped her and told her to go and play with her new mother.

'Why don't you study with your mother, Chot?' Harish once suggested to his daughter. 'She has more time than I do, she will give you better attention.'

'I've always read with you. Besides, my mother has too much work,' Chhotti said meekly.

'Not her. Mummy.' Virmati was Mummy (which she hated). Her only consolation was that Ganga wasn't called Ma either, she was Bhabhi.

Chhotti didn't dare argue. But when she brought her books to Virmati she stared at her disconcertingly, was restless and inattentive. Thinking they might function better outside the house, Virmati offered to take her to school sometimes. But Ganga would have none of it.

'She's not happy with taking just one away.' Virmati heard raised voices in the big room outside, when she was lying down in the afternoon. 'She's starting on the children. First Guddi, then Giri, and now Chhotti.'

Then the plaintive tone that Virmati had begun to hear in her dreams, 'Oh, why was I born? Surely I committed a terrible sin in my past life, that this should happen to me? Please God, take me away quickly so this disgrace can end. Then she can have all of them.'

At this point the children would begin to cry, and Kishori

Devi would scold. 'Why are you talking in this useless manner, Bahu? If you talk of dying, what will these little ones do?'

Renewed sobs, by which time Virmati invariably started to feel like a murderess. But she didn't want Harish to think she was indifferent to his children.

'I could take all of them to the Company Bagh. They don't go out much. Or we could go to Darbar Sahib.'

What was said to Harish about this, Virmati never got to know, but the next time she suggested taking the three for an outing, he said, 'When I am free, Viru. Right now, your husband is too enamoured of your company to allow you to go without him.'

As the post-monsoon heat slowly passed and the beginning of winter came on, life in Moti Cottage became more cloistered. The nights were too chilly to sleep outside. And inside the little dressing-room, family conversations could be heard by an increasingly sensitive Virmati. Her ears would burn scarlet, her chest heave with misery at the implications of some of the things she overheard. There was no escaping them either. She sat with her husband in the drawing-room, but she did not always wish to be there when his friends or his students came.

The ache in her heart lifted as she sat in the principal's office in the Yuva Vidyapeeth. The school was something she could call her own, a place where there was harmony in the hierarchy. While she was working she felt herself strong, and when she thought about home, ideas of revenge came into her mind, which she slowly put into practice. Her only weapon was her husband, and she started to use that. She displayed her power over him, needling him about Ganga, so that he would lose his temper with his mother over her. She asked him to get sweets and savouries for her, and then magnanimously made him share them with the others. She would make a show of dressing up to go out with him, and since he loved flowers in her hair, asked him to tuck a sprig of jasmine or a rosebud into her bun, just as they were leaving. She even took care to dress better than she usually did, and smiled seductively at Harish at least once a day in full view of the others.

From time to time she wondered what was happening to her. But she would not allow herself to feel hurt. She loved everything about Harish, and that included his relatives.

She had no contact with anybody from her own family except Paro. Her visits she waited for eagerly, but from the initial once a week, they became closer to once a month. Virmati was almost scared to ask her why, and noted this change in herself sadly. She who had bossed her younger siblings around without a moment's hesitation, now afraid to ask Parvati something. Or was she afraid of the answer? She did not want to think about it. She did not want to think about anything.

XXIV

It is 1943, and the strain of being the colony of a warring nation shows. There are shortages and the costs of living are rising. In the market-place, bureaucratic procedures multiply. The government seeks to introduce fixed prices as profiteering spirals. The dark face of control emerges, the black market, hoarding, raids, and punishment. A grain merchant is fined a thousand rupees because he charged two rupees extra for a maund of rice. Even sweetmeats have been divided by Mr L. P. Addison, District Magistrate of Amritsar, into first-class ones, prepared with pure ghee, to be sold at Rs 2 per seer; second-class ones, prepared with vegetable ghee, to be sold at Rs 1–4 per seer; and still lesser khoya and and oil ones, to be sold respectively at Rs 1–12 and Rs 1 a seer. Contravention of this order is punishable under Defence of India Rule 81 (4).

For a mighty empire fighting for survival, battlefronts proliferate till even the counter of an Amritsari halwai is included.

It was taking traders time to get used to their shops being part of the battlefront. All the cloth merchants of the Amritsar old city market were suffering. They had to have their cloth inspected and stamped before they could sell it, and on top of that had to pay a fee for having this done. Uncertainty and suspicion hung thick in the narrow lanes. Recently, Ram Das in the textile gully had been arrested for refusing to sell georgette to a decoy sent by Mohammad Iqbal, Chief Inspector of Civil Supplies, Punjab. The same day he (Mohammad Iqbal) had discovered and sealed 90,000 yards of unstamped cloth. Well, why didn't this Chief Inspector hurry up and stamp all the cloth that the dealers requested him to? The prices of 20,000 varieties of cotton cloth and yarn were still waiting to be fixed.

In his shop, Suraj Rai watched his son driving a hard bargain over a gold transaction. The Muslim customer wasn't happy with the price he got, but he knew he had no choice. Kailashnath knew that too, and in the token haggle, despair and complacence were more than usually pronounced, because this was wartime, and times were bad, and everybody had better accept that, quick, quick, and not want more money for gold, especially when they had dues already pending.

As the Muslim left, he spat on the step. Kailashnath noticed, and cursed.

Suraj Rai said placatingly, 'He probably needs more money. Times are hard.'

'Let him go to Jinnah, then!'

When a drowned rat was found in the well behind the house, Kailashnath was sure it was the doing of the Muslim they had lent money to.

'Next time I shall charge an even higher rate of interest. That will show them.'

'But maybe he was not responsible,' remarked Suraj Rai.

'I do not put anything past these people. Who else would poison a whole well?'

Suraj Rai stared at that gesture of hate lying inside the bucket, next to the the well everybody was free to use, and didn't know what to think. Money-lending was part of the jewellery profession, and his rates were fair. Everybody accepted that. If this was any indication of times to come, he didn't want to live in them. In his personal life, in the life of the community around him, nothing was the same. Identities, loyalties, futures and nations were becoming a matter of choice rather than tradition.

And Virmati – would he ever get over that loss? Married life will cure her infatuation, the grandfather had said while urging his son to insist on an arranged match. But to force his daughter to marry someone against her will was contrary to the very fibre of his being. What could he have done? After she had been educated, she had gone her own way, changed from the caring, responsible girl she had always been, to a stranger, deaf to reason, threats or pleading. Even now, thinking of her, bewilderment and pain enveloped his heart.

It is December. The old bazaar area of the city was decorated with arch gates, and unusually crowded. It was the day of the Hindu Mahasabha Silver Jubilee celebrations, and there was to be a procession and speeches. Suraj Prakash was alone in the shop. Judging from the crowds, he could see that the afternoon procession was going to be an elaborate affair. The licence had been granted, the bazaar decorated with bunting and garlands on the main gateways. He thought he might go and hear Shyama Prasad Mukherjee, president of the Hindu Mahasabha. The man was said to be an excellent orator, and he generally spoke his mind, even against the British.

Then he heard rumours that the licence had been revoked because there was fear of communal disturbances. Suraj Prakash thought of the dead rat in the well, and knew that revoking a licence would do nothing to prevent communal disturbance, if the will for it was there. He decided to close the shop, in case there was trouble. There was no possibility of business that day anyway.

As he finished locking up, he heard the sound of volleys in the distance, and people running and shouting. He stepped down from the shop and found himself hustled away from it. By the time he had reached the end of his gully, there was confusion everywhere. He should have locked the shop from the inside and gone up into the old house, he thought, as he now tried to turn and go back. But the lanes were very narrow, and there were people running wildly in all directions. The crowds pressed in upon him. There were people screaming from the balconies.

'What's happening?' he shouted at somebody.

'Firing.'

'Tear-gas.'

'Baoji, run. It's dangerous here.'

He started running, his eyes darting everywhere.

Behind him, he could hear firing. Perspiration began to dampen his brow. His heartbeat was hammering in his ears, and he was gasping. Ahead of him, he could see some Angrez soldiers. One of them was shouting through a megaphone. The procession was cancelled. Everybody should disperse quietly without creating trouble. But where was the room to disperse? A noxious gas started to spread. His head began to throb, and he felt sick. He leaned over into the nearby gutter to vomit, when he was hit on the back of the head. He slumped forwards, his body coming to rest over the single step leading into a cloth shop.

The house at Lepel Griffin Road was crammed with people. Suraj Prakash was laid out on the floor of the drawing-room, his body covered with a white sheet, his face turning blue and dark as the hours passed and the mourners thickened about. There were Kasturi's two brothers and their families from Sultanpur, her sister and brother-in-law from Pherozabad, other aunts, uncles, and cousins, Taiji's family, everybody from the Samaj, and half the merchants and traders from the bazaar. Lala Diwan Chand sat, shrivelled and crumpled into deep old age, next to his daughter-in-law. As each new mourner appeared, a fresh burst of sobs ensued. Like waves, the sound of grief ebbed and flowed through the night.

Towards this crowd Virmati made her hesitant way. Like other close relatives, she was dressed completely in white, her dupatta covering her head. She took off her chappals slowly and deliberately on the steps of the veranda, beyond the jumbled mass of footwear. Those whose connection to Suraj Prakash had not been very intimate, and who were looking around, could see her from the edge of the room. She was very conscious of their curious gaze, and in reaction her own face stiffened.

She remained on the periphery, leaning sideways against the wall avoiding everybody's eyes. Tears streamed down her cheeks, and her crumpled face was half-hidden by the dupatta pressed against her quivering mouth. The vague idea she had of approaching her mother was given up when she saw how surrounded she was by her other children and her sons-in-law. They formed a protective ring around her with their arms, their hugs and caresses.

Kasturi sat next to her dead husband, almost as still, head bent, eyes closed. Her tikka was smudged across her forehead, her thick green khaddar sari crumpled. Her children were sadly aware that by tomorrow, their mother's red and green would be replaced by a white that would be hers till death.

All night the family watched over the body. The father of the corpse seemed insensible, the wife quiescent and unreachable. The relatives came to embrace their passive bodies in a steadfast stream.

To them: *You must be brave for the wife/father's sake. Sad, terrible, everything is God's will, who knows the future, we are in God's hands, you do not see such men nowadays, he was a saint, a pillar of his family, community, strength, prayers . . .*

Among themselves: *What a shock for the old man. Poor thing, her life is over. How young he was. Only fifty. How did it happen? Nobody knows. He was all alone. There was firing at the procession, and tear gas. Baoji always looked pale and tired. After what his daughter did he was never the same. All last year, so silent and listless. Everybody could notice. It killed him. Definitely killed him.*

The talk expanded to include the procession: *This would never have happened if the Sarkar had allowed the procession to go on. It was a peaceful procession. They should not have stopped it.*

It is only us they bother and harass. To the Muslims they turn a blind eye.

No. In fact the Muslims can assault us in broad daylight with no consequences. Look at Haripur.

Bap re. Attacking gurudwaras, looting and murder.

At Peshawar they sacrificed cows at Bakri-Id.

Chee-chee! The authorities turn a blind eye, of course.

This used to be our golden land. Sonar Punjab.

The Angrez support Jinnah. What can our Unionist Government do?

They say there will be an inquiry.

The next morning was the cremation. The Professor arrived in time to join the cortège. He was dressed in a freshly starched dhoti and kurta, with a white woollen waistcoat and a long white shawl flung around him. On his feet were white woollen socks. Virmati looked at him in astonishment. She had not known he possessed so many articles in white wool.

Harish made his way to various family members, pressed their hands and offered his condolences. Virmati, who had hovered like a pariah on the outskirts of her family circle the whole night, was amazed to see these condolences being received in the same polite manner in which they had been proffered. He was being accepted, what about her? How she longed to break down and weep in the midst of the circle that surrounded her mother. She wanted to be in its warm inclusiveness as well.

At the cremation ground, there was a silence as the last rites were performed over the body. The eldest son circled it thrice with a mutka of water which he spilled as he went along. The corpse was then shifted to the pyre, and heavy logs were criss-crossed on top. Straw was stuffed in between, ghee poured on top and all around. Kailash circled the pyre before lighting it with a flame at the end of a long bundle of straw. As the body burned, the family members silently kept adding ghee and sama-gri, the havan process that Kasturi had performed almost every morning of her life. When the last outsider had left, Virmati approached her mother.

'Mati,' she said in a low voice.

Her mother turned and looked past her.

Virmati, choked with sorrow, gazed at her mother mutely, misery and pleading in her eyes. Trembling, she tried to touch her.

Kasturi shook the hand off. 'Why are you here?' she managed, her eyes red and swollen. 'Because of you he died. Otherwise is this the age to go?'

Virmati turned an even more ghastly shade of pale. What was her mother saying?

'*Bas, bas*, Mati,' sniffed Gunvati, trying to calm her mother down.

Kasturi, convulsed with grief, turned on her. 'Would your Pitaji have gone if he didn't have to live with the disgrace his daughter caused him?' She covered her eyes with her sari and shook her head from side to side.

At the anguish in Kasturi's tone, Gunvati and Indumati closed in around her and gestured Virmati to leave.

The next day, Lala Diwan Chand expired. Since his son's death, he had been in a state of shock so severe it seemed to deprive him of all his faculties. After the funeral he lay down and never got up. At this news Virmati felt a hardening around her heart that she thought nothing could remove. Her father had died without forgiving her, and now her grandfather too. Not one of her family cared for how she felt. It was clear that they did not want to see her, or have anything to do with her.

She didn't attend any of the rituals that marked her grandfather's passing away. Harish thought it was his duty to go, as the eldest son-in-law, and he made a brief appearance at the Lepel Griffin house without his wife. He thought Virmati's refusal to accompany him very odd, but she was adamant.

'People will comment.'

Virmati smiled her new tight smile. 'Let them,' she said.

Harish did not try to persuade her. Since the deaths she had hardly spoken to him. Both Ganga and Kishori Devi had tried to be nice to her, but her frozen look remained unchanged. Anyone who came to sympathize, she refused to see. The family thought nobody should be allowed to grieve by themselves. It was unnatural, but they could not force her to accept condolences. It was almost as though she had gone mad. Forgotten who she was, who she was married to, and all her obligations.

After the pugri was tied on Kailashnath, and the pollution of her father's death wiped away by religious ceremonies, the Professor made love to Virmati every night. It was the only way of getting close, though the ardour was missing.

The morning Virmati retched in the angan was a happy day for him. She was pregnant, he was sure. Their union had borne fruit within her womb, and now she must be true to her nature and turn her attention to him and the child.

Out in the angan, crouched next to the pump, Virmati was staring at her vomit. She moved the handle slowly, and watched the water wash the sluggish, stinking mass down the small hole in the wall, into the open drain next to the house. As she watched she felt sick of her body, which as usual asserted itself when she was most unprepared. Now it had taken whatever small shred of privacy she had left. The whole household could hear her. The whole household could put two and two together.

'What is the matter with Mummy?' Giridhar was asking his mother. 'Is she sick?'

'Nothing that concerns us, beta,' was Ganga's reply.

'Why is she throwing up then?'

'Women do that, silly,' said Chhotti. 'Even Bhabhiji did this when she was having you.'

'No she didn't.'

'Yes she did.'

'No.'

'Yes, Bhabhi, didn't you?' Chhotti turned to appeal to her mother.

'Don't trouble me,' retorted Ganga sharply, a look of fear crossing her face.

'Yes, you did. I remember. Now Mummy is doing it.' Chhotti giggled as she said this. 'What fun!'

'Bhabhi, look at what Chhotti is saying,' whined Giridhar.

Ganga slapped her daughter and shouted, 'Let me see how you laugh when some woman's baby comes and takes your father away from you.'

Chhotti stared at her mother, tears coming into her eyes.

Giri started to cry, 'I don't want a baby, I don't want a baby.'

'Don't be upset,' said Ganga silkily. 'What can you or I do? Now your new mother is going to provide you with lots of brothers and sisters and you must be very good and share everything with them.'

By this time Giridhar's cries had reached a crescendo, and Harish looked testily from his room to silence them.

Virmati's morning throwing-up at the pump continued. The children stared at her from the veranda with bland faces. Virmati felt they almost made it a point to be there. Her sharp ears could hear them talking about *gandi* mummy.

Kishori Devi meanwhile changed. Without saying anything, she substituted Virmati's morning cup of tea with a glass of hot milk, with either almonds or honey added to it. Then, almost every day there was a milk sweet with the evening meal, kheer, rubri, rasgulla, shrikhand, rasmalai – things that Kishori Devi especially made. There was even talk of keeping a cow.

'Beta,' said Kishori Devi to her son. 'Bahu should sleep with us.'

Harish looked wary. 'Why, Amma?' he asked.

'In her condition it is best,' said Kishori Devi enigmatically. 'I will move her pillow, sheets and quilt onto my bed.'

'Your bed?'

'Virmati is not some kind of maharani who needs a separate bed all to herself.'

Men were supposed to understand sexual taboos, but Harish had been in England so long that she elaborated for his benefit, 'For the health of the child.'

'But Amma, I do not see the need,' said Harish lamely.

Kishori Devi replied sternly. 'The shashtras say that a woman carrying a child must be governed by pure thoughts, loose clothes, sweet cooling liquids, milk . . .'

'It is still too early, Amma.'

'No, it is not. Her thoughts should be pure all the time. The effect will be seen in the child, the flesh and blood of your father.'

Harish was defenceless before these oblique references.

'I will recite the Gita to him every night,' went on his mother.

'By the time he is born his sanskars will be very good.'

'Amma, this might come as a shock to her.'

'Let her learn our family ways as soon as possible. No sacrifice is too great for the coming child,' stated Kishori Devi mournfully.

'But Amma –'

'With Ganga it was the same. I cannot make distinctions between my daughters-in-law.'

'No, no . . . of course not,' said Harish looking confused. What was his mother talking about? He had no idea of how Ganga's last pregnancy had been spent, of how many Sanskrit slokas his mother had recited to the unborn foetus, on which bed she had spent her nights, what she ate, what she drank, what she thought.

'So that is settled,' said Kishori Devi, getting up, muttering '*Hai* Ram, *Hai* Ram,' and groaning with every limb she straightened. She made towards the kitchen, her hand pressed to her back, as her son stood and watched, aware of her in a way he had never been before.

Virmati was appalled. Her mother-in-law had barely spoken to her in all the months she had been in Moti Cottage, and now she wanted to sleep with her. Her flesh prickled at the thought. Was she such a personless carrier of her husband's seed?

'How can you expect me to do such a thing?' she whispered bitterly in the low tone she now almost automatically used when they were in their room together.

'It is her concern for your baby,' pleaded Harish.

'What about me? How do you think I am going to feel about the whole thing? Did you say anything about that?' demanded Virmati.

'I thought you would be pleased, her showing such concern, reciting the Gita to you every night, when she is tired. She is old, you know.'

Virmati's face assumed a pinched look, the lips thinned and straightened, the eyes glassed over as though they could not see. Even her cheeks seemed to fold inwards.

'This shows great progress on Amma's part,' went on Harish. 'She is struggling to reconcile herself to reality. With our child, you will be accepted in no time.'

That night Virmati lay stiffly next to her mother-in-law. The old lady sang some slokas in a low undertone. From time to time her voice would rise, and she would snake a claw-like hand onto Virmati's abdomen to make rotating motions on it. The first time this happened, Virmati almost jumped out of her skin with surprise and horror. After that she lay rigidly, the slokas grating on her ear, tensely apprehensive of the moment that hand would touch her again. Cramps started to shoot across her back and belly. After Kishori Devi had croaked herself to sleep, Virmati lay on her back, her hands folded over a still flat stomach. She tried not to breathe too deeply. Her mother-in-law smelt of age, of sickly, heavy coconut oil, of foul, sweet breath. Resignedly, Virmati got up to vomit and then crept back to the dressing-room.

Every night for the next few weeks, Virmati would hear slokas in Kishori Devi's bed, and then vomit her way back into her own. With an aching abdomen, and a lingering sour taste in her mouth, she would try and sleep. In the day she looked wan and hollow-eyed.

'Soon this vomiting period will be over,' said Kishori Devi to her son. 'Then she will not have to get up in the night.'

'I hope so, Amma.'

'My poor boy,' said Kishori Devi looking at him with pity. 'Don't worry. First pregnancies are like this. And with boys it is even more difficult.'

'How do you know it is a boy?'

'She has the signs. I can just see it in her face and movements, the shape of her belly, the things she craves.'

Harish was not aware of Virmati's craving anything. 'What does she want?' he asked.

'Sweet, cold things,' said Kishori Devi categorically.

'I'm not so sure she actually wants . . .'

'That is what women should be given in the first three months,' interrupted his mother. 'Then Shashtika rice with curd in the fourth month, with milk in the fifth, with ghee in the sixth. Even her enemas should be of milk and ghee.'

'I don't think Virmati needs an enema.'

'We shall see. The body should be clean and pure at all times. Sons cannot be born just like that.'

I will have a girl to spite her, thought Virmati.

It's a girl, thought Ganga. She can't keep away from sour things, though Amma refuses to see that. It wasn't like that when I had Giridhar. God will make sure it is a girl. And, from once a week, she started fasting twice a week, for the long and prosperous life of her husband.

Virmati had completed three months of pregnancy when she woke in the middle of the night convulsed with cramps. Thick, dark red, rubbery clots dotted the inside of her salwar. Bent double with agony, she managed to get up, fold some old cloth into a long, thick pad and tie it around herself with a string. In no time at all she could feel the blood soaking through. Alarmed, she lay down, clenching her thighs together, hoping that if she was very careful and did not move, the cramps would go away. Perspiration dripped onto the sheet from the side of her face. Through the spasms ran incoherent thought – they mustn't know – mustn't come to know.

Virmati's moans woke Harish, whom prolonged abstinence had made restless.

'What is it, darling?' he asked tenderly. He put his hand on her face and felt the perspiration.

'You can't be hot,' he exclaimed as his fingers travelled swiftly over her, down to her salwar, and inserted themselves between her legs.

Inert and exhausted, Virmati let him do what he liked.

Harish's hand encountered a wet and soggy mass. He quickly withdrew it and put on the light to see blood everywhere. He looked at his wife. Why hadn't she said anything? He turned her towards him. Even through the pain he could see the inflexible, resolute expression on her face.

'What's happening?' he asked.

Virmati said nothing. Tears trickled from the corners of her eyelids as Harish went to call his mother.

'*Hai* Ram!' exclaimed Kishori Devi when she saw Virmati. By now the blood had begun to soak the sheets. 'Why has she let it go so far? Beta, call the doctor. Hurry, nothing should happen to the baby.'

Ganga stood in the doorway and watched.

The doctor came, gave Virmati an injection, pronounced the baby lost, and made sure the miscarriage was completed in the hospital in sterile conditions. Released the next day, Virmati came staggering home to a durrie spread on the string bed. The mattresses had all been removed by her thoughtful mother-in-law, who assured her son that Virmati would not be able to bear the sight of bedding that had been so polluted by vaginal bleeding.

'I will rip open the mattress, wash the cotton and the cover, get it beaten, stuffed, and stitched again.'

Harish stared mournfully at her.

'So soon after her father. Some women are weak by nature.'

Virmati became better, but not less dull. One abortion and one miscarriage. She was young, she told herself, years stretched out before her. Years of penetration, years of her insides churning with pregnant beginnings.

God was speaking. He was punishing her for the first time. Maybe she could never have children. She had robbed her own womb three years earlier, just as she had robbed another woman of her husband. Ganga's face, swollen with hate and fear, had followed her everywhere, the venom concentrated in the gaze of her evil eye. Maybe that was why Kishori Devi had taken all those precautions.

That brief first time she had been in perfect health, but, preoccupied with shame, she had violated her body. The time for a

246

child lay in the future. Now she felt she was left with nothing. Her job could not sustain her, and flaunting Harish seemed a pathetic gesture, signifying her emotional poverty.

Summer came, and this time no poetic distraction to enliven the company. Harish was at his wits' end. It had been over a year since their marriage and all that had made Virmati so dear to him seemed to have vanished completely. In her place was a block of wood, whose only response to the world was the passive oozing of tears. Even his most ardent caresses could not arouse her.

'Why not, darling, why not?' Harish started being more insistent.

'It hurts.'

'I'll be gentle. It won't hurt you, I promise.' Then, when she said nothing, 'Don't you love me any more?'

Eventually she submitted to his caresses, but that was all it was, a submission, and he was too sensitive not to mind.

Ganga's tread grew lighter in the house, her stares less malevolent, the scolding of her children less strident. Her husband had married the girl he had run after for five years – the witch – and much good it had brought him. The sindhoor in her parting shone brighter, her bindi sparkled on her clear white forehead.

Virmati silent and withdrawn, paled in comparison.

How stubborn she is, thought Harish. After her father and grandfather, she has not been the same. Further study will improve her. It was not like this when she was studying in Lahore. There she had a proper respect for our relationship.

Thus was born the idea of sending Virmati off to Lahore to do an MA. Harish chose philosophy for her subject. It would be a civilizing influence and induce a larger perspective on life. Part of his extensive library was devoted to European, British and Hindu thought, and Virmati could use those very books. They would read together, like they had done long ago, before things had become messy and complicated. Virmati and he had been at their happiest when he had been teaching, and she learning.

Virmati acquiesced. That is, she said nothing when Harish suggested the idea to her.

Ganga rejoiced. He was sending her away. True, she was going to study, and was not being returned to her mother's, which would have been a clearer statement, but still, the house would be all hers. Just like it used to be. Poor Virmati. What woman would want to exchange a home for a classroom?

XXV

It is now 1944. On the war front, the Allies are slowly winning. India continues to feed this effort, with money, goods and manpower.

On the national front, after the 1942 agitations, most of the Congress leaders are still in jail.

Gandhiji is released unconditionally on 5 May, 1944 at 8.00 a.m., after twenty-one months in prison, for medical reasons. Reports of his health absorb the nation. His blood vessels are rigid, the pressure fluctuates, his heart is enlarged, his condition anaemic.

Segregation rears its ugly head. In Rani ka Bagh, a new locality proposed in Amritsar, ownership is going to be restricted to Hindus and Sikhs. In Sind, Hindus are not going to be allowed to buy property. In Lahore, two educated gentlemen refuse to continue eating the food they had ordered, or even pay for it, when they discover the bearer, as well as the caterer, are Muslims.

The word Pakistan appears more and more often in the newspapers. The Sikhs are agitated. They will resist it to the death.

Any form of assault on women is still a serious matter. In Lahore, three college students are tried and found guilty of outraging female dignity. The goonda element in the city is deplored.

Wheat continues to be in short supply. People who can afford to are told to eat meat and vegetables, leaving the grain for the poor. The language of crisis is used about food.

The Japanese invasion is a threat. In Kohima the devastation that the Japanese caused is used to fan fear of the outsider, to associate our interests even more firmly with those of Britain. This strategy is not always successful, but the enemy is still the foreigner, and not the neighbour turned stranger overnight.

The atmosphere of these years is heavy with expectations.

When the war is over . . . , when shortages are over . . . , when prices are back to normal . . . , when the Congress leaders are out of jail . . . , when the Unionists finally show the League what's what . . . , when the British go . . . , when India belongs to Indians.

Virmati and Harish are on their way to Lahore. Virmati is still young enough to feel that the unhappiness of the past could vanish from her life, like the thick black smoke dispersed from the train into the damp monsoon air.

The resolution concerning Virmati's further learning has been preceded by bitterness, because family money was limited, and why should it be wasted unnecessarily on the higher education of a married woman? Ganga, who couldn't wait for Virmati to leave, resented her studying the most. She couldn't read, and Virmati was to do an MA! If that much attention had been given to her, she would not be in the position she was in today. She had taken her duties as a wife seriously, looked after the house, children, in-laws, and husband's salary, but she had got no recognition for her hard work and years of sacrifice.

The night before Virmati and Harish left, Ganga looked at herself in the mirror. She traced her features with her fingers, watching the lines they made in her smooth skin. She had good eyes, a small nose with a winking diamond pin, a fair skin, the pores a little large but the colour clear. Her lips were stained orange with paan, and her lower teeth had a gap dating from her pregnancy, but still there was nothing very repulsive about her appearance.

Now that the witchcraft had worn off maybe her chance would come. Perhaps at night – after all, how long could a man remain alone? Maybe now he would see the uselessness of an educated wife. She smiled at the short while Virmati had lasted in the house. She herself would never clear the field for anyone.

Virmati's stay in Lahore was going to be done cheaply. A sister of a friend of Harish's, whose husband was away in the INA, had a small house in Krishna Nagar, not very far from Government College. A paying-guest arrangement would provide security and be economical.

As Virmati sat in the house in Krishna Nagar, and let her eyes wander over the slightly shabby furniture, over Leela, the sister, friendly but not very educated, she felt that this is what she might have been had the Professor not entered her life. Married in a slightly shabby house, with no books or music, no paintings on the wall, no air of culture, no sense of worlds beyond the here and now. Although the lady looked happy enough, she knew there were higher things in life.

Virmati's life in Lahore was isolated. She was married with a husband, a co-wife and two stepchildren. She had had one abortion and one miscarriage. These barriers divided her from her fellows. She read, she studied, she spent time in the quiet hush of the library with its gallery running round, surrounded by books in wooden cupboards that stretched to the ceiling. At lunch-time she ate her solitary meal of paranthas, sabzi and achar sitting on the lawns and watching the traffic swirl around the district courts below. Sometimes the other girls strolled over to Anarkalli to shop or eat, but Virmati, acutely conscious of the need for frugality, seldom joined them.

Virmati's friend in Lahore, what about her? What about Swarna Lata? They met. They exchanged news about each other, the easy part of this reunion.

'Marriage. MA, Philosophy.'

'A baby boy. Rationing centres opened. Price control offenders and penal servitude.'

Virmati's negligible words became drowned in what Swarna Lata had done, ending with, 'Come and demonstrate with us against the Draft Hindu Code Bill next Saturday outside the railway station. Men don't want family wealth to be divided among women. Say their sisters get dowry, that's their share, and the family structure will be threatened, because sisters and wives will be seen as rivals, instead of dependents who have to be nurtured and protected. As a result women will lose their moral position in society! Imagine!'

As Swarna talked, Virmati's old feeling of being left out grew. Swarna hadn't changed. Obviously her activities did not threaten her family structure. The Draft Hindu Code Bill. What did removing inequalities mean? Would a new Hindu Code remove the inequalities between two wives? From Ganga's point of view, she was the one with too many rights, the one with monopoly. Their husband's semen should be shared. Virmati began to giggle hysterically to herself. Swarna Lata stared.

Virmati quickly looked at her friend, her mouth slackening into wistfulness. She had to think of her husband's good name, how he would appear to others, how his absent ears would react to any confidences she might reveal.

Lamely she said, 'I wish I could come, Swarna, but I'm married.'

'So? I'm not asking you to commit adultery. We have plenty of married women working with us. I'm married, aren't I?'

Virmati looked at her hands. In Leela's house she helped with the cooking. An old burn scar, long and brown, lingered on her right thumb. A ring that Harish had given her, a ruby set in a round of small pearls, had grease stuck in the crevices. Hands like hers, should they be raised in sloganeering? Would Harish like it?

'It's important that our voice be heard, Viru,' pressed Swarna Lata. 'Some men are planning to demonstrate against it. Won't you add your strength to ours?'

'If you think I can make a difference,' said Virmati politely.

She didn't go, though. And Swarna dropped out of her life.

At weekends, Virmati sometimes amused herself by taking out Leela's offspring, Kiran and Kaka. She preferred to do this rather than make the hour's journey to Amritsar. There was a lot to see in Lahore, and by now she was adept at locating beauty. At the mosque of Wazir Khan, she directed Kiran and Kaka's gaze to the repetitive patterns on the four minarets. She admired the extensive inlay work in hushed whispers. She pointed out how the roof, the walls, and the pillars, every inch coloured intricately in vegetable dyes, reflected the earth and the sky in ochre, yellow, white and pale blue.

On the way home she bought the children kites, and helped to fly them on their terrace.

Another time she took them to Shalimar, built by Shah Jahan in 1652. They wandered around the gardens, admiring the pools of water, and the wavering single-spiral fountains, arising out of red stone flowers.

In the central pavilion they stared at the wooden ceilings, covered with meena work, dulled over the years, and at the mirror reflecting their images. And down below there were the marble niches where diyas used to burn behind a curtain of falling water.

She grew especially close to Kiran. Some of her most intimate moments in Lahore were spent with the girl. She was reminded of Shakuntala and herself in Dalhousie. Kiran too followed her eagerly about the house, asking her about her college, waiting to grow up so she could do all the things Virmati did, and acquire the gloss and patina Virmati had achieved through Harish, education, work, marriage and suffering.

Harish did not like Virmati frittering away her energy, seeing the monuments of Lahore with Kiran and Kaka. They were bright children, he conceded, but she was mother to two children in Amritsar, and sister-in-law to someone who was practically her daughter. So why was she wasting her weekends in Lahore, when she could be showering her family with the sunshine of her presence?

For the time being, however, Harish only made his displeasure known, he did not insist on any action. The charm in travelling to meet Virmati in another city lent romance and freshness to their relationship. As though they were lovers once again, with the unhappy time wiped out.

They would often go to visit Syed Hussain. In all those furtive visits to the guest room, Virmati had never seen the inside of his house. Now that she was legitimate, she could enjoy its atmosphere of privilege. Everything in it spoke of taste and refinement, the English books, the stack of 78 rpms, Bach, Mozart, Beethoven, Schumann, Chopin, Tchaikovsky, in faded blue-and-cream dust jackets, the shinning silverware around the plates at mealtimes, and the two large, sleek dogs (Faustus and Marlowe) that padded elegantly around the place.

Virmati sat on the margin, heard Harish and Syed talk, and marvelled at their flow of words, she who had no words at all.

With his friends, or with Virmati alone, the war dominated Harish's conversation.

'Their days are numbered, Viru, their days are numbered.'

'The Allies are nearing Berlin. They definitely can't last for more than a few days now. After so many years! I can't believe it.'

'Hitler is hiding in the forest caves, they say. Coward. Didn't think twice about sending his own army to its death on the Russian front. Thank God our leaders are not like that.'

Why does he care so much? thought Virmati. It's not our war. God knows the amount of money, arms, ammunition, not to mention soldiers, we have pumped into it, but, still, how can it be our cause when they imprison us here?

'They are fighting in the streets now.' *At least their fighting is open.*

'All Berlin is on fire.' *At least it's a fire one can see.*

'Hitler is dead!' 1 May, 1945.

'Goebbels has committed suicide!'

'Total Nazi collapse!'

'Five hundred thousand Germans surrender!' 5 May.

'One million Germans surrender!' 6 May.

'It's over, Viru! It's over. War in Europe is over.' 8 May. *Thank God!*

'Now it's our turn next. Now they will have no excuse. Cripps had given a commitment. At the San Francisco Peace Conference the eyes of the world will be on Britain. There will be pressure put on her to recognize our sovereignty. After all, a fifth of the world's population is still in chains, groaning under its yoke, condemned to servitude. That is something that can cause the Allies a lot of political embarrassment given their anti-Fascist, anti-imperialist rhetoric during the war. No, Britain is now finished, Viru, finished. They have no power left, even in India. Look at the mess they are making of the food distribution. Shortages everywhere. All man-made.'

And me, thought Virmati, what about me? The war, or the end of it, rather, seems to have gone to his head. Suddenly he is transformed. He becomes visionary. His eyes are sparkling, his hair is flung about with passion. I feel so utterly left out, so utterly cold. Will there be any change in my life, I wonder?

In the holidays Harish's pressure on his wife to come home increased. He had become principal of AS College, and it was increasingly difficult for him to come to Lahore. Virmati was evasive. She had a rival whom she didn't want to see.

'What has suddenly happened to you? You are getting very fussy. I can't come here every time, you know.'

'But you like coming here.'

'Not this often. The area is too dirty and congested. Remember the tank last year.'

'I remember many things about last year.'

'I can't afford to keep you in Lahore this summer. It's two months' board and lodging for no reason.'

'I don't mind going on a holiday with you, but I will not come home.'

'Leela quite agrees with me. She thinks it better if you return.'

I play with the idea that she must have refused. That she could have said, I'm my own mistress. I will relate to you with dignity or not at all. None of this hiding and whispering and keeping my voice down and struggle over who is going to wash your underwear and who is going to clean your shoes. None of this for me.

She was, after all, a woman who had defied her own family for many years.

Perhaps the words were at the back of her mind, teasing her tongue with their shadowy sounds. She looked for an opening, but she looked timidly, for though she had escaped the marital home, an essential part of it, the marital bed she carried inside her head, and its burden was heavy. Its rumpled sheets, and tell-tale stains did much to ensure that her voice remained soft when she spoke.

In the end, my mother couldn't have mentioned that she had more of a home with Leela than she did with him.

She couldn't have, because her eyes looked confused and her face went blank whenever her daughter demanded a story about her Lahore days.

She couldn't have, because when I grew up I was very careful to tailor my needs to what I knew I could get. That is my female inheritance. That is what she tried to give me. Adjust, compromise, adapt.

Assertion, though difficult to establish, is easy to remember. The mind goes soft and pulpy with repeated complying.

'*Jeeti raho*, beti,' said her mother-in-law coldly as she bent to touch her feet. 'May you be the mother of a son,' she added as Virmati straightened, her travel dust still upon her, the brightness of the fabled city in her cheeks.

Ganga and she slid glances past each other.

Giridhar and Chhotti came reluctantly to touch their Mummy's feet.

Virmati found the dressing-room the best place in the house after all.

Harish tried to make sure she spent her time profitably. He didn't want her to fret over the family situation. He wanted to see her as happy as she had been in Lahore.

'Here, do this while I'm away.' He waved marked portions of her textbooks at her, before he left for college on his bicycle. 'We'll discuss them when I come home.'

Virmati took the books with a sigh. 'I know these bits,' she said, flipping through the pages uninterestedly.

Seeing her lack of enthusiasm, Harish added, 'It refreshes the knowledge in my own mind when I read these books with you. I could never do something like this with *her*.'

Virmati flushed with pleasure, and turned to her book with a glint in her eye.

She then spent the morning diligently copying the main points of the text in her notebook. She tried to memorize what she had copied, but it was hard work. She didn't see the point of what she was learning.

She hated philosophy, although Harish called it a noble subject. It was dull, abstract and meaningless, but studying it was her only means of escape. She wished Harish had thought another subject suitable for her. She also wished it was not such an uphill task, being worthy of him.

When it was time to go back to Lahore after the summer holidays, Virmati was secretly relieved.

Harish looked downcast parting from her.

'It is so lonely without you,' he said sadly, sitting on the unmade bed, watching as she bustled about, packing her suitcases.

'Our meetings in Lahore are much nicer,' she said, caressing him with more fervour than she had during her entire visit.

He smiled at her, but was silent during the trip to the station.

Monday, 5 November 1945. The INA courts martial open at Red Fort, Delhi. Pandit Jawaharlal Nehru is the lawyer for the defence.

Leela's family is deeply involved in the whole issue. Leela is distraught, her husband is in the INA, his reputation and future are at stake. Patriot or traitor? Why should these things always be left to the people in power to decide? Kiran and Kaka feel their reputation is at stake too. What can they do to help their absent father?

12 November is INA day. When Kiran reached school, assembly was going on. The principal was making rousing speeches. She talked about the INA, about the protests that were sweeping the country, about how the issue should be kept alive until the accused were released without a stain upon their honour. She then declared the school shut in order to commemorate INA day.

Kiran conferred with her friends. 'We must do something,' she said slowly. In the Lahore of the 1940s, it was not hard to decide what to do.

'We must have a procession,' they decided. 'Go from college to college and make everybody join us.'

Yes, yes, they must.

And the schoolgirls marched, marched through the streets of the fabled city, shouting

Lal Quila tor do
Azad Fauj chhor do,

ending with 'Subhash Zindabad', though he had vanished, and nobody knew whether he was dead or alive.

The spirit of the girls flowed out in aggregate voices, shouting to the students from Sanatan Dharam College for Women, Khalsa College for Girls, and Dayal Singh College to come and join them, and the procession grew and grew, until imperialism decided it was threatened.

'Who are your leaders?' asked the Punjab Police, as they bore down upon them.

'Nobody. We ourselves.'

Obviously, this was not to be believed. The insurgents were now using children to foment disturbance, thinking that their sex and age would protect them. They must be taught a lesson. They must be charged.

'Shame, shame!' cried the girls.

'Toadies of the British!' shouted Kiran.

A policeman advanced upon her. She turned to run, and got the blow on her arm and shoulder. Shock and injury brought tears to her eyes. 'Murdabad,' she yelled, 'Murdabad!'

'Punjab Police Murdabad!' the girls around her cried.

'Punjab Police, *hai, hai*!'

'Punjab Police Murdabad!'

'Subhash Bose Zindabad!'

The lathi charges increased, there was screaming, and a stampede. Brickbats began to fly. Blood was flowing down Kiran's arm. The hurt made her think of her father, and forced her to go on.

Meanwhile, Mr C. B. Clark, Commissioner, Punjab Police, had arranged for the principals of the three colleges to come and manage their students. All three of them understood the gravity of the situation. It would do no one any good if their students were injured in lathi charges. They realized that law and order had to be maintained at all costs. Even though our brave soldiers are facing a trial, this, my dear friends, will not help them. You have made your point.

They saw that they had no option. They dispersed. Kiran was in no state to ride her cycle home, her friends took her back in a tonga.

Leela, flabbergasted, frightened. 'What possessed you to go marching in this manner? One sacrifice in the family is not enough?' Proud that the daughter had shown herself to be worthy of the father, but never saying it, no never, because Kiran was a girl, and girls had to be contained, and the earlier this process started, the less painful it would be.

And Virmati. The child shows such courage, while I fret about my petty, domestic matters, at a time when the nation is on trial. I too must take a stand. I have tried adjustment and compromise, now I will try non-cooperation.

Through that winter the word 'co-operate' beckoned hard at Virmati. Harish informed her he could not go on like this, this was her second year away from him.

It was getting very difficult for him at home. His trips up and down Lahore were silently and continuously resented. If he brought anything home for the children, it was felt he was wasting money. If he didn't, it increased the feeling that all his time, concern, attention and finances were being swallowed up by that witch who, as it was, prevented him from giving anybody else their due.

Kishori Devi to her son: 'Beta, all of us have to make sacrifices. The end of the war has not brought prices down. If anything, the situation has become worse. Perhaps I should go home. With me, you have another mouth to feed. The rest of your family is your responsibility, but Guddiya and I can at least spare you that much.'

'No, no, Amma. What are you saying? I cannot allow anything like that.'

'Beta, I can see the situation for myself. After all, now you have to go to Lahore frequently. The ticket there and back –'

'For heaven's sake, Amma, it is only a few annas!'

'Every pice counts. Then it is not only the train ticket. Once a man steps out of his house, he begins to spend, no matter what. Besides, you should spend. She is your wife. It is only a pity she feels the need to run away all the time.'

'She doesn't feel the need. She was here for a whole year. Then you know what happened. I am the one who sent her to study.'

'Beta, you are very good. How many husbands encourage their wives to study after their marriages? She has got a diamond – a diamond from heaven! But now with two bahus in the house, I can safely leave you. How many people can you support and look after? It is not fair. I do not wish to be a burden on you. Now you let me go. Things are cheaper in Kanpur. Here, everything is very expensive.'

'There is no question of letting you go. If you leave, the whole family will have to leave with you,' said Harish obliquely, at the thought of living alone with Ganga. 'It is out of the question. Let things settle down.'

'Viru, you have to come home, darling. I pine and long for you. I need you, I cannot bear this separation any longer. Is this why we married?'

'I spent all summer with you at home,' reminded Virmati. She was disturbed by his manner.

Harish, annoyed by her intransigence, went on. 'At the end of your exams, thank God all this nonsense will be over. I have gone on keeping two households long enough.'

'That's not fair,' flared Virmati. 'I didn't ask you to send me here.'

'You make it so difficult for yourself there. I think by now you have had enough time to adjust.'

Virmati sat speechless.

'My wives now know what to expect from each other,' continued Harish. Virmati looked at him. Normally he never referred to his 'wives'. She was the wife, Ganga was the pronoun. Was Harish actually equating both of them? What had happened at home while she was away? Did she have to crawl back to that dressing-room to protect her conjugal rights?

'We are not the same,' she said, rather incoherently. 'At least that is what you always led me to believe.'

'She has her claims, just as you do,' stated Harish flatly. 'And she is not the one who is running away.'

They've got him, thought Virmati, clenching her lips and staring at her husband with hatred.

'Have you – and she?' she stuttered. 'Like last time? What excuse do you have now?'

Harish did not pretend not to understand. After a moment he slowly said, 'The situation is clear for all to see.'

'What situation? If there is a situation, I don't see it.'

'How long can I remain alone? Here I am running after you all the time.'

'Doing an MA was your idea, not mine!'

'Yes, but look at all the other things you are doing. Getting involved with Swarna Lata, with Leela, with Kiran, with anybody and everybody except your husband.'

Virmati's head was spinning. Distress enveloped her heart.

She tried to think, but it was too painful. Whatever else she did, she would not go back to Amritsar during the holidays. Direct action was needed. She refused to fight Ganga with cunning, guile or seduction. If Harish's love for her wasn't strong enough to survive an MA, it certainly wasn't going to survive a lifetime. She thought of how often he had said he would die for her, and decided men were liars. She didn't care if she never had a home, children, if she cut off her nose to spite her face. Right now, everything about her was aching so much, to cut off her nose would be a relief. At least the incision would be definite, sharp and localized.

Ganga sees her influence growing at home. She secretly exults at her husband's occasional fits of sadness, though her serious face and devoted, red bindi deny that she could ever harbour a thought that did not directly pertain to his well-being.

When she tentatively presses his legs, he does not object. She takes to doing this every day. She talks of the activities of their children, of the well-being of his mother and sister, of household concerns, and desperately tries to weave a family structure that includes them both.

Virmati said she was going to stay in Lahore that summer. She hadn't done too well in her exams, she might have to repeat the year.

Her husband said nothing. He was determined to teach his wife a lesson.

He could afford to wait. Time, like everything else, was on his side. Besides, he really loved Virmati. For her own happiness, a little harshness might be necessary. Meanwhile, he found himself looking at Ganga's breasts, squashed against her blouse, as she bent over his feet and legs, pressing them, eyes downcast, bindi and kaajal smudged. He could see the black beads of her mangal-sutra coming together, and plunging unseen into the depths and folds of that lush topography. The visual contrast appealed to him: colours, dark and pale; textures, hard and soft; size, large and small. He wondered why she wore her mangalsutra inside her blouse. One day he reached in and pulled it out gently, and was flattered by the look of abject gratitude on Ganga's face.

1946 saw unrest all over the country. The postal, telegraph, general and municipal strikes couldn't be controlled.

The Hindus, Muslims and Sikhs were agitated. Many Muslims don't want Pakistan. Dr Khan Sahib says, 'I have no desire to understand Pakistan.' Abdul Ghaffar Khan says, 'How can we divide ouselves and live?' Dr Syed Hossain, Chairman of the National Committee for Indian Freedom at Washington, states that unity has been a historical fact from the time of Akbar. Sir Khizar Hyat Khan accuses the British of being the father and mother of Pakistan. Still, the idea of Pakistan seems more of a reality day by day.

'You cannot equate us. This is ridiculous. We are the majority,' the Congress points out.

The Muslim League: 'We are equal. We demand equal representation.'

The Cabinet Misssion to India, Cripps, Alexander and Pethick Lawrence, is sent to resolve the issue. What will be the exact composition of loyalties in the future government of India? After four months of meetings, hearings and deputations, they are unable to satisfy anyone. They return to England amid accusations and counter-accusations.

In mid-August the killings in Calcutta start. They go on and on. The drops of blood in the distance come nearer and nearer. Only now it is not drops, but floods. The sewers of Calcutta are clotted with corpses, they float down the Hoogly, they lie scattered in the streets.

People die – roasted, quartered, chopped, mutilated, turning, turning, meat on a spit – are raped and converted in rampages gone mad, and leave a legacy of thousands of tales of sorrow, thousands more episodes shrouded in silence.

Meanwhile, the Interim Government struggles through endless rounds of meetings between representatives of every major party in the country.

Virmati felt afraid. She was good at ignoring things not actually under her nose, but she was deeply affected by the Calcutta ravages. Bengal and Punjab, the two states that the Hindus and the Muslims were going to fight over. If this had happened in Bengal, could Punjab be far behind?

In Amritsar, too, there were disturbances. A squabble here, a murder there. Patrols of like religions were formed. There was talk of sending Ganga and the children home to Kanpur.

There was also talk of Ganga refusing. For her husband's sake. Who would stand by his side?

Kishori Devi felt she was living in a place where the law had no sanctity any more. Two men had died in what had begun as a simple argument over the price of some vegetables. This was in the old city, but Harish's college was in the gullies of the old city too.

Ordinary events assumed an ugly communal hue.

One day, two Muslim youths started quarrelling in the crowded bazaar. A Hindu tried to separate them. The Muslims turned on the Hindu and started beating him up. Passers-by joined in the fray. Brickbats and soda-water bottles were flung about. The police were called, and they fired in the air. The crowd melted away. It was only 8 October, 1946, with another ten months to go before Independence.

'Beta, it is time for us to leave this place,' Kishori Devi told her son. 'Your kind of job you will find in any university of the United Provinces.'

'My work is here,' replied Harish with a vague look.

'After independence, there will be work everywhere. You can never want for a job,' persisted his mother. 'Bring Virmati and come. It is time everybody at home saw her.'

The idea of travelling with his two wives to his home town sent shivers down Harish's spine. He could not imagine Virmati coming willingly, though it was not a point he had to consider very carefully. She might protest, but ultimately she had to do as he said. Still, right now, he did not want to make things any worse than they already were between them. He looked at Ganga, engaged in housework as always. She was so convenient, he wished she attracted him more.

One afternoon Guddiya came from school terrified. A strange man had followed her all the way home, whistling and calling. Guddiya could say nothing else about him, but that he was young and Muslim. Guddiya was well-developed, and her mother's fears instantly increased tenfold.

She spoke to her daughter-in-law.

Then she had a long talk with her son. It was agreed that they would leave first. Harish and Virmati could follow once the house was wound up.

Virmati heard of their departure with mixed feelings. Harish was there, in an empty house, waiting. She knew, though he might never admit it, that he had chosen to stay behind for her. On the other hand, they had been married for three years, and somewhere along the way, the prize had tarnished.

For the moment, however, with the unrest in both cities, the most practical solution was to go home to Amritsar and her husband. She left Lahore next morning to start her life as a house-wife. She had not been as happy studying the second time. The city had changed, she herself had changed. Perhaps things will be different later, she thought as she left. I will come back next March, do my exams, and see about a job.

XXVI

10 p.m., 2 March, 1947. Defeated by the year-long attack on him by the Muslim League, the Punjab Premier, Malik Sir Khizar Hayat Khan Tiwana, head of a Muslim, Hindu and Sikh coalition ministry, resigns without consulting his colleagues.

3 March. The MLAs, belonging to the Muslim League, are delighted. They start to dance with glee on the Assembly floor.

> Pakistan Zindabad
> Pakistan Zindabad

they clamour, while unfurling their flag in the Assembly. Master Tara Singh leaps upon it, tears it to pieces, and on the steps of the main entrance to the Punjab Assembly pulls out his sword, brandishes it and shouts:

> Pakistan Murdabad
> Sat Sri Akal.

The Hindu and Sikh crowds respond:

> Muslim League Murdabad
> Coalition Ministry Zindabad
> Akhand Hindustan Zindabad.

By 5 March it is clear that no coalition or single-party rule is possible in the Punjab. The Punjab Assembly is prorogued.

Governor's rule under Section 93 of the Government of India Act is proclaimed.

Massive killings start on a province-wide scale.

Reading old newspapers, I live through each day as though it were the present. Reports of massacres increase steadily as Independence approaches. My heart breaks. The paper I am reading is a Hindu one, and the disbelief about the breakup of our country that they credit to Hindu and Muslim alike seems incredibly pathetic and naïve. No, no, I want to shout down all those years, what you thought was so impossible was possible. It became true. I want to wail and sob. The loss is mine as well as theirs.

I must be calm. I must be able to scan newspaper headlines with hands that do not tremble. The past has happened. Hundreds and thousands of screams have been uttered. But those deaths I am so scared of created seeds that scattered through the wind, and settled in all parts of the country, waiting restlessly under the earth. Dormant, but not extinct. And if I stare these facts in the face, I cannot cope, because I feel threatened by lawlessness and bloodshed. History makes me insecure. I am glad I am not an historian.

Kailashnath: In those days, Amritsar had a population of 300,000. Fifty-one per cent of it Muslim.

You don't have to be a genius to predict what happens to a city in these circumstances.

I remember when it started. It was 5 March. Those Muslims were well prepared. They knew how to make bombs, explosives. We had to discover ways to protect ourselves, fast.

They looted and burnt, drank our blood, destroyed our peace, and put the fire of revenge in our guts. They had always hated us, tried to poison the well once. We learnt to make bombs with rags soaked in kerosene, and gunpowder in bottles. We closed our shop and took all our jewellery home. Some of it belonged to Muslims, who never claimed it. We were lucky, there was nothing in the shop when they burned it. My wife's family had a cloth shop; they locked it and prayed to God, but in those days God wasn't listening. When they found it reduced to dust and rubble, they left and came to Delhi.

Gopinath: A few days after the Assembly was dissolved, I had to go to the station. I will never forget the sight of that train. I threw up on the platform. It was taken straight to the shed to be washed. There was blood everywhere, dried and crusted, still oozing from the doorways, arms and legs hanging out, windows smashed.

We all travelled on those trains. It could have been me, anybody I knew. After that we lived with fear. We were afraid to go out, even when the curfew was lifted. We were prisoners in our own homes.

It does no good to remember, no good to think of those things, we had to get on with our lives. If we thought too much we would go mad, as our uncle did after he fled Sultanpur. He couldn't forget what he had lost, could never find anything to do that he considered an adequate substitute for his old life, and he slowly sank into senility and uselessness.

People living outside the Punjab can have no idea. The British left us with a final stab in the back. We didn't want freedom, if this is what it meant. But we were forced to accept Partition and suffering along with Independence, as a package deal. They were always Muslim-lovers, those British. The River Ravi was the natural boundary. Lahore was the seat of Raja Ranjit Singh and we all expected the Sikh holy place to come to us. But no, they had to cleave us with their pencils, their tapes and their measurements.

But ultimately, the fault was ours. If we were stupid, greedy and uncivilized enough to allow religion to be used in this way, why blame them? The same thing is happening on a smaller scale even now, when there are no British around. People blame them for this legacy, but how long can you keep doing that? There is always the past to contend with, in one way or another, hidden or openly, one's own or one's country's. Births and deaths are messy, ragged affairs.

Kanhiya Lal: I'm a doctor and I had never seen so much blood. It was horrible. I will never forget it as long as I live.

My parents, brothers, uncles and aunts, most of my cousins,

left Amritsar in '47. After what we had seen, there was no question of staying in that hellish place, where people killed each other like hooligans.

On 5 March, the killings started, and we lay low. The birth is going to be bloody, we thought, but then things will get back to normal.

Burning, burning, Amritsar was burning. Every night, for days and days, the sky was red, we could smell the smoke all the time.

I could see them come with lathis, I could see them come with swords. We were safe, though we were in the old city, because we were a doctor's family. We treated all the sick and wounded, and no questions asked. Everybody knew that and respected it.

We tried to save as many of them as we could. To tell the truth, we were closer to our Muslim friends than we are to our fellow Hindus at present. These people have no culture.

Around this time the cholera scare was at its height. The authorities knew that in the congested conditions, an outbreak of cholera spelt big trouble. I went to work in the camps, did my duty, and when the last camp was emptied, I left too.

Swarna Lata: Partition had been decided upon. We accepted that as a political decision. But Lahore was our city. We were going to stay there, no matter who it went to.

When we heard about Rawalpindi, we all felt sick, but for some strange reason we felt such massacres could never occur in our city, where we saw daily evidence of the Hindus and Muslims living as one. I suppose there are some things one cannot comprehend. When the troubles started, we wouldn't leave. My husband kept saying, you go because of the baby. Well, I thought, the baby will be safe with my mother in Delhi. So I left her there and came back. She said I was a fool, but I didn't care. If everybody got scared and started to leave, that meant the tactics of bloodshed and terror worked.

Ours was a Hindu area. All night long, the men kept watch from the rooftops. We managed to get hold of guns. My husband learned to make bombs. I did too, though I was against the whole thing. Every evening we would see the sky red. It was rather beautiful, if you could detach yourself from it all. And those cries:

Allah – o – Akbar
Har, Har Mahadev
Bolo So Nihal

Those cries became the cries of battle rather than religion. And then, of course, the inevitable. I suppose we were also naïve in those days. We believed in man's innate integrity. Then a Muslim friend rang us up.

'They are going to get you tonight. For God's sake, leave.'

And they did come. We escaped to a friend's house. We had seen too much plundering all around us to believe that they would leave us alone. Next morning, we saw they had ransacked the whole house. Our hearts were empty, and after that there was nothing to do but depart.

Indumati: In Amritsar we went wild. Wild with enthusiastic welcomes for those who made it to safety, wild with grief for the loss of a sister city that was steeped in blood. The Mussulmans chopped our people's heads off, raped our women, cut off their breasts, all of which they claimed was in retaliation for what the Hindus were doing to them.

Everybody's house functioned as an ashram, with beddings laid on the floor while the angans were converted into langars. To feed whoever came, whoever was there.

We were all together in those days. The whole city was an open house. There was a great spirit of generosity. They gave with open hearts.

They offered money, food, clothes, transport, shelter, time and care. The sorrow and the calamity was stifled in activity, in our sympathy for those who came, having lost everything, in the gratitude we felt for having survived. We never forgot those days, but never spoke of them either, because what was there to say?

Shakuntala: I lost my brother in those times. They say he was killed by some Muslims who had a grudge against him. Somnath was always too kind and generous, and very lavish with his favours. After Partition, I came to Amritsar, where I had my house and a job as principal of a girls' college all ready waiting for me. I was one of the lucky ones.

Parvati's husband: Thousands and thousands came to Amritsar. Overnight we had become a border city, a destination much longed for and reached with relief. Walking, some in ones and twos, some in small groups, and some in processions fifty-thousand strong. We took them all. There were four refugee camps: Govindgarh Fort, the largest; Sharifpura; Company Bagh; Cantonment.

Most of them left as soon as they found a place to go. Moving further into the new India. Looking for relatives, friends, an opening. A place to settle down, and get on with life.

Some stayed, desperate for news of those who had been left behind or lost in the march. They wanted to go back and look for them. And, if they were unsuccessful, they wanted to kill. Kill anybody who was not their own. The age, the sex, nothing mattered. Those, of course, we did our best to dissuade, as we did our best to suppress the stories of atrocities that insidiously burnt themselves into us.

Money poured in. Amritsar gave and gave. Nobody had a thought to spare for themselves. Not like today.

Food was free. Mridula Sarabhai was in charge.

Later, there were those who went back for their things. Their money and their jewellery. When they saw their houses in other peoples' hands, their bitterness increased. The houses they had given up were far nicer than the ones they got in exchange.

Kailashnath: Those days. The dispossessed kept talking. Talking of what they left behind. After a while it got so I could repeat the pattern of conversations in my head. A description of the house. The locality it was in, usually good. The trees they had, usually fruit-giving. The animals they kept, usually productive beyond compare. The furnishings, usually priceless.

I'm not saying their loss wasn't real, or the bereavement less than devastating. Of course it was. All I mean is, how much can you go on hearing? Consider it your fate and get on with your life. I'll help you all I can, but spare me your stories. You are alive, aren't you? Well, there were 500,000 dead by the end of it all, and you'd better thank your lucky stars that you and yours were not one of them. With those bloodthirsty mobs, it is mother luck that you are alive to tell your tale.

My father-in-law made it from Karachi. He couldn't take it, being dependent on his daughter. Every morning he would start the day by saying I have nothing, it's all gone, all gone. Everything. I couldn't bear the droning on of that tired old voice, suddenly decrepit. Everybody who was involved in the bloodiness of Partition grew old forthwith. Yes, we came of age all right, in 1947.

Swarna Lata: How many really understood what was happening? It took us all by surprise – we never expected it – it would pass after they got what they wanted – what was the point of murdering, looting, raping, after the goal had been achieved? When the refugees came, they told stories about the killings, the abductions – those screaming girls – they spared no one, not even ten-, eleven-, twelve-year-olds – the forced conversions – people dying of hunger – boiling leaves – scraping the bark off trees – one roti in a day if they were lucky – this city felt its heart about to break – and there was nobody who could come and who was not welcome. Such moments happen but occasionally in history – when our hearts move out in love and tenderness for those who suffer, and whose suffering we ourselves have so narrowly escaped. Occasionally in history – and it is just as well it is only occasionally – the price one pays for a mass synthesis of generous spirits is too great.

Pandit Jawaharlal Nehru: The appointed day has come – the day appointed by destiny – and India stands forth again after long slumber and struggle, awake vital, free and independent.

The past clings onto us still in some measure and we have to do much before we redeem the pledges we have so often taken. Yet the turning-point is past, history begins anew for us, the history which we shall live and act and others will write about.

We rejoice in that freedom, even though clouds surround us, and many of our people are sorrow-stricken and difficult problems encompass us. But freedom brings responsibilities and burdens, and we have to face them in the spirit of a free and disciplined people.

When Virmati came home to Moti Cottage, the first thing she did was shift everything belonging to Ganga to the dressing-room. Doing this, she felt light-headed, as though she had conquered and won. Now the dressing-room was Ganga's and the main bedroom hers. All summer long, she lay under the fan while the city burned. There was nothing she could do. She couldn't go out of the house, there was curfew almost every day, and for women nothing was considered safe. The college was shut. Harish spent much time anxiously listening to the news bulletins, twiddling the knobs on the radio, depressed at the death of civilization. Otherwise he helped with the refugees, coming back from the camps with ghastly reports. Amritsar was a city washed over with the scourge of death, which reddened the skies at night and filled the air with lamentations. Like so many others, he was waiting for all this to be over.

In the evening, Virmati would sometimes fill the tank with a little water, climb down the steps, and lie down. Her mind was drained of all emotion. Her limbs were heavy with torpor. Harish would sometimes join her. Submerged in the depths of the tank, all they could see was the far-away sky and the grey walls. Often they made love. There was no one to see them, no one to mind anything they did. Virmati had never had so much space around her. Maybe this was really what she had fought for all along, space to be. She conceived.

This time, she knew nothing could happen to her. With the certainty of the nascent life within, she felt strong, and her heart moved out in pity to mankind in general. Later, when it was considered safe, she wanted to help in the camps. But Harish would not allow it. She must think of the baby, especially in the light of what had happened before. Shocks, exertion, witnessing of horrors, all this was not good for a pregnant woman. Let the country, till yesterday a colony, go to rack and ruin. Let those thousands march footsore, weary, raped, mutilated, bewildered, and lost, let them march into Amritsar in all their hordes and be herded towards various shelters. She must stay at home.

Then, one night, they heard that their neighbourhood, quiet, secluded and remote, was going to be attacked. All the residents of the street, and that included Virmati and Harish, Kasturi and her sons, daughters and daughter-in-law, gathered in Sardar Hukum Singh's house, the only one high enough to allow a watch to be kept from the roof.

The attack proved to have been a rumour, but it did serve one purpose. Virmati's mother sent for her. The times demanded from Kasturi that she carry resentment no further. Virmati shifted to her mother's, where she helped with the cooking along with the other women, because the need of the hour was to feed the scores of people who passed through their house fleeing from the mobs in Pakistan. No one mentioned the past. The present was too drastic for such luxury.

The house had to be made goonda-proof. The boundary walls were raised to eight feet and topped with jagged edges of broken glass. On the inside of the walls, coils of barbed wire were spread.

Kailash spent his time organizing the langar at home, and arranging transport for relatives who wanted to move on. As they left, more people kept streaming in. At night, there was no room to place a foot anywhere. The men slept in the verandas and on the roofs, the women and children in the angan and rooms.

The prices of everything shot up – there was hardly any vegetable to be bought. In the house the main meals were dal roti, roti dal, with some variation in the kind of dal. Two big tandoors were put just behind the kitchens. The huge gardens to the side of the house were scoured for vegetables – sarson, mooli and shalgam. When the floods came in October, the electricity was cut for days. All the grain had to be ground by hand, adding to the work.

That October, Virmati was six months pregnant. She could not be properly looked after by a doctor – they were all at the camps having their hearts wrung and senses wrought upon. Many refugees had nothing – only the clothes upon their backs. They had left everything behind, to walk in kaflas for days and days, in processions that were sometimes fifty miles long. Master Tara Singh had given away half his clothing and begged the inhabitants of the city to do the same.

Such a spirit possessed Virmati, as she moved slowly and heavily to the cupboards in Moti Cottage. Absent people had no moral right to their clothing, when there were so many needy ones crying out for cloth to cover them. First, she looked at Giri's clothes lying stacked in the children's cupboard. Kurtas, pyjamas, sweaters that were too small for him – had Ganga nurtured hopes of another? Then Chhotti's clothes – mostly school uniforms neatly folded, blue kameezes and white salwars and dupattas. Virmati took them all.

Her mother-in-law's cupboard had Guddiya's uniforms, along with the old woman's saris, petticoats, blouses, all in white. God knew there were plenty of widows in the camps who needed white clothes.

Her own things she went through the fastest. She kept five sets for herself and gave the rest away. Harish's she left alone.

Finally, there was one big steel almirah she couldn't open. Ganga had locked it and left. Left eight months ago, in riot and bloodshed, left putting a lock on her cupboard, a lock that asserted her claims, and promised she would return. How many people had escaped from Pakistan and done the same?

She would have to come back tomorrow with someone to break open the door.

The next day, back at Moti Cottage with a locksmith, Virmati stood before Ganga's open cupboard. Just seeing those saris made her sick. Each one of them reminded her of the woman, with her round face, round bindi and black kaajal-lined eyes staring fixedly at her with loathing.

The child within her womb trembled, as revulsion coursed her body.

She stretched out her hand to pluck the first sari from the pile, a red thing. Ganga liked wearing red. It was hard for her to touch it, it was like touching Ganga's skin. Finally she swept everything out from the cupboard, without going through the individual items, and tied them into large bundles with old bedsheets. The huge piles of clothes she made over to Kailashnath to donate to the camps.

Kailashnath was delighted.

'You are a generous woman, sister,' he said.

'For those in distress,' murmured Virmati.

I was born.

'Bharati,' suggested Virmati as a name.

'No,' said Harish.

'No? But why? I thought with the birth of our country . . .'

'I don't wish our daughter to be tainted with the birth of our country. What birth is this? With so much hatred? We haven't been born. We have moved back into the dark ages. Fighting, killing over religion. Religion of all things. Even the educated. This is madness, not freedom. And I never ever wish to be reminded of it.'

Harish's voice rose hysterically, and the girl was named Ida.

'But what does it mean?' asked Virmati doubtfully. 'People might think it is a Persian name.'

'This is the very attitude that has led to Partition,' said Harish irritably. 'Let anybody think what they like. For us it means a new slate, and a blank beginning.'

Virmati was left alone with the baby, while Harish worked for a while with the newly formed Kashmir Sahayak Sabha, to help combat the fires burning there.

For a while he went to Kashmir and then came back, dispirited and sick at heart.

'Is there no end to this needless violence and stabbing?' he asked. Was this price necessary for freedom?

But there was no time to ask these questions, or think out the answers. The deed was done, they would just have to go on living.

XXVII Epilogue

Ganga's leaving home, in the pressures and tensions of the moment, was meant to be a temporary affair. However, she could never return. She wept, begged, and stormed indirectly through her mother-in-law, but circumstances did not favour her. After Independence, Harish was offered a principalship in one of the new colleges of Delhi University. Amritsar had become a place to leave, rather than stay in, and the couple moved to Delhi and a much smaller house.

Virmati had just one child, Ida. Harish told her that three was a large enough family, his resources were already strained beyond his means. Giridhar and Chhotti came to live with them when their schooling demanded it. Harish carried on with his love of learning and made education an issue with each of his children. They didn't care for the whole process as much as he did, and each found a way to rebel.

Giridhar decided to go into business. He opened a small chemist's shop in Karol Bagh and married one of his customers. Both the families objected.

Chhotti, who craved her father's attention, did excel in studies, but she refused to do anything with the humanities, books or music. She joined the IAS, mainly for the cheap government accommodation that would enable her mother and grandmother to live with her. While Harish was alive, the relationship between the two houses was perpetually uneasy.

Chhotti never married. Her father thought no man good enough, and her mother dared not cross him in this respect.

Her husband continued to be Ganga's public statement of selfhood. Her bindi and her bangles, her toe rings and her mangalsutra, all managed to suggest that he was still her god.

Ida refused to show any signs of intellectual brightness.

'There are other things in life,' she told her mother.

'Like what?' asked Virmati.

'Like living.'

'You mean living only for yourself. You are disappointing your father.'

'Why is it so important to please him?' Ida protested to her mother. She wanted to please herself sometimes, though by the time she grew up she was not sure what self she had to please.

Later, she tried to bridge the contradictions in her life by marrying a man who was also an academic. Virmati could only guess at the basis of their relationship, but she did not think it comprised the higher things in life.

I grew up struggling to be the model daughter. Pressure, pressure to perform day and night. My father liked me looking pretty, neat, and well-dressed, with kaajal and a little touch of oil in my sleeked-back hair. But the right appearance was not enough. I had to do well in school, learn classical music, take dance lessons so that I could convert my clumsiness into grace, read all the classics of literature, discuss them intelligently with him, and then exhibit my accomplishments graciously before his assembled guests at parties.

My mother tightened her reins on me as I grew older, she said it was for my own good. As a result, I am constantly looking for escape routes.

Of course I made a disastrous marriage. My mother spent the period after my divorce coating the air I breathed with sadness and disapproval. 'What will happen to you after I am gone?' was her favourite lament. I was nothing, husbandless, childless. I felt myself hovering like a pencil notation on the margins of society.

For long periods I was engulfed by melancholy, depression, and despair. I would lie in bed for hours, unable to sleep, pitying myself for all I didn't have, blaming my mother, myself. Now her shadow no longer threatens me. Without the hindrance of her presence, I can sink into her past and make it mine. In searching for a woman I could know, I have pieced together material from memories that were muddled, partial and contradictory. The places I visited, the stuff I read tantalized me with fragments that I knew I would not be able fully to reconstruct. Instead, I imagined histories, rejecting the material that didn't fit, moulding ruthlessly the material that did. All through, I felt the excitement of discovery, the pleasure of fitting narratives into a discernible inheritance. This book weaves a connection between my mother and me, each word a brick in a mansion I made with my head and my heart. Now live in it, Mama, and leave me be. Do not haunt me any more.

Acknowledgements

I am indebted to the Nehru Memorial Museum and Library at Teen Murti for allowing me access to the microfilm copies of the *Tribune* (Lahore).

The Professor's comments at the Roerich exhibition in Chapter XVI are modelled on the review of the exhibition by Mr Roop Krishna A.R.C.A. (Lond.), *Tribune*, 17 December 1940. The format and speeches of the Punjab Women's Conference in Chapter XVIII closely follow the account given in the *Tribune*, 19 January 1941.

The more general accounts taken from the *Tribune* are as follows: 30 December 1939 for the account of Pt. Jawaharlal Nehru at the first All-India Hindustan Scout Mela held at Malviya Nagar, Amritsar, Chapter XIV; 18 September 1940, account of the tonga strike, Chapter XV; 1 November 1940, account of Bhalla's Shoe Store, Chapter XVI; 27 December 1943, account of the Hindu Mahasabha procession on 25 December 1943, Chapter XXIV; 2 July 1944, account of the grain dealer fined a thousand rupees, Chapter XXIV; 15 January 1944, the prices on 20,000 varieties of cotton cloth and yarn fixed, Chapter XXIV; 13 November 1945, account of the INA procession, Chapter XXV; 5 June 1945, discussion of the Draft Hindu Code Bill, Chapter XXV; March–April 1946, account of various reactions to the Muslim League, Chapter XXV; Pandit Jawaharlal Nehru's speech, Chapter XXVI, from his Address to the Nation, 15 August 1949.

The poem 'Love's Unity' is by Alfred Austin. The gravestones in Nahan are real.

My grateful thanks to the following people who were so generous with their time and memories: Sneh Lata Sanyal, Shiva Gogia, Autar Singh Kapur, Renu Malhotra, Vimla Kapur,

Kaushalya Prakash, Vidyavati Minocha, Vir Sen, Vijay Sen, Laj Sen, Satya Nath, Ravi Sen, Jyoti Grover, Ramesh Grover, Saroj Bhandari, Som Bhagat, Manohar Lal Kapur, Chhote Lal Bharany, Rameshwar Kaushik, Panditji in Nahan, Jagjit Singh Chawla, Mrs Sondhi from Ashiana in Dalhousie, and Padma Bhandari.

My thanks to the following for helping me in my research: Urvashi Butalia, Pratibha Kaushik, Prabha Sen, Gyanendra Pandey and especially Khushwant Singh, and Riaz Khokkar in enabling me to get to Lahore.

Vikram Kaul spent hours helping me transfer my manuscript from floppies to a hard disk, and ironing out the bugs. I am extremely indebted to him.

Edward Jones, Vikram Chandra and Julian Loose made the publication of this book possible. I am very grateful to them.

My writers' group supported me through the two years it took to get a first draft together by willingly listening to every chapter as I wrote it, and wanting to hear more. My thanks to Janet Chawla, Neelima Chitkopekar, Anuradha Marwah Roy, Anna Sujatha Mathai and Addison Ullrich.

For critical and editorial comments, I thank Anuradha Marwah Roy, Addison Ullrich, Vasudha Dalmia and Rajeshwari Sunder Rajan. In my wrestle with the final draft, Ramya Sreenivasan, Amy Louise Kazmin, Ira Singh and Maya Bhattacharyya were of invaluable assistance.

My appreciation to my family, Nidhi, Maya, Amba, Katyayani and Agastya.

And lastly, Anuradha, who for nine years never allowed me to lose faith in myself. Who held my hand, and indicated paths.